THE MOON IS MAKING

THE
MOON IS MAKING

By
STORM JAMESON

CASSELL
AND COMPANY, LIMITED
LONDON, TORONTO, MELBOURNE
AND SYDNEY

01446936

First published 1937

ACCRINGTON

Printed in Great Britain by
Greycaine Limited, Watford, Herts
F737

FOR
WYN AND LYN GRIFFITH

I

THE MOON IS MAKING

CHAPTER I

HANDEL WIKKER left his house at six o'clock in the evening on an errand which vexed him—since it was to ask a favour, and he hated few things worse. Hurrying along, he was half aware of the change in the air. He had been indoors for a week and during that week winter had vanished and spring, later than ever, come at a bound. The sixteenth of May. The little town, not sleepy, never livelier than in winter, dreamed most of its dreams in summer, with eyes open in the short northern nights.

Wik lies actually in two parts—called Under Wik and Over Wik—and the harbour, facing north, divides them. A deep gully runs inland from the narrow harbour for close on two miles, widening thence into a green rich valley. The stream pouring through the gully to the harbour is deep, swift, tree-shadowed; the rough fields turn steeply to yellow limestone cliffs, hollowed into quarries, with moors above. Under Wik is a huddle of small houses, for fishermen, sailors, and the workers in the shipyard, tumbling together round the harbour half-way up the grim east cliff. The bigger handsome houses of Over Wik are scattered over the west cliff and behind it. This western cliff falls softly, out of sight of the harbour, to a wide marsh, over which the sea creeps twice a day, slowly and gently, while it rushes against the rocks of the east cliff.

As you might know by the name, Wik began as a Frisian settlement. They say that the fishermen of Under Wik can make themselves understood on the coast of West Friesland to this day. *Good butter and good cheese, Is good Wik and good Friese*—spoken as Under Wik speaks it, you understand. The speech of Under Wik is common in a few fishing villages to the north and south of Wik and nowhere else. Meeting each other, the men say: "Weerst tha gang?" and the children cry about the streets: "Awa, awa," in high piercing voices, thin and pure, like peewits.

Handel Wikker believed, from their name, that his family was the oldest in the place, but the narrow stinking yards and alleys of Under Wik held many families with names as old as his own—Ormesby, Upsal, Blash, Soureby, Thwaite, Horn, Scrope, Risewarp. These had sunk.

He skirted the marsh and took a road leading uphill to a farmhouse. Had he followed it to its end it would have brought him to his brother's house, but his business was with the owner of this shabby farm.

He crossed the yard and knocked on a door. There was no answer. He knocked again, and shouted. After a time he heard slow footsteps, and Scoresby opened the door. When he saw Handel Wikker he stepped aside without a word—because he was surprised and would not show it—and let Handel walk in front of him along the flagged passage to the kitchen. He eyed his visitor's rigid back with an expression of quiet cunning. He respected him, but he trusted no one.

"Will you ha' supper with me?" he said grudgingly.

There was a cheese, a loaf, and a yellow plate on the table. Handel shook his head. He sat down and looked at Scoresby, forcing himself to a friendliness he did not feel. He wanted something from the man.

"I've come to ask the loan of your day books," he said abruptly. He glanced towards the cupboard where he knew the books were kept, nearly thirty of them, of as many sizes, in which ten generations of Scoresbys patiently had noted the day's weather, the first entry made on the cold evening of October 16, 1598. So far as Handel Wikker knew, no similar record had come down. His eagerness to possess a copy of it had grown until he could not put on with it any longer. The books had never been out of this room, no stranger had been allowed to handle them; he might stand a few feet away and look, but not lay a finger where so many Scoresbys had laid their greasy or earth-cracked paws.

For six years, from his twentieth year, Handel Wikker was the master of a whaler. During these years he made careful meteorological observations and studied the forms of snow crystals. He used to send the results of his studies to the Royal Society, and one year he offered a paper on the variation of the magnetic needle received by his audience with a considerable respect. His whale fishing prospered, but at the age of twenty-seven he left the sea and began the study of chemistry and natural philosophy at London University. During this year he published an Account of the Arctic Regions, by which he was made a Fellow of the Royal Society. But already he had turned to theology. He took degrees in philosophy and in divinity and entered the church, and after two years he was brought from the south of England to his own town of Wik to be vicar of that parish. He returned at the same time to his first love, the study of natural forms.

He was now a man of thirty-five and unmarried, of a good height, handsome, with grey long-sighted eyes, a long delicate nose, and a high forehead fringed with fair, almost red, hair. His temper was as stiff as his back. . . .

Scoresby was delighted to feel himself in a position to humble the man. How desperately he must want the books to bring himself to ask for them! He had no intention of lending them, but he said craftily, to prolong his happiness:

"What d'you want them for?"

"I'm at work now on a theory of winds and tides," Hande Wikker said, with bitter reluctance. He disliked having to explain himself to any man, worst of all to an ignorant and inquisitive fellow. But for the anxiety and the burning eagerness he felt at the nearness of the precious books he would have left without pressing for them.

Scoresby rose stiffly from his chair—at fifty he was already an old man, toothless, bent with rheumatism from the sea air in his joints—and shuffled to the cupboard. He opened the doors and allowed Handel one glimpse of the dark pile of note books, then suddenly closed it again and stood with bent head. His tiny pig-like eyes twinkled behind their lids. He was savouring a keen malice.

He ran his finger over the ledge of the cupboard and pretended to be overcome by disgust. "Kezia!" he shouted. "Hey, Kezia! Bring your duster here." There was no answer: he turned to Handel with real annoyance, puckering his dry lips. "Why, what d'y' think," he blustered. "My young gel came home yesterday—for good and all—shoo's been living i' London, I may tell you. . . . The young bezom . . . I'll right her. . . . Now you're missus here, I said to her, you'll see you keep things clean and sweet in the house, I said . . . and don't order anything without I tell you and we'll clag together like peas in a pod. . . And now what! Where, where?"

"How old is your daughter?" Handel asked civilly. Tense with anguished desire for the books, he did not hear Scoresby answer: "Seventeen. Shoo's seventeen." He sat stiffly in his chair, his eyes piercing Scoresby's body as though it were a mist.

"I can't sit here all night. Are you or aren't you going to lend me the books? I'll pay you a reasonable price for the loan of them for one month. Come—speak up."

The vehemence with which he denounced sinners in his pulpit was part of his nature. He did not ask, he commanded God to smite them. And when he bowed his head on his hands in prayer the relation between him and his God was that of first officer and captain, absolute obedience tempered by self-respect. He could no more flatter Scoresby into parting with his books than he could steal them.

Scoresby was nettled—the more so that Handel's manner made him feel small. "Since you put it like that," he said shortly, "you shan't ha' them. You may look at them, one at a time, when I ha' time to show them to you. I'm not unreasonable."

Handel rose to go. Though he was angry his sense of justice forced him to thank the man for his offer. He went home trying to stifle his rage and disappointment; he struggled with himself not to hate Scoresby.

A few days after, he was walking in the cool of the day to his brother's house. He passed Scoresby's farm, and his anger started up for a minute. He forgot it in the delicious mildness of the evening. A dazzling sky sprang behind the hill; the road turned and doubled on itself a score of times to come to the top of the hill, and at one of these turns he passed a large field of sheep-cropped grass with a grove of chestnut trees masking the farther side. They were so crammed on every branch with their waxen blossoms that no leaves were visible. Each tree was a single pyramid of ivory-yellow clusters, blazing against the sky. A fire of branches had been made under the nearest tree and a column of blue smoke rose towards it; the figure of a girl crossed and re-crossed the smoke, bending to lay more branches. Handel Wikker stood still to watch. Suddenly a fountain of lear flame sprang. A soundless wave rippled in his body and fell back.

He turned and went on, but he did not go to his brother's house; he took a steep lane, slippery with mud, to a grove of oaks called indifferently Upsal Wood or The Stone, from a grey boulder of granite lying at one side of the grove. There is no granite in these parts; geologists say that it was carried here during an ice age by a glacier moving to the North Sea from the other side of England. Handel believed that neither time nor ice moulded the shallow receptacle on its upper surface, but the flints of savage priests for their bound victim. He often came here, oftenest on windy days. The noise made by a wind in the trees and the sense of being lifted away from the earth, gave him a sharp sensual joy. He had asked himself whether it was not in fact an impure joy which ought to be put away. But the effort to surrender it made him dull and heavy; he no longer felt confident of God's mercy when he prayed. He went back to Upsal Wood and again his ears were unsealed and his eyes opened and he heard and saw God.

He stayed in the wood for an hour, until eight o'clock. To-night there was no wind. It was mild, the sky cloudless, the air cool and soft. The birds were singing as loudly as in full day. When he turned to walk back, the light, still clear, had the kind of shiftiness and deceit which comes into it before dusk. He reached the field of chestnut trees a little before nine o'clock and stood still in the road to look at the fire. The girl was moving round it. The flame had vanished, though a little smoke still went up.

The daylight was now almost gone, and the birds silent. The sky had turned the colour of pale water.

He had stopped near the gate into the field. Seized by an inexplicable curiosity, he opened it and began to walk towards the trees. Only the topmost flowers were still visible and colourless, like the ghost-candles seen in country churchyards after dark. The dew soaked his ankles. He felt a spider's web across his face. As he came nearer the girl turned to look at him. She was leaning against a tree, her arms hanging by her sides.

"I saw your fire from the road," he said gently.

Whether from shyness or surprise she did not answer him.

She was very young, thin, with a narrow rosy face; her eyes were large and black, with thick brows, her mouth small. Her hands were small enough but scratched and dirty. She was as beautiful as the trees, the fountain of fire, and the naturally impudent spring. Handel thought he had seen her somewhere before, but his memory refused to give him a definite answer. It offered him instead the eyes and soiled neck and fingers of a woman in Hammerfest, and the gestures of another, with the lights and guttural voices of a street sunk in night and the cold of winter.

What streets, what cold of what winters? The years since he left the sea were womanless from choice and because no earthly woman was as attractive as natural philosophy. Spring betrayed him. The deceitful union of sky and shamelessly swelling earth, the warm air with its slight savour of salt, and the girl's scratched hands, offered him harmlessly a pleasure he would have rejected at once if it had appeared in a reputable shape. His heart beat too heavily and the joints of his wrists ached.

"Do you often," he asked, "light bonfires at night?"

"No," she said. Her voice was clear. She half smiled at him, parting a little her red, childishly-soft lips. Her clothes smelled of wood smoke.

"Then why to-night?"

"To see—to see——" she broke off, laughing and seized with shyness: the blood rushed over her face and throat, to her shoulders. "In fact, I wanted to see how a fire would look against the chest-nuts."

"You might have set the copse on fire with your silliness," Handel said in a loud severe tone. The pleasure it gave him to speak harshly to her vanished when she took it simply as a matter of course.

"Oh, no," she said calmly, "the earth is far too wet."

Actually the patched earth where they were, immediately under the trees, was dry and bare: a warm scent of dusty earth rose from it, mingled with the smell of leaves and the slight fragrance of the blossoms—so slight that it is only when one is standing, as it were, in a tent of them that it is noticeable at all. At moments the overpoweringly sweet smell of hawthorn drowned all others. On the crest of the hill facing, the trees were black and motionless; the sun, which was already high on the other side of the world, had left a trace of smoky ash. Everywhere else the sky was still pale, pricked by a single star. A stream which was actually a long way off made itself heard dashing over stones.

"What is your name?"

"Kezia."

Again, the name sounded familiar. He touched her hand. A subtle and disintegrating warmth moved in his veins. "Kezia," he said loudly.

"Yes?" she said, looking at him with her slight smile.

"You're not afraid?"

"I live here. These are all our fields."

She stood idly in front of him, one arm lifted to a branch of the tree. Her eyes were half innocent, half teasing. She was certainly not afraid of anything he might say or do.

"You're Kezia Scoresby," he burst out. He turned to go, shocked into his senses by the realization, and in his momentary sanity he reflected that if he went away he could see her again; and he would know then what he wanted. What did he want? To marry? A single shudder passed over him; he closed his eyes. The thought of leaving her had been enough to fill him with an irrational, torturing fear that he would never see her again.

Kezia took her hand from the tree. Seized by curiosity, she moved nearer to him and laid her hand on his arm. She knew who he was, she had heard him preach, and her first impulse had been simple surprise that out of the pulpit he spoke like an ordinary man. When he looked at her again she saw that he was not only a man, he was an archangel; his eyes—it was perhaps the first time she had really looked at a human eye—were surely quite remarkable. The excitement of making and watching her fire moved through her body. She began to tremble, and to expect —here her mind failed her, but she felt that she would be hurt and ashamed if he left her.

He did not leave her. His arms moved to touch her of their own accord. "I love you," he said abruptly. "Hey, what do you say to that?" She did not say anything. She stood beside him without, so far as he could see, showing fear or surprise.

There was now no light; as it receded, the rays given off by the earth itself sprang up. They were visible to Handel Wikker's sight, and it crossed his mind that the sky had the form of a woman bending over the earth. He heard the stream rushing in the distance, and a leaf moved lightly over another in the darkness of the tree. His blood moved like a river flooding against its banks. He felt that he could not contain it. This, he thought, is the sole cause why we were made.

"I should go," he said absently, without altering a muscle of his intention to stay.

"You had better stay now," she said kindly.

"I'll make this right afterwards, Kezia."

She had begun to be a little afraid now that her longing, as vague and formless as the tree into whose depths she was looking up, had taken a shape. It was exacting. No idea of running away crossed her mind, because she was willing to be taken and made different. The fear was only in her body, which at one moment seemed distinct from her, and lost, and in another enveloped her in a fog, through which her lungs laboured for breath. It was a part of her body that said awkwardly: "This will never be made right, never."

Handel felt no doubts and indeed no pity for what he was doing. He was now only a man, and one who knew better what he was about than he did the first time he lay with a woman. He had lived twice as long as Kezia.

It was without any feeling stronger than self-horror that he went the next day to see Scoresby and tell him he wanted to marry Kezia. Scoresby was startled and immediately suspicious. Throwing his head back, he wanted to hear when Handel had seen her, why he was in such a hurry to marry, whether the girl expected it, how long? who? where? His little eyes became hard and bloodshot and his fat sallow cheeks quivered. His unwilling respect for Handel Wikker vanished. "We'll ha' Kezia herself," he exclaimed.

She came in, looking at Scoresby, and Handel loved her again. His relief and self-will took possession of him and he began to speak to her father in a way the older man resented at once. He was touchy as well as conceited and suspicious. If Handel had been another sort of man and had come in with a wink and a nod probably he would have agreed to anything, and amused himself only by making gross speeches to them both. He was actually afraid to speak out, and he grew sourly angry with Handel's overbearing voice and manner.

"I'll think on it," he grumbled. "I'll think on it and let you know."

They were all three standing in the passage leading to the kitchen. With a sudden movement, Scoresby bustled his daughter inside the kitchen and himself after her, slamming the door in Handel Wikker's face. "You'll hear from me when I think fit," he shouted. He had bolted the door, and after a minute's angry consideration Handel turned and went home.

He shared his house with his widowed elder sister. Mrs. Semiramis Jordan was now a woman of forty-five, short and heavily-built. Her liveliest feature was her eyes; they were black, small, and invincibly malicious. Her husband, who had been fifty-five when she married him, died in six months—and five months before the birth of their child. He left thirty thousand pounds to his wife.

After his death Semiramis kept repeating: "It's of no account. When the boy's come we'll ha' a man in the house." The child was a girl. Semiramis was bitterly annoyed, but she had her christened Merry—this, as she told everybody, was to make the best of a bad job. . . .

Merry Jordan grew up like her father, tall and thin, with grey eyes and fair, almost colourless hair; she was happy, nervous, of a lively rebellious mind. A year ago she had married an artist who was visiting the town (there is a plague of them every summer) and left Wik. Semiramis was outraged. When she realized that nothing she could say would better it, since Merry was twenty-one, she said to her: "If you live I hope you'll ha' ten bairns and not a bite to put in their mouths." She meant this kind wish with all her heart, and her daughter who, in spite of much, was strangely bound to her, shivered. Then she laughed and repeated it to her husband as a joke. She thought that when her mother showed herself cruel and spiteful it was not her real nature. . . .

Her brother Handel was the only person who could silence Semiramis's tongue. Even he could not do it at once. When he told her he intended marrying Kezia Scoresby she let him feel the rough side of it. She thought he was making himself common —"to marry a gel off a farm! Nay, it's not even a farm. A pigsty! I'll not ha' her in the house." She pretended to have heard that Kezia's aunt, with whom the girl had been living in London, had turned her off when she saw that she was no better than she should be.

Handel told her to hold her tongue; and his authority silenced her for the rest of the day. In the evening Kezia herself came to the house, driven there by her father in the cart he used about the farm. He marched in with her, and holding her by one arm made a gesture of handing her to Semiramis. "Here, missus, your brother's had t'gel, it seems. He'd better keep her—I'll not."

He was out of the house before she recovered from the shock of his impudence. Hurrying to the window she opened it and screeched after him to come back and take his gel home. He drove off, doubled up in the cart, racked with laughter. Poor Kezia stood leaning against the wall in dumb fear.

Handel came into the room and found Semiramis, like a hawk with a captured pigeon, plucking the last feathers off her prey. It was perhaps the best way it could have happened. Kezia was so thankful to see him, anyone, that she dropped into his arms, and felt only the exquisite comfort of his body on hers. He held her for a minute. Semiramis was silent, but her black eyes were starting with spite and hostility. Nothing surprised her, not even the evidence of her own eyes that Handel was lost, ruined. She would have denied even the awful weakness she felt at seeing the downfall of a man whom she had considered just, noble minded, severely incapable of the sins she conceived everyone else to be committing the whole time. And there he stood, in his vicar's clothes, oblivious. Controlling herself, she thought: He has forgotten his God, he has sinned in the evil flesh, and he has shamefully insulted me, me, Semiramis Jordan. If God does what's right, as he would if I had anything to say to it, he'll be punished.

She was still too much afraid of his severity to say more than: "So I'm to lower m'self to the ground now, am I, to suit you?" when he told her she must behavè herself. Grumbling, she had the second-best bedroom made ready; and in front of a servant she compelled herself to be almost civil. Alone with the girl, she would say:

"Hey, Miss Scoresby—if that's your name——" and wait for Kezia's, "Yes, Mrs. Jordan," before finishing an unnecessary remark. "That's a good coat o' yours: when did m'brother give it to you? Ha'n't he given you anything?" And after a few minutes: "*What* did you say he gave you?"

In spite of her anger and of the scorn she felt for Kezia she curbed her tongue outside the house better than she did in. To acquaintances—she had no friends—she said shortly: "My brother —th' vicar—is gettin' himself married this month. The gel hasn't a mother and she's staying in th' house until t'wedding." She told the same story in the shops when she was ordering material for wedding clothes for herself and Kezia. According to custom, the clothes were made up at home by a dressmaker named Boulby's Anna, who worked for the good houses; and to her, too, Semiramis repeated: "Y'see, Miss Scoresby's h'orphaned"—an agitation she was not able to unload played the devil with her h's.

For once, it was not Semiramis's fault that scandal was spreading in the town. There had been more than one witness of Scoresby's arrival in his dirty tumbledown cart, and he spent the next day— which was a market day—telling every soul he met the story and how he had thrashed Kezia to make her tell her poor old father the truth. At night there was hardly a house in Wik but knew a great deal more than the truth. It ran from mouth to mouth, and for one who disbelieved it there were ten to point out to him Kezia's living in the vicar's house. If there were no truth in the tale, why was she there and not at home with her father, quietly and decently preparing for her wedding? It was bad enough in all conscience that Handel Wikker should think fit to marry a girl as ill suited to the place she would take; the circumstances of it made it a scandal such as Wik had not enjoyed for many a year.

Semiramis sent out invitations to the wedding. She did it without telling Handel and flatly against his orders. He wanted no one there but his two sisters and his brother; he could have done without them, but that he had no excuse to keep them off. When he heard of the invitations he was speechless with annoyance. He need not have troubled himself—they were declined, all of them except the one which by some oversight had been addressed to Mrs. Vansittart, wife of the singing master at the school: and she, after accepting, sent a message by the servant to say that she was in bed with a severe colic. This was a hundred times worse than if she had refused at first.

The week before the marriage, Handel was walking along a cobbled street in Under Wik; he was pelted suddenly with fish-heads and stones from one of the dark, stinking yards. Someone the same night scrawled a grossly life-like drawing on the side door of the vicarage. When he came into the pulpit the next Sunday he saw that the church was almost empty except for Vansittart and his choir in the gallery below the organ; the free pews were half filled, but the square pews, like rooms, belonging to Over Wik families, gaped at him from their crimson-padded chairs and hassocks.

He had altered the hour arranged for the marriage; but when he came out of the church with Kezia, half Under Wik was waiting to stare and jeer at them. Afterwards, his only memory of his wedding-day was Semiramis's face, like a stone of offence: she stared at him with a strange air of grief below her fury.

"You've tied a knot with your tongue you'll be matched to unloose with your teeth," she said. "I hope you're satisfied."

"I'm not answerable to anybody on earth," Handel said, shortly.

"If you had to marry her, was there any need to go about it as you did? Why not ha' spoken civilly to her old fool of a father? You could surely ha' waited, to give him time to come round. But you must go up there, as hoity-toity as if you hadn't a right to be on your knees crawling before God Himself to forgive you for your *common* behaviour. But how did you speak to him? I know you, Handel Wikker."

"Then you should know enough to hold your tongue now," Handel said. He held the door of his library open for her to walk out. She went without looking at Kezia, who was leaning against the window, playing idly with one of the crimson tassels of the curtains. Like a child, she had come to an end of her capacity for active unhappiness, and had withdrawn mutely into a world in which Semiramis's spite and Handel's incomprehensible fury and his refusal to repent were forces of Nature with which it would be useless to try to contend. Looking out of the window, she saw a boy whipping a top—he was not very clever at it. Her husband's hand on her wrist recalled her: with a timid glance she saw that he was smiling, and her heart leaped with joy. All her body seemed to become light with it.

CHAPTER II

SEMIRAMIS was the oldest of four children: her sister Ann came next, born after three years; then Ezekiel Wikker, after a further two; and five years later, and last born of all, Handel.

Ezekiel Wikker, a man now of forty, had become a wealthy landowning farmer, increasing the farm which had been their parents' property into a sizable estate, by making good use of the money he inherited at the same time. When he married he built a wing of three vast rooms to the original building and re-christened it Upgang House, but his wife did not live to enjoy these honours—she died when their only child, a daughter, was a few weeks old. Shortly after her death, he dismissed the indoor servants, engaging in their place a single woman from the village. She was called Soal, Martha Mary Soal; she was a dry, placid woman, plump, with thick long chestnut hair. Before Bessie Wikker was a year old she had a half-brother, of whom after they were babies together she saw very little: he lived with his mother in the kitchens and for some whim Ezekiel made Soal wait on the little girl, whose nurse and foster-mother she had been, in the newly-built sitting-room. Bessie learned early that she was not welcome in the kitchens, and she sometimes passed two or three days when she was a child without speaking to anyone—if her father had gone out or Soal was in one of her wry-tempered moods.

This year she was ten years old; she went to the village school and she had begun to read the books thrown heedlessly into a cupboard in the sitting-room. She read *Combe on Digestion*, and Josephus's *History of the Jews*, and two volumes of an account of Albert N'yanza, by the first Englishman to set eyes on it—but, "How," he exclaimed, "can I lead the more tender sex through dangers and fatigues, and passages of savage life? A veil shall be thrown over many scenes of brutality that I was forced to witness, but which I will not force upon the reader;" and with a glance, respectful yet mild, towards his "fair readers," he excused himself for describing incidents and scenes which might offend a sensitive mind by beseeching them to reflect that his young wife had accom-

15

panied him in the frightful discomforts and dangers of the journey, which lasted for more than four years.

Ezekiel Wikker attended his brother's wedding, but he made the excuse that it was entirely unexpected to save himself the trouble of sending a present. The next morning he rose very early, at five o'clock, and walked round the fields nearest the house, looking carefully at the fences. His land was the only creature— he thought of it as a living being—on whom he was prepared to spend money. His daughter had one frock for the winter and another for summer, and Soal helped her to make her own calico and flannel underclothes, but there was not a foot of rotten fencing or a broken-down gate on the whole eighteen hundred acres. He paid his men fair wages, and even during the harvest they fetched their own meals: he provided nothing—not even a glass of ale.

He came back at six o'clock and found Soal setting milk for butter, in shallow dishes in the dairy. He called her away to give him his breakfast, of wheaten porridge, bacon, and potato cakes. Following her out to the larder he watched her cut half a dozen thick slices from a side of bacon, the flesh almost black and the rind covered with a green bloom like an almond. He took a piece of string from his pocket and measured accurately the length of side which remained.

"That's to see you don't feed yourself and that boy o' yourn on the fat of the land," he said, looking slyly at her. "You're too fat, d'y'hear, and so is he. It seems I'm to look after you—at your age!—or else you'll brusten yourself, eating and drinking until you can't breathe. Why, it's shameful."

"You can choke yourself with your string for all I care," Soal said, with friendly good humour. She had half a side of bacon hidden in the loft, with sugar and currants, and a few other necessaries.

"Is that a way to talk to me—haven't you any respect?" He shook his arms at her, and brought one doubled hand down, crack, on to the table. Soal looked at him with honest fear and admiration and shrugged her shoulders. He was very strong and full bodied, with a red flush in his cheeks, black and self-confident eyes, and a heavy resolute jowl.

"Why should I respect you?" she said; "you're too much like every other man—you're only larger, noisier, and greedier than the rest. Tell me something—is it going to rain?"

"Yes," he said, at once. He could always feel the approach of rain. "I want that roll of sailcloth from the loft. Shall I moil up and get it, or will you? if you're not too fat and careful."

"I'll go." She had covered the bacon under a heap of sacks and pushed it behind a chest, but he would smell it—he had an extraordinary sense of smell.

"I've sold it. I gave two shillings for it at a sale and by God when I got it home I found it was rotten. I've had only ten shillings offered for it—ten shillings for nearly eighteen yards of the best canvas! It's pure black-hearted robbery, and if she knew how rotten it was, she wouldn't pay that. How's any honest man to live and feed a houseful of women when he has to give away eighteen yards of cloth at sixpence a yard? Tell me that." He took her by the ear and looked at her mournfully, but he was in high spirits. "Bless me, you're a fine woman," he said; "you're more like a whale than a Soal, but I'll overlook it. If the Guernseys all calve easily to time, I'll give you half a crown—no, a shilling— to go into Wik. Say I never stint you!"

"You'll do as you please," Soal said, with a dry smile. She moved away, glancing at her plump shoulders in the mirror as she did so. She thought herself well enough off here. There were ways of getting round him—she would to-day take more flour than she needed for the potato cakes and hide part of it in the pantry. He followed her when she went to the sack and dipped her basin in it; then he levelled the flour with his right hand and pressed the other on it. This hand was deformed by the loss of one finger and the curiously twisted shape of the thumb, so that it left a mark on the brownish surface of the flour there was no imitating: he would know at once if she went to the sack again this morning and punish her for it in some way.

After breakfast he went out again and rode over that side of his estate which touched Scoresby's land. Here a long field belong-ing to Scoresby, over a hundred acres, thrust itself between two of his. It was a maddening sight; it completely spoiled this side for him. He could scarcely bring himself to look at it or think of it. For ten years now he had been trying to persuade the other man to sell, but it was the largest and oldest part of his farm—it had been marked on a map of 1680 as Scoresby's Field. Scoresby refused to part. To add injury to insult, he neglected it most years, and weeds crept from it into Ezekiel's wheat—it was like a rotten tooth between sound ones.

Scoresby's house was more unkempt than ever; a wretched-looking horse was grazing in the field nearest the house and reaching over to snatch at the grass in the garden, and a cart with one wheel off and a splintered shaft lay out in the yard. It was the very cart he had taken to drive Kezia to the vicarage. Last night he was celebrating the wedding in Under Wik, and driving into his yard afterwards he struck the gate post and rolled head first into the pond. The icy water brought him to his senses and he went indoors and tried to pray, but the few words he could call to mind were little use—For what we have received, may the Lord make us truly thankful. He repeated them doubtfully several times and they brought him no comfort.

He came out when he heard Ezekiel's horse, and stood blinking and coughing in the sunlight. "Hey, this is a poor business," said Ezekiel, staring round him at the cart. From the cart his glance travelled over Scoresby himself, his soiled jacket with the green from the pond dried on it, and a red and yellow handkerchief covering his head, except where a large rent allowed to be seen dirty grey matted hair and grease.

"Oh, it's nothing," Scoresby said, cheerfully. "I've a better cart on order; it'll be here next week or some day. I don't take any account of that."

This was a lie, and Ezekiel knew it to be one; but he told so many lies himself that he would have been surprised to hear the truth spoken in an awkward moment. He turned his horse, to get a view of the field he coveted, and said carelessly:

"You've let the thistles get into that field again. I'm going to put a man in to pull them. Ha' you any objection?"

"None, none," Scoresby said, waving his hand. "I intended to see to it myself, but I've been busy—you see, I've nobbut m'self in the house, I can't ask you in—that brother o' yours seduced my girl and took her off. I ought to have thrashed him, but I didn't want to bring disgrace on the Church."

"She's married and no harm done," Ezekiel said shortly. He felt that his brother had made a fool of himself and a sense of discomfort, unusual in him, filled him when he thought about it. "I rode over to speak to you about your field——"

"Yes, about the thistles," Scoresby said slyly.

"No—devil take the thistles, we'll pull them for you—it's too good a field to be in the state it is, you ought to be ashamed——" he cut himself short, and began in a coaxing voice: "The fact is.

you ought to sell; you can't manage the field, you're not getting younger—I'll give you a fair price for it. What more do you want? I can't keep on asking about it, time's money. I want to set men to work—in short, my dear chap, you really ought to sell it—you'd be doing the best for yourself and"—his eyes blazed with longing—"for the field. Come now, why don't you?"

Scoresby squinted up at him with what was almost a simper.

"What a pity t'field isn't a young silly gel," he said rapidly. "Then you could creep in one night and have her, without paying —like y'r brother. You're alike."

Ezekiel's face turned a dark colour with disappointment and anger. "You miserable sinner," he said. "You starved, rotten hoop of a man, you're not fit to own a blade of grass of your own, let alone a field like that. But I wouldn't buy it off you now if you came to me on your knees."

He began to move off quickly, but not quickly enough to avoid hearing Scoresby call after him: "If I want to sell any of my fields I've had a better offer; I've had scores of offers for it— but I'm not selling. I tell you I'm not selling a single foot, not a foot."

Instead of going home, Ezekiel rode over to the north side of the marsh, where his sister, Ann Wellhem, lived with her husband. Soureby Bog Hall took its name from that corner of the marsh: a vast field of coarse grass and reeds stretched from the garden to the edge of the marsh, and in bad weather the sea came up to the fence separating garden and field. Now, in May, the tides were low and gentle, and the field was covered with vivid green hummocks of grass, spotted orchis and the somnolent bog buttercups. A bridle path followed the curve of the marsh, above flood level, and climbed the hill at the opposite side from the house. Half-way up the hill, among the first houses of Over Wik, it became a narrow road and climbed steeply to the top, crossed the width of the cliff between the best houses, declined among shops, and fell down the other side to the harbour and the bridge. Driving a heavy old carriage along this path, over the rough short grass and stones on either side of it, was neither safe nor easy; but Mrs. Wellhem preferred to go on doing that rather than pay the cost of making a road to the house. She was more miserly than Ezekiel. He was fond of her; she and Semiramis,

of whom he was a little afraid, were the only people in the world
he respected.   Between him and Ann there was less than two years;
in childhood they had been allies against Semiramis, who pinched
their legs and arms in bed as a punishment, and stole their things
from them.

Ann Wellhem was small and slight.   Her eyes were the only
noticeable part of her face; they were a pale greenish-blue, set
widely apart; an innocently malicious light came into them when
she was speaking, as though a wick had been turned up for the
occasion.   She wore an appalling red wig, and carried herself
with dignity.   The strangest thing about her was precisely her
dignity: no one treated her rudely, neither the tradesmen whom
she cheated out of their money nor any of her wide circle of
acquaintances.   Even when her hat, with the wig caught in it,
blew off and rolled away along the sea wall in Wik, the retired sea
captain who returned it to her saw nothing absurd in the way in
which she beat the dust out of it before arranging it again over
her wisps of real and still reddish hair.

Her husband, William Wellhem, had a weakness of the bone
which bent his legs outwards; he was no taller than his wife, and
entirely and helplessly under her will.   He had none of his own.
The money he inherited from his father had been lost a year
after the marriage in the bankruptcy of a shipping firm and he
was dependent on her for everything.   He had less than fifty
pounds a year of his own money left.   Out of this he had to clothe
himself and to pay her for any extra trouble he gave in the house.
Since she was the judge, he found himself at the end of every
month not only penniless but in debt to her for such items as
"cleaning a second pair of boots"—"wear of carpet in doorway"
—"wear to sheets caused by restlessness on the night of May
fifteenth."   He had never summoned the spirit to defy her.   One
afternoon, when they were walking together on that part of the
west cliff known as the Piece, Sir Thomas Money stopped to
ask William how he was.   He had scarcely begun to answer
when Ann rapped him on the head with her knuckles and
said:

"There's th' head and th' hair, Sir Thomas, but there's nought
else."   William merely walked on, with bent head and legs.   His
name in the town—but it had not come to his wife's ears—was
Sweet William.

They had one daughter, Lily.   It was always a matter of

speculation in Wik whether William had known at all what he was doing. She was the same age as her cousin, Bessie Wikker —a lean silent little girl, with her father's long face and melancholy blue eyes.

When Ezekiel rode up to the house he saw his sister stooped over a bed of strawberries in the lower garden. Turning his horse into the yard, he walked up to her and began to pour out his troubles.

"Ann, I've made a fool of m'self again—I have—it's this evil temper of mine, it'll be the death of me one day—I shall go too far, and my veins will burst with rage, and that'll be the end of me. See what happened to me this morning. I went to see that fellow Scoresby about his field, I sidled up to him as if we were dear friends, I praised his farm, I told him what splendid wheat he had, and his clover, and the rest of it—I was speaking in a voice like milk, and I said all that, upon my honour I did— and what happened? All at once I lost my temper with him and told him the truth; I answered him according to his folly, and I shall have to begin again from the beginning. My pride has brought me low—as Solomon says—*an angry man stirreth up strife, and a furious man aboundeth in transgression.* Yes, he says—*Seest thou a man that is hasty in his words? there is more hope of a fool than of him.* Me, *me*, that's me, myself, Ezekiel Wikker at your service."

His sister looked at him with affection. "You should send your solicitor to see Scoresby."

"No, it's no use. I'm too simple to have any dealings with solicitors. They'd cheat me out of my money. They'd join with that brute Scoresby to rob me of everything. I'm done for, Ann—shot—scalped—skinned—and all because I'm a contentious man and can't hold my tongue when I'm provoked." He was enjoying himself richly in this catalogue of his vices. His eyes twinkled, and he danced with excitement in front of her, on the path. Catching sight of an early strawberry among the leaves, he bent to pick it, but she was too quick for him.

"No, you don't," she said sharply. "Leave those alone— they're mine."

"Can't you spare, what, one?"

"No, I can't." She smiled very slightly. "If William saw you eating one of them, he might get it into his head that he could take them himself." Bringing her head near to his, she said:

"I played a trick on him last Friday. What do you think, two friends of his from London, a lawyer and such another fellow, had the impudence to call here. I ordered a chicken to be killed for them, for their dinner, and as soon as they left I handed him t'bill for it, three shillings; I got his money and gave him an honest receipt. Then what does the fool do but leave the receipt lying on a chair, so I took it, and swore to it he'd never paid me. He was a'most crying when he fetched out the second three shillings. Six shillings for a bird so old I a'most broke my teeth on it! And their faces!—serve them right for coming."

With reluctance, she invited him to stay to dinner. He went in with her. They found Sweet William already seated meekly at the foot of the table. Ann looked at the loaf on the serving-table with a suspicious sharpness, to know whether he had been eating anything. There was no butter on the table; when Ezekiel asked for it a piece no larger than a sparrow's egg was brought in, of which Ann allowed him half.

"D'y'know what Semiramis says?" Ezekiel smiled. "That you start the week with a pound of butter and finish it with two—you've scraped it on, and scraped it off again, crumbs and all."

"I'll have a word to say to Semiramis," she said mildly. "And you, you needn't sit there simpering. When your wife, poor young gel, was dying, you used to eat her food. And you the stout healthy man you are!"

Ezekiel was not abashed. "But what do you think—isn't that the very reason? Judge for yourself, don't I need more food than anyone else? Look at my stomach—why, it's eight times the size of yours or William's. What does a poor weak creature lying in bed all day want with cream, eggs and beef juice? I needed that food; I shouldn't be alive here now without it."

"Well, you needn't come here often and think you'll be asked to dinner every time," said Ann. She leaned forward to look into the dish in front of her. "William, do you want any more of the pudding?"

"It'll do for my supper," he ventured.

"No, that it won't," she said, with a short laugh; "if you can't eat it now it will be warmed for my dinner to-morrow."

William said nothing. The servant carried away the dishes

and Ann retired to her room, after seeing that there was nothing Ezekiel could take. He stood up, and opened the window. Trees, grass, and the wide silent marsh shone in the strong sunlight as if varnished. The sea lay beyond the marsh, smoke-coloured, an untrodden field. Everything was somnolent, glittering, at peace —everything except William Wellhem, who crossed the garden as slowly and sadly as a snail, in his dark clothes. Thinking of the six shillings, Ezekiel felt sorry for him. But how, he wondered, did he come to marry such a woman as Ann?

CHAPTER III

HANDEL was turned out of his church; or rather, instantly and without questioning, at the request of the Bishop, he laid it down. There were awkward and unpleasant scenes in the church on three or four Sundays; the scandal, instead of being forgotten, spread more widely and began to creep into the newspapers. At last, after he had received a number of letters about it, the Bishop sent for Handel to discuss the trouble.

The Bishop was at least twenty-five years the elder, but he had an air of suavity and innocence with his authority. The two men liked each other. Handel told him, with the greatest coldness and brevity, that his marriage to a young girl, the daughter of a farmer, had become a cause of offence. After a few vague sentences, the older man asked him quietly: "Was the offence just?"

Handel was looking through the opened window into the garden. A glorious plane-tree stood close under the window, with sweeping branches like green glossy steps, but its leaves were covered with dark blotches and dried at the edges. He looked from it into the Bishop's steady, shrewd little eyes, and said gently: "Yes."

An expression of profound unhappiness and distaste crossed the other man's face. He broke the silence to ask Handel whether he desired to make any further explanation. No, Handel had nothing, no palliation of his sin to offer. His only duty was an absolute obedience. The only thing he could do, to save trouble, he did. He resigned his church, although he did not leave Wik. Indeed, it never occurred to him to go away. He was a poor man. He had spent—without thinking about it—all the money his father left him, and all his large earnings when he was the captain of a whaler. He bought any instruments he needed for his experiments; he had once travelled six thousand miles to watch an eclipse, and he paid the university fees of no fewer than five poor scholars, the sons of merchant officers whose fathers had been drowned at sea. When he left the vicarage he had only a hundred and thirty pounds in the world.

Semiramis behaved very badly. The vicarage was old and shabby, and she had had a modern range fitted into the kitchen, and had replaced several ill-fitting doors and window frames by new ones. Without waiting, she had all these torn out, and the old ones, which had been mouldering in an outhouse for three years, botched into the gaps. When she left with her spoils, the house looked as though a storm had rushed through it.

She bought a large house in Over Wik. Handel refused for Kezia's sake to live with her in it, and took a two-roomed cottage on the unfashionable east cliff. It stood alone, at the head of a steep road called the Garth, and looked down over the crowded roofs of Under Wik to the harbour and the new shipyard. A field of almost three acres went with the house. Handel began at once to dig it over, and to build a third room to hold his books and where he could carry on his researches.

It was September when they first went to the house, and the evenings were made glorious by the sun, which sank behind the opposite cliff and sent its level rays straight in at the windows of their rooms. For ten minutes every evening they were caught up in a radiance which transfigured everything it touched, the walls, the separate blades of grass in the field, their faces. It was as though suddenly they had found themselves living in a suburb of the City of God.

When Handel Wikker was working in his garden, he had time to think over what had happened since the evening of the sixteenth of May. He drew a distinction in his mind between the obedience he owed the Church and his obedience to God. The Church, he thought, must avoid even the appearance of evil, but God need not. He is above the necessity for such carefulness. Therefore his position regarding God, the obedience he owed to Him, was quite different from his duty to the Church. He did not feel that in lying with Kezia he had committed a sin for which God need punish him. But he was dumbfounded by it. He could not explain what had possessed him—it was as though his soul had suddenly lost its senses and gone mad in him. And if such a thing could happen to him, Handel Wikker, what became of his simple understanding of good and evil? He did not know. But at least he knew that there was nothing evil in Kezia or in their life here.

He was not convinced that what he had done was evil. The Church, through its Bishop, had condemned him rightly—he was a stone of offence to them—but God, he thought, could easily

c

read his heart and what He read there was certainly not anything of which He need disapprove. Indeed, there were moments—and these were usually in the evening—when Handel *demanded* that God should approve of him.

He had begun to think that man is capable of anything, of any act or feeling. Now he believed that God had willed him to know this and, therefore, had cast him down. This was just —he accepted it; he accepted God's right to use any means to bring a man to his knees; and in return he required that God must accept him. That, also, would only be fair.

With Kezia he was happy as few are happy. Returning to the house one evening, he saw her a moment before she heard him. She was leaning on the table in their living room, spreading the cloth, smoothing it idly with her roughened fingers. Her slender body was already altered by their child which she was carrying, and her face had become thinner and more beautiful. The delicate bones of her forehead were clearly marked. She was not browned by the sun; her neck was white and slender, like the neck of a little girl. She stretched it forward, and stooped across the heavy table; she was smiling a little at her thoughts.

Turning, she saw Handel in the doorway and gave a little cry of joy. "You're early—I'm not quite ready. The kettle's not boiled yet. You must wait; you're really early."

"I know," he said, coming into the room. He caught hold of her. "Are you as happy as you look, Kezia?"

"If I look happy——"

"You do. Are you?" He glanced round the room. "You're not lonely here? I don't spend much time with you—not as much as I should." He was startled to hear himself speaking in this way.

Kezia did not answer at once. She leaned on his shoulder, but not with her whole weight, and seemed at a loss for words. At last she said quietly: "I don't expect you to spend time with me, as you call it. You have other things to do—I don't mean your work in the field. I mean your books, things that have nothing to do with me. If we had not come here"—she hesitated, and could not bring herself to speak of the vicarage—"it would have been different. You would have lived your usual life, and I —I should have had a small share of it. Here in this house you notice me." Her face changed, and she began to smile merrily. "There's really no need, I assure you. I am very well off. Much better off than when I was living in London, with my aunt. Or with my father," she added, with a slight air of nervousness.

"My dear Kezia," Handel said gently. He looked at her dark shining hair and stroked it: he felt himself trembling with a tenderness he could not express, and a sudden acute fear. This was perhaps the first time in which he thought of her as having a life of her own—a life that went on in his absence, and could bring her pains and loneliness, as well as what was no doubt the satisfaction of being his wife.

This thought recurred to him one grey February afternoon when he went into Wik to fetch the midwife for her. This elderly woman, Mrs. Waind, lived in a house which seemed to be tottering into the harbour. It had one foot in the water, and leaned crazily forward as though the next moment must see it fall. The midwife herself lived in the upper of two rooms. The lower was occupied by her father, a man of ninety-six, bed-ridden for years. Since he had no use for his wooden leg (a shark had snatched off the real one in Sydney Harbour, to his extreme surprise and annoyance—he was never tired of repeating: "One minute I had two legs, and the next th' shark had one and I had th' other. E-ee, th' sinner. . . .") he lashed it out of the window with the Blue Peter at the end. One flood-tide his room was awash; he floated through the window on his bed, and only the leg saved him from being carried down the harbour and drowned.

Mrs. Waind promised to come at once, and Handel returned to the cottage. At three o'clock in the afternoon the light was already going, but as he climbed the Garth he found it brighter up here than in the narrow mist-haunted streets of Under Wik. The grass was heavy with moisture and a trickle of water poured down one side of the Garth to lose itself in the grey water of the harbour. He had sent a message to Semiramis, and she came when the midwife had been in the house an hour and already regarded it as her own. When on duty she was no respecter of persons. Semiramis looked her over with a contemptuous, "Ha! so you're here, Waind, are you?" and went upstairs to the bedroom to see Kezia. The doctor arrived at the same time, and he, too, went upstairs, followed by the midwife, who found the stairs a trial and complained loudly.

The room, lit by one lamp, was crowded with so many people in it. Handel stood close to the door and looked silently at his wife. She was half-sitting up in bed, her hair drawn tightly in a plait; she looked even younger, and unfamiliar. Her hands held the sheet up to her shoulders, and she gazed from one to the other of her visitors in alarm. Her cheeks were flushed. When the pains came she closed her eyes, biting her lips to keep silent.

"Now, doctor, you're here in good time," Semiramis said, smiling. "What d'you make of her?"

The doctor—a Scotchman, with a reputation for drunkenness and severity—took Kezia's wrist, but did not begin to count her pulse. "You're all right," he said, dropping it. "You're doing splendidly. How d'you feel?"

Kezia raised her eyes, which seemed darker because of the shadow thrown by the lamp, and looked at him. At the same moment she felt a pain which was really agonizing; she cried out, and caught his arm. "Must I?" she whispered half unconsciously. She looked at Handel.

"Come, come," said the doctor, with loud kindness, "you're not afraid. The pains are good for you. Don't you know that? You will soon, you will soon."

He went out of the room, and Handel followed him. "You could give her something to deaden the pain?" he said. He had been horrified by the look on Kezia's face when she seized the doctor's hand.

"I could, but I'm not going to," the other man said promptly. "Don't lose your head, my dear sir. The whole process is perfectly natural; the pain is natural—it's nothing—women like to make a fuss, but I can assure you it's nothing. Mrs. Waind will send for me when she wants me." He took himself off.

Handel shut himself in the little room he had built at the side of the house, and tried to finish an article he was writing when Kezia had sent him for Mrs. Waind. But he was unable to forget his wife's face—she had looked at him with reproach, like a child who is being tortured—and he had to shut his ears to her cries. The grey afternoon became evening; the hours passed slowly, with no change except that Kezia cried more and would not answer him when he talked to her.

Towards midnight he went into the living-room and found his sister and Mrs. Waind drinking tea together. They were sitting close to the fire, their skirts turned back over their knees, and talking now in a friendly way. The midwife's face was covered with tiny beads of sweat; she sucked sugar off the end of her spoon and poured the tea into her saucer. Semiramis sat stiffly, with

a look of excitement, her lips moving a little even when she was
not speaking.

The swollen elongated shadows of the two women met together
on the ceiling in the circle of pale light cast by the lamp. "Pain
is the curse of Eve," Mrs. Waind said. She blew on her tea in
the saucer and sank her nose in the brown ripples.

"Why aren't you attending to my wife?" Handel said sharply.
He had felt dismay and a sudden suffocating anger when he came
in and saw them.

"Your wife is asleep," answered Semiramis—before the other
woman could recover from a fit of coughing. "What's the matter?
Are you choking?" she said to the midwife. "Come, control
yourself, my good woman." Handel went out.

Kezia was not asleep, but her pains had ceased for a time,
and she was lying with closed eyes. She opened them suddenly
and saw that the lamp had begun to burn unevenly and was blackening the side of the glass. She watched it for a moment, and the
thread of smoke wavering in the draught, and the yellow flame.
It appeared a long way off, as though a vast dun-coloured plain
lay between it and her. She felt terribly lonely. She dozed off
and seemed to wake again with darkness all round her. Somewhere in this darkness an old woman was crouching, and Kezia
knew that the woman was about to suffocate her. She gave a
feeble cry. In the same instant she awoke fully. The lamp had
been turned down, and Semiramis Jordan was in the room, standing
quite near the bed. Bending over Kezia, she said: "Are y'awake,
girl?"

Too afraid of her to make any reply, Kezia said nothing. Her
pains began again at that moment, and she turned her face from
the light.

"You'll ha' a boy," Semiramis went on. "He's due—since
there are only gels in th' family. If you take my advice you'll
ha' him circumcised in three days—the sooner the better."

Kezia looked at her in growing horror. "But I don't want
him to be hurt," she murmured.

"You'll do as I tell you, or I'll ha' nought to do with him.
And mind you, Kezia, I can give him something. I ha' more
money than I want, and only one gel—and she's not to have it."

Kezia looked round the room, at the lamp, and at the older
woman's black, inquisitive eyes. These eyes seemed to bore into
her flesh, as if it were no longer any shelter for her baby. She

began to cry quietly, this time not for herself; she was crying for
the child. "Let him alone," she said in a low voice, "I want him
to be left quiet and not hurt." The door opened and Mrs. Waind
came in.

"What's this! Crying at your age! Why, how old are you?"

"Eighteen."

Semiramis stood up and walked stiffly across the room. "She's
ovver-tired," she said, in a severe voice. Her short, heavy body
came between Kezia and the light and it seemed to the young
woman that she had at last been abandoned. She closed her
eyes.

Handel fell asleep in his room. He slept uncomfortably, leaning sideways in his chair, and woke in the remote light before dawn.
The house was silent. He opened the window and leaned far out.
The air was clear and cold, stinging on his cheeks and on his eyelids.
He loved Wik, and never more than when he saw it at some moment
like this, when perhaps no one else was looking at it. In the stillness he heard sounds and voices from the shipyard. They were
preparing for the launch at twelve o'clock, and he felt suddenly
that he would like to see the ship again before she left; he knew her
owner, and the master who was taking her on her first voyage had
once been third mate on one of Handel's ships.

The door opened and his sister put her head in. "So you're
awake, are you?" she said shortly. Her face had a peculiar
severity and sullenness, and her black eyes were lively. She looked
at him with a motiveless hostility. "You'll be wanting your
breakfast."

"How is Kezia?" As he spoke, a cry from the room upstairs
made him start, and he felt a cold shiver in his spine. "It's still
going on," he said, without actually knowing what he was saying.

"Yes, there'd be something wrong if it wasn't."

He went upstairs to Kezia. She was flushed and haggard.
Her cheeks seemed to have fallen in, and her eyes were staring—
she was quite ugly. The midwife had just tied a roller towel to
the end of the bed and was thrusting it into her slack hands.
"Grip your hands inside that, woman, and pull on it when the
next pain comes," she ordered. Kezia clenched her hands, but
without pulling, and moaned, rolling her head from side to side.
She looked at Handel with no recognition in her look. "Pull, I
tell you; pull," Mrs. Waind said, angrily.

Handel touched Kezia's forehead. It was cold and slippery

with sweat. But this is dreadful, he thought. "Can't you do anything for her?" he said, turning to the woman.

"Your wife ought to be doing something for herself," the woman answered. She looked exhausted. When Semiramis came into the room Handel suggested that he should go for the doctor, but both she and the midwife poured scorn on the idea. "*I'll* tell you when I want the doctor bothering us," cried Semiramis.

She pushed him out of the bedroom. Vexed and disturbed, he left the house and hurried down the Garth to the shipyard. The ship that was to be launched was a four-masted barque, beautiful and very light—it was well named *The Cloud*. In the yard the flags were already up, lifted to the winter sunlight by a light breeze. Tiny pointed waves lapped the wall. Smells of iron, of new rope, of the mud under the water, mingled with the fragrance of new wood—a platform for the musicians had been put up that morning and the yellow curled shavings were blowing about the yard.

Handel spoke to one of the men, who replied: "Yes, and she's reckoned one of the handsomest ships ever built—and an iron ship at that. But for all of it, she's a killer. Killed one chap, yes, outright, and broke the arm off another, snapped it across when he wasn't looking. Nor she won't change, either."

Handel waited in the yard for some time, but at ten o'clock he went back to his house, half afraid and half hoping to hear that all was over and his child born. But Kezia was still in pain, and her cries had become terrible and inhuman. He went outside to escape them and stood listening guiltily to the noises of the launch. The music came up to him in snatches, with other sounds, voices, excited cries, and suddenly a burst of cheering, which rose, swelled, and died into a murmur as the masts of *The Cloud* moved forward, passing slowly out of his sight.

Without thinking he started to hurry towards the Garth, so that he would be in time to see her move down the harbour. Semiramis's voice reached him when he had taken only a few steps. He turned back quickly.

Kezia's son had been born—but before he had time to ask how she was, a man came, running and breathless, to ask him to come at once to the yard. There had been an accident. An apprentice had plunged into the water to pick up the floating blocks, as was his duty; no one saw how he managed to get himself struck by the gliding *Cloud*, and by a miracle he was still breathing and alive when they dragged him out. He wanted a parson—"Get me, he says, go up running and get me Handel Wikker; th' new chap may be a better Christian, who knows? but he couldn't sail, could he, his ship in all weathers? His ship home, he says, the round trip."

Semiramis cut short the man's half-incoherent words to ask whether the doctor was down there in the shipyard.

"Ay, he is," the man stammered.

"You can tell him we've done without him," she said to Handel, with a spiteful air of triumph.

Handel hurried to the yard, thinking as he went of Kezia, with joy and relief. Under his breath he repeated, "Kezia, dear soul—wait for me; wait a minute."

The youth was dead when he reached the yard, and the doctor leaning drunkenly against the wall of the sail loft looking at him. He had been at the breakfast at eleven o'clock, before the launch. When he saw Handel he remembered that his wife was in labour and without asking him any questions he left the yard to go and see her. He could scarcely walk up the Garth, wavering and slipping, and twice stepped over his ankles in water into the ditch at the side.

He was met at the door by Semiramis Jordan, who hurried him upstairs. Kezia was dying. He could hardly have saved her even if he had not been drunk; and when Handel came she was dead. The child was alive and crying loudly—from hunger, the midwife told them; she was giving him drops of milk and water on the end of a clean rag.

The young woman's death had almost sobered the doctor, but he was not yet sober enough to be surprised when Semiramis seized him by the arm as he was leaving the house, and exclaimed: "I'll not ha' him circumcised. Do you hear me? I'll—not—ha' him touched at all." In his bemused state, he found everything natural. He felt sorry for Handel, extremely sorry—but what could he have done about it?

Other people were sorry for Handel, and many of them chose to forget that his marriage had been a scandalous and disgraceful business. They were prepared to send flowers and carriages to follow Kezia. But then Handel vexed them again by arranging to bury her at sea. The truth was that here now the master mariner—he had the words, "Kezia, wife of Handel Wikker,

Master Mariner, of this parish, Born 1865. Died 1883," set on her coffin—took charge of him, as if the last eight or nine years of his life had been nothing. The rest of the truth was that he could not endure the thought of the young girl lying *under* the earth. He turned to the sea to help him out, as naturally as if he had never left it.

After three days she was carried down to the fish quay and put on board a cobble. The day was Saturday, a day when by custom the men at work in the shipyard were given beer and farthing rolls before knocking off. This noon they had actually voted to do without, and were on the quay to see the young woman go.

The boat took her three miles out, beyond the buoy. There she was lowered overboard. The sea was exquisitely calm, and the coffin slid through the water like a fish, flashing swiftly out of sight. The master of the cobble noticed a change Handel made in the service. After the words, "We therefore commit her body to the *sea*"—he added, "that takest away the sins of the flesh."

He stood a long time looking after her. The water rose to him in just such pointed waves as he had seen in the harbour on the day of the launch; bubbles of light sprang from it, at random, in arrowy flashes, so that his eye was shot through with them. Looking into these strange depths, so clear and so impenetrable, he saw his spirit broken and dispersed by its fall with Kezia into the life-breeding water.

II

CHAPTER IV

ONE fine morning in June Ezekiel Wikker came to see his brother. He had driven from Upgang House, through the town, and at the bottom of the Garth he was forced to get out of the trap and walk. The horse could not pull him up that hill. He had to walk beside it, to see that it did not slip and bruise itself on one of the loose stones. He was not only out of breath when he reached the top—he was very angry. He walked into Handel's room, beating the dust off his sleeves with his hat, his face scarlet and swelling.

"Look at me!" he cried. "Do you know a bigger fool? To come up here in this heat, crawling up the road on my knees, sweating—my heart in my mouth. I'm fifty-one—yes, d'you hear? Upon my word, if I die of a stroke to-night you'll be a murderer, brother Handel—it's your devil's fault, you shouldn't live in this God-forsaken place."

"It suits me," Handel said, with his slight smile. "But why give yourself the trouble? If you wanted me I could have come."

"Did you come last month when I sent? Or the month before? You ha'n't been for eight months. Semiramis says you read, and dig potatoes, and read, and walk at night, and read—what the devil do you read?" he asked, with cunning innocence. "You must ha' every book in the world in your head." He leaned forward, his eyes bright with a peculiar eagerness and curiosity. "Everything—you must know every trick under the sun. That's what I want—I want you to tell me how to get my hands on Scoresby's Field. There must be something. I've heard of a woman dropping something in a field—so that everything died—grass, beasts, rabbits. You must ha' read about it. Tell me, I say, tell me."

Handel shook his head. "No," he said, severely. "No, there's nothing—and you ought to be ashamed to ask. I wouldn't tell you if I knew."

"You live an unnatural life," Ezekiel muttered, with an ironical calm. "You don't know what shame is. Now *I* do. I'm often sunk with shame—the thoughts that come into my head! God

37

knows where they come from. I don't." He hesitated, something
that was almost genuine diffidence came into his voice. "You
should look round and get a woman here. Kezia's been dead
ten years—at the least. What's the good? Walking at night,
and the rest of it—you'll be out of your mind before long, and
then where will you be?"

"Out of my mind," Handel said. He was setting his dinner
—bread, cheese, and a lettuce—when his brother came. A way to
get rid of him was to ask him to stay and share it. Ezekiel glanced
once at the table, with distaste, and went away. Semiramis,
although he was far from anxious to see her, would give him a
better dinner, and perhaps a glass of port—if she were in a generous
mood. He turned in the doorway, to say:

"Ten years is a long time. No doubt you're a finer character
than I am—I couldn't stand it. Nor will you, if you starve yourself—and walk when you ought to be in bed, with a decent woman,
yes, within easy reach."

Handel watched him out of sight—because it was pleasant to
stand in the sun and feel the salt in the air stinging his face. A
sea-gull flew overhead, its wings dazzling against the blue sky.
Then he went back into his room, to his dinner and the *Summa
Theologica*. He carried morsels of dry cheese to his mouth on a
piece of bread, and half-way through he dropped knife and bread
and began to walk up and down the narrow room. It was terribly
untidy, with books thrown about the floor; a dish carrying the
cheese had been set down on the window-sill a week since—no
wonder it was dry—boots had been dropped among his papers,
and dust lay everywhere. The other two rooms were tidy, but
in this one he declined to disturb his papers.

*"God therefore neither wills evil to be done, nor wills it not to be
done, but wills to permit evil to be done; and this is a good."*

Thomas Aquinas was peculiarly dear to him—he even felt
that he understood him as intimately as a younger brother may
understand an elder, because although they are unequal in mind,
they had the same nurture. But, again like a younger brother,
he rebelled—against Saint Thomas's serenity and certainty. The
evil and cruelty in the world are too much—no one has the right
to feel certain. The frightful tortures which we inflict on each
other, without pity, the slow piecemeal killings, floggings of
prisoners behind locked doors, twistings of genitals, cruelties that
can only be recorded without details, too foul and indecent. And

almost all of them glorified, in the eyes of those who do them, by some vague or well-defined idea of right. The victim is guilty. Therefore it is necessary, it is an act of virtue and goodness, to treat him with beastly cruelty. Why seek in the past? Even here in Wik—this month, this exquisite bright June—the father and mother of a little girl were found by neighbours to have crucified her by fastening her wrists and ankles to hooks in the wall, with thin rope; she hung from three o'clock in the afternoon until eight, when a woman who had been uneasy since she had heard stifled cries ("Don't, I'll be good, oh don't!") looked through the window of the kitchen and saw it. The child had misbehaved herself, said her father calmly: he had punished her to teach her a lesson. Why not? . . . *wills to permit evil to be done* . . . what does it matter in the universe if a little girl, defenceless in the hands of the two people she looks to for protection, is fastened by her soft wrists and ankles to nails and left hanging for five hours, while her care-free gaolers walk about in the sunshine? They talk with people in ordinary voices, like human beings. Ditchburn, the Under Wik butcher, related that they had bought a piece of lamb in his shop and asked in a kindly way after his wife, who had been ill. No, they were not monsters; they were normal human beings—but perverted by their own minds.

Animals do not torture each other for moral and irrational reasons. They kill in order to live; and if like a cat they play with their victim before killing it, even that may not be as it seems, a cruelty which is almost human, but some bodily necessity—the chemistry of an animal's body may demand the stimulation of its organs. It is only men who kill each other for an idea. That which raises us above the animals is at the same time that which makes us disgusting and intolerable.

Opening his window, Handel leaned far out. The clear, light air quivered with arrows from the sea. A cloudless blue sky sprang overhead; and the dry hot scents of the field lying between him and the edge of the cliff crushed him with happiness, in which he recognized one of those memories, of youth itself, which disturb, intoxicate, and in the end sadden.

A sensible man would be content with a world in which such happiness is possible. At sixteen Handel Wikker would have kicked his legs in it like a colt. But he was forty-six. And the ordinary world, lovely beyond bearing when one is in the mood for getting drunk, was a source of sheer horror and grief to him in any of the other moods. Helpless against the cruelty which men enjoy doing, the little girl placed her crucified hands over his eyes. Everywhere he saw nothing but darkness.

He shut the window when his papers began blowing across the floor, and went upstairs. Everything of Kezia's had vanished from their bedroom. He had given away her few dresses and clothes; and there was nothing else. She had brought nothing with her when she came—and left nothing of which he could say: "This reminds me of her." Her son had no feature to which anyone could point as hers; not a look or gesture. Semiramis— he was living with her—used to nudge visitors and say slyly: "Nothing of them thieving lying Scoresbys in him, hey?"

There was not any corner of the house in which he could imagine he saw her again. She had left no mark on it. Living, she was restless and eager. She did not sit still for a single hour; she ran into the garden, ran back again, talked to herself, often laughed, played tricks on him like a child; and succeeded somehow in not making a nuisance of herself. She was scarcely exacting in the way an older woman would have been. She did not expect attention. Some days he hardly noticed her from the moment she awoke in the morning until last thing at night; then in the darkness or by the light of a single candle, she was really a woman, not a child or a young girl. She opened to him with an untroubled self-surrender in which no vestige of fear remained. If he recalled her, it was in one such moment; and then, in horror of himself, he put the thought out of his mind, and rushed from the house.

He was convinced that her death was caused by his sin. It was his punishment—visited on her innocent flesh. He felt that God had punished with extreme severity. Being what he was, he noticed more clearly the cruelties of God to other and greener souls, less able to bear it. But it was true that in killing Kezia He had gone too far with his punishments. Why not say He was unjust?

Pushing aside the loaf, he knocked the jug against which the *Summa* had been propped. Fortunately it was empty. He gathered up the broken pieces; stooping to smooth out the leaves of the book, he read: "*similarly the fornicator has merely pleasure for his object, and the deformity of sin is only an accompaniment.*"

His mind was no longer clear, as it had been clear when he left the sea to begin the studies that led him from natural science to theology and the tall three-decker pulpit in the parish church

of Wik. He was torn by every form of doubt; of himself, of his
honesty, of his place in the world. Why labour to teach virtue to
an animal who delights in inflicting pain? Why not let the cruel,
the weak, the stupid, destroy this world among them, and save
one life at least—one's own? He had scarcely brushed the fringes
of knowledge—why should he not spend the rest of his life learning, and die with at least one tangible satisfaction: that he had
added to the store of real knowledge, scratched together slowly,
patiently, at the cost of life, by men who do not want any other
delight? That might be the only reasonable way of living. All
others illusory.

And yet——?

He knew that was a lie. His mind, and that ass his body,
cried out to him for a satisfaction which did not, to procure itself,
trick him into shutting his ears to the noise of cruelty and folly.

I must do more! he said to himself; day and night he said it.
But since his mind was not certain, what could he do to help the
others—more than nurse them when they were sick, rob himself
of sleep, scold, advise, and when nothing else was any use, take
them his own food? He did all these things, and he knew they
were not enough.

CHAPTER V

THE same week he travelled up to London to attend a meeting of the Royal Society. After the meeting in the evening he was walking across to his lodging, and he realized that he was hungry. He had forgotten to eat since the early morning. He looked for a cheap restaurant and found one in Glasshouse Street, behind Regent Street. A few men were there eating and drinking at a long table, and while Handel was waiting for his food a woman came in alone and seated herself near him. She seemed to be known there. The waiter put his hand on her shoulder when she spoke to him, and served her with a friendly smile.

"Need something to keep you on your poor legs all evening," she said to Handel. She had a quiet, rather hoarse voice, and a smile in which if there was no humour there was a world of good temper and slyness. Her full body was drawn in at the waist, and her cheeks painted. She might have been thirty. She had Kezia's large black eyes, with the slender arched brows.

He was startled by this discovery and continued to stare at her in surprise and anger. She was going to make some impudent remark, but changed her mind and looked at him with a timid, submissive smile. Seeing that he took no notice, she turned her attention to her food. She ate greedily, her tongue working over the morsels of bread and flesh, to draw the last lingering savour from them. When nothing was left, she looked round her with a sly smile. Taking courage from the fact that Handel was still gazing at her, she said in a drawling voice:

"What about standing me a drink of port—or even coffee I could do with if it was good and strong."

Handel called the waiter and told him to bring two cups of black coffee. She thanked him, with a laugh that showed the inside of her mouth and her red moist tongue. Taking a florin from her pocket, she laid it on the table between them and said quietly: "My last—see?" Kezia's eyes in her wide face were suddenly vacant, as if for a moment they had looked down and seen—nothing: darkness. She noticed that he frowned, and thought, with contempt, "They're all alike—they don't want to know anything is wrong: if I was to drop dead now not a soul in the place would be anything but vexed—yes, and afraid to his dirty stomach of being mixed up in it." An unaccustomed bitterness seized her—unaccustomed because she was naturally lazy and easy-going, and enjoyed her life.

When she rose to go, Handel followed her. He was scarcely conscious of her, and did not notice it when as if by accident she brushed her body against his. He walked with her through two or three dark shabby streets until she stopped at a house no shabbier than any of the others. They passed a child sitting on the narrow fœtid staircase. The woman spoke to her, and the child shrank away from them, flattening her thin body against the wall.

The room was dark; she fumbled for a moment and a thin jet of gas spurted behind the globe. It showed him a large bed with a canopy, a washstand, and some other pieces of furniture, submerged in the frowst of walls, carpet, bed hangings—as though everything in the room were the same colour, and that the colour of dried clay. The woman busied herself making tea.

"Queer how that child won't ever look at me," she said calmly. "She's the same age as mine. Look, I was writing to mine this evening, and almost forgot it was time to go out." A sheet of paper and pencil were lying with a soiled garment on the bed. She picked them up together. "It isn't that I'm at all fond of her—you can't be fond of what you don't see, can you?—but I write to her now and then and tell her to be a good girl and not mess her clothes—and I'll give her a present some day—signed, your loving Mother."

She spoke with a rough good-humour, as if inviting him to laugh at her. Handel felt an extreme pity. It made him anxious to speak to her, and while he was hesitating she came and stood beside him, leaning heavily on his arm. His pity changed suddenly into sharp physical longing. He did not want simply to possess her—he felt a suffocating impulse to degrade himself as vilely as possible with this woman. He threw out his arms.

Moving away from him, she went over to the bed and began straightening the soiled covers. Then she turned her head to smile at Handel. He moved nearer to her. She made a simple gesture of invitation, almost the gesture of a child, and unfastened her bodice, drawing her arms out. Handel moved back in horror of himself and what he was doing. For the first moment he saw the room as a room, squalid at that, and the woman as a living human being, whom he had been going to injure.

He spoke to her in a low voice, which nevertheless he could not make sufficiently gentle. She stared widely at him, and said: "Are you going?"

"It's time I went. I ought not to have come."

"You mean you don't like me," she said slowly. Her bare arms hung down, yellow and shapeless, heavy, the arms of an older woman.

Handel became conscious of the noise of London outside the room, and of the whistling of the gas jet behind his head. "I had evil thoughts; you reminded me of—another person. I ask you—I apologize," he said sharply. Almost against his will he felt sorry for her again; it was more than sorrow—a mortified grief. He recalled that she would expect him to leave her money. Before he had put his hand into his pocket the woman leaned forward; lifting her hands, she spat in his face.

"So much for your apologies," she said. Hurrying to the door, she unlocked it clumsily. "Get out of my room." Her face worked, and she began to cry, quietly, drawing in her breath as though she were afraid of making any noise. "Go, go—for mercy's sake," she repeated. When he had gone she locked the door again and sat down on the bed.

She was still crying. She cried because she knew now that she was growing older and less attractive and because she was deeply, mournfully offended. But to her it seemed that she was crying because once years ago she had given all she had, all her savings, to the man she was living with and he had not only left her immediately afterwards, but when she saw him the next day with other men he had made fun of her to them. After a time she lay still, looking at the gas jet until she fell asleep, in her clothes, on the top of the bed.

When Handel left the house he walked for a long time, two or three hours, without noticing where he was going, in a torment of self-loathing. Regent Street was a maze of yellow light and shadows; in the warmth of the June night women, like the woman he had just left, sauntered between the gas lamps in silk dresses and jackets, carriages jostled each other in the road, men and women crossed the areas of light and were lost in the intervening darkness; all the feverish energy of an ant-heap rumoured in his ears: he walked through wide streets becoming emptier and darker, into a side street with high walls, past a church, past men bawling outside a lighted public-house, through streets flaring with gas jets, and slippery with refuse and odours, the stream of men, women, children, surging between two lines of booths like dirty scummy water gleaming in the light from a lamp. What possessed you? Why did you go there with her? There was no answer, it was "the muddy concupiscence of the flesh." He turned, bitterly humiliated, from the thought of Kezia's eyes in the woman's face. His humiliation was mixed with an exasperated anger because he had tried to ask her forgiveness and had come away in the end without giving her money. He had no idea where the house was or the street. He had followed her without looking.

He became calm suddenly, his mind emptied both of his contempt and his suppressed anger. It was as though a process which had been taking place in him over a long time had now reached its last stage—or as if a new one were beginning. Strangely, at this point, he could recall no feature of the woman's face and no detail of her speech or the room. He remembered only the least humiliating moment—when she spat in his face. At that moment hers had taken on the look of childhood: as though what had happened to her in her own person had been too much to bear, and she had gone.

CHAPTER VI

BESSIE WIKKER, at twenty, was a smiling young woman, childishly rounded in face, with lively greenish-brown eyes, and a round head of waved brown hair. She had had no upbringing to speak of; at the age of fifteen, Ezekiel considered her education complete and refused to let her go back to school. He told her that she was to look after his house and see that Martha Soal wasted nothing; at the same time he gave her two pounds for herself, rubbing it into her that she would have to make it do a year. After this, Soal treated her for a time with a sullen scorn, until she saw that the girl was as helpless as any infant to look after herself. Then she was sorry for her in a careless way, and tried in small things to make her life easier. The truth was that Bessie had a mute obstinacy at the core of her soft lively nature, and no better defence.

Every year, when February came round, she was forced to remind her father of her allowance of two pounds. It was every penny she had, for clothes and her own needs. Her soul fainted within her as the moment approached, but she was upheld by desperation. I must have the money, she would repeat to herself, rolling her eyes like a young nervous horse, and certain that she would rather die. She was never able to ask for it in a natural voice.

This year the day of reckoning came on a Sunday. As she dressed herself in her cold bedroom, she thought about the ordeal with a last-minute courage. She was always very slow, both in dressing and putting up her hair; and although she knew that her father was waiting she did not hurry over any part of the ritual. This was the fruit of her obstinacy. It was also despair and folly. There would be trouble. And where another girl might have thought, Why aggravate him? Bessie's thoughts ran, Why rush towards it?

When she came down into the hall Ezekiel strode up to her and took her by the arm, holding her, silent and quivering, at arm's length from him. "So this, this, is the great event I'm

46

kept waiting for, is it? This miracle of beauty and elegance, this pomped show! What do you mean by it, eh? Just tell me. Words, girl, words. Move your tongue."

Soal, at work sweeping the breakfast-room, called out boldly: "And now she's come, why aren't you off?"

"Hold your tongue, woman." He pushed his daughter towards the door and climbed with remarkable nimbleness into the high dog-cart he used on fine Sundays to take them into Wik. Bessie seated herself on the other side and listened with bent head, until his passion seemed to be running out. Then she lifted her head, and said in a rapid and breathless voice:

"This is the day you give me my allowance, father."

Ezekiel gazed at her with eyes like black stones starting out of his face. "Your *allowance*, girl?"

"Yes, father."

"Do you know what," Ezekiel said; "you're out of your wits, you're positively mad. Talking to me of allowances. . . . *What* allowance? Do you think this is a time to let your female tongue loose, do you want to provoke me beyond bearing? You—you —why, I don't know what you mean. If you're not mad, you're shameless." Seizing the whip, he sent the mare a cut across the hindquarters that started her flying along the road as if she were possessed of a devil. "You must be doing it to provoke me. You—you—you. You want to get me into such a state that I shan't hear a word of the prayers, or anything else. Yes, you, you're forcing me to sin by even entering a church in the state I'm in. You ought to be ashamed of yourself—you wretch—if you had a grain of reason in you!"

Gripping the edge of the seat as the dog-cart flew over the ruts and stones in the road, Bessie repeated in an unnatural voice:

"You always give me two pounds in February. You always give it to me in February."

Seated in their pew, in the gallery behind the pulpit, she strove to seem calm. At the other side of the panel on which she was leaning was an ancient wooden-floored passage, with a low window at the height of her eyes: it looked out to sea. The masts of a ship passed slowly across it in the weak sunlight, and in spite of her childish unhappiness her spirits rose swiftly and suddenly, like the gull swooping between the ship and the cloudless sky. After all, I am not going to live with him for ever, she said to herself. Soon I shall be free. She thought of marriage, of love, with a vague, delicate longing. Who would marry her—she who scarcely saw or spoke to a man, old or young—she had not the faintest idea. She was only confident that it must happen.

Turning her gaze from the window, she looked again secretly at her father, at his thick back and neck held stiffly upright, at the veins crossing his temples, at the coarse black hair on his cheeks and the red full lips. I hate you, she thought, trembling: I hate you and I wish I could kill you. At the same instant she felt an extraordinary sensation as though a hand were stroking her body; it confused and alarmed her, and she made an effort to give her thoughts to the sermon. It was as dreary and meaningless as always; she turned back to the window and the gulls for relief, until the moment came when, with closed eyes, she heard ". . . and the fellowship of the Holy Ghost, be with us all ever more, Amen." Signal for shuffling, coughing, creaking . . . smoothing and rustling of women's dresses.

Ezekiel pinched her arm so cruelly that she bit her lip. Did anyone see my disgrace?

After the Sunday dinner with Semiramis Jordan, he called Bessie to him; putting his head on one side he spoke to her in a half-coaxing voice.

"If it was my last two pounds—would you ask me for them?"

"They're not your last, father," Bessie said, with the sharpness of despair. "You know you give me them every year—and I need them—I can't buy anything, anything, unless you give me my money." It's little enough, she thought. She was on the edge of tears.

"But what d'you want to buy? Eh? More clothes? Do you spend two pounds on clothes? It's a pound too much, my girl."

With an air of profound reluctance, he tipped two sovereigns out of his pocket, caught them and handed them to her. Unable to speak, she took them without thanking him and hurried out of the room. Ezekiel threw himself back in his chair. "No milk of human kindness," he exclaimed. "A cold, spiritless . . . crying, give, give—the daughter of the horse-leach."

He heard Bessie speaking to her aunt outside the door; opening it suddenly, he bawled: "A thankless tooth! Do you think I can live without respect or affection? Don't I need kindness, as much as any other man! I'll teach you a lesson, one you won't forget in a hurry. Ugh!"

The following Thursday, market day, he drove himself into Wik and returned towards six o'clock with a woman he had persuaded to come home with him. She was a Mrs. Bell, a woman of forty-odd, who had been living in Wik for less than a month. Come from heaven knows where, with no luggage but a large dress-basket and a dog, she established herself in *The Swan;* this was a public-house on the harbour, in Under Wik, where no respectable woman would ever have gone—or would have stayed when she had spent an hour there.

Mrs. Bell enjoyed it, the noise, the tipsy men, the piano played from morning till night by a one-legged Dutch sea-captain living in the house (he took a room for a week and stayed the rest of his life, living on what he addled by playing; the first officer took his ship home).

She was a plump, rosy woman with a bosom like an over-sprung sofa, and swinging ear-rings. She would come into the bar in the evening and stand her round of drinks with the habitués; then, with a glass of brandy for herself and another for her dog (who liked his nightcap as well as any human), she retired to her room. This side of *The Swan* leaned over the water, and at low tide Mrs. Bell fed the sea-gulls from her window: they came about it in a screaming cloud of wings, while her dog barked, the Dutchman played his piano, beating time on it with his wooden leg, and Mrs. Bell laughed her rich booming laughter above it all.

Her dress-basket was carried into the hall by young Richard Soal, and Ezekiel opened the door of every room downstairs and shouted to Soal to light the lamps—he even had the candles lit up on the twelve-branched chandeliers in the drawing-room. Mrs. Bell sat on her dress-basket and looked curiously about her. She caught a glimpse of Bessie flying up the stairs out of sight, eyes wide open with fear and surprise, and said nothing.

Ezekiel stood in front of her, his black eyes sparkling, hands on his thighs. "Now what d'you say? How d'you like your home, Mrs. Bell? Hey? It's a sublime sight, isn't it? Then upstairs we have by way of eighteen bedrooms—Did I say eighteen?

I meant twenty-eight, forty—as many as you like. Will you come up, missus?"

Leaving the dress-basket, Mrs. Bell poked her head into each of the ground-floor rooms. She saw shabby carpets, mildewed wallpaper, and massive immovable mahogany furniture. She walked up to Ezekiel and slapped his face lightly.

"Y'old liar," she said loudly. "You told me you had twelve large rooms downstairs and more than fifty bedrooms, and you promised me ten for myself. What have you to say to that, you devil?"

"You wouldn't have come if I'd said fewer," Ezekiel retorted with an air of gravity. "Fifty was the least you'd come for—I might have put it lower, but is it my fault you have such exalted ideas? It doesn't signify now you're here, and I never heard that two needed more than one room to roil in. As for the rest, it's all yours—the chairs are yours, the curtains, the wallpaper, the kitchens with that fat doup of a Soal in them—all, all yours for the time being. Now, shall I show you over the place?"

"You'll put my trunk in the trap and I'll go straight back to *The Swan*," Mrs. Bell said drily.

"What, now? What, without a trial?" he said, downcast, or pretending to be. He began to implore her, even falling on his knees and clasping her round her ample legs—"like bed-posts," as he said, looking at her slyly. She boxed his ears as they never had been boxed, and set the dog on him, only holding it by the leash.

"Take my trunk," she said again to Richard Soal—the boy had been standing in the doorway, watching the scene with a half-sheepish merry smile—"and help me up into the trap, and I'll get myself home. If I can't drive I'll learn as I go."

Ezekiel was too fond of his horses to let her go alone; and even his impudence was not equal to showing himself at *The Swan* with her that night, two hours after the congratulations poured on him (along with a glass of brandy) when they left. Young Soal drove her, and returned still smiling sheepishly and as silent as usual.

Ezekiel postured before Martha Soal in the kitchen until out of weakness and fondness she said grimly: "You and your dozzil! A rare fool she's made of you and you the fool to let her. I'll forgive y'this time and it's the last, mind."

"What a savage beast she was!" he said, grinning. "What a fool, too! To throw away the good home I offered her. And *I* was a fool to be taken in by her. I ought to be ashamed—at my time of life—running after strange women, and with a fine woman like you waiting at home. I ought to go down on my knees, but I shan't again, it doesn't at all suit me—and you don't want to see me make a holy barzon of myself in front of two women the same night? I've led an evil life, a wicked, sinful, scandalous life," he said, with profound enjoyment. "Now let me depart in peace."

CHAPTER VII

ONE morning at the end of February, Ezekiel looked out and saw Semiramis's personal servant hurrying towards the house, her black skirt wind-whorled round her knees. She was a middle-aged woman called Skelton, almost an idiot, and astonishingly faithful. Others said she was simple-minded: no one else could have lived with Semiramis for twenty-five years. He went out to meet her. Looking at him with a vague smile, she said that Mrs. Jordan wanted him to come at once, she was at her wit's end to know what to do with young Mr. Andrew, who was behaving like a fiend from the pit.

"What he needs," echoed Skelton, "is a man to do his business for him." She stood submissively in front of him, with her foolish patient smile, and wavering glance.

"Where's his father, hey?"

"Away," said Skelton, "away. Am I to say you'll come?"

Ezekiel was about to set off to keep an appointment at his bank. He wore his frock-coat and top-hat, and he was carrying a heavy ivory walking-stick. A closed carriage from the livery-stables in Wik had been ordered, and he and Skelton shared it in silence—she was mutely afraid of him, and he had nothing to say to a plain, bony woman. He was annoyed by having to sit opposite her for three-quarters of an hour.

Semiramis had watched for his coming from the window of her room. At once she began bitterly to complain of ten-year-old Andrew Wikker's conduct. He had disobeyed her that morning twice, and when she went to him in his bedroom to thrash him for it, he ran away from her round the room—round and round like an animal: driven into a corner at last, he struggled with her for the stick while she beat him with it, until she was quite done and had to leave off beating. "I feel that babbish now, a'most dying," she said in a loud voice. "That boy will kill me."

"I don't know what I can do," Ezekiel said drily. "Andrew should live at home with his father if you can't manage him. Where is he?"

"Sitting in his own room at the top of the house," answered Semiramis.

She let him go up alone. There was a double flight of stairs to the top floor, and as heavily he climbed the lower one a slight sound made him look up. He saw Andrew seated on a step of the top flight, silently watching through the banisters. The boy's reddish hair stood up over his head like fur, his lips were folded closely together, his large grey eyes, dilated by fear or anger, watched sullenly the man advancing towards him. Ezekiel stood still. The boy had the air of a young animal, desperate, stubborn, frail. (Actually, he was very strong.) An unfamiliar pity touched Ezekiel. He looked up at him in silence, ruddy face and black bright eyes so pressing themselves into Andrew's mind that he remembered it all his life.

"Hey," he said, "you can't give your aunt all this trouble."

Andrew did not speak. He looked through the railings with a passive indifference. After staring at him for a minute, Ezekiel turned and went down. "You've punished the boy enough," he said quietly to Semiramis. "You're too old to indulge in these scenes. Why isn't he at school?"

"He would ha' been if he'd taken his thrashing in a proper and decent manner."

Ezekiel turned an eye upon her like a tom-cat, but full of meaning, and offered to take Andrew to Upgang House for a week; and so he returned home a few hours later with Andrew seated, still silent, beside him. He handed him over to Bessie. "See what I've brought you," he shouted. "You s'd mind he doesn't snap."

Bessie took the boy into the sitting-room and knelt down in front of the fire, holding him by the arms. "Why is it so long since you've been to see us?" she said, laughing. "You'll stay now you've come, won't you? My poor young Andrew." She threw her arms round him and kissed his cheeks, holding him so that he rocked on his feet. She was delighted beyond everything to have someone in the house, was it only a little boy of ten. Towards her Uncle Handel she felt a romantic affection, and sometimes thought of herself as his wife and with a delicious sadness imagined her own death-bed.

The boy drew back. He did not like to be held closely; it made him feel uneasy. When she left him to get his room ready, he slipped off quietly and went along to the kitchen. He found Soal making a large flat loaf, and a little to his horror she was mixing it not with water, but with blood from a small basin standing beside her on the table. To reassure him, she began to say that it was for the Shrove-tide sowing, and the blood was from a young calf killed that morning. He felt relieved, and still a little startled. His breath seemed to harden in his throat and his legs shook.

Next morning he went out with the men, and craning his head forward, lips pinched into a line, he watched Ezekiel break the loaf over the first field. The earth-coloured fragments fell among the furrows, indistinguishable from the clods of earth.

He wandered away by himself, along a lane with water gleaming in the deep ruts; he was looking for some sign, an uncommon reed, a wind-flower or a hawk, to mark the day. Coming to a narrow rushing stream he stopped, squatted down, and amused himself by damming it with barriers of soil and leaves. An unreasoned happiness filled him, and he thought he could live for the rest of his life here if he were only left alone. The faint line of the sea, a good three miles off, exalted him as though he were discovering it for the first tme. Used to hiding his feelings, he only gazed at it with a half-dreamy, half-sullen look on his face —round but for the long chin: his high cheek-bones gave it a look of the north and of forests; there was a dark ring round the pupils of his eyes and it made their full gaze pointed and intimidating if he were in one of his tempers.

It was dark at four o'clock. Three hours later, when he was sleepy and contented after his supper, he looked up and saw Richard Soal beckoning him in the doorway. He went with him through the kitchens to the yard, and was first astonished and then alarmed to see a long narrow hole, as though a slit had been made in the ground, immediately below the door of the cow-house. A dead calf was lying on its side in the yard. It was very young and its head seemed a good deal too large for its thin body. Soal herself was waiting to lift the calf into the hole—it fell there on its back with its legs up, and she helped her son to fill in the earth round it. The feeble light from one lantern set on the ground threw such shadows that he thought the calf had been wounded in the side.

There was something pitiful and terrible in its being shut

away in the ground. His throat swelled and in spite of himself tears came into his eyes. He turned to go in. Bessie had run out in search of him; seizing his hand she drew him into the house and tried to comfort him. "Were you afraid?" she said eagerly: "never mind, you shan't be hurt."

"Don't, don't, our Bessie," he said testily, although glad enough of her company at the moment.

She told him the calf had been born a month before time: it was the second mis-birth this year, and was the cause they buried it in that place and posture—to prevent these accidents. "Will it?" he asked doubtfully.

"You must ask Soal that." She had a quick, merry, gushing laugh in which he could not help joining.

She helped him to undress. Seeing him quickly asleep, she opened the window of his room and leant out. The night was so clear, so bright, that she could see the most distant of the moor fires; there was a smell of peat smoke in the wind, and the air winter-thin and fresh. A restless spirit entered into her with the sharp, light custard-wind from the east. She wished she were free to run out, seeing herself as small and nimble as a young fox scampering through the dark wood of night. Her body felt light; when she moved she blundered against the walls and door like a moth seeking its way out. She walked quickly and carelessly. She had long legs, thin wrists, small waist, and a round full breast: with the body of a young woman, her face, voice, and gestures were those of a child.

Nine o'clock struck. Wishing to hear some other body's voice, she went down to the kitchen. Soal had the calf's heart on the table in front of her and she was thrusting into it nine new pins and nine needles. It was part of the precautions against another premature birth. With a serious face, she showed Bessie the piece of witch-wood—mountain-ash, it was—in her pocket.

Her son, leaning against the wall, watched her with a half-ashamed smile. Richard Soal's eyes were light-coloured, his mouth was pale and too full; he had Ezekiel's long insolent nose. It gave his boyish face a hint of dignity. He was nineteen. Since he worked on the estate without wages, he had only the clothes Soal could give him; she rapped and reeved for him where she could, and he was wearing leather breeches that had been made for his grandfather, his mother's father, and handed down as an heirloom. He was silent and awkward: only his mother knew that he intended to become a great man.

Without any clear memory of having been told, Bessie knew that he was her half-brother. She scarcely ever spoke to him: this was not from indifference but because his reserve, perhaps it was shyness, intimidated her.

She sat dreaming in the warm kitchen: the dark of night; some man, his features indistinct, holding her at the waist between his two hands; Mrs. Bell's smile and long-swinging ear-rings; wild geese strongly flying over the house at dusk, their wings arched against the iron sky; a dress covered from neck to hem with narrow frills. Her face changed, became alert and childish. She felt a happiness like the slow unfolding of a leaf in her body, below her heart. She thought vaguely, I am going to live splendidly—to live—yes, to live. . . .

Soal made up an enormous fire; at midnight a deep bed of hot embers received the heart. She had first fastened the doors and the windows; she closed the shutters and stuffed cloths between the cracks. No light must show outside; she expected that before long something unpleasant would be trying to force an entrance.

Whilst believing her, Bessie felt distinctly uncomfortable. She was not bold enough to wait near the fire. She felt a good deal safer leaning against the wall farthest from the windows, with Richard at one side and the door into the passage on the other. The back of her neck pricked as though it were being stroked by a hand with rough-skinned fingers. Nothing happened. In that hot fire the heart was quickly consumed, and a jet of greasy smoke sprang from it, to hang grey and wavering above the fire.

She began to think about the icy cold of the staircase and of her bedroom. Glancing up she saw that Richard was looking at her with an eager and heartless smile. Yawning with complete abandon, he stretched himself, and laid one arm round her shoulder. She did not move and he began to rub handfuls of her hair between his fingers, as though its softness delighted him. Soal was looking closely into the fire and did not see them. The blood ran into Bessie's cheeks: she felt extraordinarily happy and light-headed and shut her eyes. At once the darkness into which she plunged was alive with flickering downy flames, but the strange thing was that neither they nor her happiness had anything to do with the young man. In a few minutes she glanced at him, smiled lightly and teasingly, and walked away.

She ran upstairs to her room. Undressing quickly, she blew the candle out before the shadows it cast into every corner became too alarming. Her cheeks burned, but she was shivering with cold. Once last winter she had dared to light a fire in her bedroom. Ezekiel had punished her by making her sit every morning practising her scales without a fire, until her fingers froze and went dead and knocked helplessly against the keys.

CHAPTER VIII

SEMIRAMIS JORDAN'S house in Upper Wik was pervaded by a curious smell, neither pleasant nor unpleasant: the smell of old furniture, and too-long-worn silk dresses; meals following one another for years without the rooms in which they were eaten being aired; medicines, of which she kept an enormous quantity; and, above all, the slightly musty smell of Semiramis's own body, never washed, and saved from becoming too obnoxious by the fact that she was becoming thinner and drier with the years. She would soon be only bones with a little flesh held to them by her wrinkled skin, every wrinkle pitted with tiny black specks —so numerous that she seemed to be growing swarthier as she grew older. Her brother Ezekiel used to say that if her hair were washed it would be found to be grey, but at fifty-seven it was still as black as in her youth.

One morning in April she was in her bedroom with Skelton. The woman's dark eyes, without a flicker of intelligence in them, dingy faded balls, were fixed on her mistress with passionate intensity, like an animal, as though she took in what was said to her only by watching the expression on Semiramis's face. Semiramis was looking through a pile of underclothes laid on the bed, in search of a garment so old that it was only fit to be given away.

At last, with reluctance, she chose a pair of black woollen drawers, darned and shapeless, and made Skelton put them on. "Now," she said when, clumsily and hurriedly, Skelton had drawn them over her legs under three or four layers of petticoat, "let's see that they fit you. Can you bend?" Skelton bent. "Can you stride?" and Skelton stepped out, forcing her lower limbs to imitate the airs of a guardsman while her face kept its look of rapt credulous simplicity. No sound of rending followed these exercises and she was allowed to keep the garment, although her mistress would actually rather have given her money to buy new than part with something of her own. But that would have been a bad precedent.

58

When Skelton had gone she looked out of the window and saw her sister, Mrs. Wellhem, coming to call on her. She knew at once why: some days since she had mentioned to Ann that on Friday she was having the dressmaker come in to sew for her, and Ann had seized the chance to bring a garment of her own to be made up at the same time. She would have to pay the woman for her work, but she avoided having to feed her; it was worth all the trouble of coming here from her own house. Semiramis did not object to being made use of in this particular way. She was generous and would give away anything except her clothes, which rightly she regarded as too intimate a part of her to be thoughtlessly abandoned. She would take out and wear a garment she had had thirty years, quite indifferent that it was out of date, dirty, or in rags. And apart from not taking offence at her sister's habits, she was pleased to see her for several reasons, not the least lively of them being that no one else called on her.

She had no friends. Her sharp tongue frightened away other women less quickly than her habit of telling any lie that delighted her at the moment. She was completely without scruples. She would destroy a woman's reputation sooner than look at her: as the young wife who had been accused of drunkenness; and another, to whom Semiramis pretended she had lent silver teaspoons never returned; and a third singled out as an immoral wretch, knew to their cost. Thus, although she paid calls herself, and these were regarded by the victim as worse than an attack of colic or the visitation of a devil, no one came to see her except an occasional newcomer to Wik who had not yet been warned. These rare birds were greeted by her with every sign of favour and affection, and dismissed, with their ears burning from the shocking tales to which they had listened, almost ready to pack up and fly from the Gomorrah which Semiramis had revealed under the simple and charming town where they had come to live.

Ann came in, crushing under her arm a length of cloth she had begged from someone else. "If Boulby's Anna is making for you she can run this up at the same time," she said with a crafty smile.

"For me?" Semiramis said innocently.

"No, what are you thinking of? You never wear cloth; you think yourself too much of a lady. This'll do for me to go out; it's warm, it'll wear, and I suppose you're not going to object if I ask her to work for me and pay for her time?"

The dressmaker had made herself at home in the dining-room. The long mahogany table was covered with the black silk for Semiramis's dresses. She had a new dress made twice a year, always of black silk, and always a tight-fitting pointed bodice, stoutly boned, hooked from neck to waist, and a full skirt. But she never took both halves of a new dress into use at once; she would join a new bodice to the skirt of the old one she was wearing, or arsy-varsy, but that not until the new garment had been hanging in one of her cupboards for at least a year and become impregnated with the familiar rich smell. Since she never threw anything away she had already fifty such dresses to choose from, all bought since her marriage, and in various stages of impregnation and decay.

Boulby's Anna was a notable figure in the town at this time. It was always said of her that she knew enough about the hidden lives of families in Upper Wik to blast open the cliff if she chose to speak. She never did speak. Not even Semiramis had succeeded in making her gossip about her other customers, and women who would have shunned her like the plague seeing her come out of Mrs. Jordan's house, if they had not known her genius for holding her tongue, felt quite safe and even tried slyly to make her tell them whether it was true that Semiramis had scales on her back like a crocodile. In vain. Boulby's Anna died without spilling any of the poison with which she was full to the eyes. She was a tall, dark, commanding woman, with a black moustache, and a tendency to epilepsy. She went into silent fits, during which she could neither speak nor move. Her hand remained clenched on any article she was holding, it might be an arm or a tea-pot.

The sisters planted themselves in chairs near the window, so that they could see who passed along the road. It happened that the only person to walk past was that Mrs. Vansittart, the wife of the singing master and choir-leader, and mother of four daughters. Semiramis looked after her and sneered.

"There she goes, fadging along. Look at her waddling," she said cruelly. It was true that, owing to the muscles in her sides having given way, the poor woman heaved herself along like a goose. She had a sallow, creased face, which had none the less kept the look of a kindly mischievous child. Her small eyes twinkled with good humour and insight; she was gentle, stubborn, and aware of her clumsiness.

It was astonishing that she and her slender delicate husband had produced four tall and remarkably handsome daughters. The Vansittart girls, aged from fourteen to twenty, were acknowledged beauties; they were also excessively proud, and because the young men who might have proposed to a penniless girl were too inferior to be endured as husbands they pretended to despise all men and at dances either sat out, each lovely scornful creature the replica after an older or younger model of the others (they were like a frieze painted by one of the Brotherhood), or danced civilly and condescendingly with men as old as their father. Their names were Lizzie, Sarah, Julia and Lucy, names which belonged to so many merely pleasant or intelligent girls in Wik that it was strange to see these radiant creatures answering to them as a matter of course. "Make the tea, Lucy": the supple rounded arms of a dancer stretched towards the kettle.

Mrs. Wellhem stretched her thin neck at the side of the window. "Them brazen young girls will come to nothing," she said drily. "They make ower much show for a hundred and ten pounds a year."

"I heard he had more," said Semiramis. "His wife buys old clothes at t'back door and sells them. As well as what she gets begging in other people's houses."

There was not a shred of truth in this story, which had sprung into Semiramis's head when she saw Mrs. Vansittart stop in the street to speak to a poor woman.

No one else passed the house, and she turned her malice, like a pointer trained to follow any scent, on her sister. "I hear y'had a scandal in t'Chapel on Sunday," she said mockingly. She and Ann were brought up in the Church of England, but where Semiramis had remained in it, Ann, partly to annoy her sister and partly because she could lord it there at less expense —subscriptions and pew rents being naturally on a lower scale— had taken herself after her marriage to the Congregational Church. She never failed to resent Semiramis's disdainful references to it as 'Chapel.'

"I hadn't heard anything," she replied coldly.

"Oh, yes," Semiramis said, with her cruel smile. "Your minister, if that's what you call him, your fine Mr. Howard, B.D., B.A., preached a disgusting sermon on Sarah and Hagar, of all tales for an unmarried man to brazen out. I wonder you ha'n't heard; th' whole town's talking of it."

"Married or single, he needn't be ashamed of reading his Bible."

"Ay, he may *read* it," Semiramis said, with an air of disgust and scorn; "we may all stand up in t'pulpit and tell what we've been doing, so that decent women don't know where to look for shame."

She was distracted from tormenting her sister any more by Skelton's coming in with the glasses of port and biscuits Semiramis relished at any hour of the day. When she had handed them, with her usual air of stupid benevolence, her mistress said: "Skelton, show your drawers," and Skelton coyly withdrew her skirts to show a few inches of hideous black ribbed wool. "I'll be bound you're glad of them," Semiramis prompted her. She wanted the dressmaker to hear of her generosity. But Skelton replied with one of those speeches which caused her hearers to wonder whether she was as vacant and innocent as she looked. Lowering her skirts, she smiled slyly and said: "All we want now is a high wind." Even Semiramis was taken aback for a second by this ill-timed jest, and in the meantime Skelton had left the room.

Boulby's Anna had cut the bodice of Mrs. Wellhem's dress and she now pinned it on to her. Unluckily, one of her attacks seized her just when she was kneeling down with her hands on Mrs. Wellhem's waist; they grew rigid and clasped her as in a vice: the dressmaker's head fell back, her eyes turned heavenward so that only the whites showed—in her dark flowing dress she looked like an ecstatic embracing the knees of her saint. Time ceased for her. There was nothing to be done, and while her sister was held there unable to move, Semiramis prowled about the room, snatching up—so that it tore—the bodice Ann had taken off to be fitted, and knocking open as if by accident the bag she carried everywhere, stuffing into it any trifling object she managed to pick up during her visit. A handkerchief and a pair of kid gloves belonging to Semiramis fell out. She sent her sister a glance of malicious joy.

Mrs. Wellhem's eyes started. "I must ha' taken them up by accident," she said faintly.

"I saw you pick them up from the bed as you went by," Semiramis said drily. "You could ha' had 'em if you'd had the honesty to ask. Do y' steal every house you go to or only here?"

At this moment the dressmaker came out of her trance and went on calmly fitting, taking from between her lips the pins she had been gripping there like the singular ornaments of a savage. She gave no sign of having noticed what went on round her and it was neither family loyalty nor discretion that prompted Semiramis to remove the gloves into her own pocket in silence; it was rather a feeling she would have been astonished to hear named—sisterly love.

CHAPTER IX

HANDEL still kept his three-roomed house at the top of the Garth. He lived in it alone. There was room actually in it for his son, but he preferred to leave the boy with his sister on the ground that the east cliff was too far from Andrew's school. The truth was that he did not wish to introduce, into a life he deliberately made as bare as possible, anything that would interfere with it. He believed that Andrew was happy with Semiramis, and the boy, like all children, took his life for granted and did not dream of enlightening him.

One September evening this year he was walking to his house, accompanied by four of his friends. The air near the harbour was still and very warm. Through narrow gaps between the houses on the waterside they caught a momentary glimpse of bright dancing waves, pointed like arrow-heads, and of a ship lying at a wharf, motionless, her masts naked, her decks dry and white; gulls rocked idly on the water and stood as still as wood on the ancient mooring posts. On the other side the houses were piled one on top of another against the cliff, separated by flagged horizontal walks and steep crazy steps springing at the ends of narrow yards and passages as black as pitch.

When they began to climb the Garth all this vanished. Nothing was visible between the hedge except a sky of such transparent blue that the fleecy clouds passing over it, one after another, seemed to be reflections. Slowly, as they neared the top, this sky became wider and like a bubble enclosed not only the town, now again visible below from another angle, and the harbour which at this height became smooth and glassy and the colour of smoke, but the line of the cliffs covered with a vivid green turf, and a sea, sleeker and more unwrinkled than the sky, in which two or three distant ships appeared to be hanging motionless. The sun was still above the cliffs, and the light had the nostalgic clarity of early autumn, when it offers each line and colour with a piercing distinctness, as if to say, "Look well, you will never see it like this again."

The air at this height had an intoxicating purity; it seemed, like the light itself, to belong to another world. Handel and his friends stood for a minute in silence at the top of the Garth to breathe it in deeply. The schoolmaster, Mower, threw himself on the dry short grass and flung his arms out. Handel alone was neither hot nor winded.

"Now you see how much higher we are here than on the west cliff," he said smiling. "Yet this is still Under Wik. Those houses there, which seem high enough when you toil up to them from the harbour, are Over Wik only in name. I always believe when I'm there that I can smell the marsh at the far side."

"All the same if I lived here I should need a new pair of lungs," Mower groaned.

"You would grow them."

They walked one behind the other between Handel's rows of blackcurrants and lettuces to the grass verge in front of the house. He went indoors and fetched out three chairs and a wooden stool. There was nothing else in the house on which they could sit except the table. No one thought the worse of him for what had come to be regarded as the eccentricity of a scholar. But it was not only from his growing scientific reputation that he drew the respect with which many—the better sort of people in Wik—treated him. His authority made itself known in other ways. Positively it seemed owed to a quality each man felt without naming, his courage in not averting his gaze from some inner crisis—of despair? of regret?—which showed itself only in an ironical indifference to everything he might be imagined to have valued—time to do his work, a suitable room, right ease. He was at the beck and call of any poor or hurt man, woman or child; at forty-seven he still spent time as recklessly as if it were only money.

Mower, the schoolmaster, was more intimate with him than the rest. What had grown between them, from respect, was simply love, the absolute dependence of one soul on another. A lean red-headed man, with a wide mouth and a long ugly nose, Mower bragged and blustered when he suspected that he was not liked and became humble only in the little circle of his friends. To Handel he showed a mind as ruthless and confused as a child's, and sensibility and goodness. He sat on the stool with his long legs spread at an extraordinary angle. An ironical smile gave his face the look of a country satyr, or a gargoyle leering over the town.

"I'd live here myself if I weren't married," he said. He

blushed at the thought that this might seem a criticism of Handel
for bringing his wife up here. "My life is a failure," he rushed
on. "I work like an ox. But the years have slipped past without
giving me a single one of the things I expected with the greatest
confidence when I was twenty. I was going to write history—I
couldn't persuade anyone to publish even a text book. Say what
you like, I've had visions. I saw Jesus Christ in the face of a
man with a spade digging the street; the clay he threw up was a
burning yellow, the sun set fire to the houses, and there he was in
his yellow corduroys, Christ to the life, and a drop on the end of
his nose, and his hands blue with cold, black starved. I was young
and I felt dumb with joy. Now look at me, lank, pale, a weak
stomach, and my wife gets me to help her to sort rags in the evening for the crazy-quilts she makes to sell to her friends." He
coughed with disgust.

King turned to him with a polite sneer. The editor of the
Wik Times, the only local paper, he had been educated above his
intelligence, and he was morbidly afraid of slights. It was perhaps
this which had made him a liberal in a town where every man
of importance was conservative from the womb and would remain
conservative until the blood turned in his veins and began to flow
the other way. He felt at his ease with Handel, so much so that
his speeches were sharper than usual and he was intoxicated with
happiness.

"If you'd gone home with him you'd have rejoiced in a complete holy family, six or seven brats and a wife with her womb
dragged down below the orifice, all living together in two rooms
in Ash Yard. One half of the town is sunk in dirt and the other
in a complacence nothing blunter than a knife will alter."

"What Mower saw we've all seen," Handel said. "The
exquisite patience of poor men is as dreadful as the blood of
Christ dying."

"No doubt," King said, smiling. "But Christ died to some
purpose. These others might as well not have been born for all
the meaning there is in their lives. To be poor, to be cheated,
to live for sixty-three years and toil to earn a mean living during
fifty of them, and at last to die, in the vilest discomfort—do you
call that life?"

He was answered by the vicar. Taking Handel's place when
he was disgraced, the Reverend Charles Vawn was moved to know
him first by curiosity, then by a polite delicate pity he felt for

him. It was inconceivable to Vawn that the other man did not suffer the torments of hell when he thought of his disgrace, and he hoped by his constant politeness and by inviting him to the vicarage two or three times a year to console him and pour oil in his wounds.

"All these poor creatures are equal before God."

"But not before you," King retorted joyously.

Now that the sun, ringed with tongues of flame, rested for a moment on the edge of the other cliff before plunging down out of sight apparently into the marsh, a haze, half luminous, half opaque, flowed from it towards them. Fields, houses, cliff, swam in their tide of light above the darker smoke of the town. The faces of Handel's friends were transfigured by it. A street lamp, suddenly lighted in Upper Wik, showed weak and ragged. All at once Handel's memory recalled to him the woman he had been about to lie with in a dingy room behind Regent Street. He saw her simple, inviting gesture. Invitation of one prisoner to another to draw as close as possible to the wall shutting each in his cell, beyond hope, beyond pity. The miracle of this woman's life, from her birth to her obscure death, surpassed any of those over which Vawn glibly passed his tongue when he preached. Vawn's habitual slight cold smile and pale eyes gave to his face the air of one of those peevish Madonnas to whom the Annunciation seems as welcome as an east wind. Not for the first time Handel was vexed by it into speaking hotly.

"Mower saw Christ as a shivering workman, but some artists have painted Him at His Resurrection as a lion. Christ the lion. Our comfortable Erastian Church, with its well-lined belly and its natural kindly feeling for the powerful and rich, has nothing to say to either. The lion if He sprang would consume the heart and liver of the bishops, and Mower's workman would rather get drunk any day than go to Communion."

Finding these remarks in the worst of taste, Vawn smiled coldly. Handel was astonished to see a look of pain contorting Vansittart's face. The music-master was usually silent in company; he was nervously afraid that he was a bore.

In fact he was. When once he opened his mouth to begin talking he was forbidden to stop; sentences flowed on and on in a maddening gentle monotony until someone brutally cut in. . . . He began suddenly to talk about music as a proof of immortality, the only certain proof, since all the others depended on faith and reason; both these could be deluded, but in music, in penetrating into the warmth, the darkness, the secrecy of that mysterious other world, one not merely felt but knew that one was absolutely and eternally at peace, safe from harm, excused effort, mysteriously warmed and fed; in short, a god.

Lolling in his chair, Vansittart talked, moving his long delicate fingers with the lightness of butterflies circling round each other in the sunlight, oblivious, or seeming to be oblivious, of the yawns neither King nor Mower made the slightest attempt to hide.

At last Handel got up from the ground and went into the house. "Forgive me," he said mildly, "my dear fellow; I'm going to fetch a bottle of wine."

He came out again in a minute with four glasses gripped bowl down by their stems between the fingers of one hand and a bottle of Rhine wine in the other. The wine, when he raised a glass to the light before handing it to Vawn, was exactly the colour of the fine luminous veil now slipping from the air; to hold it again between their hands gave each of them an illusion of warmth and keen happiness even before he tasted it. Vawn made the cold, not unfriendly grimace, which passed with him as a smile; King and Vansittart drank it almost drop by drop, without venturing a word; only Mower let himself go in a roar of joy.

"That's good, my boy, that livens me. How long have you had it?"

"Nearly long enough for it to settle down," Handel answered. He did not go on to add that it was a gift made to him by a man to whom he had presented the fruits of ten years' research in meteorology. Bringing out the second bottle he thought slyly how vexed they would be if they knew that the other ten were making merry the hearts (and heads) of certain silly bedridden old men and women.

"Not a finer pleasure in the world than to drink a glass of good wine," said Mower, "on a warm still evening, with a fine open view at your feet, and nothing between the top of your head and the sky, and the ashes of the sun burning out, and no voices except ones you've chosen to hear."

"A little music——" began Vansittart timidly, but smiling.

"Not a note, by God! You want to make hysterical German babies of us. A nation," shouted Mower, "which has never been able to think except with its long-winded gut, and that accounts for practically the whole of German philosophy. For the quite simple reason that they go in for music at the most horribly unsuitable times. Music is one thing, and talk, with wine, is another. Only ill-bred people mix them."

Vansittart did not mind in the least being called ill-bred; he was too modest on the surface and too arrogant below it, but he flushed a dark red at the insult to his "other world." In another second he would have begun on one of his endless sentences, in which the relative clauses followed each other like sheep trotting along a lane, and if they did not madden his listeners sent them to sleep. Before, stuttering with grief, he could get out more than a word, King said hastily:

"There must be no women, either."

"Why not?" Mower said; with his second glass he had risen into a happy and truculent mood.

"Obviously not. The perfect company consists of men, all friends, with no seeds of rivalry among them. The wine, the air, the view, even the fire of the sun, would be altered and spoiled if a woman were dropped in. We shouldn't recall this as a perfect hour, free of constraint, because we should all in some way have been irritated or stimulated by her to be not ourselves but men with a woman."

His voice dropped into a silence as unexpected and profound as the well of the sky, now becoming more remote, cloudless, and of a deeper blue, in which the first star, infinitely weak and delicate, seemed to float almost submerged; the impalpable tide which had carried away the last traces of the dying sun had also spread above the earth a light fog: it hovered above the town and without diminishing the light gave it the deceitful brightness of water, altering the colours and shapes of the houses and so darkening the gully that runs inland from the harbour that it reminded Mower of the opening of the *Inferno*.

Nel mezzo del cammin di nostra vita. . . .

"*In the middle of the journey of our life,*" he said, translating airily, "*I found myself in a dark wood, having strayed from the right path.*"

He looked at Handel with a demure smile, but his friend's face was cold and forbidding. Mower felt disgusted with himself and, utterly depressed, he thought, What have I said? How can I have offended him?

"The world is fortunately less dark than in Dante's lifetime," Vawn said smoothly.

"No," Handel said in a curt voice. "No. You're wrong, my friend. I know, because I have bad dreams. If only I were an artist. . . . In my dreams I see children struck down and slain by hawks in the streets of the cities; a living man holding back his entrails with his hand; I see death in the shape of a gull come up to the window; I see stones and dry rocks breeding serpents, eyes swinging from trees; I catch sight of my mother's face bent towards me in one of those moments when, thinking that I was asleep, she allowed herself to look at me with a love she thought excessive (I was her youngest) and so tried to hide, and before I can even smile at it that always gentle face becomes vacant, coarse, indescribably vulgar and stupid. One night I fell asleep and dreamed that I was standing in a poor room looking at a young woman with her newly-born child; she was naked to the waist and I saw her ribs and the transverse bones of her arm; the breast at which she was nursing her child hung down like an empty purse, a dry, withered skin; I saw the child dying, and I saw in her womb another, like a worm, waiting to be born. Again, another night I found myself in a dark wood, not Dante's; what I had taken for leafless trees turned out to be the living skeletons of men, not each a single man but to one tree many bodies, inextricably twisted to mimic the branches of trees, their eye-sockets imploring, or warning, and a voice, the voice of all those, crying, Son of man, save us, save us and spare us! And I, in that kingdom of death running from one to the other, asking How can I save you? When I woke up tears were running over my face. I wasn't ashamed or surprised. It was not, as one says, *only a dream;* such dreams are prophetic. I fall into them when I'm awake, in whatever moment I think of that huge and dreadful sea of cruelty, never drying up, never full enough. If there is no other hope of ridding the earth of cruelty, I mean the bloody-minded and stupid cruelty of rich women towards poor, of the powerful towards the helpless, of jailers towards prisoners, we ought to pray in our churches for the end of man. Though but a fragment of His creation, as St. Augustine says, the fragment poisons all the others. I feel in the anguish of my bones themselves that a judgment is on the way. But of what sort I can't see."

Vansittart had turned pale.

Squatting now on the grass, Mower said dreamily: "I remember when I was a child—I suppose about four—I cried because my two sisters were fighting, I thought very savagely. It filled me with such horror that I couldn't help sobbing. The one who was defeated slapped me when I tried to help her up afterwards—it gave me something else, on the whole much less alarming, to waste my tears on." He laughed in a loud, noisy way. Ho ho ho!

"When I realize that Beethoven is dead," said Vansittart, "I think that I'm going mad. . . ."

"And then you play the A minor quartet and are transported to heaven," said King cruelly.

Handel had gone a few steps from them in search of a sprig of tarragon—Mower had asked him for a leaf of it for his wife—and with his back to them he looked at the fast-fading coast-line. A few lights near the water at the most distant point marked a fishing village where he had stayed with Kezia for a week after leaving the vicarage.

The sea was now a dark formless field between the land and the sky, and among its endless furrows four or five specks of light crept so slowly that they seemed to stand still. Ah, my love, Handel thought, seeing the young girl as she stooped in the darkness towards the sea, standing among the stony roots of weeds growing to the water's edge. This dryness of my life since you went is not broken up by any spring or goodness of water.

He turned back, the sprig of tarragon in his hand, and as he did so saw his four friends in a light as severe and astonishing as if they had been gathered up by El Greco himself into one of those scenes which, more than anything in nature, suggest the coagulation of the air into forms as clear and violent as the artist's idea. The wall of the house directly behind them was cut in half like a cracked rock by the open door and the window placed directly above it. Their features too, eyes, nose, mouth, temples, altered and emphasized by the subtlety of the light, seemed splitting open to allow another face, the true seed of the outer, to show through. He laughed and said:

"We blame men who are cruel, stupid, ambitious, for the evil they do, but forget to blame ourselves; in whom there is at least as much evil, if scattered, so that it makes less show. There is a goat in me; a vulture in King's sincerity; a wolf, as well as gentleness and pride, in Mower. Here's your tarragon; don't lose it, even this year it grew badly; there was sun but too much wind."

"And what animal did you notice in me just now?" said Vawn. His acute mind had guessed better than Mower that Handel was unhappy; at the same time that he felt less sympathy for him.

"You're too well guarded," Handel said, with a smile. He was discreet enough to hold his tongue when it was a question of telling Vawn that his delicacy of mind existed side by side with the mental forms of greed and vanity.

It would only have been unkind to talk to Vansittart about the vague but truly terrible fear, the sickness of uncertainty, which coloured the instinctive goodness of his nature. Very probably he was unaware of it. And (apart from his goodness) he would be too modest to ask.

"Think of all the exquisite moments in life before you talk of ending it all," Mower said. "Wine, for instance, drunk in the best company. As we drank it this evening. The sight of a terrific dawn, when one is young. Certain books."

"Beethoven," murmured Vansittart.

"The cock would crow and burst his neck before you denied," Handel said kindly.

"The love of wisdom," King said. He sent a sly look at Vawn.

"Sleep," Handel said, "that country into which the poorest can enter and be free of its wide as of its narrow streets, its palaces and solitary rooms, its ecstasies and terrors. We meet there, in surroundings which only for a short time resemble those in which we expect to find them, friends whom we have not seen for years, but they have altered, grown older perhaps, or plainer, as though all these years they had been living and changing under the eyes of our other self, which consequently is not surprised and recognizes them at once. They are kinder to us than they were in the past, just as sometimes the one friend we love most and see every day or week and trust without thinking about it, in a dream wounds us and makes mocking fun of us when we beg him not to behave to us like that." He half glanced at Mower. "We ourselves are not in our dreams indifferently any age, but almost always younger, with smooth skins, able to run, jump, dance, play Bach with our own gut-cords, rise from the earth by simply willing it, and hover like gulls in the night sky. We not only re-visit the past, never so dark as that other abyss on the forward side of night, but find ourselves in cities and country of the most ravishing beauty. The other night, as I slept, I saw that the cliff behind the marsh was covered with trees on which every leaf was a tiny curling flame. There are the terrible dreams, out of which one wakes covered with sweat, but I believe that in these, too, one is hearing about the future and not about the past, living in it in some way I don't understand and with senses which send in their reports in code. It is worth a little terror to push off into space and meet days and years still on their way to us and not yet ready for inspection. They show up clearer that way; one sees the essentials which, when the time comes, will be obscured by irrelevant details; it is like seeing off a crowd of young men who have volunteered to fight: one sees too much, their smiles, the glint of a button, all the common details of everyday life surrounding them, the usual sky, the ground, the flags, but what we don't see at the time, and most of us never think of, is the warm quivering flesh, the heart, the lungs, the entrails, the subtle brain, which is going to be torn in pieces and suffer and die. My bad dreams are telling me something about the future which, when it comes, I might miss, or perhaps it is so far off in time that I shall be dead before it happens. And what I don't understand is this same word 'happens.' How often does an event happen? If it is happening to me now to see and endure some frightful calamity, and then later on it happens, as we say, 'in reality,' how can we know that that ends the series? How many more times must the same event 'happen' before the original evil is exhausted, and can go back whence it came? And where did it start from, unless in my very heart and mind, and in yours, and in its victims?"

"That will take us farther into space than your dreams," smiled Vawn.

"It will. Don't be alarmed, I'm not going any farther, it's quite late enough. And sleep is the supreme good. Think only of those towering sky-piercing cathedrals it makes us visit. The blueness of its seas, the unbearable delight of its symphonies which, unlike life (we are not all like Vansittart), never bore us and may last hours or seconds. Think of those waking moments when we are half asleep and possess both worlds, neither of them able to harm us. That is when we become infants again, lying in a room and able to enjoy the sunlight without being conscious of anything else in it; free, yet guarded; alive, yet peaceful. I shouldn't be surprised if at death we enter just such a state for a time before our minds sink at last through time into peace."

It was now almost dark. The sounds of the deserted country-side, a clock striking the half hour, a belated cart moving along

a lane a mile from them, the note of the half-submerged bell buoyed
out at sea to mark a line of rocks below the water, suddenly became
clearer, as though they had only been waiting for his voice to cease
to make themselves heard.   A gentle odour of thyme and southernwood rose from the damp earth.

Vawn stood up, politely, while Mower rose with a groan, rubbing his thighs.

"My God, how stiff I am," he said ruefully.   "All my joints
ache."

"You should try——" Vansittart began.   Mower's large hand
was clapped over his mouth for a moment while the other gripped
him by the arm.

"Come home, and hold your tongue.   I won't drink celery
tea and I won't rub on any of that filthy red stuff you gave me
last year.   Besides, I can't reach the worst spots."

"My wife rubs mine," Vansittart said slyly.

"Well, mine doesn't, see?   Good night, Handel; God bless
you and keep you from dreams."

"Good night, good night."

"Good night."

Handel listened for a minute to the noise made by their feet
on the stones of the Garth.   He smiled involuntarily at the last
echo of Mower's voice, floating up from the blackness into which
they had vanished from sight.   Picturing them stumbling along
the narrow street by the harbour, he looked up and saw the first
shaveling moon in the sky, as sharp as a finger-nail.   His glance
travelled in a downward arc over the sky to the hills and there,
passing over valleys in which the scattered villages were dropped
between inhospitable moors, over roads he knew by day as steep,
with stone hedges, and gouts of water springing at the side, over
his brother's land, The Stone, the field where he saw Kezia, and
in less than a minute came back by familiar ways to the town,
sunk in shadow, clinging about its harbour which remembered
the Saxons and no doubt kept quiet in its mud the bones of some
of them centuries after they were murdered by the Danes.   A
few street lamps were alight, but the town itself, the houses, the
harbour, the wharves, were in darkness.

He went in, rinsed the glasses they had used, put a few sticks
where they would dry for his fire in the morning, and went to
bed.   He dreamed that, climbing the sides of the gully behind
the harbour, he had seen Christ hanging from a Cross made of

stone, like the stone used to mark a boundary on the moor; drawn nearer against his will, he saw that Kezia was leaning against the tree, her head hanging turned over her shoulder; his agony was soothed, but before he had spoken to her the scene became a room with a little child sitting on its po and looking up at him; there was a bed in the room and beside it a woman with indistinct features, the walls of the room darkened as with fog; she opened her arms in that strange gesture, simple and lascivious, and lay down on the bed. He bent over her, and through the watery transparent surface of her body, swollen like the sail of a ship, he could see the child crouched looking up at him. It is mine and hers, he thought, his senses invaded by an exquisite pleasure: the woman's belly broke open, bursting like an ear of wheat, and the child moved its tiny limbs and began to talk to him; delighted by its voice he took it up; it was at first charming, and immediately became shapeless and inert: he was in a street, perceiving it at the same time with his ears in a phrase of music which altered quickly and subtly to revive in him the sentence "now the way from the River was rough": it was obliterated by other words— "she lived as soon as she was born." These words seemed to him extraordinarily important and he clung to them as he was drawn slowly and irresistibly upward along endless corridors and plains and through level after level of a grey aqueous air, far above which, as through a dissolving mist, he caught a glimpse of daylight. For a moment while he was still struggling with the folds of some garment which brushed his face, the same ridiculous words sounded in his ears, abruptly vanishing when he opened his eyes. He looked at his watch. It was five o'clock. He rose and went downstairs to wash himself from head to feet in cold water, standing in the scullery in front of the sink. He had drawn the water over-night. He lit the fire, hung his kettle over it, and went out.

The sun was not yet up, but behind the house the sky was covered with tongues of flame, lying one over the other like the scales of a fish. Some of them had floated off into the upper air, and the blue curtain of the sky stretched behind and above them as though it were the backdrop in a theatre which had caught fire only at the foot, while above it the illusion of vast blue distances remained glowing and serene. There was an exquisite emptiness and freshness in this world. It was an hour propitious for courage. Nothing moved, except the seagulls diving with sharp cries from a great height on to the waves.

Handel turned to go in. A plume of smoke rose from the chimney of the house, very frail in the light. Not far off, if he could have stretched his arm down to it, a faint stain of smoke was beginning to spread from the Under Wik houses through the limpid air, soon to be shaken, as by a passing wind, by the bell calling the shipyard workers to begin work. At this moment Handel felt in himself a conviction that wherever he went, whatever happened to him in a future he welcomed, some part of his life, some drop of what had been a single, irresistible jet of force, would remain immovably here. A boy, just growing to man-hood, will walk through Under Wik and unknowingly think one of my thoughts, to the undoing and turning towards another goal of his whole life; or a girl will be born to-morrow in one of those houses, grow up, laugh, marry, suffer, and one day will come upon a shred of my substance and be penetrated by another keener, more exquisite happiness than she has yet known. No doubt I shall live for ever. Though I die without understanding, I shall live until I understand every secret of life seen in the blade of grass staring from my eye-sockets.

He was filled with a keen satisfaction in realizing that he was immortal so long as one person remained to whom, as to him, the air of Wik was a subtler essence than any other, living, salted, potent, a fragrance of which it could be said that however dry the roots of a tree in the ground yet through the scent of water it will bud and bring forth boughs like a plant.

CHAPTER X

AT the same hour, at cock-light, Ann Wellhem was dressing herself for one of her journeys. At this time she used to travel a great deal, setting off from Soureby Bog Hall in the clumsy old-fashioned carriage she kept, and sleeping away perhaps four nights. It was what she called cadging about. She would be content to stay harmlessly at home for weeks—then one day the fever would seize her, and until she was able to be on her way the life lived by William Wellhem and her servants was one of constant strain and terror. She detected and denounced every innocent stratagem to which William resorted to give himself an illusion of freedom, chasing him out of a room in which she found him sitting and wearing out the chairs, counting his cups of tea, fining him. Only one servant, Horn, a woman with a child whom she nourished on her scanty wages, had stayed in the house for longer than three months. Horn never attempted to leave, not even when her room was searched three or four times a day and her food cut to the bone. She took a grim pride in her mistress's habits. Tyrants are not always hated; their very meanness and cruelty endears them to a servant who can reflect, 'I may be nothing but at least I wouldn't carry on like that.' Horn was stiff-necked, and despised the younger women who burst into tears or a rage when Mrs. Wellhem was in one of her states.

"Aren't you ashamed of yourself?" she would say to the girl who, snivelling or red in the face, was packing her box to go. "Aren't you ashamed to take any notice of the old crambazzle? Don't you know what's matter with her?—she has a little beast, a lop, in her stomach, jumped in when she was asleep; it can't get out and it sends her clean daft whenever it starts to hop round."

Flea or no flea, some lively body was at work in Ann this morning as she dressed. She felt it like a feather lifting and falling softly below her waist; she hummed joyously, drawing on to her skinny body an astonishing number of garments, odds and ends of wool and flannel, fastened with strings, buttons, safety-pins, like a precious casket.

As soon as she was dressed she went round the house locking up every cupboard and drawer, after laying out for her husband and the servants provisions to last a week. She also laid out six matches, one for use each day, and counted the lumps of big coal left in the outhouse. All this was somehow in the nature of a religious rite, a sacrifice (of other people's comfort) made to the gods to ensure her safe return. The day on which she had left the tea canister unlocked a wheel came off the carriage and she was thrown on her nose in the ditch and all but stunned.

She drove herself. The carriage had been brought out and cleaned of straw and the droppings of hens flying in and out of it in the shed, and it stood in front of the door. The horse, a broken-down bay the colour of her wig, was resigned now to leaving the rank marsh grass that blew him out without feeding his spirit. Just then, Ann saw the Congregational minister approaching the house on foot.

"He's come for something," she exclaimed, with profound annoyance.

Looking about the room she made certain that no crumb of biscuit or drop of wine remained on the sideboard, and tucked out of sight the flask she was taking with her for emergencies. The fire in the grate was almost out, since William would not require one in her absence—if he felt cold he could sit in the kitchen with Horn. She kicked the embers apart so that scarcely a glimmer remained when Horn came in to announce that Mr. Howard was waiting in the hall, and would be obliged if Mrs. Wellhem could see him for a minute.

"Did you tell him I was going off?" Ann said in a harsh voice, raised so that the minister could hear it.

"Yes I did."

"He ought to know better than to come yarning into people's houses in the morning. Half his religion consists in wasting other people's time. Very well, let him come in, but he's not to stay—so leave the door open."

An elderly man, kind and incapable of holding his own even with the deacons of his church, Mr. Howard came in with less assurance than Daniel. He had come, moreover, to ask for a subscription towards the cost of heating the church.

"My good man, so you've succumbed to the evil one at last," Ann said in a resigned tone. "I warned you and I warned the others, at the last deacons' meeting, who it is has put into your hearts to talk of warming the church. We know whose thoughts must be eternally of heat and fire. Don't expect me to subscribe. I told you."

"But you yourself complained of the draughts in your pew," Mr. Howard ventured.

"Exactly. And on cold Sundays I stop at home."

"But if everyone did that——?"

"They'd be none the worse," cried Ann triumphantly. "Half of 'em go to church out of vanity and the rest because they have nothing else to do on Sundays. You can't tell me anything about Wik, my dear man, but I can tell you that the worst hypocrites are those who pretend they're pleased to see you. Ah, here's my Lily. My little lily-pot, my pure white lily, so unlike other girls, Mr. Howard, so unlike. Are you ready to start, my darling?"

Lily Wellhem was now a young woman twenty-one years old. She was taller than her mother, with colourless fair hair, and the same greenish-blue eyes set in a long face. In the family she sided with her mother against the unfortunate William, yet in some subterranean way she resembled him. It was as though William had gone to ground in his daughter and the flashes of spirit she occasionally showed were really his outbursts of defiance, rare —and smothered at once by Ann's indulgence. Ever since the girl was born she had treated her as though she were made of glass. Mr. Howard spoke to her without getting an answer. She stood near the window, with downcast eyes and a strange expression of timidity and malice on her pale lips. She might not have been listening, but when her mother said, "Come, we're going," she made a swift and joyous movement of her head and smiled without raising her eyes. Possibly she was really shy and timid. She had never been allowed a friend, lest she should become rough or deceitful. The only person, except her parents, who spoke to her was Horn; the other servants all believed that she was "a bit off her head" and told tales about them. She was never separated from her mother except at night when she went to sleep.

Turning the minister out of the house Ann drove off with Lily and their dress-basket inside the roomy carriage, leaving him to walk back to Wik without bite or sup in him. Her usual practice was to drive to a house in the country—cousins and second cousins of the family were as thick for twenty miles as brambles—and stay until her stomach was upset. She had no

false shame in announcing on her arrival that only one thing
short of a death in the family would dislodge her. Fortunately
for her unwilling hosts she had a weak digestion; five or six days
of meals where she could never resist over-eating was enough to
send her home; and she and Lily would take to their beds, each
with a bread poultice on the offended quarter, and lie there until
its sufferings reached a stage when other remedies could be
tolerated.

On the outward journey she made a habit of stopping at cottages
and farmhouses to ask for a drink of water. While it was being
fetched her sharp eyes ferretted into every place they could reach,
perhaps a valuable old chair or a chest rewarded them; then began
an exercise of her wits in which oftener than not she was triumphant. Pointing a finger at the chair she said boldly:

"What will y'take for that, hey? It's not worth much but I
like the look on't; I'll take it off y'; I'll give y' half a crown for 't.
What d'y' say?"

The extraordinary thing was that unless the chair in question
happened to be cherished as a relic, she was as like as not able to
coax it away from a woman who knew as well as she did that she
was being cheated. The woman would try to put her off—the
chair had worm in it, it was rotten, it was not worth sixpence.
"I know that, my good woman," interrupted Ann kindly. "You see,
I'm offering you five times what it's worth." As soon as the woman
began to seem distresssed Ann knew that she had won. Bending over the chair, with a caressing movement of her neck which
was like that of a stoat burying its face in the fur of a rabbit's
neck, she hurried out with it to the carriage. Actually there
was something of the stoat about the whole business, from the
way in which both women had played their parts—one pursuing
and the other, trembling with a mysterious weakness, offering
up her blood in the form of a valuable chair. There was nothing
weak about these women at other times, that is what made it
so remarkable and disturbing.

On this journey Ann found nothing worthy of her skill, but
she begged a jar of pickled walnuts from a woman and was annoyed
when she noticed that they were mouldy. Arrived at her aunt's
house she gave her the walnuts, with a smile of innocent benevolence. "My own bottling." She stared blandly as she said it at
the name, clearly written on the label, of the real owner, confident
that no one would point out to her an obvious lie. Early in her

life she had grasped that a direct lie told with simplicity and
assurance will go down in all but the most ill-bred company. Her
own assumption of good manners was so natural that she could
speak her thoughts with outrageous sincerity; she could even
have worn the bread poultice in public, without any loss of
dignity.

At nine o'clock that evening she retired to bed, and after she
had seen Lily into bed in the adjoining room, hanging over her
with the solicitous care she would give to a new possession when
she had got it safely into her hands, she began to undress. But
first of all she prayed. Her prayers were always calculated not
simply to trick the Almighty into conferring benefits on her for
nothing—she considered it merely common sense to take for
granted that He had no time to look narrowly, or as she would
say, meanly into her claims—but also to pay off persons who
had offended her. Thus, to-night she omitted Semiramis and
Handel from her petitions and began directly with Ezekiel, for
whom she prayed that he might be brought to think less of food
and drink: she prayed, carelessly and almost brutally, for her
husband, and then for Lily in terms of the most fervent love.
"My precious daughter, my balm of Gilead, my day star. Lord,
Thou knowest she is not as other girls. Cherish her, Lord, as
You would Your own."

A still deeper and more imperative note entered into her voice
when she entreated that a table she had bought the week before
might not turn out to have been restored. A hidden listener
would have understood that he had been mistaken in supposing
that her one and only passion was for her daughter. But it was
not even in her possessions that her sharpest terrors and joys
resided. The secret smoke of her petitions ascended when she
prayed for herself. Then—by way of adroitly distracting His
attention from anything less answerable she might have done—
she would elaborate some small kindness, perhaps invent it from
the beginning, proffering it to His notice in the most favourable
light until she had convinced herself, doubtless convincing the
Almighty as well, that no better Christian than herself deserved
His blesssing. "Bless me, O Lord," she murmured, "bless me,
for I am worthy."

She rose from her knees at last, satisfied that all would be
well, and began to take off her clothes. First she laid aside her
shawl, then the stuff bodice and skirt, the black moiré petticoat,

the first of three long-sleeved woollen under-bodices, the flannel
petticoat, another bodice; she unclasped the grey-coloured stays
which embraced her, with stout shoulder-straps holding them up
over her breasts, in a massive web of whalebone from breast to
thigh: and now, standing in nothing more than an under-bodice,
two flannel chemises, and three pairs of woollen drawers, she
lifted her thin arms into her nightgown, discreetly shrouding
the removal of one pair of drawers. Between September and
May she slept in all the other garments.

Unlike Semiramis, she did, four or five times a year, wash the
whole of her body, after taking due precautions against chill:
even then, from decency, she never glanced at it.   So that she
had no more idea than the most casual stranger what sort of a
lean dry larva of a body now lay curled up inside all these swaddling
clothes.   Her mind was turned inward, revolving in ever-narrowing
circles of satisfaction, from the outermost one of all, the thought
of four or five days' free lodging, to an inner obscure room of
tranquillity and bliss, a place of warmth and germination into
which nothing obtruded except impulses of worship and malice,
malice towards others and worship of herself, the twin poles of
her being, systole and diastole of her blood in the teeming darkness
of her mind.

CHAPTER XI

THE west cliff at Wik, lower and greener than the east, had all the finest residential houses, set in terraces and crescents along its length. Between the gardens of the houses nearest the sea and the crumbling edge of the cliff, there was a stretch of green short turf known as the Piece. It was common land, and from time immemorial ladies had walked there after Church on fine Sundays, trailing their long skirts on the grass. On weekdays children from Under Wik came to disport themselves; sometimes they fought like devils and then, at the sight of a manservant sent out from one of the big houses, they fled with whoops and calls (Under Wik children at this time swore horribly) to the shore or the yards—slippery with fish scale and refuse—opening on the harbour.

One fine morning, at the end of September, Ann and Semiramis walked there together. It was Semiramis's fifty-seventh birthday: Ann had sent a single egg in by Horn with the message, "Mrs. Wellhem sends you this egg with her love, but you're not to expect any more, since they're hard to come by." An hour later Ann herself turned up for dinner. "Did you get the egg?" she demanded.

"Yes. We'll eat it for our dinner," her sister said coldly.

"Ha. That's a poor sort o' dinner to offer a guest."

"It was a poor egg."

They went out. Semiramis had only just had a bathroom put into the house. The house had nine bedrooms but until now no bathroom; she was intensely proud of having put one in. It was a large room, built over the kitchen, the walls covered with a thickly varnished paper in a design of red and yellow vine-leaves and little birds, the window of stained glass with the languishing heads of two saints facing each other in the upper half, and Japanese matting on the floor. A dozen times a day she spent several minutes in the room, trying the taps; a smile of joy came into her face when, more splendid and startling than any natural waterfall, the water gushed from them into the brown marbled

83

bath.   Skelton heard her speaking to herself; creeping noiselessly
to the door she caught the words: "——if I catch *that woman*
laying a finger on it except to clean, I'll have her thrashed naked."
She could not doubt that she was the woman for whom the punishment was intended and slipped away again, stunned and grieved,
not for herself but at the revelation of Semiramis's cruelty.

Semiramis did not intend to use the bath.   She had long
since persuaded herself that she had not the strength to survive
the shock of water on any part of her body except her hands and,
at rare intervals, her face between her eyes and chin.   But she
now felt, in speaking to anyone whom she chanced to meet in the
street or in shops, a purely voluptuous thrill in bringing it bodily
into the conversation.   When she went into the grocer's she would
say to Greene, who was also a leading tenor in the choir, so that a
devout church-goer felt a faint shock in hearing the cry "*O taste
and see,*" welling out in the tones she had last heard saying: "And
a pound of candles, madam, and what else?"

"You may send me something for cleaning taps—t'best, mind
you.   Th' taps *in my bathroom* are made of a new special metal
—none of your common kitchen taps.   See to it yourself, Greene.
I'll not ha' just anything."

In the draper's, at the long narrow shop on the pier, in which
every intended marriage was known and discussed a month before
it was made public, by the prospective bride's mother coming in
to speak about linen sheets and tablecloths—even an approaching
death could be deduced from the wife or other relatives asking
discreetly whether among his rolls of cloth Mr. Charlton had a
really reliable fast black—in the draper's, Semiramis seated herself on one of the high chairs and had pair after pair of curtains
unwrapped for her inspection, finally sweeping all of them aside
with the remark, spoken at the top of her loud grating voice:

"None on 'em's suitable for th' window o' my bathroom.   I
wanted a bit o' fine muslin with bods on it."

"Why birds?" said her sister inquisitively.

"To match th' wallpaper, what do you think?"

"Oh, I thought perhaps you were becoming light-minded
in your old age," Ann said with a smile, terrifying in its implica-
tion of a pitiless and as it were involuntary malice; her lips barely
moved and her eyes had become glassy and inscrutable, as though
she were thinking of anything rather than what she said.

"And how old do you make out I am?" Semiramis said curtly.

"Yes, you're three years older than I am, I know that," Ann said in the simple friendly tone she adopted to persuade an on-looker—at this moment old Mr. Charlton himself, plump and whitened by the obsequious juices he had been secreting during half a lifetime—that she was innocent of offence.

"Then you know which of us is going downhill quickest— ha' you a bathroom in your house? I think you ha'n't, so your advice is useless. I'll say good morning, Mr. Charlton; if you should come by a length of curtain muslin——"

"With a pattern of birds," Mr. Charlton said, rubbing his hands with his usual zeal and animation.

"Ay, with bods—you can send it up for me to try *in t'bath-room.*"

In silence the two sisters climbed the steep road that would bring them to the Piece. Many of the people they met on the way knew them and bowed slightly, with cordial smiles, guarded and unnaturally bright, on their faces, and hurried on without waiting to chat, as though seeing them were a reminder of important business needing to be done at once, or as though the two of them were walking past surrounded by a bubble of impalpable glass through which they could be seen but not approached.

The air on the Piece was fresh and lightly stinging, with a breeze from the sea. It forced them to move quickly, and if Semiramis were not still offended she would have suggested turn-ing back. Suddenly Ann, who was walking nearer the edge of the cliff, said:

"There's your young Andrew down there."

Semiramis came to the edge and looked over gingerly. The earth here was waterlogged and unsafe. The boy, scrambling up the long cliff, leaping from tuft to tuft of rough grass to save him-self from falling into the soft dark-red clay, was Andrew Wikker, Handel's son. He looked up and saw the two old women peering at him, and waved his arms.

"He'll break his neck," Ann exclaimed.

"Nonsense. The boy's well enough. He may do as he likes."

"He has eleven years of sin behind him, the young brute," said Ann. "Brute" did not mean more than if she had said "child" or "servant." All these words denoted a being to whom sin, in the shape of theft, lying, and disobedience, was second nature.

In the meantime the eleven-year-old sinner had taken a cir-cuitous path which would lead him to the top of the cliff at the end nearest the town. They turned back to intercept him. He was up first and came bounding to meet them. His thick reddish hair stood out round his head in curls as stiff as though they were made of copper wire; they partly hid a broad, very prominent forehead, under which his eyes seemed deeper set and colder than they were. His body was thin and supple; he sprang back like an eel when he was being thrashed. How often that happened only Semiramis and Skelton knew; to both women he was a disturbing and incalculable being, an energy they found as difficult to control as if a flame had escaped from the grate and were capering about the house.

Skelton tried to manage him by bribes. She gave him little cakes she had made and sandwiches of brown sugar, and when he was punished by being sent to bed without tea or supper she crept to his room with part of her own food for him. In return he treated her with a contemptuous affection. Sometimes he laid traps for her; when she fell into them he stood and laughed his high screeching laugh until the poor woman believed that he was a devil sent especially to torment her.

His good looks were another source of uneasiness to her mind, as bewildered in her head as a bat in a closed room. How could any boy appear so curiously and piercingly beautiful, with a white skin and eyes as cold and filled with light as a grey sky, and yet behave in the way this boy behaved, with fixed stubborn pride and cruelty, if he were actually only flesh and blood?

To Semiramis he set problems of a subtler and more painfully acute sort. She struggled continually to break down his will, not because she thought he was sinful, but because every time he defied her she felt as though her heart were being squeezed in her side. He doesn't care what happens to me, she said to herself; he is growing up, he will leave me. She would coax him to stay at home with her instead of running out to play with his friends Charles and Isabel Mower. When he resisted her and went, she sat in her room turning in her mind the innumerable other sins he had committed until she could no longer contain herself. He came running in, rosy from the air, and she fell on him with terrible looks and voice because he had scrubbed the toe of his boot.

"Your poor father," she said, "scrats the money to pay for your clothes and you go out on your pleasure and wilfully destroy them." When she had thrashed him with her own father's malacca

cane until she had no breath left, she would ask him gently if he
were sorry. If he said, "Yes," she forgave him, pressing her dry
roughened lips to his cheek while he closed his eyes to endure the
pungent sour smell of her hair and clothes. Usually he declined
to repent. Then days went by without his being spoken to, his
little efforts to start a conversation were all ignored, and even
Skelton was afraid to do more than squint at him, with a depth
of reproach and fear in an eye as divorced from the rest of her
face as if she were holding it out to him in her hand when she
handed him a dish.

He was afraid of the dark. To cure him of his fear, and to
indulge in herself an unconscious cruelty which was nourished
by boredom, Semiramis stood outside his bedroom door one night
when she knew that he was awake, and groaned horribly. She
had been going to burst into the room when he cried out, and
laugh at his mistake. She groaned for several minutes. There
was no sound from his room; at last, losing patience, she went in.
The bed was empty. Only after a time she saw Andrew kneeling
on the window-sill with an arm groping outside it to reach the
drainpipe. When he heard her, he almost fell, recovered himself, and turned his head slowly and awkwardly. He looked at
her with fixed, absent eyes, as though he were looking through
her at something behind her head. He made Semiramis think
of a young bird; a creature so fragile, and yet so stubborn, so wilful,
so capricious. His eyes suddenly dilated, in an expression of
fear and hatred. She spoke to him.

"What are you doing? Why is the window open?"

"I opened it—you can see," Andrew replied firmly.

"Were you trying to get out?"

He did not answer, but looked at her with the same expression,
while watching his chance to dodge past her and reach his bed,
which now appeared to him safer than the floor. Semiramis took
him by the arm and pushed him towards the bed. "Get in."
Andrew obeyed. "Now lie down and go to sleep. And if you
lay a finger on t' window again I'll have bars put across it so
that you can't reach."

She went out, leaving the door ajar. The staircase was in
darkness, and when she reached the lowest flight of stairs she
heard someone breathing loudly in the hall and saw a bulky figure
trying to creep quietly towards the kitchen.

"Is that you, Skelton?" she said, in a low voice. Advancing

across the hall, she came close enough to Skelton to see that she was shaking all over. "What's the matter?"

"What did he say?" Skelton whispered.

"He said he'd opened t' window. He was going to climb out."

"Yes, and he'll kill himself."

"What d'y'say? what d'y'say?" Semiramis said inaudibly. "What nonsense."

She gripped Skelton's thick arm, and the two old women stood close together, listening for some sound in the darkness and silence of the house. Upstairs in his room, Andrew listened. He heard nothing, but he felt certain that something was going on somewhere in the house and he no longer dared look towards the door. After a time he fell asleep. . . .

While they were walking towards him Semiramis remembered that the day before he had been out playing when the steam-roller came panting up the hill. It was a new dangerous purchase by the County Council. It was preceded everywhere by a man carrying a red flag to clear the roads. The children scattered when they saw it. Andrew came flying into the house, bolted the front door, and set his back against it. "Don't be afraid," he said to his aunt, "I'll protect you."

She told Ann the story with a derisive yell of laughter. It was her way of showing off his spirit and her pride in it, while concealing even from herself her fearful love. In a dim way Andrew realized this: he knew that she told the story because she was pleased, but he suffered no less an agony of humiliation in her loud-voiced mockery. His Aunt Ann, whom he detested, joined in, and the two of them laughed until his ears were burning.

Walking beside them he tried to speak in a steady voice to make them believe that he did not care what they said about him. Alas, the subject he hit upon was the worst one he could have chosen. They were walking past a huge notice, scrawled in red chalk, of a Salvation Army meeting. "WAR Has Been Declared." The word War was in letters a foot high, filling three-quarters of the space.

Andrew pointed a finger at it. "Just look at that," he said with a little laugh.

"Why, I believe he thinks it's real," Semiramis said. "He thinks there's going to be a war," and she went off into a screech of laughter, her toque slipping over her ear as she bent sideways. Her sister smiled sardonically.

"It doesn't mean a real war," she said to Andrew.

"I know that," Andrew said sharply.

"Ha! Is that the way you speak to a lady?" Mrs. Wellhem snapped. "You're bringing him up very strangely, Semiramis, I must say."

"I knew it wasn't a real war," Andrew repeated, anxious to make it clear that he was not completely a fool. He failed to notice the significant frown which Semiramis had turned on him. Hold your tongue, was what it said, in unmistakable tones.

Mrs. Wellhem opened her pale eyes widely. "So your aunt was making a mistake?"

Andrew realized that he was in disgrace already, but he was quite unable to understand why. With fatal stubbornness he persisted: "I knew at once; I knew it was only the Salvation Army."

Semiramis's eyes sparkled with anger. Giving his arm a violent pinch, she said: "Go straight home, you. I shall thrash you when I come in."

When Andrew was out of hearing, Ann Wellhem said: "You won't thrash him, will you? He didn't do aught, and he's onny a little lad. You s'd let him off this time." Her heart had been mysteriously touched by something in Andrew's face, the sudden flicker in his eyes when he turned to go away. If he had protested or cried she would have said nothing, but his very silence gave her a feeling that all was not well.

With much argument, and by reminding her sister that it was her birthday, she wrung from her a promise to forgive him this time.

The two sisters sauntered towards Semiramis's house. In the warmth of a sheltered road they raised their veils, loosened their furs, and with joy felt the sun on their cheeks. Energetically and amiably they disputed whether the four proud Vansittarts would become whores or washerwomen when their father died. It did not occur to them that Providence could be so lacking in common decency as to allow these girls to marry and lead peaceful ordinary lives.

G

CHAPTER XII

ANDREW'S life was divided as day from night by the door of his aunt's house. Inside the house he grew up in a state of siege, perpetually watchful for his freedom; one day he was defeated and the next, withdrawing further into himself, he tried to repair the harm done to his defences. Outside he became a schoolboy, neither popular nor unpopular with the others, many of whom thought him "cracked." He was too mischievous and unruly to be a favourite with the masters, in spite of his intelligence: singing-master Vansittart, who was fonder of him than the rest, said: "The noise Andrew Wikker makes when he laughs is not in the least human," and when it started he put his hands over his ears.

He grew tall and very bony. He was noticeable not only by his height but by the shape of his head, with its short and stubborn nose, deep-set eyes, and big rounded forehead. His hair made this prominent forehead more extraordinary; before going out in the morning he struggled to flatten it—he once stole one of Skelton's pudding-cloths and went to sleep with it knotted tightly round—but it stood out from his head in a stiff bright fleece. In time he took to brushing it off his forehead, and since in his schoolfellows' eyes it was the least peculiar thing about him he was not laughed at.

One Saturday afternoon in spring he was hurrying to pick up Charles Mower for their usual walk when he heard his name shouted from a window above his head and saw a boy named Frankland beckoning him to come in.

"What do you want?" he called impatiently.

"Just come in a minute," the boy said; "we want to ask you something. It won't take a minute."

He went in reluctantly and ran up the stairs to the room where he found Frankland waiting with another boy in his class. He saw at once that they had some game on and he did not go far into the room.

"Well, what is it?" he asked.

He listened, frowning, to a long confused question about his father: had he really been a whaling captain and if so had the jawbone of a whale, which was being used by Sir Thomas Money as a gate-post, belonged to one of his whales? "Is that all you wanted to know?" he said in a contemptuous voice.

"No, there's something else," said Frankland. His eyes sparkled behind the thick lenses of his spectacles. "There was someone else in your family, someone whose father wouldn't keep her in his house, and so he sent her away in his pig cart, and that someone had to get married in a great hurry. Do you know who I mean?"

Andrew was at first surprised, then seized with a blind rage. He ran towards Frankland, knocked his glasses off with a blow on the side of his head, and joyfully hit him on the other as he drew back. The sensations he felt were so pleasant that he went on raining blow after blow on the boy's head and body. Stunned by the fury with which he had been attacked, and half-blind, Frankland crouched close to the wall, with his arms stretched across his head and face. His friend had come to his rescue and received an unlucky blow on the nose. He was busy mopping up his own blood. Delirious with joy, Andrew struck the wretched Frankland without pity and without realizing what he was doing. It was the sudden opening of a door in another part of the house which brought him to his senses. He dropped his hands and stood looking in surprise at Frankland's swollen and disfigured face.

"You've broken his glasses," stuttered the other boy.

"It serves him right," Andrew said lightly.

He ran out of the house into the street. His cheeks were burning and his heart beating violently. He had forgotten where he was going, but in a minute he remembered and tried to think quietly. There were two ways of reaching the Mowers' house: one, the longer, would lead him by back lanes where he was less likely to be seen. He took that. He was out of breath, and when he came to the narrow passage between two lanes, he stood still leaning against the wall. It was the high brick wall of Sir Thomas Money's garden. Directly over his head, between him and the glowing azure of the sky, not in the least dimmed by it, but burning steadily with their own deeper flame, hung the yellow drops of a laburnum. He stared at them until the air round him seemed gilded with their peculiar lustre, wherever he looked he saw varnished gleams of light, as yellow as though the sunlight had run together in blobs and clusters among the scarcely visible leaves. Slowly he became calm: another happiness took the place of the one which had turned to disgust at the sight of Frankland's distorted face. He felt that he could look at the laburnum flowers for ever. It was as though the longer he looked, the closer he drew towards some riddle of which the answer was to be found precisely in their fiery conjunction with the blue of the sky and the dazzling whiteness of a cloud hovering directly above them. He remembered that Charles would be waiting for him and hurried on.

There was no one in the little garden of Mower's house except Isabel Mower. The child—she was small and very thin and, although she was thirteen, seemed two or three years younger—was kneeling on the grass border with a book which she had not even opened. She looked up at Andrew with her small sparkling smile —it was like winter sunlight on water. Her heart-shaped face had more finish about it than children's faces have usually; each feature was firmly drawn and delicate: even her smiles had not the vagueness of childhood, but expressed an extraordinary range of emotions, from affection to irony.

"Where's Charles?" asked Andrew.

"Coming," she said. She made room beside her on the strip of worn grass for Andrew to sit down. It was close and very still in the garden.

He began to feel sleepy. He took her book out of her hand and, turning the leaves, began to talk to her about it. She was not interested. She only smiled, and folded her little slender hands in her lap, waiting patiently until he had finished. He could see by the way she moved her eyes to look through the leaves of the tree above their heads, that she was bored by his attempt to amuse her. He closed the book and looked at her gently and kindly.

They sat there in silence until Charles came out of the house.

Charles was vexed that his father had kept him. He said nothing about it, ashamed because at seventeen he was still treated as a child. Dark and sallow, he had dark-brown eyes redeemed from softness by an ironic gleam, a long nose slightly twisted to one side, and a long shapely mouth. The hint of weakness in his looks—it was to be found less in any one feature than in their full, rather feminine modelling—was corrected by an abrupt, jerky manner.

Two years older than Andrew and years more civilized, he was his only intimate friend at this time. It was perhaps thanks to him and to his enthusiasms and lively mind, as well as to the chance of living in a place as beautiful as Wik at this time, that Andrew was able to look back on his childhood without bitterness. And to think first of such things as the lilacs and laburnums lining the streets behind the railings in small shabby gardens, where a border of exotic shells or a rare kind of fuschia might announce that a house belonged to the wife of a sea-captain; of the scent of new wood in the shipyards; and of long glittering summer after-noons spent on the edge of a sea of which the treacherous currents were marked by the changes of light and colour on the surface from green to an opaque blue, in places to a blue so clear and dark that it was nearly violet, or by the sudden emergence of a line of sharp-toothed waves, each throwing back against the sun-light pouring on it from above a barb of pure white light in an air already quivering with a brightness like fine dust.

"Are you coming, Tib?" Charles said to his sister.

She sprang up, and the three of them, Tib loitering behind until she was told to look sharp, started to walk along the sands.

The tide was out and they walked over a ribbed shore, dark and wet. The shallow pools left behind by the sea were warm, even now in May when the sea was still cold as ice. A hedgeless tossing field, it stretched away on their right, steeply hanging above their heads to lean on the horizon. There it was apparently grey and smooth; here it blashed on the shore, opening and closing its great jaws; at one minute you saw a green throat, the next a slaver of foam a mile long.

Andrew half closed his eyes, so that he could feel himself a speck of living matter; it might be a gull's feather, incessantly washed over and penetrated by this windy thunderous element. He opened them again widely, as if by sight he could swallow it, so that wherever he went he would take it with him. He knew that his mother had been buried at sea and he believed this made him in a sense the sea's child. A certain note to be heard in it on languorous summer evenings, deep, soft, sustained, sibilant, he had long ago decided was his mother's voice. He listened for it when he remembered, with an attention which seemed to draw him through his ears towards something of the greatest importance, that he never quite managed to hear or see. The effort left him weak and empty. The awful miseries into which, for no reason, he was sometimes dropped, blackening the air and driving him to all sorts of follies to escape them, were accompanied in his mind by a sense of being surrounded and suffocated by lifeless waters; he could do nothing to help himself except wait for them to subside. So, too, the moments of ecstasy when he flew straight to a peak of bliss like a drop of water to the sun, came with and left behind them the uninvited thought of a wave gleaming in sunlight, its sleek sides slippery with foam and endless sweating drops of light.

When they turned to walk back—they were due at the Vansittarts for tea—he was caught by the look on Tib's face. The child was not taking any notice or listening to them; she might have been walking quite alone. At this moment she was standing looking into a pool between two rocks, her delicate face poised, with its air of aloofness, like a bird on a slender stem. She seemed suspended between sea and shore, with the sky for a background. Andrew's heart started alert, almost with fear.

"Don't dawdle, our Tib," Charles shouted. "Hi—we're going back."

She came to life at once and skipped over the pool with a sideways flirt of her legs, and was away scrambling up the cliff before her brother and Andrew had ploughed over the sands to reach the foot. At the top they sent her home and went off to Vansittart's little house at the end of a street looking down into the harbour. This, with the streets falling steeply from it to the pier, was the shabby part of Over Wik.

But from the sitting-room with its bay window the Vansittarts looked as sharply as a stone is cast outward and down over the roofs to the harbour, the wharves, the east cliff with the houses clinging to it, and the green field above. When the setting sun shone on this field it seemed the one celebrated in the hymn— *There is a green hill far away*—so bright, smooth, glowing, and rounded was its arm laid above the houses. They could watch the ship growing on the stocks in Wik Old Yard, and the ceaseless traffic of the wharves; they saw the Norwegian timber-boats moving slowly up the harbour. The heart of Wik was beating just below them in shipyard and wharves. Its strong eager life, alert and rousing, came up to them day and night as they slept and as they worked, talked, and ate together in the familiar room.

This sitting-room of Vansittart's house was unlike any room in Wik. To begin with, it was used for meals, and as music-room, studio for Lizzie Vansittart's paintings of flowers on trays, plaques, and finger-plates, sewing-room, and it had been the nursery. It was what any Wik housewife would have called "dauby." The couch had broken springs, the wallpaper was a nondescript yellow and covered with pencil scrawlings to the height of a child's mischievous arm; every shelf, cupboard, and corner bulged with a miscellany of objects, new or old, necessary or unnecessary, fans, boxes, sheets of music, plates, reels of cotton, mending, paint-brushes. It must sometimes have been tidied, or it would have overflowed into the passage, but no one had ever seen it look any different.

Vansittart was alone in this room when his wife told the boys to go in. He was stooping near the window over a small, oddly-shaped violin. It was not, he told them, a violin; it was a viol. He held it up between his hands and showed them the differences. Its six strings were tuned as in a lute; they were lighter, longer, and less tense than in a violin. Its wooden body was very thin, and the ribs deep.

"There are a million fools who think that a viol is an imperfect violin," he said fiercely. He trembled with anger. "Don't forget now I've told you that it's different and perfect in itself. Music written for the viol is never played properly now. You don't even know what the Sixth Brandenburg Concerto ought to sound like, because you mutilate it by playing it on instruments the Master never intended you to use. As for earlier music, as for Lawes, and Byrd and Jenkins——"

He broke off with a guilty look when his eldest daughter came into the room. She looked at him and at the viol. A smile turned down quickly the corners of her red beautiful mouth, as red as a strawberry, and her eyes sparkled.

"Do you know what he paid for it," she cried. None of the Vansittarts had any proper shame. "Fifty pounds. He earns a hundred and ten pounds a year. The money is what our mother has been saving for years and he takes it to buy that—a viol! Sometimes we haven't even a shilling for food."

"But, Lizzie," her father said, in a pleading voice, "you don't know how ethereal and abstract music can be unless you've heard Byrd's Fantasy for Six Viols. Just as you don't know what music Bach drew out of the clavichord when you play a piece he wrote for it on a clumping, noisy, woolly-toothed horror of a piano."

"Well, you haven't got six viols," Lizzie said coldly. "And our mother wears the shabbiest clothes ever seen in Wik."

She came over and stood behind him—she was much taller than he was, black-haired, black-eyed—looking down at him with a mingling of love and rage that made her face that of a mother punishing her joyously loved child.

His true mother, his wife, had heard the last sentence as she staggered in carrying the black-japanned tray with its load of ill-matched cups and saucers, the blue teapot and the pile of bread and butter. She glanced sternly and reproachfully at her daughter. Clearing with the back of her hand a space on the littered table, she set the tray down with such energy that the things bounced off the humps into which it had warped, and slid and rattled. Ruin was only averted at the last edge by Charles Mower's quick deft fingers. Mrs. Vansittart forgot to thank him.

The dark eyes, clouded by experience, yet living, in her crumpled greasy face, flashed a look of fury at her daughter. Emily Vansittart was the meekest creature in the world and with all the stubbornness and strength of the meek. Nothing roused her except an attack on the happiness or dignity of her husband and daughters. If the girls quarrelled she flew to help the one who seemed to be most in the wrong. But her daughters, although they loved her, were independent of her on the day each was able to walk, and to think, I, Lizzie, Sarah, Julia, Lucy Vansittart am as beautiful as anything I see. Only her husband depended on her still, brought her troubles when he had nothing else to bring, and still at night lay in her arms as trustfully as when she first gathered him there.

"I won't have it, Lizzie," she said defiantly. That she was a comical sight only made her more intimidating. "And as it happens, it was I told your father to buy the viol. A chance like that doesn't come every day. . . . You girls have never gone short of food, or clothes, or fun, yet you grudge your father his pleasures. No, no, it's too much."

"Very well," Lizzie murmured.

She began, silently and biting her lip, to arrange the cups on

the table.   Her mother and father looked at her and at each other,
and all at once she smiled and began humming, the tension was
broken, and in the same moment the door opened and the other
girls flew into the room.

It seemed to Andrew that they all talked at once, as purely
assertive as a lot of birds.   Sarah—the second daughter and the
most beautiful, a lively radiant creature, white-skinned and scarlet-
cheeked like the goose-girl in the story—chattered to the two boys,
teasing Andrew about his hair, and asking Charles if it were true
that he was going to London to be a lawyer.

"No; I wish it were," Charles said moodily.   "My dad says
I have to be a solicitor and learn here, not in London."

"You'll be a catering law-monger," she laughed, "as Milton
says."

"Why, have you read Milton?"

"Good heavens—what do you think?   My father said it . . .
let me see—how old are you?   Seventeen?   Terrible—and Andrew
is younger.   You must hurry up, my sweet child," she said softly
to Andrew.   "I meant to marry you, and here I'm twenty-three
already—I shall be an old maid before you ask me."

Her head was on a level with his; to look directly into her eyes,
their blackness so full of light that it was like looking into the
perspective of a strange world, made him breathless.   A year
younger than Lizzie, she was more womanly; her high rounded
bosom and thin wrists forced themselves on his notice, so that
he was afraid to look at her.   She knew that he was becoming
confused, and it seemed to amuse her.

All the bread and butter had been eaten, and Vansittart could
no longer nurse his viol without playing it.

"What shall I play?" he asked his wife.

"Play your own piece, father," she answered.

He held the viol between his knees and looking fixedly at the
window, played.   At first Andrew noticed its peculiar tone, clear,
sweet, and reedy, but then he was caught by something in the
music itself.   He was too ignorant to understand it, but he began
to feel the same strange absorbed pleasure that he drew from the
effort of listening for his mother's voice in an undertone of the
sea.   This was different only in that the sound seemed to spring up
within his mind like a jet of pure water of which each glittering
drop destroyed the memory of the one before it.   And yet the
thread of brightness remained.   His pleasure in it changed to

sadness and made him wince as though the notes were knives, then returned altered and piercing, so that the marrow of his brain seemed to be dissolving in an unearthly happiness. His outer ear was telling him all this time that Vansittart's "piece" was unlike any music he had heard, and that although it had what he thought of as a tune it was not a tune he would ever remember or even like. There was, indeed, nothing to like in the music. It existed almost in another world; its notes gushing inside his brain were independent of his feeling; he could not control them unless he put his fingers in his ears, and if he were asked to describe the piece he would only have said that it was a very queer noise indeed, scarcely music at all.

He sat feeling a little dazed when Vansittart put the viol down. Fortunately nothing seemed expected of him. Mrs. Vansittart took up a stocking from her pile of mending, and as a sign that their quarrel was forgotten Vansittart put his hand out and pulled Lizzie's little ivory thin ear. Julia Vansittart had edged towards the door. She now opened it noiselessly and slipped out.

"She has a box of chocolates in her room," Lucy whispered to the two boys; "she's so fearfully greedy that she eats them alone —and she's conceited, she thinks no one looks so smart in a dress as she does. You should just see her trying on before the glass. Sarah and I die of laughing."

"Where has Julia gone?" said her father. He looked at the two boys with an anxious and timid smile. "We aren't entertaining you," he said sadly. "The girls shall sing. Yes, yes, yes—go and bring your sister, my little Lucy; don't be lazy, run, run."

Standing in an uneven line from eldest to youngest, they sang in German a song of which he did not understand a word; but from its first note he was led, alone in ecstasy, into a darkness and stillness which seemed to him familiar, as though he were returning to it with joy yet with grief that he could not, for longer than the sounds, unseizably lovely as they were, loitered in his mind, there remain. . . . *Über allen Gipfeln ist Ruh.* . . . He tried, by keeping his eyes fixed on the singers, to make sure of carrying away at least something, some sign which later he would recognize, of its peculiar and miraculous charm. Each girl was like yet unlike her sisters; Lizzie, tall, fiery, her eyes too large and brilliant, so that the rest of her face, even her fine wide mouth,

appeared insignificant, like the face of a clown who in exaggerating
one feature has obliterated all the others; the lovely Sarah; Julia,
at twenty an overgrown child, with black curls tumbling over her
white forehead, gleaming black eyes, a chin white and too full
for the perfection her face would have had; Lucy the youngest,
the most reckless and vivid, with the smooth glowing cheeks
of a healthy boy.

Their shoulders touched as they stood with their backs to the
window. They were set, as in a Florentine painting, in a landscape
of clear brilliant colours, small houses climbing up the side of a
hill, the enamelled green of a field, and just at the level of their
clasped hands, an arc of bright water, the shape of old Wik become
a lively frame for their abounding, rosy youth. The thought
sprang into Andrew's head that if he were so far distant, as far as
God, from the earth and yet able, as no doubt God was, to overlook the least item on it, he would not only see the whole of space
with its several worlds at once but the whole of time; past and
future would run together into one endless moment, in which, more
securely than in a painting, the four Vansittarts singing together
would be caught and held. And not only they, but the pure
silvery jet of sound springing from their throats, the patches of
dark rust on the rim of the iron tray, the childish scribbles on the
wallpaper, and yes, the houses of Under Wik with their glaze of
smoke and sunshine, the idly rocking masts of a Norwegian barque,
the voices of men and hammers in the shipyards and on the busy
wharves, and his own aching tremulous happiness.

"That," said Vansittart, "is the essence of pure music. It
was written by a man who was often hungry and dirty. Like
me. We have all seen pure water springing out of the bog. He
is one of the greatest musicians who ever lived. I love him. He
is my brother." But an unhappier brother, he thought, remembering that Schubert had written, not once but a hundred times *Ach!
so muss ich ganz allein.* . . . He looked at his wife for a moment
and thought, I am not alone.

She was hurrying out, moving in her flat clumsy way to look
after the soup. When Andrew and his friend were going they
met her in the passage. The strong smell of cabbage came
from the kitchen. Blushing, she shook hands with them and
said:

"It smells dreadful, doesn't it? It's a very old one. But I
must use everything in the soup. It's for the poor."

She could hardly have expected them to believe the lie. The reason she told it was not because she was ashamed of their poverty, but that she could not resist trying to make her husband out cleverer than he was. She knew that in Wik a man was reckoned stupid or clever according to the money he made, so day by day, to people who knew as well as she did every penny she had to put in her purse, she pretended to have so much money that in order to get rid of it she would have to give some away.

"Are you coming back with me?" Charles asked, when they were in the street.

"No," Andrew said. He added, with a feeling of reluctance: "I'm going to see my father." He was afraid that his friend would say, He doesn't often ask you, does he? But Charles's thoughts were on something else.

"They're mad, aren't they?" he said.

"Who are? The Vansittarts?"

"Yes. Fancy paying fifty pounds for a second-hand fiddle, and as balmy poor as rats. Poorer than we are, by a long chalk. The girls are all right. I'd like to make up to one of them, Lucy or Sarah, if it wasn't that I've had enough of poverty and scraping and saving, pretending to lead a decent life. When I marry I'm going to marry a rich woman and don't you forget I said so."

"I'm not going to marry at all," Andrew said.

Climbing the Garth to his father's house, he felt cheerful at the thought that for one evening he was not going to sit opposite his aunt at supper, evading her endless string of questions and watching her choose out the best morsels and transfer them to her plate before serving him. He felt happy and peaceful in his father's house, for one reason because Handel Wikker was always too busy and preoccupied to say: What have you been doing with yourself? Who do you speak to? What have you heard? Yet he would never ask to live with him. And it was not only from shyness, from the profound diffidence he would have felt in thrusting himself where perhaps he was not wanted, but because he lacked the courage to tell Semiramis that he disliked living with her. Sensations of unresolved fear, tenderness, and hatred existed side by side in his feeling for her; he would have been capable of striking her and in the same moment of throwing himself into her arms in an agony of remorse. To escape for a few

hours to his father's house was like escaping into the open air
from a cell.

Handel was preparing their supper of eggs and cheese and
bread. While he boiled the eggs, Andrew told him of his own
accord about the viol and Vansittart's piece.

"It was the oddest noise I ever listened to," he said, confessing
freely. "I couldn't make it out."

"Neither can anyone else," said Handel. "He played it in
London at a private concert, there were musical critics in the
audience, they told him it was rubbish and he half believed them.
He believed anyhow that he had better not try again."

"Is it rubbish, then?" asked Andrew.

His father was silent for a minute. "I think it is the most
remarkable music of our time," he said. "I don't know how much
he has written down, I'm afraid that most of it exists only in his
memory, and since he will get no encouragement, and since with
one thing and another he has very little time, it is probable that
you and I and a very few others are the only people who will ever
know that a great musician lived here in Wik out of his time.
Mark, I do not say before his time. The poor fellow may just
as well be a couple of centuries after it. There are times when
an honest artist is made to suffer. All men are born with the need
and longing to create something. In a time when the channels
are open so that the waters, as the prophet said, return not but
water the earth, all men can create in newness of life. Then the
true artist, who is their example, is at his ease. He is honoured.
But at other times it is not life but *death* which is going in a moment
to be born. The wheels grind backwards, destroying and killing,
the waters are hid as with a stone, it is the kingdom of death,
the hard winter of the soul, and the artist suffers in it: struggling
to live, either he creates forms of death because they are what
he sees, and he is reviled by the common people whom they alarm,
or he makes a terrible effort and finds in himself a fresh serenity.
But not a creature understands him, none of them is able to make
the effort, as hard and painful as a birth. He will be hated.
And so when Christ said, Father, forgive them; for they know not
what they do, He was doing, with an infinite effort to subdue
His fear, what Vansittart struggles to do in his music, He was
creating out of His agony of mind and body a new, different serenity.
This, this only, is what His vicars have never been able to forgive,
they have never forgiven Him for His success. They won't have

it at any price. They have always found excuses for dodging it.
An archbishop will lie rather than confess that to a Christian
killing is forbidden; he will pretend to be a Christian when actually,
like any savage priest, he is saying, There is a time to kill. This
forgiveness, which Christ discovered in Himself when He was
dying, is not a creed but the supreme personal achievement of
an artist creating a new way of life, which the archbishops repudiate
and which in their hearts they detest. Much as those critics,
who think they know all about music, loathed and rejected the
work of poor Vansittart's genius, because they don't understand
it—their ears are as full of hard wax as their minds of dishonest
ideas."

He put the eggs on the table, found some salt and poured it
into another egg-cup, and they sat down to eat. Andrew was
hungry; he ate three of the four eggs, and talked, breaking off
shyly when he felt that he had talked too much, and beginning
again reassured.

His father watched him with a curious smile. He could see
in him more than one Wikker, something of himself and of Ezekiel,
a hint even of Semiramis's instinctive malice. But in vain he
searched for any trace of Kezia in her son. Yet it was there,
and he missed it because only a woman would have seen that
Andrew was afraid, not of hurting people, but of seeing them hurt
and would do anything to avoid it. Handel guessed, however,
at a certain coldness in the boy's nature, a rather cruel simplicity.
His mind was airy, but it was a cold air, like the frostbound darkness and stillness of a northern night.

When it was time for Andrew to go home, his father went
with him as far as the door. It was a still night; above Wik the
sky was broken into dark violet-hued clouds, lying in an archi-
pelago of pure light. The first quarter of the moon was visible
between a greater and a lesser island, as it were a sail becalmed
between their two shores.

"The moon is making," said Handel.

"I don't know what that means," Andrew said. He felt
ashamed.

"Why, it means that it is waxing towards the full. You know
they say that when the moon is making, queer people behave more
queerly than usual," he added slyly.

"Wik is full of mad people," Andrew said. He was thinking
at the moment of his two aunts.

He ran off. He looked back from the top of the lane and saw his father standing in the narrow doorway. The light from the passage was behind him so that he was only the dark shape of a man. He had stretched his arms out, his hands on the sides of the door; he might have been hanging. Andrew started irrepressibly with fear. Turning his head, he began to run as hard as he could, in order to forget that he had had so unlucky a thought.

CHAPTER XIII

Two years ago Handel Wikker had begun to preach a gospel of repentance, as simple and, to tell the truth, as hard as his thoughts. He had meditated so long on certain words that they had ended by telling him what he wanted to know. A word such as "forgiveness" no longer meant to him what it meant to his hearers. It meant an action which *they* must perform. In striving to make this clear he used few words and those often in a sense slightly different from the common. The effect was that his words became alive and flew into people's minds. They were not understood but they were remembered.

He preached in the evening on Sunday. To avoid offence it was spoken of as an "address." The place was the neglected Temperance Hall near the East Wharf, a large shabby building, badly lit by a few dusty windows, and used on week-days as an auction room. As time passed these addresses were talked of over a still wider area. In summer the large airless hall was crowded with visitors who enjoyed his abrupt eloquences so much that they were able to feel they were taking a strengthening holiday not only from work but from their usual religious tasks. During the rest of the year it was filled with curious or earnest persons, chiefly Dissenters, wandered in from the Wesleyan, Wesleyan Methodist, Primitive Methodist, or Baptist chapels, and with a large sprinkling of rough men and women from Under Wik who had never attended any church. It was this, as it were, outcast half of his congregation which gave him qualms he was not able to stifle. For years he had been cherishing and admonishing the sick and broken of Under Wik; but with these others, uncouth, foul-mouthed, quarrelsome, he had had nothing to do. He was surprised to see them coming in ones and twos to sit at the back of the Mission Hall.

Occasionally a man would accost him after the service, and smelling strongly of sweat and of fish, ropes, or drink, would thrust his face with its broken teeth and discoloured flesh against his and begin to argue stupidly about the address, repeating himself, and dully striking one raw-knuckled hand on the other. Invariably Handel felt a surge of repulsion and anger. He did not say: "Get off my bridge," but his voice and manner became brusque, and he cut the inarticulate wretch short.

At the end of May, he received a letter inviting him to go and see the Bishop, the same who had been forced to turn him out of his living sixteen years back. He went.

In the evening, after he had dined, and they were drinking coffee together in the Bishop's study, he felt a sudden tormenting hunger for the finer things of the spiritual life as he now felt and saw them in this room, bookcases filled to the painted ceiling with decently-bound books, thin plain coffee cups, a good *fine*, the reward at the close of the day of long hours given over exclusively to the mind and perhaps the soul.

Through the windows of the study he could see one edge of his host's private garden, the level grass with its border of white and purple lilacs in bloom, the bed of herbs, and the magnificent plane tree he had seen rippling in sunshine on his earlier visit. Only the rim of the high wall caught the setting sun, and by its subdued yellow glow made the rest of the stone appear to be sunk under water. The garden itself was in shadow, and filled to the height of the wall by the watery shifting light, one plane of colour sliding into another as though reflections from the sky and its clouds were meeting others springing from the depths of the pool.

At this moment, when he was comparing the way his friend lived with his simplicity in speaking and writing, the old man began to talk about him. He talked openly and mildly about the possibility of his "dear son" coming back into the Church—as though Handel must certainly have known all along that that was why he had been invited to stay the night. Simply in order to discuss it—and to have his mind and heart probed with a gentleness which was all the more searching because it began with the Bishop putting himself humbly and firmly in his "son's" place. There was no turning him out, and he meant to look into everything.

Handel suffered an extraordinary exultance and an extraordinary humiliation. Never had he felt so sharply, with an almost sensual pricking and quickness, the dignity and the beauty of the visible church, founded, not in the blood of martyrs but on the subtle brains and enduring purposes of men who had been in their way workers in the use of a singular power. He was before a sudden frost had nipped the trees, shrivelling and tearing the young blossom. Now in the wind they were dashed like the waves, to and fro under the sullen sky.

They won't come, thought Handel. At that moment he saw Mower and Vansittart struggling towards him, with bent heads. He hurried in again, put a light to his fire, and was holding a newspaper to it to draw it when they came in. The paper caught fire at once.

The room, since it was very low and small, was soon hot, and it was between mouthfuls of smoke blown down the chimney by the wind that Handel told his friends his news and asked their advice. Not that he would take advice.

Mower let himself go scornfully about the Church of England.

"I have no respect for bishops," he shouted. "They are superb dialecticians, they are spiritual princes who live in the greatest material ease, and the fact is that the country could bear the loss of all of them in one day far more happily than it could bear the loss of, say, all the scavengers or all the common schoolmasters like myself."

"Now you're talking the most irrational nonsense," Handel said sharply. "There is an argument for conformity which is quite unanswerable. Whatever else it is, the Church is one of the pillars of order. Upset it and you will have begun what may end in revolution. Scavengers don't make revolutions, my dear John—nor schoolmasters either."

"Revolution? A damned fine thing!" roared Mower.

"You don't believe it," Handel said, with a cold smile. "You don't want universal anarchy, and you can't keep only a little of it, to gratify your more respectable lusts."

He thought of his own. He now believed that he held within himself some inferior being whom he ought to discipline. He had injured Kezia, indeed killed her. But he would not injure her further by speaking about it. Even to Mower he gave the impression that he had forgotten the scandal of his marriage. Whereas the truth was that after Kezia had died he began looking for her to ask her to understand him.

"You haven't given me your opinion," he said to Vansittart.

"I know nothing; everyone else knows more than I do," Vansittart answered, with the shyness, simplicity, and good nature which made everybody in Wik despise him and think him a fool.

"Yes, but what is *order?*" Mower said almost quietly. "What is real organic order, the order in a blade of grass which prevents it from growing into a beetle? My life is what you would call orderly, but I tell you that I'm a raging maniac, a fornicator, a coward, a murderer. . . ."

But what are they talking about? Vansittart wondered. The only thing we know about life is that it goes out. Bach and Schubert are dead. The only truly good person I know will die. At the thought of Emily's death he felt the terrible anguish which he had so *organized* that its only expression was the kind of smile his face wore when he was composing one of those pieces of music he knew better than to play again in public.

"I am beginning to believe that I know nothing about my own nature," Handel said quietly. "One must discover what is real in oneself."

When he was alone, he found himself thinking of Kezia. He was seized by a nostalgic sickness of desire. It was not so much for her as for the clarity and simplicity of those days which now seemed to him, perhaps because of their bareness, of long stretches of time when nothing happened, and because of his tireless strength then, to have been of a special flavour and value. He had squandered them at the time so carelessly that scarcely a moment remained intact—the impression of a clear sky, of lasting sensations of cold, hunger, warmth, but of their hidden essence, nothing, not one drop of a fragrance which should have lasted a lifetime. Even Kezia's face had become dim, tumbled over day and night, by the waters of memory.

ought to be praying for yourself. As for t'field, you can't take it with you unless you eat it, and you needn't think your bones under it 'll spoil it for me. I'll give y' a word in passing. Hi, there, I s'll say, can y' hear me? how d'y'like t'taste of your field in your mouth? I'll plough up to your damned toes, and we'll see if y' lift 'em."

Scoresby was so deeply offended by this form of mockery— he had not been joking about his grave—that he turned and walked away, declining to answer the remarks Ezekiel shouted after him. Irritated, Ezekiel threw a clod of earth, which fortunately missed the old man, who stumped on without lifting his head.

Ezekiel's annoyance was shot through by secret thrills of pleasure, which came to him from the scent of the lilac in his buttonhole; it reminded him, without his being aware of it, of his own sleek cared-for fields. He felt well and strong. By contrast with the miserable poor ghost of his enemy, he was consciously revelling, as he strode back, in his own rich flesh, quivering with the life he felt about him in the germinating fields, as though it were the seed of his own body he had cast there.

He went home and ate a dinner which began with a shoulder of new young lamb; he devoured almost the whole joint, smacking his big red lips over its creamy fat: then he ate the breast and wings of a chicken, a quantity of sausages, each a mouthful for him, a rhubarb pie, eight cheese cakes, and drank a quart of his own ale, warm and spiced.

"I told Scoresby this morning he couldn't eat his field, but by God, I've eaten half a one. Ha'n't I now? And I feel better for it. And mind you," he said to Soal, "you're not to stuff the rest of those cheese cakes, or give them to that boy of yourn. You may put 'em on the side and I'll eat them later."

His own greed delighted him. He was vexed when he caught an expression of timid scorn on his daughter's face. Her coldness and disapproval hurt his pride and made him for less than a second uncertain of his joyous contempt for all he understood by respectability. Looking round for some way of punishing her, he remembered that she never played now and sent her to the piano to practise.

"You'll practise for an hour while I rest," he suddenly shouted at her. "Why did I pay for lessons for a whole year? Go on, play, girl, play. And put life into it. You're as cold as a stone."

"Mayn't I practise this evening instead, father?" Bessie said desperately. "I was going into Wik."

"And what were you going to do? Amuse yourself? Sing in the streets?"

"No. I was going to walk on the Piece. The band plays there this afternoon."

"Oh, ay; I think it does," Ezekiel jeered. "And so you and all the respectable decent women in Wik must trail up and down the Piece, showing yourselves off like the hussies you'd be if you was let loose. By God, I believe if the only way you could get husbands was by walking naked on th' pier you'd do it. Modesty isn't what saves us from you. . . . Sit down, girl. Sit down and play until I allow you to leave off."

He fell asleep, and for the next two and a half hours Bessie's fingers blundered over the keys, listlessly, except when a spasm of indignation sharpened her disappointment and drove her to crash noisily on several notes at once, without, however, waking her tormentor. She was half afraid and half longing to disturb him. He slept, and snored, and woke finally with a start at a moment when Bessie had begun playing with more spirit than usual.

He listened for a moment with his eyes widely opened and vague; a strange look of surprise and a softened, foolish smile flickered in them. "I thought you were my mother," he muttered.

"May I stop now?" Bessie said. She thought he was still half asleep.

"If you want to. I won't be hard on you."

It was too late for her to hear the band playing on the Piece, and she wandered out of the house in a mood of despairing rebellion. She felt it shameful that at twenty-five she should be bullied still as if she were a little girl; but except at moments where a flame seemed to light up her body suddenly, and failed again almost at once, she was far too much afraid of him to protest.

She had become thinner in the last year, but her high, rounded bosom and thin arms and wrists were still those of a girl who might become stately in due time. Her long and delicate neck seemed to be pulled backwards by the weight of her hair, and her eyes had still the brilliance and the unwavering, rather stubborn expression they had had when she was a child. She walked quickly, with slight jerky movements of her arms.

There was a gap in one corner of the hedge, leading into the

CHAPTER XV

In the fifteen years that Andrew had been living with his aunt her daughter Merry had never once been home. She was living a kind of life of which no one in Wik had heard more than rumours. And since to believe them would have involved believing with the same motion that a perfectly commonplace girl born and brought up in Wik had turned out to be extraordinarily talented, they were regarded, naturally, as flatly untrue. How was it possible or likely that Merry Jordan, whom everyone remembered as a lanky talkative little girl, could be the same person as Mrs. Jordan Smith, well-known in England and America as an eloquent writer and lecturer on—of all ridiculous and faintly indecent things—Women's Rights.

If it were proved to be true it would simply mean one of two things: either that her fame was largely an invention of the over-credulous, or that she wrote a great deal of nonsense, which only the donkeys who inhabited the rest of the known world would swallow. Charitably-minded people, and ordinary people in their charitable moments, inclined to the first theory. The others, that is, most of the natives of Wik, preferred the last as more in keeping with what they suspected of the world. It was clearly impossible that both notions were wrong and that Semiramis Jordan's daughter had indeed turned out differently from anyone else in the town.

Semiramis herself took no interest in the newspaper reports which from time to time Merry posted to her in London and America. To her, Merry was merely a daughter who had made an unfortunate marriage and did well not to show her face after it in her mother's town.

The letter from Merry saying that she and her husband were coming to Wik—"coming home," she had written, with a pathetic inability to understand her place in the scheme of things—arrived at dinner-time. It gave Semiramis the most violent indigestion. She quivered with annoyance as she read it, and when Andrew chose this moment to upset his glass of claret and water she leaned across the table and slapped his face.

The boy jumped up, knocking over his chair.

"Clumsy young fool!" cried Semiramis; "go into your room and stay there until I call you down."

It was a cloudless July day, and a half-holiday. Andrew's reply was to walk out of the house, leaving his aunt speechless with fury and the pains of her internal disorder. In the evening, when he returned, she had been watching impatiently from the windows of her bedroom. She came out on to the landing, a terrifying figure in nightgown and shawls, and thrust her inflamed face into his. He had never noticed before that her left eye was beginning to be filmed by cataract, so that all her stubbornness and all her malice seemed to be concentrated in the other.

"Where have you been? I sent for your father; he'll talk to you to-morrow." Andrew did not speak. "Do you hear me, Andrew?"

"Will you let me alone?" the boy muttered. He tried to slip past, but she had planted herself at the foot of the stairs leading to his room and he could only have reached them by pushing her aside. He felt an instinctive repugnance to laying his hands on her.

"You've been up to no good. You're as full of tricks as your mother. She never opened her lips without lying, and she was a filthy slut. My brother was took in by her."

As Andrew retreated this woman came forward. He seized his chance to spring past her and run up the stairs to his room. He would have locked the door, if there had ever been a key in it. All he wanted to do was to avoid thinking; he hurried into bed and lay there, his gaze fixed on the dark star-strewn field he saw when he was lying down and looking sideways at a corner of the window, until he felt himself sinking into a delicious confusion. Now he had only to turn round and bury his head in the sheets and he would be asleep in an instant. But, alas, he could hear, above the sound made in his ears by the waves of sleep advancing towards him with the whispering lapping noise of the real waves he had been listening to during the past hours, a cautious turning of the handle of his door. A ray of light from the lamp in his aunt's hand struck into the room. Andrew pretended to be asleep. It was no use. Pulling the sheet from his face, the old woman brought the lamp so close to it that he felt its warmth, and his eyelids, shocked by the light, lifted of themselves.

He lay blinking and dazzled in the yellow glare, screwing up teeth and gums.   Barely allowing Merry time to finish her sentence, she said:

"Hm.   Ha' y' noticed I've had brand-new pew cushions put i' t' church?   It was in th' Wik paper I sent to London.   You'd get it, I suppose?"

"Yes, I read about it," Merry said energetically.   After all, she said to herself, it's quite natural that she should think more about what goes on here.   Her own triumphs seemed to her in retrospect a little exaggerated and insubstantial.

On the other hand, she had been afraid of her mother behaving so rudely to her husband—whom at the time of her marriage she had called a "thief and a blackguard"—that he would want to leave at once.   She had reckoned without Semiramis's rooted belief that men were a superior order of beings and ought to be waited on and flattered at any cost in female comfort.   In the seventeen years since she had seen him, Stephen Smith had ceased gradually to be a thieving scoundrel and became instead one of these noble creatures.   The transformation was fixed by Stephen's own behaviour.   He quite naturally assumed towards Semiramis a half-helpless, half-insolent manner which fitted in very well with her ideas about men.

It was so long since she had had a man living in the house that she had accumulated vast reserves of an emotion which in a young woman would have been coquetry; it revealed itself in an eager willingness to provide Stephen with the kind of meals, wines, and cigars he enjoyed, in asking him a dozen times if he was comfortable, if he needed anything.   And if what he said he needed was not in the house she would send Skelton, Andrew, or Merry herself scurrying out to the shops to buy it.

Stephen and his mother-in-law became almost fellow-conspirators.   Semiramis declined, from no other desire than that of disappointing her and keeping her in her place, to ask Merry about her life, but she was devoured by an almost sensual curiosity about it.   The kind of information she wanted was not any she could have got from Merry by questioning her.   She did not want to know how many people had listened to a lecture on Female Suffrage, but whether her daughter had expected to have children and why she had none.   And did she still cry when she saw a dead bird; and was it a fact that in Manchester last year she had had both cheeks publicly slapped by the irate wife of a politician, who was convinced that women have no rights, except the right to express themselves in these natural and primitive ways—a view with which Semiramis was in entire sympathy. Not for worlds would Merry have confided in her mother a single one, even the least intimate, of her inner disappointments, fears, hopes. She knew too sharply, from memories of her childhood, what ruthless and mocking use would be made of them.

She warned her husband not to answer any questions, of which the obvious purpose was to place in her mother's hands weapons like those she had sought for and used with such effect during the years when Merry had vexed her by being a stubborn, sensitive little girl. Stephen easily promised to be on his guard.

But he was not safe, he never had been, against a desire to make himself agreeable, to show off in the company he happened to be in at the moment. Merry knew this about him, just as she knew that he loved her as much as he was capable of loving anyone. She depended on this occasion on his loyalty, forgetting on how many occasions she had depended on it in the past and been let down.

One afternoon Semiramis found herself left alone with her son-in-law for several hours. She began by asking him about his painting. He had almost ceased to do any work since Merry began to make three or four times as much money as he could earn by working when he felt like it and borrowing, when he did not, from an indulgent mother. He had great facility in the use of colour, and no other talent whatever, and no taste. For several years he had not painted more than one or at the most two landscapes during the year, but he was always on the point of arranging a show of his work and discussing it with persons whom he imagined could be of use to him in getting it noticed in the press.

"I'm afraid I haven't done much lately," he admitted, with an air of frankness. "You know it's not very easy to combine painting with marriage, when one's wife is in London one week, Leeds the next, and on her way to America the week after."

This wilfully and violently exaggerated account of their life —they lived quietly in London for months at a time—caused Semiramis to lift her eyebrows and draw down still further the corners of her thin lips.

"You ha' to go too, do you?" she said. "If she must, must she, gad about like a fast woman, can't she go alone?"

Stephen looked pained. "But she's my wife," he said ingenuously. "I can't let her travel about by herself."

"Yes, I can tell you—but ought I to? Ought I to give away another woman, even if she is my mother?" She looked at him with her soft, dazzling smile, inviting him to laugh with her. He was too anxious.

"I beg you to tell me."

"Very well. The truth is, and you mustn't believe it simply because I tell you, my mother detested yours because she believed that this girl was enjoying something she had never had and never would have: sensual joy. Extremely respectable people always imagine that any relation between a man and a woman which has not been publicly announced and, as it were, disinfected, must be more and wickedly exciting. They feel they've missed something and they respond by pouring their hate and disappointment on to the lovers. Naturally, they put it all on to morality." She smiled ruefully. "I have never been able to understand what's moral and what isn't. Even what I think is obscene most people don't, and they find obscene what I think funny or natural. Cruelty, possessive greed, stupidity, are not immoral when they're being used to bolster up society. Irregular love always is. Always. It's very mystifying. Most mystifying of all is the idea of 'regular' love—what *can* they mean?"

She laughed breathlessly, like a child.

Andrew had kept his eyes fixed on her while she was speaking. He wanted to be sure that she was not putting him off with lies. Now, although he was not confident of her seriousness, he believed that she was speaking to him as to an equal, and he felt a strange sudden elation and pride.

"If only you lived here," he burst out, "it wouldn't be like it is."

This time his cousin did not say, Like what? She nodded, and sent a penetrating glance over his face. She was sorry for him, yet she felt that he was hard enough not to be deeply scarred by her mother's severity. She did not know that he suffered more from Semiramis Jordan's devouring love and need to have absolute power over him than from any harshness. Beatings are very likely to twist a nature out of its straight course, but they do nothing more. The child Merry had often been thrashed, as they say, within an inch of her life. Since she had survived it with no visible damage, she thought—sad as she felt for him— that Andrew could. But then Semiramis had not loved her.

"My mother's great quality," she said, with sudden energy,

"is that she is wholly herself. I think all the Wikkers have this uniqueness . . . what do I mean?—they are originals. They are themselves. They are not echoes of anyone or any group of people. They don't take their ideas from newspapers or from what are called 'leaders of opinion'—I suppose because they run faster before the wind and shout the loudest. My mother, your father —every Wikker is the same, and you and I belong to them—are self-centred in a good and bad way. They are deeply, perhaps grossly, rooted in their own earth. Their faults are pride and indifference to other people."

"Is indifference to other people a sin?"

To talk and be talked to without the faintly sneering, faintly inquisitive kindness of the men and women he knew (except his father) excited Andrew in the same way he was excited when the wind rushed from the moors with a strength that set his legs capering and the blood to rush through his veins to his head.

"If it is indifference to their sufferings. Yet even in that they're partly right. One shouldn't identify oneself with the sufferings of other people. That is really an outrage. In doing it you outrage yourself. In the end—unless you're crucified first —your own outraged nerves and body turn on you with hatred of everyone and everything. I've seen that happen."

She was silent and Andrew could not think of anything to say to her. He took up a handful of the dry yellow soil, yellow from the limestone in it, and let it trickle through his fingers. The quarry thronged with colour, the rough dark green of bramble-bushes, grey-green of the mountain-ash weighted with its globes of scarlet fruit, the harebells, spurts of pure, transparent blue thrust in among the tufts of bell heather and the wild thyme; on the edge of the quarry, directly above their heads, brilliant spiky yellow gorse sent down wave after wave of a bitter oily scent distilled from it by the heat of the sun.

A dozen questions he wanted to ask her were humming—a swarm of bees—inside his head. He could not fit words to them. In a week or two she'll go off and I shall have no one to ask, he thought, almost in despair.

"Do you resent being asked what you're going to do?" said Merry, eagerly and gently.

"No. But I'm not sure," he stammered. His face had a strange blankness, as if he were determined to feel nothing, nothing

"Ay, I'll be bound you laughed on th' other side of your face when you were slapped.   If I had my way a married woman would stop at home, not go gadding about th' country like a bad lot.   A pity you ha' no bairns, but with the life you lead it's no wonder.   You'd be better praying than crying ovver it, if you ask me."

"But I haven't asked you," Merry said gently.

Her husband had slipped out of the room when she came in. In a few minutes she went upstairs and found him pretending to be hard at work preparing a small canvas.   She watched him with a smile, knowing only too well that if she reproached him he would fly into a rage to defend himself.   Yet she could not let this pass.

"Why did you tell my mother that I had cried because we haven't a child?"

"Surely I'm at liberty to tell her what I like?" he said haughtily.

"You promised you wouldn't discuss our affairs with her."

"I'm not aware that I promised. . . ." he drawled.   "In any case, she's your mother.   If I'm to talk to her at all I can't refuse to answer perfectly natural questions."

The grain of truth in this silenced Merry for a moment.   She was helplessly given to seeing herself in the wrong: perhaps because she had been in the wrong in her mother's eyes since the moment she was born.   It was Stephen's strongest hold on her, apart from the tenderness she felt for him and his easy kindness (when he was not offended), that he was able continually to put her in the wrong.   She was impulsive, heedless, untidy, a freak, and she had never conceived.   None of his faults, his egoism, disloyalty, sulkiness, was blacker than her inner conviction of sin.

She sat silent and discouraged in the window until Stephen laid down the canvas and said:

"Your mother is a character."

He meant that he was willing to overlook his wife's last words if she said nothing more.   Merry had no vanity: she did not care how a quarrel ended, and if to end it quickly it was necessary to sacrifice justice to peace she made the sacrifice at once, and all the more cheerfully because she had learned in her childhood that justice is only another name for power.   Justice generally leaves one of two men or women dead; where mercy, without justice, would have kept both alive. Her spirits flew up at once. She laughed at herself.

"You married into a family of *characters*, my poor Stephen. But every family in Wik is as bad. You don't know yet what the Wik character is—or you would come among them as a strong man armed. Their self-centredness can be crude, gross, bestial, coldly cruel. Yet they have so much courage and force of life that one only wishes they could be civilized."

"You might," said Stephen, "wish the same about the rest of the world."

CHAPTER XVI

HANDEL did not make his decision until five months after his visit to the Bishop. His friends, even Mower, thought he was reluctant to give up all hope of returning to a way of life which had suited perfectly his feeling for authority, decency, order. But this feeling, powerful in him as it was, did not count for so much as another—the fear that it was not humility, not conscience, which made him hesitate to return, but pride. Yes, pride.

At last, one afternoon in September, he walked as far as Upsal Wood and stood there to pray. So high up and alone, with the wind hissing in the oaks as water hisses past the bows of a ship, he might have been on the bridge, an officer consulting his "old man" with independence and respect. His lips did not move. He prayed inwardly in silence. "You know my heart," he said; "tell me what right I have to stand alone: as I want to stand. Who orders me to return? Do you? To what must I return?" He felt an inescapable repugnance towards taking up again a way of life which would check his freedom of mind. He wanted to be free to examine the nature of every thought that came to him, to take nothing for granted, not even the scriptures—still less the words of a church whose conscience shows so much energy and subtlety in finding reasons which permit, no, command, it to be on the side of the wealthy and powerful.

"With what hope? Do You tell me to leave Wik, to leave the men and women who already depend on me?" He saw the steps at the end of the stinking dark alley, their stones worn to the shape of a cup by five centuries of use, the passage, the room, the bed; the man lying there was alone all day until Handel Wikker came in, changed the bandage on his groin, emptied the slops, and remained for half an hour near the smell of that wound. "With what fruit? To be known? To forget the reproach that sixteen years ago I resigned, because of a scandal? I would rather forget nothing, I would rather remember, of these years, every minute as if I were living it again with full knowledge. You do not order

130

me to go away from my place. If I could find You it would be here, near this stone, or walking on *this* sea. *For whither should my heart flee from my heart?"*

When he had thanked God for allowing him to do what, without knowing it, he had already decided to do, he noticed for the first time that the ground near him was covered with acorns. He stooped and took up one of the double sprigs. There is something, to men as to children, so entrancing in the neatness and simplicity of an acorn in its cup: it seems that some use ought to be made of it. Every autumn when he was a child, Handel had gathered a score of acorn-cups and kept them in the vague hope that he could make something from them as charming as they were to look at and touch. Now, turning the sprig in his fingers, he felt a thrill of that mystery and delight. As if nowhere else in England were there oaks and green acorns he exclaimed:

"How could I leave?"

Before writing to the Bishop he went to see Vawn. The vicar disapproved sharply of his decision. He said so. In his disappointment with his friend he became cold and impatient.

"You seem to me to be behaving recklessly and without taste," he exclaimed. "What would become of authority if everyone behaved as you do?"

"What *is* authority?" Handel said.

He smiled, but his voice was faintly arrogant and contemptuous. He was probably not aware that he was arrogant. He had been accustomed for so long to having his own way that he did not take contradiction well.

"You know what it is. . . . And you know, or you used to know, that societies can't be kept stable by religion alone. What's absolutely needed is a strong hierarchy. . . . When a man like you refuses to keep his place in this hierarchy you bring in an element of disorder. You rebel, do you? You think you have the right to your freedom—but it's utterly anti-social!" He looked with his cold smile at Handel. "You're not going to take offence?"

"No; not I," Handel said brusquely. "I agree with you— up to a point. There must be an order. But I'm not satisfied that you, my dear fellow, and the Archbishop and the Bishops, are working hard enough for your living. Your consciences are too sensitive on points of order and too easy about war and poverty."

"You're talking now like a radical."

"I can even bear that," Handel retorted. "You can't sail away from the facts by calling them names. It's deplorably a fact that the contrast between Under Wik and this room—it can't be worth less than eight hundred pounds on board—is becoming offensive to me. I say that if there really are not enough rugs, couches, and bookcases to go round, one of Christ's vicars ought to be doing without so many of them. No doubt this is very crude and, as you would say, disorderly, but there it is. I can't any longer bolster up an order I don't like the look of. My heart rebels and my head tells me that a Church which has identified itself with wealth will come to stink in the nostrils of sensitive men."

"Too much violent nonsense," said Vawn, "is talked about our society. Men like Sir Thomas Money don't become rich by robbing the country—what nonsense—but by serving its needs."

"Latimer would not have said so," retorted Handel. "In his day the Church spoke her mind. And it was not the mind of bankers and shipowners."

"The Church has not changed. It is you, my friend, who have changed."

Handel's eyes started coldly. "I?"

"You enjoy rebellion. If I had been your spiritual director I should never have allowed you to become a priest."

Handel stood up.

"Why argue? You and I, Charles, want the same thing: a Christian country. We must go on differing on the means." He looked down at his shabby clothes without seeing them, or the stains and dirt which offended Vawn. He was quite unconscious of having spoken with a deadly and smiling indifference, as though Vawn were a child.

The other man swallowed his anger. He even felt a condescending pity for his friend's wrong-headedness and dirty shabby clothes.

"You wouldn't allow an ignorant fisherman to argue with you in church," he said, with a slight smile.

"No, certainly not," Handel said. "Why should I?"

"So you believe in a hierarchy? After all?"

"I believe we are all workmen," said Handel mildly. "Every man to his trade. I don't want to live in greater comfort than the others. That's all, that's all."

He took himself off. The same evening he was walking to his brother's house: passing the kitchen garden he saw his brother's son by Martha Soal leaning against the wall, practising his flute. Of the kind you meet beggars playing in the street, it was Richard's dearest possession. To speak strictly, his only one, unless you cast into the account the clothes his mother begged for him from her relatives or cobbled together out of his father's cast-offs.

Not seeing Handel, he began to play a little melancholy air, as simple as death itself: it had the sound of the light wind which steals out between dark and dawn; it was thus a sound nearly as old as the earth. It had recurred—like the phrase which turns up again and again in a piece of music as though it were the key to a secret which the music itself is just failing to unlock for us—so many times since the creation of the world that it had no longer any close connection with time. It was rather the immortality of time to which it lent speech for an instant; it was pure time, pure existence, everlastingness in a single phrase of five notes. This sound, the same when it was given out in Nineveh, in Thebes, squeezed in itself the whole of Handel's life. In it he was the child in the womb who had ravished Kezia, lost her, sought God in his own heart, suffered, died. He regretted with sharp grief the death of the body, of its ears which hear, its eyes which see, and its hands which touch, hold, reflect. If, he thought, the soul could make a better habitation for itself, doubtless it would, and I suppose it regrets leaving it.

The young man caught sight of him. He looked up with a sulky face, blinking his short-lashed eyelids, and stopped playing. He furiously disliked being overlooked in one of his moments of free, unselfconscious absorption and happiness. It destroyed the happiness for him; it reminded him that he was to all intents a serf, that he worked without getting any thanks for it on land which ought to be partly his. He resented anyone who, like this man, stood to him in an unadmitted relation—unadmitted, he thought, because his mother was a servant. For his father he felt fear as well as dislike.

Against his will he felt himself bending his back before the fixed, remote stare of Handel Wikker's grey eyes. He felt embarrassed and impotently sore and angry.

"Why have you stopped? . . . who told you you're not fit to be heard? You play well enough."

Soal turned his face aside. "Because I chose to stop," he said rudely.

Handel Wikker looked at him, understood what was passing in his mind, pitied him, and left him without more words. The young man did not want comfort, or wisdom, or politeness; he wanted what he would have called his "rights"; and Handel had not been moved to tell his brother that he ought to provide for his son.

CHAPTER XVII

ONE evening in winter Ezekiel drank so much brandy at *The Swan* that the landlord was afraid to let him go home. The pupils of his eyes had almost disappeared, and when with a great effort he managed to focus them on some object he advanced towards it with a sideways motion and spun round at the last instant to catch it. The other drinkers were in fits of laughter. Taking counsel with his wife, the landlord sent a boy for Handel.

Ezekiel frowned when he saw his brother coming into the room. "Go away——" he said, "you're unlucky."

He refused energetically to stay the night with him, and when Handel said curtly that in that case he had better put up at *The Swan*, he leaned forward, drew the landlord's head towards his mouth as though he were going to whisper in his ear and suddenly, letting out a piercing yell, fetched the unfortunate man a blow on the crown that knocked him out. Handel turned and went out.

The idea of kicking him sprang into Ezekiel's head. He staggered towards the door, but it was too late: his brother had gone. I'll go myself, he thought. He went down into the yard, told the boy to get his horse, mounted, by a miracle of balance, and muttered: "Go home, go home," in the belief that he was talking to someone else; this someone else was very dumb.

The mare was a strong mischievous brute, not very clever; she knew her master well enough now, and set off at an easy walk. The moment she put her foot on the cobblestones beyond the yard she felt that she was walking on glass. There was a black frost, invisible and smelling of fear. The streets were empty. Shuddering, she picked her way along the middle of the street, taking the easiest way out of the town. Ezekiel sat quietly, the reins in his hands, his head sunk.

He did not come to himself for an hour, by which time they were in the lane leading from the marsh. Suddenly at this moment he lifted his head and looked round him. The shock was too great. The earth rose and struck him between the eyes in a welter of fields, clouds, walls; trees rushed across a sea of light and fell on

135

him, he saw falling rocks, and when he turned his head he saw the marsh behind him covered with a stretched, glittering skin, pulled all ways by invisible muscles into fan-shaped creases and whorls, channels or watery serpents, moving, slipping, frightful.

At first stunned, he put his arms over his face and began to whimper, but in a minute or two curiosity drove him to take another look. This time, because he was prepared for the torrent of light and darkness, he was able to hold it off. It became still, as if frozen. He ventured to look up. The space between earth and sky was filled with lines of light, crossing and intercrossed, an infinite number, a web incessantly spun and quivering. Enormous stars were formed by it, and so were a multitude of objects nearer his eyes, trees, blades of grass, and the plumes of breath from his mare's nostrils. He felt an astonishing exhilaration. "Well, by God! I never saw it look like this before," he cried.

He was in bliss. A wide ploughed field he was passing stood up before him; its furrows ran upright, leaning against the sky like a vast board on which an artist had drawn lines tapering towards a point. He checked his horse in order to look at it, his mouth open, amazed and delighted to see that between every furrow the earth rose in pointed waves, alive and running with light. Now he needed to dismount and stand over the ditch. He felt an extraordinary pleasure when he perceived that he was himself a source of light, and walking excitedly back to the mare he gave her, for pure friendliness, a smash over the hindquarters that sent her flying up the road. Her legs sprawled as all four feet slid on the icy flints. She was wild with indignation; by the time she had recovered herself, miraculously still on her feet, she was a mile nearer home. She trotted on cautiously, keeping to the grass at the side, and left Ezekiel to come home as he pleased.

He stood gaping after her for a minute. He did not feel the cold, bitter though it was: the brandy in him kept it out. He was still excited by the strange aspect of a road he knew perfectly well. Seeing a leaf lying on the ground in front of him he picked it up, lowering himself with infinite care until it lay in his hand. Its long skeleton entranced him.

"Look at you," he exclaimed. "You're a warrior, you are. What muscles!"

Now he could not get up again. He began to crawl along the road on his hands and knees, stopping frequently to gaze round him at the play of light on all sides.

"Brother Handel, you're a fool. There are more ways home than one."

His body felt immensely swollen but not heavy. As he crawled he reached a gate into the ploughed field, and stopped to look up at the furrows from this angle. He was struck now by the depth of darkness between each wave of earth. Impenetrable, it seemed to him rich and mysterious. He felt that he must lie down in one of the furrows. He imagined himself sinking into it as in a feather bed, but warm, dark, all enveloping. A sudden feeling of sadness overtook him. He shook his head sorrowfully from side to side.

"You, you Bessie, you treated me badly. Yes, badly."

Since Bessie was the name of his daughter, his dead wife, and of the mare, it invoked an image in his mind strangely compounded of all three. He thought he had the plough with him, drawn by the mare with his wife's face and, mistily and surprisingly, female hindquarters. Grasping the cross-bar of the gate he dragged himself up, opened it, and stumbled into the field, where he fell flat at once.

"Whu-up, old girl, whu-up," he muttered, only slightly put out to see, floating in the air before him, as though distraught, his wife's round startled face below the ears and forelock of the mare.

On his hands and knees, he crawled along a furrow, dreaming that he had brought his wife out here for a night a long time, years, ago. Nothing of the sort had ever happened, but he saw himself embracing her in the darkness, and a flame quivered in his belly. "Brother Handel," he murmured, chuckling, "you think I'm a fool—but I've seen sights to-night you'd give your soul to squint at. . . . Therefore, my beloved brother, the first man is of the earth earthy, as it says."

The icy cold rising from the hard earth stung him as though he were burning. He imagined that he was enveloped in flames and rolled on the ground to put them out. Rising with difficulty to his knees again, he felt the earth heave under him.

"It's come to me," he said, with terror. He closed his eyes.

Nothing happened. He opened them again, and saw an apparition, a naked shining child, standing in the field a few yards in front of him. Surrounded by light, the child moved his arms, turned and seemed to smile. "God save me," Ezekiel said joyously, relieved beyond words: he had looked to get a son on his wife, and here he was. Joy gave him strength to stand on his feet again.

J

He stumbled forward and began to prance round the child, singing: "Ring-a-ring-a-roses, pocket full of posies. Tish-a, tish-a, we all fall down."

He fell flat. When he lifted his head the bright boy had vanished. There was nothing within the circle of his glance except icy furrows running against the sky, and a round moon sending out claps of thunder across the frozen crystal of space. Disappointed, he wept. Then he began laughing.

"I can do that," he said.

He felt sleepy. He drew his knees up to his stomach and let himself fall asleep, vaguely conscious of burning sensations in his wrists and in the cheek pressing the ground. His breath came in a cloud from his parted lips.

He would have died of the cold if his son had not found him in time. Lying awake, Martha Soal heard the mare coming down the road. She listened. She heard the mare whinny outside the yard, and slipping a skirt and jacket over her nightgown she went down, unbolted the side door and looked out. There was no one in the yard, no sign of Ezekiel, and in the frost-bound silence she heard the mare scuffling her feet at the other side of the wall.

She ran out, catching her breath in the black bitter cold. There was not a breath of wind. The air seemed frozen, and the stars supernaturally bright. Holding her jacket round her with one hand, she opened the yard door and saw the mare standing there, her ears pricked against the moonlight, shivering with cold and weariness.

Leaving the doors open, Martha ran back towards the house, calling her son as she ran.

"He's thro-wn," she called. "He's thro-wn. L-y-ing some-wheres."

Her piercing voice startled the mare. Throwing her head up, she began to whimper again with terror. In the stillness, the air was crossed and recrossed by the long-drawn invisible arcs of the two sounds, as by flying jets of steel, the voice of the woman ringing in mid-air against the terrified whinny of the animal. Richard Soal ducked his head as he came out, feeling a kind of horror of his mother's voice.

"What is it? what's up?" he cried; he shuddered, feeling the cold on his half-sleeping flesh. "What's the good of screeching like that? You'll wake Bessie."

He shut the mare in her stable and went off down the road,

expecting to find Ezekiel lying in a ditch. The moon was now directly overhead, filling the whole of space with its white searing light. He could see both sides of the road as clear as daylight, and when he came to the gate swinging open and looked across the field he saw a dark body which might have been a sack left there. He knew there was no sack in that field.

As he stumbled towards it across the furrows he saw the light on Ezekiel's bare hand, flung out away from his body. It seemed endowed with a being of its own. It lay there like an animal, isolated from the body that had given it birth. Ezekiel was snoring. "Come, get up," his son said. He bent down and rested his hand on his father's cheek. It was icy cold. "You'll freeze," he said softly. "Make sharp now . . . get up."

Ezekiel slept on. Bracing his legs apart, Soal heaved and strained; he succeeded in dragging the man's body into a sitting posture, but it fell back, like a stone striking the ground. The earth was as hard as iron.

The shock partly roused Ezekiel. He opened his eyes. Although he had no idea where he was, he struggled to stand up: his son helped him. He collapsed again immediately, groaning and laughing—there was no life in his body, his legs were frozen from the knees. Soal dragged at him again and somehow managed to draw his father's arms round his neck, and staggering under his weight, gasping, bent double, he got as far as the road with him. Here he was forced to rest, and Ezekiel at once began to slide down on to the ground; only by an agonizing effort was the young man able to pull him up so that he lay like a sack of logs on his son's back, feet dragging on the ground. His head lolled from side to side. His arms dangled in front, across the young man's chest; gripping them, and straining all the muscles of his body, Soal stumbled along the road.

It took him more than an hour to reach the house. Once there, he let Ezekiel drop heavily on to the floor of the kitchen and himself lay helpless, feeling as though he had been beaten. His mother was not concerned with him. She fussed about, wrapping Ezekiel in warmed blankets and slapping his face and legs with a rag soaked in paraffin.

After a time Richard Soal sat up and watched her. She had struggled to lift Ezekiel on to the settle, but strong as she was it was quite beyond her strength. He lay on the rug near the fire, where she had at last dragged him, swathed from head to foot in his blankets.

"Is he frozen still?" his son asked in a sarcastic voice.

"Not him. He's sleeping like a babby."

"Why the devil didn't I leave him to freeze to death," growled the young man. He yawned, feeling weak and half-dazed. "He's brokken me. . . . What was he up to in th' field? If he hadn't been muzzy he'd be dead. 's' too old."

His mother did not reply. She was pouring water into the kettle, looking over her shoulder as she did it at her master's body lying against her feet.

"How old is he?"

"He's fifty-six," Martha Soal answered. In her voice was all the exasperation, and the deep unwilling tenderness a woman feels for her son who is behaving badly and foolishly. She had no anxiety to spare for her actual son; he dragged himself across the room, his hands on his back. Her whole attention was given to the vast cocoon of blankets, from which at shortened intervals a snore like a trumpet blast issued and rattled the irons in the fender.

III

CHAPTER XVIII

FIVE years later, on a cold February morning, Ann Wellhem awoke to hear Horn trying the handle of the door. She had overslept herself. Putting her legs slowly out of bed—they were thin and fleshless like bones—she walked stiffly to the door, unlocked it, and returned to the bed. Before Horn, carrying cups of tea in her hands, reached the side of the bed, Ann had whipped a linen doily from beneath her pillows and dropped it over William's face, where it lay passively between her and the wall. In all the years that Horn had been bringing tea to Mr. and Mrs. William Wellhem in bed she had never seen her master's face exposed nakedly on his pillow. The doily always covered it. She did not hand him his tea. The second cup was set down on the night table, and as soon as they were alone again, Mrs. Wellhem lifted the doily and handed William his tea with the words:

"You may sit up."

A grey light filled the room, coming between the curtains. The bed, an enormous structure made of mahogany, with yellow rep curtains on three sides, was covered with a quilt lined with dark-brown fustian. At night it was turned lining upwards, so that the limbs of the sleepers seemed to be disturbing a covering of earth, and when they sat up side by side, wearing flannel nightgowns identical except for the frill which adorned Ann's, they might have been posing for their own gravestones.

Ann's red wig lay on the night-table. Her own wisps of colourless hair, as scanty as William's, were kept in decent order by a bonnet made of white calico. Although she was sixty-three, the ghost of a coquetry no one had ever seen in her, least of all William, showed itself for a few minutes while she turned her head from side to side in this bonnet, sipping her tea, and staring about the room with her pale eyes still filmed with her dreams. It vanished as soon as she was out of bed.

"Now," she said, sternly, to her husband.

Obediently, he got out of bed, and tottered across the room to the chair on which night after night, since his wedding night, he had folded his clothes in the same order, sacred to married life. As his wife did, he dressed, at least to his trousers, without taking off his nightgown. At times, as when he was buttoning his shirt, his head as well as his thin arms were sucked under the boiling folds, and a convulsive struggle took place before his long bony forehead and scared eyes reappeared.

On the other side of the room his wife was going about the business more nimbly. Clothed, except for her bodice, she threw the nightgown aside and dipped her fingers gingerly into one of the jugs of water on the double washstand. William waited humbly until she stepped back, then he wrung a flannel out in water and passed it weakly over his face.

"Don't splash," his wife said from force of habit.

It was a large, high room, crowded with massive pieces of furniture, which stood about like marine monsters half submerged in an atmosphere thickened by rigour and decency. When William was left alone in it, by his wife's withdrawal, he moved more freely; looking at his face in the glass he became almost animated, but it was a sad animation, and he made only feeble gestures, glancing round as though at any moment he might be detected in a life of his own.

When he left the room it became completely inanimate, without even the hints, which most rooms offer, of having once been lived in, until Horn entered it to make the bed, and remove from beneath the valance two objects which no one would have been surprised to find there. An ordinary and terrifying proof that life nevertheless went on in this room.

Later in the morning Ann, who was busy turning out a room on the first floor, became certain in her mind that William was up to mischief. She had left him downstairs alone, seated harmlessly in the breakfast-room. Everything eatable and of the smallest value was locked up and she had the keys in her pocket, but the idea that he had found a morsel of something tormented her.

She could not bear it for very long. She made up her mind to creep down and surprise him.

"I want you to stand on the landing," she said to Lily, "and you must sing loudly, as loudly as you can, so that your father doesn't hear me on the stairs."

"What shall I sing?" Lily said with a gloomy abruptness.

"Oh—sing anything you like," her mother said impatiently.

Not for the first time she wondered whether, at thirty, her

daughter was really such a comfort to her as when she was a little girl, eager, with the native malice of a child, to join in conspiracies against anyone.

Lily Wellhem moved obediently across the landing. She stood directly in the light coming from a large dusty window, of which the upper half was covered with a waxed paper in imitation of stained glass. It gave a greenish tinge to the pallor of her skin, and with her hands clasped at the waist, half-way on a body as flat as two boards clapped together, she might have been any watery and virgin saint in the copy by a bad modern artist of a Primitive. She looked obliviously into space, ignoring completely the gestures with which her mother, infuriated by her lack of spirit, tried silently to excite her.

Finally she made up her mind and began to sing. *O fair dove! O fond dove! Dove with the white, white breast,* she bawled. The words, or her rendering of them, brought a gleam of melancholy and spiteful fun to her face.

Half-way down the staircase, Ann Wellhem stretched her lean body over the banisters in a dangerous attempt to see into the breakfast-room from here. The door was open to a space of five inches, but William, alas, was not visible in this gap.

She crept down and tip-toed across the hall. At the door of the room she looked back and encouraged Lily by frenzied signs. *Leave me alone, my grief is my own,* floated over the railings in a voice dry, flat, surprisingly sonorous. She could see half the room and by pressing her face against the crack between the hinges she saw the other half, but no William. *And my heart. . . .* Her curiosity and her suspicions were so inflamed by all this—was it possible that he had crawled under the couch?—that she poked her head boldly round the door: and came face to face with William flattened against its other side.

Husband and wife gazed at each other in silence.

After a minute of this silent communion Ann withdrew, still without speaking a word, and hurried upstairs. Telling Lily, she gave way to a choking fit of laughter, clutching her daughter's arm and driving her nails into it in an access of joy.

"Behind the door," she repeated, stupefied. "After all, he must have heard me coming . . . you and your *fond dove* . . . behind the door. You should have seen his face! . . ."

She was annoyed on the afternoon of that day by a pastoral visit from the new Congregational minister. This poor young

man was only twenty-three, and Wik was his first parish. He
could scarcely have had a more savage introduction to his preaching life. He was shy, but—he was the son of a London cobbler—
alert and shrewd: he had been underfed all his life and suffered
terribly from the cold when he came north.

When he was ushered into the breakfast-room by Horn, the
first thing he saw was his hostess, frantically picking several un-
burned pieces of coal off the fire. Scarcely more than a layer of
cinders was left to warm the room. At the same time she was
scolding her husband with fury—not only had he put the coal on
the fire without being told to, but he had placed the poker upright
against the bars of the grate. In Wik this was believed to
encourage a fire to burn brightly.

"Do you think it makes any difference?" young Mr. Sele said,
trying to smile. He was shivering violently with cold.

"We shan't run any risks," said Ann sourly. She made the
young man sit down at some distance from the miserable remains
of the fire. "If you're cold, why do you come out? No one, you
may be sure, wants you in their houses. You'd better stop at
home in future. And what's more, I shan't mind telling you
that when Mr. Howard left I gave him a piece of my mind. I
told him, and I told the deacons, that I hoped and prayed it would
be a long time before we got another regular minister. Th' church
is happier and more spiritual and Christian without a minister
living in th' town, pushing himself into people's houses. However, there's one thing—we paid Mr. Howard too much. We
shan't make that mistake with you, so don't expect it. . . ."

She ignored his incoherent reply. An almost dreamy look came
over her face, as though she were scarcely conscious of the venom
with which she was speaking to him.

"It's a wicked town you've come to, Mr. what's your name,
Sele, is it?—a queer name—a wicked, filthy town. Ha' they told
you yet about th' couple Mr. Howard married and th' bride was
on'y leaving the altar when she let out a yell fit to kill you, plumped
down, and th' child was born there and then before his eyes?
He could ha' had t'christening as well. . . . Another loving pair
had their child handed in to them at t'carriage window as they
drove away from th' church. . . . And you'll find them deacons
are fairly brutal. *They'll* lay it on you. I daresay your heart'll
ache before you've been here a month. . . ."

Taken aback, Sele glanced at the faces of William Wellhem

and Lily. Neither seemed in the least embarrassed. Lost in thought, the younger woman sat with a strained, shy, cold smile on her lips. When his wife ceased talking William Wellhem looked up timidly, all the time rubbing his long, feeble, bony fingers on his knees.

"Did you say you were from London?" he said in a low voice, evidently afraid that the young man would laugh at him.

Sele nodded. "I was born there."

"Then you've seen Buckingham Palace!" In his eagerness the poor man forgot that he was in disgrace already. "When I was quite a young man I saw it once. What majesty! They say that actually every room is furnished. I used to stand there and——"

"William! Go to the kitchen," his wife said. "Visitors don't come to this house to see you. Sitting there gaping like a great animal."

To the minister's astonishment, William stood up and shuffled out of the room, looking so wretched and downcast that the young man longed to be able to hurry after him and console him. He felt himself grow red all over with shame. The look of triumphant hatred on the old lady's face, as she sat and watched her husband crossing the room on his bent legs, shocked him to the heart. Just then the door opened again and Horn came in bearing the tray of tea things. Mrs. Wellhem turned pale and said in a voice quivering with annoyance:

"What do you mean, you blockhead, by bringing in tea at this hour?"

"What hour?" Horn said stupidly, dumbfounded. "It's four o'clock, isn't it? You always have tea at four." She set the tray down on the table with a stubborn jerk. "But I haven't brought *him* a cup," she said, pointing with her elbow at the minister. "Is he to have one?"

"Yes, I suppose he must. Go and fetch him one."

There were only two pieces of bread and butter and two small cakes, and the young man did not venture to take either. He thought that a refusal might soften his hostess. Any softening that took place was imperceptible. While he was sipping his tea and trying to edge his chair a little nearer the fire, she flung at him:

"I don't mind saying I've heard nothing good of you. You were seen behaving most ridiculously in the street, and laughing,

by almost all the deacons on Saturday morning. It's a poor do
for us Congregationalists if we're to be judged by you. . . . Mind
what you're doing," she said suddenly. "Back, back, the fire's
not for you."

"Will you have another cup?" Lily said to him, speaking as
though she were ashamed of her mother's rudeness.

"No, he won't have another cup," Mrs. Wellhem said. "He's
eaten nothing and he shan't have another cup. . . . He can
pray if he likes, though."

"Do you wish me to pray?" asked Sele.

He was mortified. Against his will, yet deliberately, he snatched
at the chance of reminding her that he was someone rather more
important than an ordinary young man, than the clever son of
a poor Radical cobbler. Suddenly the image of the dark narrow
room, with its smell of grease and leather, in which, sharing the
one hissing gas-jet with his father, he pored over text-books, rose
into his mind and filled him with the most poignant unhappiness.

"I will pray if you wish it," he repeated coldly.

He did not realize that Ann Wellhem was impervious to im-
pressions which came to her from outside.

He knelt awkwardly at his chair. Mrs. Wellhem said at once
that she was too old and poorly to think of kneeling, and Lily,
"my precious Lily," had hurt her knee and must on no account
bend it. Horn was brought in and knelt.

After he had buried his face in his cold hands for a moment,
Sele prayed, half aware now that the "Our Father" to whom he
was speaking had become a sallow workman with thick spectacles
and hands colourless, dirty, broken-nailed. "Teach us Thy
charity and patience, and take us in Thy hands to-day and every
day, and save us. Amen."

Comforted and ashamed, he thought he might leave now.
When he took her hand Mrs. Wellhem pulled him down and said
in his ear:

"I'm not sorry you prayed. She's a wicked woman, that
woman—that Horn. The lies she tells! However, it's true I
often offer up a little prayer for her myself."

He had scarcely left the room, to be shown out by Horn at the
side door, when Semiramis Jordan came in; she was quivering
with excitement. She had driven from Wik in order to be the first
with a story that, as it happened, she had a better right to tell
than anyone.

"Ha' y' heard t'news?" she cried.

"You're too late for any tea," Ann said at once. Hearing her arrive, she herself had whisked into the kitchen with the tray. Her meanness, assuaged by the thought that no warmth had been wasted on Mr. Sele, was now alarmed to think that Semiramis would ask for fresh tea to be made if she saw the pot.

"I've had tea. I said ha' you heard t'news?"

"What news? I daresay I know all about it."

"Why, it seems yon Vansittart—you know who I mean, th' singing master—wasn't properly married to the woman he's been living with all these years. Th' real wife turned up this afternoon on t' second train—she's a fine big woman, as bold as brass, and I can tell you she set them girls to rights——"

"How do you know it's true?" Ann said languidly.

She rejoiced in other people's misfortunes, but it annoyed her intensely to hear a scandal of this nature which she had not nosed out for herself. She could almost bring herself to hope it was not true.

"It's as true as I ha' my dress on."

"My dress," was a short term for the complete tale of garments Semiramis used to speak of as "my memorial clothes," a regal black silk skirt, bodice, jacket, and black velvet toque, each lavishly braided and festooned with jet. She had taken to paying visits of condolence with the assiduity of a vulture, for no worse reason than that she had these garments. They were made for her a little over two years since, when the old Queen died. Semiramis felt then that she had lost in Queen Victoria an elder sister and spared no cost in her mourning. Nor had any bereaved family since then been spared Semiramis. Misfortune on misfortune.

"Well, it seems that. . . ." Calling at the Vansittarts' house this afternoon, at three, Semiramis arrived on the doorstep at the same time as "the real wife": Lucy Vansittart admitted them together; and so, until she was turned out, she had the exquisite happiness of collecting at first hand the savoury dish she had already carried through Over Wik before hiring a carriage to bring it with her to her sister's.

"It seems that when Mrs. Vansittart—I mean th' one we've been calling Mrs. Vansittart for these thirty years, filthy creature —died last week, and they had t'funeral, a notice was put in t' paper. Someone posted it to a friend in London, not knowing, and this friend showed it b'chance to a woman of the name of

Vansittart, and t'woman laughed out and said, 'Yes, it's my husband.' It seems she'd been passing everywhere as a widow, but t'truth is she ran off and left Vansittart t'same year they were married—I shan't blame her for't, poor soft thing as he is —and he took up with this other woman, this Emily something, and brought her here as his wife. . . . You should ha' seen th' look on t'faces of them gels. Three on 'em, Lizzie and th' two youngest, came for t'funeral. Two on 'em's married, so I suppose they ha' names now of their own. Th' others 'll have been calling themselves Vansittart—they've no right to. . . . I didn't happen to hear what their right name was. . . . That young Lucy, if you please, asks Mrs. V. to leave the house, but, 'Oh no,' she says, 'oh dear, no, here I am and here I stay—for as long as I please. If anyone's to be turned out,' she says simpering, 'it's you gels. I'm your father's wife,' she says, 'and you know, don't you, what you gels are.' That brazen Lizzie turns to me and says, ay, she says, 'You'll have t'kindness to go, Mrs. Jordan.' I was just turning over them Nanking plates they've allus had on t'sideboard, they're genuine, it seems, and she pushed me to t'door and slammed it—not before I had a good look round, and saw Julia crying on t' stairs and Lizzie fiddling at her mouth with her hands . . . like this, look . . . I allus knew they'd come to it. . . .''

Ann's cruel, greenish eyes sparkled with mild joy. It was long since she had seen so satisfactory an instance of the truth of that grim Wik saying—"they'll come to it," or "it'll come to them." In both versions "it" was the justice kept in store for all who by pride, beauty, excess of one sort or another, transgressed the everlasting Wik law, "Be ye careful."

"Them gels 'll have to go," she said, smiling. "They'll not be able to hold their heads up in Wik. It shows you."

She glanced at her daughter, who had been listening with the slight smile which lay over her face like winter sunlight on paper: revealing no depths, it was less a smile than an uneasiness of the light on her pale flesh.

"My sweet Lily doesn't understand what we've been talking about, do you, my love?"

"I understand very well," Lily said, in a dry voice.

But she got up and went out of the room. Relieved of her presence, the presence of a virgin of thirty, the two old women gave themselves up to ransacking the dish for its choicest morsels.

They savoured them in common, and they kept for any that were a trifle "high" a particular gesture, smiling, nodding, and tittering in the same instant, with as much eagerness as if they had been starved for months. They had no pity on the four girls, each of whom in turn they stripped, not simply of her name but of her clothes and made her cower naked in front of two pairs of merciless eyes. But they seemed actually to hate poor inoffensive Emily Vansittart, as though she had injured them by appearing to be happy and by dying before she was found out. Their wishes flew after her gentle ghost, pursuing it in whatever place it had found shelter. They recalled her absurdity, her hats, her pretence of "feeding the poor" whenever she was seen coming home on Saturday evening with a basketful of the bruised half-rotten vegetables she had gathered up in the market before it closed for another week. But at one moment Semiramis said, with a twinge of feeling:

"As for yon Vansittart, I'm sure I was sorry for him. He was sitting by himself and when one of th' gels spoke to him about a purse he said, 'Ask your mother, she always has it.' He must ha' forgotten she was gone. He looked lost in himself all that time."

"It's true he never had much gumption," Ann said.

She was incapable of even so little pity for a person who did not belong to her own family, and who was known, too, to be entirely without shame or common sense. Invited to play at a party, he would turn up wearing his "better" suit and look as though he wanted to be invited to sit down to supper with the guests. To him, too, as to his four proud girls, *it* had come at last—and serve him right.

CHAPTER XIX

In early April, when Andrew Wikker came home from Cambridge, he had almost agreed that he hoped to stay there for the rest of his life. He knew that he was working well, he knew that a career in his own college would offer itself to him and at the moment he thought he might just as well take it. It offered him as well as a living, meagre but enough, the leisure he wanted in order to write. And more than all, he would grow into a life as unlike life in Wik as any he could think of.

He was twenty years old this year. And although Semiramis no longer came into his room when he was asleep or waking, he knew that she searched it thoroughly as soon as he went out. He was allowed to lock his door, but she had another key which fitted it, and one day when he had locked a few papers into a drawer, its lock was broken, mysteriously, no one knew how, and the papers turned upside down and torn. She questioned him during meals, and at whatever other moments he could not escape her.

"What ha' you done this morning? Who ha' you seen in t' town? Where did you say you were going to this afternoon? What's yon book you've got there? Who did you say had written to you?"

He was perpetually afraid she would find out what so far he had managed to keep from her—a new friendship.

There were people in Wik who saw nothing in Isabel Mower. She had straight hair, of no particular colour; she was very thin. Andrew thought that she was enchanting. She was not tall, her features extraordinarily delicate, her lips bright, her eyes bright and very clear; she had a firm rounded forehead and a short chin. He remembered all this when he was in Cambridge; the twinkling grace and neatness, and the expressiveness of a face which even in repose kept its smiling air of irony and candour. She was quite fearless. She did not tell lies, not even the fibs which came naturally from other girls when they had to excuse themselves to their parents for breaking the rigid code Wik had drawn up for the conduct of "decent respectable people."

After she began to be grown up—this year she was eighteen—
he rarely saw her. But one evening this spring he called and found
her in, alone. Had he stopped to think, he would not have invited
her to come and look at the sea. He did ask her—and she skipped
off at once to put on her outdoor things.

They walked along the cliff edge as far as one of the paths
running down to the marsh. They were lucky. No one who
knew them was out walking that evening. They sat down on the
grass with their backs to the last houses of Over Wik and looked
at the unwrinkled sea. Tib's hands folded in her lap were rough
and small, working hands.

"I didn't want to be in love with you, Tib," Andrew had
said.

The girl did not answer until she was comfortably seated.
Then, looking at him with a smile, she said:

"Yes? But are you?"

"You knew I was."

"No; I didn't. I love you. But don't be angry about it.
We needn't do anything and you can still do as you like, without
thinking about me."

Andrew looked at her sharply. "Oh, can I?" he said. "I'll
be shot if I can. I think about you when I ought to be reading,
so what are we going to do?"

Tib laughed a little. "My dear child, we needn't do anything. You will go on working at—at whatever you work
at—and I shall stay here and wait until you have time for
me."

"Come, let's go home," Andrew said.

They walked to her house in silence, and Andrew went home
without waiting to see Charles. He was disturbed and angry
with himself. To close his eyes and think of Tib was either an
exquisite pain or a lacerating joy: he was not sure. But to think
of marriage—worse, of all the talk, the questions, the meetings
with her relatives and his own, the ghastly and, as he felt, lewd
ordeal of a wedding in front of the shrewd, piercing satirical Wik
smile.

Even that was not the worst. Where was the sense in escaping
from his aunt's house to shut himself up with another person
—this time for the rest of his life? He could lie to and evade his
aunt. He could not evade Tib: she would have the right to watch
him and to know what he was thinking. It was the most charming

trap in the world, but it was a trap. He groaned, and thought that she was not to be trusted.

He did not see her alone for a week. Then one afternoon he called at the house to leave a book for Charles; she was sitting in alone mending the flounce of a skirt. She answered the door with it in her hand.

Without speaking a word he walked in and sat down in the little sitting-room. His heart continued to thump violently during the moment before she shut the front door and came back into the room. She only said quietly:

"Did anyone see you?"

"No. There was no one in the street when I came in."

"Well, stay now you are here." She looked at him with her bright, quick smile. "I am always glad when you come."

He frowned with the effort to think clearly about her, although she was sitting beside him.

"Do you want us to marry?" he said in a curt voice.

She had a way of lifting her hands, palm upwards, to express any feeling for which she had no words. Lifting them, she said quietly:

"Just as you like, my darling."

Something that was almost anger with her seized him. Was it so easy and simple for her?

"You don't understand what you're saying," he said. "Marriage isn't sitting at home, and sometimes going for a walk —and sewing. Perhaps it would be difficult and hopelessly wrong and detestable."

"I know all that," Tib said. She looked at him. "Why do you think about it? I am so fond of you. If you wish to marry we will. If you don't——" And she lifted her hands, with a faint smile.

"I've always wanted to live alone," Andrew muttered—he knelt down and crossed his hands on her knees and laid his head on them—"and I can't—live—without thinking about you."

He felt himself becoming dizzy, the warmth of her body through her dress intoxicated him with joy; with an effort he knelt without moving, and little by little his head cleared and his breathing became more even. He got up and stood looking down at her. She did not seem to know that he was behaving badly. She smiled at him.

"I must go," he said.

He walked out of the room and let himself out without hearing her call, quietly: "Good-bye, my darling." Neither did he notice that a woman was seated in the window of the next house, gazing into the street. There was no amusement so much in favour in Over Wik as the one spoken about as "sitting in the window." If you were a married woman with little to occupy your time, you spent at least four or five hours a day simply watching, from a comfortable chair, everything that passed in the street. It afforded endless matter for the speculations which, had they become visible, would have been seen spreading from end to end of Over Wik a tissue of inconceivable toughness: nothing escaped through it, no action, no gesture even, unless it took place behind doors and drawn curtains. Even then some rumour of it might touch a corner of the web and be instantly transmitted to a score of minds; before evening the whole town would know exactly how and when Mrs. Jordan intended to drink the bottle of brandy she had ordered more than a week since and taken secretly to her room. The elderly lady who watched Andrew come out, knew for certain that Isabel Mower was alone in the house; she knew where Mrs. Mower had gone, and since she had been sitting in the window throughout the whole afternoon and had left her post for not longer than two minutes at three o'clock, she knew almost to the minute when the young man had called and been admitted, without her seeing him.

A little later in the afternoon she would be saying to Mrs. Mower: "I see your daughter had a caller this afternoon."

With great calm Mrs. Mower answered: "That's quite likely. She and her father were both in. I was out—we're getting ready for the Conservative bazaar."

"Mr. Mower was out too, I fancy. I happened to be sitting in the window and I saw him go."

"I always think yours is a very pleasant window."

"Yes. That young Wikker it was. Andrew. He was in almost half an hour. I don't think a young gel should have visitors. I'm not saying your Isabel *meant anything by it*, but gels are very thoughtless, and this is a rare town for gossip."

"It is indeed," was Mrs. Mower's tart comment. She withdrew.

The rage she had not dared to let loose on her neighbour broke when she was scolding Tib.

"No decent girl allows a young man into the house when she is alone. You'll find yourself disgraced through the town," she repeated, stupefied that she was having to say this. It was as if she had heard while she was out that Tib had set fire to the house. "It's impossible. I ought not to have to tell you," she said bitterly.

Tib remained calm. "I don't feel that I have done anything wrong," she said. It was all she said.

Mrs. Mower was forced to think that in some ways her daughter was very stupid, almost wanting. It did not—because it could not —occur to her that she was seeing one feeble sign of a change, as subtle as it was irrevocable, in the atmosphere of Wik: perhaps of the world.

When she reflected that before very long Mrs. Jordan would hear the whole story she groaned in deep mortification and anger. "That poisonous tongue of hers!" exclaimed the poor woman.

Andrew was sitting in his room before supper when Semiramis came in. She was in a fine rage, eyes darting black looks and lips compressed.

"I hear you've been making a visit this afternoon," she croaked at him.

She was out of breath. Her vigour, at sixty-six, was horrible and astonishing, but the five flights of stairs to his room tried her, laced as tight as she was.

"Then you hear more than I've told anyone," said Andrew. His grey eyes tried to outstare her. It was no use. Those dull black pupils were as insensitive as stones to any simply human influence.

"I daresay, but it's all over t' town that you and Mower's young gel were carrying on together this afternoon as bold as brass, in front of t' window of her room. I wonder you're not ashamed to come into a decent house after making yourself th' laughing stock of th' whole town."

"There's not a word of truth in it," Andrew said coldly.

His anger was so great that he would willingly have killed her. He felt the veins in his head and wrists swollen with it, and he could scarcely see anything. His sight cleared suddenly and he saw his aunt's face with appalling distinctness, the skin of her cheeks, old, yellow, and covered with blackened veins and wrinkles, the gummy eyes, the black hairs on her upper lip, the flecks of grey spittle, the eyelids like some strange mechanism or like sightless eyeballs. An almost dispassionate curiosity made him look at it as if he were going to paint a picture of old age.

"You may say so, but it happens I've heard different. Someone saw you going in. And t' gel's no better than she should be;
it seems she's known in t' town already for her goings-on. You've
a queer taste if you make yourself cheap with every little
whore in th' place as soon as you come home. You take after
your mother. Th' Scoresby gel. She was just such a one as this
gel of Mower's, both on 'em nasty filthy creatures, not fit for a
decent man or woman to speak to."

Andrew was suddenly able to see that her rage and her bitter
tongue were both the expression, the only one she had, of a profound unhappiness. Her mind was a cauldron of unholy jealousies,
which she mistook for rules of morality. She did not know that
she was unhappy.

He did not like her any better for being unhappy—why should
he? Not knowing how to get rid of her—he could not turn her
out of his room—he walked out. He went to see his father and
told him he did not want either to go on living with Semiramis
or take her money to live at Cambridge.

"I can't keep you at Cambridge," his father said at once.

Andrew listened with his cold and detached attention while
Handel Wikker explained that his writings—he wrote in various
scientific journals on such things as the effects of magnetism on
the compasses in iron ships sailing in the southern hemisphere—
brought him in an income, with his lectures, of a hundred and
sixty pounds a year. He wrote and lectured also on points of
doctrine and Christian ethics, but he would have thought it
indecent to take money for this part of his work. While he
talked Andrew looked at him with a slight smile. He had a
respect and affection for his father which was rather that of a
disciple than a son. He used to tell his friends: "My father
is the greatest man I know, and the most ridiculous and impossible."

At fifty-six Handel had few marks of age. He was tall, and
there was little flesh on the broad skeleton beneath it. He had
become extremely slovenly. His hair was uncut and straggled
over his collar, his clothes were shabby, and the disorder in his
three rooms was so great that if he bought a new book he had to
look everywhere for a place to keep it. The tottering piles of
books on the floor and on every chair reached so high that he
could not add to any of them without bringing it down. He had
never noticed the state he was in.

"If you can live on eighty pounds a year you can have it," he said calmly.

"Then what would you live on?"

"Oh, I can live easily on the rest," said Handel airily. "I've discovered a way of getting books for nothing. I write to the secretary of the Royal Society and he sends them to me. He's been doing it for the last six months." He looked up and smiled brusquely and shyly. "Don't mind taking the money, my dear child. I haven't spent more than ten pounds on you since you were born. Your aunt has done everything."

"I can leave Cambridge and go to London," Andrew said.

"You must do as you like. . . . We'll talk about it again to-morrow. . . . You haven't had any supper—we'd better have some now. Do you like eggs scrambled with herbs?"

He chopped the herbs, then broke four eggs and began to beat them, talking all the time.

"I don't think it matters what you do—you say you want to write—so long as you work and think with the greatest rigour. Question everything. Force yourself to recoil from every idea. Thrust everything outside yourself, feelings and ideas as well as people and sunsets. Don't mix yourself in what you write. And don't begin to believe that you have any right to a satisfactory life simply because you were born. If in ten years' time you are not more dissatisfied as well as more detached than you can be now, you are not progressing. In the meantime I advise you to learn calm and patience. . . ."

The bowl in which he was beating the eggs was too small, and splashes of yellow froth flew over the edge on to an open book. He became very testy about this, and poured the half-beaten liquid into the pan. Stirring it gently—he was too careful to spoil anything he had taken the trouble to prepare—he said:

"Don't be afraid of losing an emotion or an idea by examining it. Examine it as, if you were an anatomist, you would a vein in a body, then place it back in the body and watch it at work. . . . You're surprised that I have opinions about writing. It's true I'm not a writer, I'm a preacher and lecturer who sometimes publishes his notes. But living as I do I have time to think about everything. . . . I admire precision. Most people, most Englishmen, detest it—that is why English literature is filled with magnificent clouds which resemble buildings, and no buildings that look like clouds. To please me you couldn't be too precise or too rigorous and sharp-eyed." He looked at his son with an intimidating smile. "You'd better not listen to a word I say, unless you're content to be poor all your life. If you're wise you'll stay at Cambridge, take your degree, and find work you can do without losing your self-respect, a readership, or else some routine job in a government office. Then you'll keep five or six hours a day to work at your own hard tasks—literature—whatever you like—and you'll be free to write as you feel."

"I can't stay either at Cambridge or in Wik," Andrew said. "I can very well manage in London on eighty pounds."

The thought of escaping from Tib was a relief piercing him with its agony.

CHAPTER XX

THAT year a late spring, the fields waterlogged, a black frost night after night nipping the young roots.

After his son left him Handel worked for several hours until he felt sleepy, but then to his surprise it was almost light. He thought it would be a waste of time to go to bed, and lay down on the sofa in his room, his hands clasped behind his head, looking through the uncurtained window at the leafless branches of an ash. After a time it seemed to him that he had left his room and was standing, without awareness of ground under his feet, near the tree. Looking down he saw its roots thrust far into the earth, so deeply that they must have penetrated under the sea, and their joints curled round bones, shells, stones, implements once warmed by living hands: many strange worms moved under and about the hands of the tree laid under the earth; and below them he saw the constellations of another sky. But when he looked up the branches drew him as flames lick up with their breath straws; was he made air, and there was formed of him a tree, a bird, dissolved, re-formed, in the currents of his body: and again, above him, he saw the stars he knew best as a sailor. With all this he had no sense of motion; the stillness shaped itself in him like music in a dream, flawless, quietness itself, joy itself.

He came back into his mind to find that he had slept, if it were a sleep—he was not conscious of closing his eyes—for two or three minutes. His mind was clear and alert and his body cool. He stretched himself. That was as good as a night's rest, he thought. He got up, washed himself from head to feet in the cold, iron-stained water, as he did in the morning, and put on his stained shabby clothes without looking at them.

His working day was not often less than eighteen hours, often twenty. He visited his friends and dependants in Under Wik, prepared his lectures and sermons, and made his own researches. He had become in a sense famous. The offer of a Dissenting pulpit in Manchester was made to him, and after he had refused that, of another, better known, in London. He could have had almost any, and become a figure in Nonconformity, but he had chosen his freedom: he preferred it.

In his preaching he preached a sort of liberal evangelical creed which he had imposed on the sayings of Christ. His long meditations, his struggles with himself, his mortification, had come to this—in trying, according to the command, to put on Christ, he had *put himself* on Christ.

He took hold of the words: "I live, yet not I, but Christ liveth in me," but the stress fell with a subtle difference, as certain substances change their nature though not their form under heat, and it became "liveth *in me*." Christ *in me* spoke from the desk placed on the bare platform of the Temperance Hall on Sunday night, admonished sinners in their houses, and washed their floors when they were sick abed.

This month a young man, who said he was a Socialist, came to Wik and tried to hold a meeting at the Dock End. No one in Wik had ever seen a Socialist before and few knew that such persons existed. He vexed his listeners—about a dozen men without work and as many fishermen—by telling them that they were slaves. They were going to prove that they were not by throwing him in the harbour. Handel turned up scarcely in time to save him. He was dangling over the icy water in the arms of two men, his clothes torn and his forehead bleeding from a stone.

Handel took him home with him for the night. All but the two men who were holding him had made off when they caught sight of Handel in the circle of light thrown by the street lamp at the Dock End. The two men listened, their sullen hands hanging down, to Handel's opinion of them. His voice and authority cowed them.

The young man sat shivering in Handel's room while Handel warmed up some soup and gave it to him. He had washed the blood and dirt from his face, but his jacket was beyond hope—it was a heap of rags and he eyed it ruefully. He had nothing else with him, neither staves, nor scrip, neither bread, neither money. The shilling he had been keeping for his night's lodging had been stolen from him during the assault.

When he was warmed, and when Handel had given him a coat rather better than the one he was wearing himself, he began to look about the room, rather puzzled by it, by the books, the disorder, and the fact that Handel, an educated man, a gentleman, was living here alone.

"I can see you're not used to looking after yourself," he ventured.

"I've been doing it for twenty years," Handel said.

The young man did not answer. He was thinking that his mother would have laced him with more than her tongue if he had let a room get into this state. His head ached, but he was comfortable.

"Where have you come from and what is it you're doing?" said Handel. "Who sends you out?"

He listened with curiosity and disapproval to the young man's account of himself, a Yorkshire factory-hand turned agitator.

"I joined the Party two years ago. At first I worked for it in my spare time, now I'm paid. We haven't anyone in Wik, and I came to see if I could find one or two to form a centre. . . . You saw what happened," he said, with a slight smile. His mouth was long and curiously expressive, almost a woman's mouth: his hands were those of a workman. "If you hadn't come along——"

"What little I know about your Party I don't like," Handel said. "You talk a pernicious nonsense. By reason, everything can and will be changed—poverty, crime, ignorance. The world is becoming richer; civilized nations no longer make war on one another. . . ."

"But only on uncivilized people like the Boers," the young man interrupted softly.

"The mere fact that people were found to protest against it proves that conscience and reason are alive. This is 1903—in ten years' time we shall be ashamed of having made war, in twenty war will seem impossible, in thirty——" He turned to snatch a pan from the fire before it boiled over on to the coals.

"May we be here to see it," the young man smiled. He leaned forward. His dark eyes dilated suddenly, revealing a hopeless anger, a bitterness so irrefutable and so keen that Handel was startled by it. "Do you know a shipowner and builder in the town called Money, Sir Thomas Money? He, like the world you mentioned just now, is becoming richer. But in Middlesbrough I was with chaps that have sailed in his ships. They sleep worse than dogs, and are fed on what would turn the stomach of any starving dog. His ships sail short-handed and he doesn't even

spend money to keep them seaworthy—it's sometimes more profit-
able for a ship to sink than to float and be repaired."

"Frankly, I don't believe it," said Handel. He controlled
his voice. "You poison ignorant men's minds with these
stories."

The young man shrank a little. Lowering his gaze, he said:
"Ah, but listen. When I was a child I thought that to freeze
in winter and stifle in summer in one room, to be dirty, was simply
to be alive. I ate coarse, sometimes tainted, food without knowing that there was any better in the world. When my mother
died, in fact of hunger, I thought it an ordinary thing. There is
not enough food, I thought; my mother gave me hers and died.
Now I know that I was cheated, that my mother was murdered.
I asked myself, why didn't I know it before? And the answer
—*Because no one had told me.* Now if you gave me all the money
in the world to hold my tongue I couldn't do it. It would burn a
hole in my head—now that I know. I must tell people, even"—
he smiled again—"if they try to drown me for telling them the
truth. Why"—he lifted his head and stared at Handel with a
sort of shifty boldness—"one of these days the dumb will speak
and the deaf hear them. It will be no joyful day for those who
know and don't speak."

Handel realized for the first time that he was a Jew, a sickly
and stunted Jew. A memory, like a shadow detaching itself
from the shadows in a room, turned in his mind slowly. He felt
pity and distaste in the same breath.

"You suffered and you were ignorant," he said in a low voice;
"your ignorance has led you into a life which will only disappoint
you, if it does nothing worse."

"You mean, if it doesn't land me in prison. But I've been
in prison. I was arrested in Middlesbrough in December.
A policeman kicked me in the groin and I have a running
abscess."

"Let me look at it," Handel said.

The young man took off his clothes with reluctance, because
he had no underclothes worth speaking of. Handel put a dressing
on the sore place, gave him a vest and some drawers, and later a
cup of strong tea, because the pain of removing the old dressing
had started him shivering again. There were the marks of other
sores on his skinny legs. No doubt he was in an unhealthy state.
Handel could not hold his tongue either.

"Violence is used against you because you provoke it," he said
sternly. "You incite other men to violence. It is only because
you haven't the power to do it that you have not treated Sir Thomas
Money as badly as you were treated yourself. Why should the
Moneys of this world listen to reason when they can point to you
and your like to prove that violence must be met by violence?
What have you gained? Suppose there were a million of you,
suppose that you could take arms into your hands—what would
you achieve by it but the loss of everything so far gained, the
sensitiveness, the knowledge? Imagine a revolution in this
country, Englishmen killing each other—the bitterness, the cruelty
. . . there is no cruelty so vile as the cruelty stirred up in a family
by its quarrels——"

"It is not a family," murmured the young man. "This country
is not a family. If it is, how does it come about that every mother
is not dying of hunger?"

"In another twenty years such a thing will be impossible."

"If I thought so, perhaps I could think my mother did not die
for nothing."

Handel stared at him. "You had better stay here for a few
weeks," he said. "I may be able to heal your abscess and your
mind at the same time." The last thing he wanted was to share
his house with anyone, least of all with an ill-educated, sickly
fanatic. "You'd better stay," he repeated.

"And hold my tongue?" smiled the other. "No, thanks.
Besides—you don't want me here." He shrugged his shoulders.

He was dropping with fatigue. Seeing it at last, Handel took
the lamp up and showed him upstairs to the bedroom. The young
man did not ask whether it was the only bed in the house; he took
off some of his clothes, only keeping on the underclothes Handel
had given him, and fell asleep. Handel slept on his couch in
the third room; he was used to it, and as soon as he awoke he could
see the branches of the tree like birds with their feet caught in the
ground, and the field of coarse grass growing to the edge of the
cliff. Light ran off the tree as off the points of waves and placed
its feet in the footsteps of the wind in the grass.

The young man left after his breakfast of tea, porridge, and
bread. Handel never saw him again, nor, for many years, did
Wik. Before his meeting with its violent end, he had been writing
on the wall of the shipyard opposite Sir Thomas Money's house.
He wrote, "The workers have no country and one language."

Anyone who noticed it thought that it must be a joke, but the point was never explained. Perhaps he had been coming to that in his speech when they stopped him. The next shower washed it off, and with it all memory of him.

Handel had intended to speak to the men who were listening on the Dock End, some of whose faces he had seen before they hurried off into the darkness. But they kept out of his way, and in a few days he had forgotten.

A sick man who thought he was dying, a sick mother whose children were becoming more like savages every day, a wife whose husband had beaten her insensible, waited to hear that Handel was in another house in the yard to send to him: "Could Mr. Wikker step up to Mrs. Rudby's for a minute?"

The message was usually carried by a child, lost, as they say, in muck, or by a woman hastily wiping on her apron hands wrinkled from the hard salty water. Sometimes he was vexed by what he saw when he had stooped under the blackened doorway of one of these rooms, as sunk in time as in the side of the cliff. Then, as the women said, he fair let them have it. Men that he skinned with his tongue turned sullen or sheepish, but the tired women liked it. It gave them a keener joy than they had felt since the first touch of love. Handel did not love them. He was occasionally brutal in his anger. Yet he had an exquisite and surprising sweetness which showed itself at times, and for which in Under Wik there was no name. They would say:

"He come gentle."

When he had the right of it—no one certainly would have cared to try to put him in the wrong—he could not endure any contradiction. If Christ was the Master, His first officer expected to be obeyed by the others. He was merciless when he knew you were pretending to be what you were not. Some better-off women in his congregation—a half of his hearers lived in Over Wik—came to him smiling and said they were going to clean the Temperance Hall, which was very dirty. He thanked them. Some days after he went into the hall and found three poor women on their knees scrubbing. He asked them who employed them and what they were being paid, and found that they were to scrub all day for a shilling each, with a loaf and half a quarter of pound of tea between them, and they were doing it for this wage because it was God's work.

He flew into a rage, paid them out of his pocket, and sent them home. On Sunday he preached on "the Devil's work," and his four charitable ladies turned hot and cold in turn. Two of them left his congregation, but the hall remained unwashed.

This month of April, 1903, was remembered as the month and year of the Great Storm. A day of light winds after a gale tempted the fishing fleet to go out, and during the night the wind got up with the suddenness of a hurricane. With the first light the women were running through the streets to the east pier. The seas washed over it and they huddled at the end nearest the cliff, craning their faces to the mountain of grey broken water standing against the sky.

Towards nine, two of the boats were seen making for the harbour: first one, and a minute later the other, hurled by the wind across the bar between the piers, overturned, the boat ground against the stones of the pier and every man drowned. No woman heard the woman standing beside her cry; but only her own voice thrown against the wind. Scarcely had a creature turned away when the boys on the cliff top ran down, screeching in their gull-like voices: "On t'rocks," they shouted, "on t'rocks. Awa!"

Three of the boats had been driven on to the line of sunken rocks a quarter of a mile from the foot of the east cliff. A narrow gully ran inland at this point, with banks of wind-bitten grass and sedge growing into the sand. Between the men clinging in the boats and this grass, flecked with foam—which they could see when the wind made a break in the waves—a murderous sea raged and cut off rescue. No swimmer could last in it for more than a few minutes or seconds.

Those on shore could see the men. They saw that in one boat a boy was lashed to the stump of a mast, and knowing the boats as well as they knew the shapes of their own bodies they soon knew who was in them: the boy's mother stood at the edge of the gully looking at him; the younger boy who was holding on to her leg under her skirt, as if it had been a tree, could hear what she was saying. She was saying:

"Hod up, now, hod up: hark tiv thi' mudder, and hod up, there's a brave bairn."

The wind began to take off a little about noon, but no boat could get round to them from the harbour, and the one lowered from the cliffs at the end of the gully was taken up and smashed when it touched the water. It became a question of time: if the men could hold on, and if the boats held. But drenched by icy water and frozen by the wind, first one and then a second loosened his hold and dropped off. He could be seen for a moment in the water.

The day passed. The boy's mother was still standing a little in front of the others. Straining her eyes into the grey light she thought that he was no longing standing against the stump of the mast but hanging from it. She raised her voice:

"Hod up. Hod up when thi mudder tells thee."

It grew dark. She could see nothing.

Handel went from one woman to another, telling them to go home until the morning. But how could they? One or two of them slept, in spite of the cold and their grief. There were other watchers, both in the gully and on the cliff; most of these went home to sleep in their beds and were back before light. When light came the boats were there, but on one was only the boy, whom everyone but his mother could see was dead now; on another, no one; on the third, one man. The women for whom there was no hope now did not therefore go away; they stood and waited: it was as if their veins felt what was passing in the veins of the two women, one old and one younger, who could go on hoping. There was less of a sea on, and it occurred to Handel that if they formed a line of men from the shore, as long a line as anyone could stand in that sea, it might encourage this man to try to come at the shore. He was as tall as any man there. He went first, feeling the strong icy currents plucking at his flesh and the clenched arms of the man next him. When he had gone as far as he dared he stood still. He felt an extreme excitement, like a knife in his stomach. At this level of the water and blinded by spray, he could see nothing, but he knew as soon as the man jumped and began swimming because the news ran from mouth to mouth along the line. The next thing that happened was that a man taller and broader than himself had come in front of him. Handel gripped him and recognized Thomas Money and stood straddling between him and another man until the man they were trying to save was rolled, still half swimming and alive, into the reach of Money's hands and dragged ashore. During this brief time Handel felt at once anger and a sharp intimacy with the man who had come in front.

"I never felt water as cold in my life," Money said. He slapped his thighs. A man, a groom, was holding a flask out to him: he took it and offered it to Handel.

Handel had just taken it when a woman pulled at his wet sleeve. The mother of the dead boy was struggling against the women who were trying to get her to come away.

"You may all go," she said, "go and shut yoursen indoors wi' what you can. But I s'll stop."

Handel spoke to her and took hold of her arms. They were like withered branches but surprisingly strong.

"You have other children needing you in your house," he said.

"Who needs me worst, them or him?" she said fiercely. "Am I to let him hang there by hissen? Am I to shut t'door and lig in bed wi' him hanging? He's onny a bairn, and he's been a day and night there. He was allus a good bairn and I s'an't leave him to t'sea. And so I tell you."

"Very well, I'll stay with you," said Handel.

He sent the other women home. Money had been listening with an indifferent curiosity. He now turned to go away himself, but sent the groom running back with the half-empty flask and the message that if Mr. Wikker was going to stay there and freeze he might be glad of a little brandy. Handel kept it.

He and the woman were alone at the side of the gully. The grey sky, grey water, the grey and white screaming gulls, circled round the boy. Handel tried to remember him, and could not. In his mother's mind he would have a face, hands, gestures, a voice, making him unlike other boys she knew of; she knew the feel and shape of his body as it hung there, in the water, head drooped forward as it drooped when he was born.

Hours passed. One of the women, whose husband was drowned, came back just as it was getting dark and waited a little. She went away at last, and the mother knelt down and began sobbing. Handel spoke to her, wiped her face, and wrapped a shawl round her that the other woman had brought and given to him. He did not try again to get her to leave, and during the night she fell asleep: he could tell by her breathing. He was holding one of her hands, and the strange thing was that he did not feel the cold. Just before light, when the air was uneasy with the first change, she woke up and asked him if he could see anything.

"Not yet," he said gently.

"No more can I, but t'boat's gone," she said.

"How do you know, if you can't see it?" he asked her.

She did not know how she knew. The light came gradually and Handel saw that the boat had broken up during the night, though the other two were still there. A body had been washed ashore, but not the boy's yet. The mother looked at it, called it by its name, standing with her hands on her hips, and then said to Handel that she must let the lad's wife know. They went towards Wik, the woman stumbling, and clinging to him. There was now no wind, the day calm, and the air alive and clear.

CHAPTER XXI

ONE morning in May, as Soal was walking across the yard to the wash-house, she fell and broke her leg. She was alone at the back of the house. For a long time, an hour, no one heard her cries.

She lay on her back, looking at a dazzling white cloud which never moved although it changed its shape as another and another white fleecy cloud swelled behind it, and thinking of her son. He had been dead two years—he died of enteric fever in South Africa. No one had asked him to enlist; he went into Wik one market day and that night he didn't come home, nor any night. The next they heard of him he was going to kill Kruger.

Did he kill him? Soal wondered. She stared at the cloud until her eyes began to burn and she imagined that her son was looking at her over the edge of it. She whimpered. Why, if he could see her, didn't he stretch an arm down and help her up?

Bessie Wikker came out of the house. At the sight of her Soal cried out angrily that she was being left to die. "A heart of stone," she muttered, "you have a heart of stone"—and as Bessie was stooping over her, trying to make her comfortable on the ground, the old woman pinched her sharply, then closed her eyes and pretended to be dying.

"Get me something to drink—get me a drink of tea," she said in a weak voice.

"You know I can't do that—*he* has the key of the caddy in his pocket," said Bessie. So that she should not make herself tea when he was out, her father carried the key about with him.

The men working on the farm were not allowed to enter the house, and she had to walk some way to find a boy and send him for the doctor. When she went back into the yard, the old woman said spitefully: "You took your time. I suppose you wouldn't be sorry if I died."

Bessie did not answer. She stood at the gate of the yard and kept her eyes fixed on a distant gap in the hedge. Anyone coming along the road to the farm was visible for a moment or two as he passed this gap and not again until he arrived. She might have been looking out for the doctor. Her expression was strained and half-sullen, as though a desperate struggle were going on in her mind.

She was thinking about Charles Mower. Three weeks ago she had seen and spoken to him for the first time, in the house of a married school friend. Twice since then the young man had taken a walk along this road in the early evening. He had to walk more than five miles from Wik.

On the first of these occasions Bessie met him by accident. They talked for a few minutes, and Charles said in a careless voice: "I often come this way in the evening. The view up here's charming, don't you think?"

Every evening since then Bessie had seated herself, at six o'clock, in the window of her bedroom, and with head resting on her hand she watched the gap until it was too dark to see anything at all. So few people passed along the road. It was impossible to mistake the shepherd or one of the labourers for Charles Mower: his graceful figure and bare dark head—he carried his hat in his hand during these country strolls—were recognizable half a mile away.

When she caught sight of him the second time, after watching vainly for eight evenings, she felt a pang of joy which made her feel giddy. Her hands shook violently as she put on the hat and jacket she had laid ready on the bed. But when she met him she was able to talk with a gaiety that would have astonished her friends. Her father would have been even more astonished. She felt quite safe from him: in the long light evenings he rarely came in from the fields until nine o'clock, and then, without troubling about her, he sat down to eat an enormous supper for at least another hour.

Although it was impossible for Charles to appear during the morning, she could not help watching the gap at every minute when she had nothing to do. Her mind continually reminded her of it: she would leave a task half-finished to run upstairs to her window and stand in it without moving, looking at the few yards of road and recalling the young man's face when he saw her. He had smiled as if overjoyed. His left hand holding the hat and his gloves had made a gesture of greeting. He bowed. Closing her eyes, she saw him more clearly, and now it seemed to her that his smile had held a faint trace of mockery. She shuddered.

Soal felt neglected. She began to groan angrily, to attract

attention. Bessie came over to her, and kneeling on the ground began to rub her hands and speak to her in a soothing voice.

At this moment Ezekiel came in shouting and waving his arms. He picked the old woman up, and staggering under her weight, while she screamed with pain, he carried her into the house and laid her gently on the kitchen settle. Tears of pain and anger were running down her face. He took out a big bandana handkerchief and wiped them away.

"Come, come," he said to her, "you're not dead. Fetch her a drop of brandy."

"You have the cellar key, father," Bessie said.

"I'll bring it myself," Ezekiel said sharply.

He came back with a bottle of brandy and measured out a little into a cup. Making a great show of kindness he supported Soal's head on his arm while she sipped the raw spirit and coughed and choked over it.

Her thick grey hair had come down, and it lay coiled over her shoulders, seeming more alive than her body, which had become flaccid with age and her secret grief. No one knew how often she remembered her son, but she no longer had the heart to steal food and hide it in the attics. What was the use of it, to eat alone? When she stole, it was to annoy Ezekiel. She hated him now, and blamed him for the young man's death: if he had treated him better, if he had only once spoken of him as a father of his son— but, no, not a word; the boy might have been picked out of a windy ditch for all the kindness he had for him. When she thought of her life, her bitterness was past bearing in silence and she would talk about it to herself, her face working. "He told me lies and made use of me," she said once. "I and t'boy, we were nothing."

All the same there was a bond between them. When he supported her on his arm, she could not help a weak smile coming on her face.

"I'm dying by hair-breeds, master," she whimpered.

"You'll be all right," Ezekiel said in an encouraging voice. He was completely indifferent to her sufferings, but he was always ready to pose as a kind generous creature if it gave him no trouble. And in truth he did feel for her at the moment the interest he would have taken in a sick beast.

Bessie had drawn aside and was looking at them with surprise and contempt. She could not understand how Soal could bear to be touched by Ezekiel, when only yesterday she had been calling him a murderer and a liar. In spite of what was taking place in herself, she did not understand that a physical domination leaves its marks on the memory, as ineffaceable as the sunken tracks followed by Roman soldiers crossing our fields and downs. She thought that her father was a hypocrite and Soal weakly silly to be taken in by him. She'll be hating him again to-morrow, she thought, shrugging her shoulders.

She caught sight of herself in the small cracked glass on the wall near the settle. A frown was drawing together her dark eyebrows, and her skin, in the bright light, seemed dull and pale. My life is running away like water in a house with two old half-mad people, she thought with despair. I'm not young. But for *him*, but for the life I lead here, I might have been married and in my own house.

Two days ago, visiting her friend, she had managed to find out that Charles Mower was twenty-two. Although she had known he could not be older, she felt a deathly weakness come over her when she heard it said. She was thirty.

"If t'boy was onny alive," the old woman muttered.

She thought that, seeing her like this, Ezekiel might give way to her so far as to put a plate up in the village church with the young man's name on it.

"He would have been if he hadn't been such a fool," shouted Ezekiel. "Twenty-six years he lives here, quietly and decently, doing his day's work, and didn't I give him a guinea for himself every harvest for five years? Five gold guineas! Think what I could do with five guineas now if I had them. Then one day off he goes and is snatched up by a thieving shark of a sergeant; they shout at him and make him run about until he knows how to run after a Boer he can't see, then they send him out to do what? What do you think? Why, set fire to farms! Twenty-six years he works on th' land and then they teach him to bo'n it up, and he dies, thinking what a fool he is and crying, mother, mother, like they do when they shuffle off in strange countries. . . ."

Soal's mouth trembled, and she began to cry, lying helplessly back, the tears wetting her red wrinkled face.

"There, there," Ezekiel said, smiling good humouredly, "he meant it for t'best, and he believed what they told him. He was a fool, but he's in heaven. If you're anxious to see him you've only to die yourself. A broken leg—at your age it's a serious thing, you may die to-night——"

"What's that nonsense you're telling her?" the doctor said, in his rasping voice. He had come in at the front door, walking into the house as he always did, without knocking or ringing. "Get out of this room and let me look at her," he went on. "You'll stay," he said to Bessie.

She blushed, and came forward nervously. The doctor's brutal, jocular manner gave her the feeling that he despised her because she was a woman. His big body and arched nose had been familiar to her since she was a child. He had come to see her once when she had some childish illness; he was very drunk and leaned swaying over her bed, supporting himself with a hand on each side of her shrinking body. She thought he was going to fall over her and crush her. Yet he had been gentle. He was touching Soal's leg now as carefully as if it were a baby, and talking to her in a quiet voice to keep her still. The old woman looked at him with fear and entreaty in her eyes, as dark and empty as the eyes of an animal.

Turned out of the kitchen, Ezekiel prowled up and down the passage that led from the kitchens to the big draughty hall muttering to himself: "Heaven, indeed! A nice figure I shall cut there, with nothing to eat and nowhere to put it."

He felt ravenously hungry. When he heard the doctor coming out of the kitchen he invited him to stay to lunch, and shouted furiously to Bessie to look sharp and bring out everything she could find in the larder. She did that, and left them to eat it.

Dr. Nock had had no breakfast. He helped himself to cold goose, cold lark-pie, and cold juicy lamb, and filled his mouth with as much as it would hold. He stopped eating only in order to drink off another glass of the fine burgundy Ezekiel had put on the table between them—four bottles of it. A savage inward dissatisfaction with himself, embittered by thoughts of what he would have been if he had not come to Wik as a young man, was only assuaged when he was eating and drinking.

Ezekiel was filling his glass and pressing more goose and lark-pie on him, and talking with a sly eager emphasis, his sparkling eyes fixed on Nock's face. Only a few words and phrases penetrated to the doctor's mind through the savoury smoke of goose-fat and burgundy—". . . an old scarecrow of a man, you'd hardly need touch him he'd die of it. . . ." He does himself damned well, thought Nock bitterly: how old is he—sixty? Goes into Wik for a woman once a week—and bullies his daughter. ". . . always dosing himself—scare him and put it in th' bottle for him to drink. . . ." Poor creature, she'll go off her head when she's forty, very likely, and no one 'll notice it in Wik, they're half of them fit for Bedlam. ". . . dead as a stone. . . ."

"What's that?" Nock said; "who's dead?" He listened for a minute, and burst into a roar of harsh laughter. Ezekiel had been trying to bribe him to poison off old Scoresby, so that he could get hold of Scoresby's Field.

"You miserable sinner," he said; "you should be asking God to forgive you for all the lies you've told and your cheating and bullying and the rest of it, before you die of a stroke." He stood up, still laughing loudly, and left the house.

And he's swallowed three bottles of wine, the best part of a goose, and all the jelly out of the pie, thought Ezekiel furiously. He rushed out of the dining-room, upstairs, and found Bessie trimming a hat in her room. She had so little money for clothes that she saved every scrap of ribbon and lace she had ever worn and used them to make changes in her few dresses and hats. When Ezekiel came into her room he went to her wardrobe, took out all the clothes she had, and threw them garment by garment out of the window.

"You're too vain," he said, looking at her maliciously; "you're like a silly bird fancying himself a peacock. Now go and peacock as Nature made you."

Bessie said nothing. Clenching her hands together on her lap, she looked at her father with a mingling of stubbornness and timidity. A strange light had come into her widely-open eyes, as if a candle were reflected in them.

When she was alone, she waited a moment before running to the window to see the fate of her dresses. They were lying in a ditch at the side of the road, except one, which was caught on the tall hedge of holly and privet. Her room was at the side of the house and the road ran directly below its windows. A labourer, one of her father's ploughmen, walked along the road and looked from the scattered garments to her window with an air of stupefaction which vanished when he saw her. He went on. Overcome by shame and despair Bessie went downstairs and ran out to recover the things before anyone else had seen them. The dress which had caught on the hedge was torn; tears sprang to her eyes. She had so few clothes.

She had to look after Soal and prepare cold food to take the place of that eaten by her father and the doctor at lunch. It had been meant for Ezekiel's supper, which he took at any hour when he happened to come in. There was still a round of beef and a dish of jellied eel, and when she had roasted a pair each of ducks and chickens she thought she had enough. The men were milking now; she forced herself to go into the yard and take from them the supplies for the house; she knew that they would all have been talking about her clothes thrown in the road. It is enough for a dumb animal to see anything in this place for everyone to hear about it, she thought bitterly.

At six o'clock she dressed herself and went out. Whether Charles came this evening or not, she could not stay in the house. When she had gone half a mile along the road she saw him in the distance. At once her heart began to beat so violently that she could not go on. She leaned against the gate into a field which sloped down to the stream at the side of the orchard, and tried by closing her eyes to become calm. A quarter of an hour passed before she heard his steps on the road, and then his voice.

She turned with a start of surprise and said in a clear loud voice:

"What a lovely evening! I couldn't sit indoors!"

Charles Mower had the reputation of a clever but affected and dandified young man. For one thing, he read a great deal. It was even said that he read French novels. He was extremely good-looking with his dark hair, and dark, slightly staring brown eyes, gleaming with an inquisitive irony and lively good humour. He either knew or pretended to know something about literature, and despised dancing and skating and the common amusements of young men in Wik. In return they jeered at him, not without an uneasy fear that he was shrewder than he appeared, and would get on in the world.

As he looked at Bessie Wikker, with a smile made charming by the shape of his mouth, he wondered how many evenings she had waited there, hoping to see him. His quick glance took in every detail of her looks; the top-heavy head of soft hair, badly arranged, the faint lines pulling down her mouth. Yet she's not so bad, he thought critically; her eyes are very fine, and when she laughs one can't help laughing with her. He made a joking remark only in order to hear her laugh and remind himself of its soft merry note, throaty and yet clear. Her figure was good, too, a little heavy, perhaps, beneath the waist—it was not a bad thing in a wife. I shan't need to feel sorry for myself, he thought calmly. Nor will she. I shall make her life pleasant.

"Need we go on standing here?" he murmured.

He put his hand on the gate, near her arm, which was resting on it. She moved quickly and clumsily aside.

Then she said energetically: "We could go into the field if you like—or into the orchard." A patch of red had come into her cheeks.

Crossing the field with him she noticed for the first time that the hedge was thick with may; long branches, bearing their jewelled flowers, trailed over the grass, reminding her of the ruffled hem of Lady Money's gown sweeping behind her across the grass of the Piece after church: a light mist from the river was beginning to creep along the foot of the hedge, as though it were the scent of the hawthorn called out and made visible by the level rays of the sun which was sinking behind them; pouring light into the cleft fields, it threw the overwhelming blackness of its shadow on the moor between Upgang House and the sea. The air had that uncensored clarity, as though brightness were welling into it from all the forms of nature, trees, grass, rippling water, even the dust in the road, and as though these might at any time break loose and float towards a sky calm and more remote than ever, of a fine evening in spring. The chestnuts were in flower; and already some of the cherry trees in the orchard were covered with a white dazzling cloud of blossom. Since it was very late this year, spring was leaping and rushing into flower and leaf to make up for lost time; there had never been so many orchises in the grass; along the banks of the stream were reflected, as though in water, the little moons of primroses, the deeper yellow of flags; every stem of grass and thin half-furled leaf was a jet of pure vibrant colour, the throbbing of a life too long held back by the frosts of winter.

"There is a gate into the orchard," Bessie said.

It was never used and might be padlocked. Her heart sank. She gave a sigh of relief when she saw that it was only fastened by a bar. Charles drew it back for her. She walked through into the orchard and looked round her almost boldly. Nothing so far had gone wrong, and she began to feel a joyous excitement only in having escaped from the field, where anyone passing along the road might have seen them.

Charles spread his thin overcoat on the grass and invited her to sit on it. "But it will be spoiled," she said nervously. "The grass may be wet."

"Nonsense," he said, with a brusqueness made intimate by his smile. She felt herself trembling when she sat down; she was ashamed to look at him.

"Your father has a great deal of land, and it must be very good land," said Charles, in the tone of a man making idle conversation.

"Oh, yes," murmured Bessie.

She really knew very little about it. The mention of her father chilled her with fear, at the same time that it woke in her the small flame of anger and rebellion she had felt when he threw her clothes out of the window. Her eyes grew bright and hard, and she threw her head back so that her slender rounded throat swelled a little with the effort.

"Do you want to live here all your life?"

She glanced at him, startled. "Oh, no. I——" Confused, she broke off, turning her head away so that he should not see that she had grown scarlet with shame. In another second she would have been saying: "I hope I shall marry and have my own house." Her head throbbed.

"But if your father were to die you would have the whole of this charming place to yourself," Charles said. He waved his hand as though he were presenting her with the orchard.

"I suppose so," she said, with a sigh. "Yes—of course." To Charles's surprise, she began to laugh. "Sometimes I think he never will die. He's so strong, it's impossible to think of him as dead. And yet he's over sixty."

She spoke with a reluctant admiration, and for a moment a reflection of her father's gross face appeared in her delicate one, like the image of a hill reflected in a shallow pool.

Charles Mower did not answer, and afraid that she had shocked him she was silent, watching him furtively through her eyelashes. He seemed to her beautiful, and with an innocent sensuality she imagined herself laying her hand on the nape of his neck, with its point of dark soft hair.

Unconsciously she lifted her arm and stretched it towards him, then coming to her senses, drew back, hoping he had not noticed her gesture. He had noticed it, and he looked at her with a smile which made her blush with its mixture of kindliness and irony.

Her hand had fallen on to the coat, between them; he put his own over it, and bent towards her. She had time to think, almost with anguish, that he had not said anything but the most ordinary things—not a word about love. Can he love me? she thought. She felt herself stooping towards him without any conscious movement of her body. Then she saw on his face, already so near to hers, a smile in which she read triumph and, strangely, pity. A memory of Soal and her father rushed into her mind. She started up.

Her foot caught in the braid of her skirt, and if Charles had not sprung to his feet almost as quickly she would have fallen. He steadied her with his arm. She recovered herself at once, and began to walk towards the house.

When she had gone a short distance she heard him say in a quiet, drawling voice: "You know I can't come if you go that way."

She did not turn her head. Before she had reached the door into the garden she stopped, scarcely able to breathe because of the terrible pounding in her throat. An impulse stronger than herself forced her to look round. The young man was still leaning against the gate into the field. She waved. Without waiting to see whether he would take any notice, she caught her full skirt together in her hand, and began to run feebly, her legs trembling, towards the house.

CHAPTER XXII

The letter from her son-in-law sharpened Semiramis's appetite for her breakfast. She laid it open beside her plate before taking in her fingers the devilled leg of chicken. She read the first page, turned it over with the bone, and muttered her way to the end.

". . . if I had the least influence with my wife, to persuade her to obey her doctors and rest, I have no doubt she would outlive me. The muscles of her heart are weak, but it is not diseased. But as you know she's abominably stubborn, and convinced that the world will come to an end unless she attends at least one committee a day. I have no doubt that women have rights, but as Godwin says apropos of Fénelon and the parlourmaid, one must keep one's sense of value. . . ."

"Godwin and t'other 'll be some of her nasty trashy friends," Semiramis said mildly. She belched, and wiped her fingers. "It seems it's come to her. There's never been any such thing as a weak heart in t'family. Very like it's in her father's family—a poor rotten lot." She swallowed one last mouthful of soaked bread, and pulled the bell.

"You m'get t'two back bedrooms ready," she said, staring at Skelton. "Mr. Stephen's coming to-morrow. He's to have t'big room since Miss Merry's used to t' small. She thinks she's nobbut poorly, it seems. I should be surprised if she's not putting it on."

When husband and wife arrived the next evening, Merry looked haggard and exhausted, but Semiramis barely glanced at her after she had seen that Stephen had his left arm in a sling.

"What's happening?" she demanded in a harsh voice. "What ha' you done to yourself?"

"I sprained my wrist when we were starting this morning," Stephen Smith said languidly.

It was a very slight sprain, and the flesh over the bone was hardly swollen; but Semiramis behaved as if he might faint at any moment. She made him sit down, had a glass of the old brandy fetched to him, and sent Merry running to the top of the house for

a bottle of florida water, to soak bandages for the injured wrist.
It gave her an inexplicable satisfaction to treat him as if he were
a child, or as she thought Merry ought to behave towards him.

Merry was neither hurt nor astonished that her mother did not
trouble to ask how she was.   She had not come home in search of
kindness, but because thoughts of Wik came to her, unasked, by
day and by night, asleep and awake.   With the clearness of regret
—the most intense regret of her life—she saw the end of a cobbled
street, water lapping an old mooring-post, a toy-shop.   If I see
them again living, she thought, I shall be satisfied.   For some time
she had suspected that her strength was almost at an end.

There was no day now, almost no moment, when she was not
happy.   Happiness dropped from the air on her, jetted in yellow
drops from the laburnums.   She looked, without fear for the first
time, directly into the eyes of any man or woman who spoke to
her, and saw with liking or pity the worm of the mind struggling
in the flesh.   Always slovenly, she began to take pains with her
dress.   She tried new ways of doing her hair, and sat up at night
to read, and re-read, taking pleasure in the shape of words and the
roughness of paper.

Her childhood unfolded for her in moments which came only
by chance.   At the moment when she drew her finger over the
rasping surface of a silk glove she lived through a series of summers,
each one of which had its own sharp taste lingering in her mind,
the mind not of the child to whom a still older Wik had given the
shape of its narrow houses, the salty freshness of its air, and something of its ironic indifference to all the rest of the world, but of
a person who was equally a stranger to the child and to her present
self, and yet knew no other life than theirs, and no other body
than this one it had formed with trouble such that when it was
forced to leave, it would surely desert it only with bitter tears.

She went out to Upgang House.   She had once hoped to be
able to help Bessie, but it was now too late.   And Bessie had become
cold and reserved; she was afraid that if she once began talking
to her cousin she would tell her about Charles, and she was determined not to do that.   She would never tell anyone of her
madness.

Merry gave up trying to talk to her as soon as she realized that
the younger woman was for some reason afraid of her.   The time
was past when she would have persisted until she broke down
whatever enmity or fear lay between her and another woman.

Now she looked, and immediately turned away, with respect. She scarcely knew Bessie, and the knowledge which her death in her gave her about other people was useless: it was too direct.

"I'll go out across the fields," she said, with a smile. "I suppose my uncle is about somewhere." Her cousin offered, out of politeness, to come with her. "No. Let me go alone," said Merry.

She went out through the kitchens, and stopped to talk to Soal. The old woman was now being looked after by a little girl from the village, half an idiot and very willing. She ran into the yard when she saw Merry. Soal looked at Merry with a fixed hostile stare, thinking that she had come to spy.

"There's nothing here you can take," she said, frowning. "Drat that silly girl—what's she gone out for?"

"I'll send her back," Merry promised. She looked at Soal's dark eyes and at her forehead, which was almost as smooth as a young woman's except for one very deep wrinkle. It seemed to her that she saw a red wrinkled child, covered with fine hair, crouched behind it with its knees drawn up against its body and arms folded. "I was grieved when I heard about Richard," she said slowly. She used his Christian name to show that she thought of him as her cousin.

"Keep to your own side of the pot," Soal shouted. She was angry.

"Very well, I will," Merry said, smiling.

She went out into the yard, and found the little girl squatting there on her heels, and reluctantly sent her into the kitchen. What a life for a child, she thought, sighing.

She had begun to feel tired, but the sun pouring down on a field of young corn revived her; she seemed to feel it moving diligently in her veins and in the sharp blades of wheat. The wheat shone as if it were still bright with dew, and tiny creeping plants covered the earth under it, like spiders' webs of another kind. At the farther end of the field she saw her uncle.

It had never occurred to her that he was an old man, and she was surprised to see that his hair had become grey since she last saw him five years ago. He had altered in other ways—but these had not so much changed him as brought into relief the very qualities he had always tried to hide by making use of others, more amusing or more presentable, which they dimly resembled. He had always pretended that he was a man of quick passions, easily angered and just as easily appeased—a buffoon. But now, with less vivacity, his eyes revealed the coldness, the never satisfied greed and cruelty, with which he had lived his life. Only his mouth, still red and full like a child's, retained a curious innocence, as if in spite of himself he was not able to take seriously either his own passions or the unhappiness he inflicted on people.

He spoke to Merry with genuine kindness. He could see that she was ill, and although he detested the sight of illness—because it alarmed him about himself—he forgave her for it quite easily. In spite of the long winter, his wheat had come on well and he was feeling remarkably strong and healthy. He felt almost an affection for Merry. If she had been his daughter, he thought, she would have understood him and not frozen him with her coldness and respectability.

"How are you? You look well enough," he lied.

"I'm going to live to be ninety," Merry said, with a laugh. "In another ten years I shall be able to drink with you, bottle for bottle, at *The Swan*. We'll astonish the town."

"We'll do it," Ezekiel said, grinning. He took hold of her arm. "You're nothing but bone," he grumbled. "You'd better live here and grow fat."

He showed her the new barns he had built, "to last five hundred years," and pressed her again to come and stay—"but without your husband," he said slyly.

Merry encouraged him to show off, and to boast to her about his land and his unparalleled strength and cunning. He felt no shame in front of her. And she, who knew very well that he was a tyrant who made his daughter's life wretched, and lied and tricked and bullied cruelly to get his own way, could not help feeling admiration and a quick bold liking for him. It's his immeasurable tenacity, she said to herself, and his zest, the greedy passion his body feels simply for living. With a little difference *I* should have been like that.

In the carriage on the way home she felt ill, worse than when she came to Wik. She said nothing about it, but went upstairs to lie down after sending word that she did not want any supper. After supper Stephen came up to her room and asked her if she would like the doctor. Although she now felt a horrible nausea and pain, she said:

"No."

Stephen seated himself beside her bed. "There are at least a dozen letters for you downstairs," he said.

"I'll read them in the morning," she murmured.

"I can't think why, knowing you're ill, all these people write to you," he said peevishly. "You're not indispensable."

Merry turned her face away to hide a smile. During the last few days she had realized how deeply he resented the fact that she was well known, and that her illness inconvenienced hundreds of people who were used to working with her. But, instead of being hurt, she was touched by his weakness; it made her smile. She even blamed herself for his lack of responsibility. If I had done less, she thought, he would have been forced to make some effort and he would not have passed his fortieth year with a face as smooth and characterless as that of a boy. Nor would he be a failure. If I die, she thought, he will suffer all the more. Now, suddenly she realized that his habit of evading troubles went too deep. He would never change; he would always look about him for someone, some woman to take the blame for his existence, or he would fritter away his life in plans which never came to anything. It is my fault, she thought quickly. She felt a blind love and pity for him, an almost lacerating tenderness.

"You've been happy with me, haven't you?" she said.

"Perfectly happy," Stephen said lightly. "Of course, you've had your own way about everything," he added, with a slight smile.

"No," Merry said. She forced back her tears. "I only did what I had to. I couldn't have lived a quiet family life. Forgive me."

"There's nothing to forgive." Stephen stroked her hand. "Now don't let's have a scene," he said gently, anxious, partly for her sake, and partly for his own, to avoid any kind of emotional tension. "You know I couldn't do without you. We're very happy."

After a moment Merry said, turning her face away, "I love you."

"Then go to sleep, my darling. If you're not better in the morning we'll have the doctor."

His bedroom opened off hers, with another door on the landing. He went to bed. He was feeling deliciously drowsy—"the wine," he thought, ". . . . yes, it's certainly the wine:" but when he was barely asleep he heard his wife groan and say: "Oh, Stephen," in a deep hoarse voice that made his blood run cold. He sat up in bed, shuddering, and listened. She said nothing more. After a minute he called gently:

"Are you all right?"

There was no answer. She was speaking in her sleep, he thought. He lay down again. His heart gradually quietened, and he went to sleep. In the morning when he awoke he remembered it, as if it had been an unpleasant dream. He dressed himself, and not hearing his wife, he went into her room. Merry was lying with a calm look on her face—calm, and vacant as well: she was dead. She had been dead for hours.

Unable to believe it, he touched her. It was quite enough.

He backed out of the room: tears were pouring over his face in a warm stream, and he wiped them away with his hands, and snuffled loudly. He must find Semiramis and tell her at once. Even in his distress he remembered to keep it to himself that she had called him and he had not gone. I may have dreamed it, he thought.

Semiramis looked at him for a minute without speaking. Her face became very red, and slack, and he caught sight of her blackened gums. Closing her mouth tightly, she left him standing crying in the dining-room and went to Merry's room. It was years, many years, since she had thought of her daughter as a child, but now between two movements of her wrinkled lids she saw the thin eager little girl watching her with her pale eyes, pale and yet brilliant. Winter sunlight moved over the sliding grey waters. "Hey, where am I?" she said, uneasy, afraid to look at the bed. A pang divided her body.

She stooped forward, gripping the quilt in her hands, and whispered: "What's coming?"

The pain ceased and did not come back. She felt empty and weak, but alive. Straightening herself, she looked firmly at Merry, to be certain that Stephen had not made a foolish mistake.

At once, in the same moment in which she was certain, separated from it only by a breath, she felt anger against the calm woman in the bed. Merry had always escaped her, always defied her. Even as a child, even when she was being thrashed, even when with tears brightening her eyes she tried to be reconciled, she kept something back. Her nurse said of her: "She's artful, she's a deep one." She set herself up to be different, Semiramis thought. Yes, from the first—presenting herself in the place of the son with whom Semiramis had been living for nine months.

"Her name in t'papers did her no good," the old woman said jealously. "No good. You came to no good," she repeated.

M

With one more glance, taking in the length of Merry's body under the clothes, she left the room and went downstairs.

She found Stephen sitting at the table, his head in his hands, and the dish of bacon and sausages growing cold. Ringing the bell furiously, like an alarm, she had it taken back to the kitchen to be warmed up. "You're no better than a fool," she said to Skelton, her voice rising. "A fool, a fool. As if there wasn't enough trouble in th' house without you setting food on t'table to get cold. Look sharp about it . . . then right yourself to go out—I want you to fetch t'doctor."

In a softer voice she urged Stephen to eat, heaping his plate with the morsels she would have kept for herself on an ordinary occasion. He had had a cold for the last two days, and she made this the excuse for giving him brandy in his coffee, and making him lie down in the sitting-room after the meal. Her tenderness for him was genuine. There was even a trace of coquetry in the way in which she helped him to more food and urged him towards the couch. Since he came, she had taken into use a new dress, with an enormous brooch of diamonds and rubies set in heavy gold. She threw a pleased glance at herself in the mirror behind the couch. In the same instant she felt a twinge of contempt for the man who had given way completely and allowed her to do anything she wished to him. But she continued, with fond anxiety, to comfort him.

When the doctor came she waited for him in the dining-room, while he went into her daughter's room. She was meditatively picking the two bacon bones on her plate when she heard him coming down, and hastily wiped her fingers.

"Well, doctor?" she said harshly, her face red with excitement and emotion.

"Why, I knew that," she said, when he told her that Merry had died of heart failure. "She ovverdid it with her carryings-on and she's come to it. It serves her right."

A blind grief seized her as she was speaking, for the first time realizing that Merry had *gone;* but not for a fortune would she give herself away to the man she always spoke of as "yon drunken scoundrel Nock, or whatever he calls himself."

"Since you are here, you'd better look at Mr. Stephen Smith —her husband—he's a h'artist, a famous h'artist. You'll mebbe have heard of him. Th' poor lad's lost in a cold—and now with t'shock of this happening . . . yes, and I must see about getting

Windus and his men up to measure t'body. I tek it you'll send in your Mrs. Dodgson or Hodgson or whatever her name is—and I hope she's fit to do t'job—I hear she made a rare sight of that Mrs. Agger when she came to lay her out; her own husband didn't know her after it. Drunk, it seems."

The doctor looked at her with distaste. "I see you're standing the shock very well," he said.

"When I want your opinion of me I'll ask for it," Semiramis said.

She went upstairs, meaning to go to her bedroom, but an impulse drove her to look once more at her daughter. It might be the last time she saw her as she was, since already a change had taken place in her. Stooping over the bed, Semiramis suddenly felt giddy. It was as if she were looking into the mouth of a tunnel, filled with darkness and cold winds. She became aware of her hands pressed on the sheet, of their dry wrinkled skin, glazed, yellow; of her trembling knees. With fear she thought, But I'm old, I'm an old woman. She thought that her life ran out of her body at this moment; she almost saw it, a creature like a mouse, running from under her skirt and scurrying across the floor under the window. She clapped her hand on her body.

One slat of the blind had stuck, and the light came through the gap in a wavering rectangle on the bed. A little higher up and it would have fallen on Merry's hands. Semiramis remembered her as a calm smiling baby, sitting placidly in the sunlight. She looked again at the dead woman's face and saw on it an expression of joy.

Whatever else, she was happy, she thought grudgingly. For a moment, she clung terrified to the edge of the bed.

"*Don't go*," she said.

Her courage revived, and with it all her malice. If you'd thowt less of them other women and their rights and more of yourself, you'd be alive now, she sneered. *I* shan't die, she thought; I shan't die yet of a long while.

Looking furtively at Handel she thought, He must have his hair cut before we go so far as that. She turned her face aside to conceal the sarcastic smile that crossed it at the absurdity of the thought.

Her husband came into the room at this moment. If he were surprised to find his wife talking to "that preaching radical," as he called Handel, he hid it under a brusque, friendly manner. "My dear sir, you should have kept it," he said, as soon as Handel began to speak about the flask. "I am certain you could have used it to better purpose than I shall. Why not keep it?"

"Thank you," Handel said, a little taken aback by this affability, "if I needed it I would keep it. But, in fact, I don't."

Tea was brought in, together with a decanter of whisky for Sir Thomas. Handel refused whisky, but sat holding his cup of weak China tea without drinking it. He was wondering how quickly he could leave; he had a great deal to do, and he was annoyed with himself for having stayed. Why did I do it? he wondered. Almost mechanically, his mind turned back to the problem in which he had been engrossed immediately before he came out: he sat stirring his tea, and pondering, and only became conscious of what had happened when he saw the look of irritated astonishment on Sir Thomas Money's face. Then he realized that for some time Money had been speaking to him and he had not heard a word.

"I beg your pardon," he said, with a smile. "I'm afraid I was not listening. It's an abominable habit I have fallen into—through living a great deal alone. There's no excuse for it, and I dislike the idea that I'm becoming eccentric."

What the devil do you think you have become? thought Money, only half placated. "I was merely saying that it surprised me, when I accompanied my wife to your—meeting—the other evening, to see that one of your active supporters is that scoundrel Lamb—a fellow always making trouble in my yards. He's a proper sea-lawyer—like all these so-called secretaries of unions. But perhaps you approve of his politics?"

"I know nothing about them," Handel said, urbanely. "What I do know is that you employ a bullying agent to collect your rents in Under Wik. A man who falls behind with his rent for any reason, is likely—if he's been active in his union—to lose his job in your yard—I suppose to make certain that he can't in future pay rent to any landlord. Unless he can get relief. Otherwise he or his family go to the workhouse."

He had spoken in an indifferent voice, in which the edge of irony was sharp enough to prick without drawing blood. The other man felt only a quickened interest in him: nothing that Handel Wikker could say to him, nothing anyone could say, would sow the smallest seed of uneasiness in the shipbuilder's solid body. He knew what he was doing, he had never at any time made a serious mistake; he never would. At the same time he enjoyed meeting a man who disapproved of him—provided, of course, that the man was not in a position to give him actual trouble. It heightened his sense of his own powers.

"Perhaps I ought to let them drink the rent money and say nothing about it," he said slyly.

"No need to go to those lengths," said Handel, "but you might listen the next time Lamb comes to you. He's a reasonable man. He no more wants trouble in the yards than you do. A steady decent man, trying to educate himself, saving to send a boy to college—why should you imagine he wants to create disorder? In the end you'll have to deal with your workers on a different basis than you do now. The spirit of the times is with Lamb, and against you . . . the future. Why not meet it?"

Money did not answer at once. He, like his wife, whom gossip said he treated brutally, had no respect for conventions. Unlike her, he knew how necessary they were to him. He knew, with an acuteness which differed from Handel's in being used for aggression on all fronts, that there was no mark of the dangerous agitator on the lined forehead of secretary Lamb, that a little flattery, one man of the world to another, would go a long way with a man of his temperament. It so happened that Money was incapable of flattery. If he could, he would love to run the union secretary out of the town and be shut of him for good. He hated the sight of him in his neat clothes, and of his colourless face, timid and obstinate.

"Good God, Wikker, you know nothing about it," he burst out, with an exasperated gesture. The veins in his throat swelled, and he tried by forcing a smile that showed his strong yellow teeth to control himself. "The spirit of the times is what *I* like to make it, nothing better or worse. Anything voted on ". . . it was the general will . . . well, perhaps it was only the will of the majority . . . but you know how it is in these things . . . the democratic spirit of our . . . iberal. . . ."

The sounds of the band, and faint cheering, rose as far as Handel's room. Sunk in his work, he scarcely heard it: towards evening he remembered with a mingled feeling of irritation and guilt that he ought to be dressing to go out to dinner. He had a dark suit folded away: he took it out, looked at it without noticing the creases, and put it on. He had remembered to go the day before to have his hair cut.

When he reached the streets near the harbour he saw that a crowd had gathered to watch the fireworks, although these would not begin until ten o'clock. A light warm wind had risen, and with it life began to run quickly in the town. The bare-footed and half-naked infants of Under Wik ran screeching about the wharves, the flags rippled with the sharp noise of bullets against the house walls, and in the harbour the water broke up into a myriad points and splinters of light, and started against the eyes in a quivering torrent, blinding, hard.

Handel turned his back on the harbour and was climbing the steep street into Over Wik when he saw his sister, Ann Wellhem, with her husband. They had come to a halt at the other side of the street. Ann, very warm and red in the face, was waving her sunshade above her head like a weapon. He crossed over to them.

"It's you, is it?" Ann said coldly. "I'm just sending William home."

"Didn't you come to see the fireworks?" Handel asked.

"We did, but I've had enough of him," his sister said grimly. "I don't want him hanging round me, and if *I* don't want him no one else does. He shan't stay. I said *Go home*," she repeated, in a terrible voice, and lowered the sunshade to poke her husband with it on the legs. "Go home!"

With one last glance, mournful and unavailing, into her face, William turned and walked slowly away. From the back, because of the deformity of his legs, his frock-coat descended almost to his ankles and laced boots. His head had sunk forward, and the coat seemed to be out walking by itself. In effect it was—since whatever spirit Sweet William possessed before he married was long since dead and there remained only an old envelope of bone and dry flesh. Who can say what it felt, or of what, that shocked on-lookers, it was insensible?

Handel hurried away. It cost him an effort to think kindly of his sister, and he was already late. There was nothing he could do. He overtook and passed William, and saw with horror that tears were trickling over the old man's large face, bony and vacant. . . .

The dinner-party was smaller than he had expected: he was the sixth and last guest and he had the impression that his being there at all astonished the others, who were all—or seemed to be—intimate friends of Sir Thomas and his wife. Again he wondered why he had been asked, and more drily, why he had come.

He found himself seated on Lady Money's right, but these subtleties of politeness made so little impression on him that he hardly noticed it. He did notice, since he was not blind, that she was wearing a very handsome dress, with a necklace and brace-lets on her thin arms, of rubies, which were surely those for which Sir Thomas was said to have paid ten thousand pounds at the time of his marriage. He was struck, too, by the curiously physical warmth she was able to create round herself by little more than smiles and gestures. Her eyes glittered with amusement, and she had a way of stretching her long neck back when she laughed —which reminded him of a hawk about to strike, and then— by an extraordinary leap of his mind—of his sister, Semiramis Jordan.

He began to feel towards her a friendly interest, held back by distrust and contempt. He was not conscious of this last feeling. It took shape in his mind only as complete indifference to her anxiety to please him—he could feel this anxiety whenever she asked him a question and listened with a lively air of humility to the answer. He knew he was wasting his time here—and yet he was not impatient. Cool—and detached, but he was willing to like her better than if she had been less, yes, less attractive.

The dining-room, a long room with mirrors and floridly-carved panels, was at the side of the house; it was darkened by a thick hedge of cypress planted close to the windows. So, although the evening outside was still light and the air drenched with that luminous glaze of the setting sun in June, when it is stronger than at mid-day in winter, candles had been lighted on the table

"We oughtn't to talk about these things now," Handel said, with a touch of contempt. "Do you know the name of your husband's agent?" he went on, smiling. "It's Palmer—that's the Old Testament name for a kind of locust—*That which is left of the palmer worm hath the grasshopper eaten.*"

"Why do you smile?" she said in a low voice. "There are moments when I hate humanity so much that I would like to crush it out."

Handel shrugged his shoulders. "I believe in reason," he said. "One shouldn't hate people or try to love them—but treat them reasonably. That's quite enough."

"Would you try reasoning with a wild beast—or a locust?"

"But the locust, this rascal Palmer, isn't acting on his own," said Handel quietly. "Your husband is responsible for him. You are responsible."

"I don't understand anything about it—I don't know," she answered, dropping her head. "I wish I did—will you help me to understand?" She blushed. "Oh! Don't laugh!"

"I shouldn't dream of laughing."

"Then don't despise me for being stupid. Help me."

He made her some sort of promise, very much as he would have promised a serious child rather than risk hurting its pride.

The young woman who was seated next to Thomas Money leaned forward at this moment and said:

"You look splendid, Sarah. You ought always to wear colours —they suit you."

"Oh, Sarah is too lazy to look after herself," Thomas Money interrupted, with what seemed a brutal geniality. "You know, she was a governess before she married me and she's not used to spending money on clothes or to taking a bath more than once a week. Her back is actually dirty sometimes." He began to laugh quietly, and the young woman smiled with an air of discomfort. It was better to take such remarks as a joke. They were not actually much out of the ordinary Wik humour, except that the cruelty was a little too apparent.

"But why not tell them how persistent you were," Sarah said indolently, looking at him.

"Were you a governess?" Handel asked her in a low voice.

"Yes. I taught French and Italian."

He was about to ask her something more when Money interrupted him with a question.

"No, I don't agree," Handel said easily. "People like you are a liability to the country so long as you refuse to admit that you have duties, so long, in short, as you are merely and shamelessly acquisitive. I haven't the least respect for your intelligence and acumen and the rest of it. I can't see any essential difference between you and some offensive little boy cheating his school-fellows out of their pocket-money—it's the same impulse."

"No, by God it isn't——" began Money. As always, when he was drunk, he could talk with a clearness and good humour impossible to him in his sober mind. He became eloquent.

Listening to them, Sarah gave herself up to the excitement of feeling this man so close to her that if she touched his foot she could apologize for it as an accident. I respect him deeply, she thought; he is not like any man I have ever known. She thought with a familiar bitterness of her life, which since her marriage had become even narrower than when she was a governess. I might have done so many things. She felt the energy of her body, its sensual potency which she could have used. Looking furtively at the other women at the table, her only friends now, she despised them. They don't think; they are content to be only what they are, that is, nothing at all, where I, I still want to know, to change. This life I live is intolerable; I ought to go away; I ought to hide myself and take some other name, and begin again.

She felt discouraged at once. Her imagination refused to give her any details of a new life, or of any action that would be unpleasant, or troublesome, or would force her to become poor and uncomfortable. She had been both. To-morrow, she thought confusedly. I'll think about it quietly to-morrow. She began to watch Handel Wikker again, with a stealthy, passionate intensity, looking at the firm lines of his mouth and thinking, Touch me with your mouth; kiss me; let me feel your hands and body: it's all I want.

She began to talk to the stupid, fat-necked young man on her other hand. By turning her head slightly sideways she could listen to him and still watch Handel in one of the mirrors. A curious smile crossed her mouth at the thought that the young man had no idea what she was thinking while she seemed to be listening to him with a close attention. Narrowing her eyes, she gave herself up to the voluptuous pleasure of imagining a scene in which Handel at last did everything she wanted. Her smile at this moment was scarcely comfortable to the young man; he hoped doubtfully that she was smiling at something he had just said—not at him. She turned her head and looked at him with her clear, disconcerting eyes.

"What did you say?" she asked him.

"I was only saying," he said boldly, lowering his voice, "that it's queer to see this preaching fellow dining here. I thought he was above such things."

Her smile became definitely cruel. "Oh, not at all," she said. Bringing her lips close to his ear, she added: "You're quite mistaken. He enjoys a decent dinner as much as anyone—not to speak of other temptations of the flesh and the devil."

She went off into a fit of laughter, in which the young man uneasily joined, avoiding her eyes.

Soon after ten o'clock Money took his guests on to the lawn. It was scarcely dark yet, but the men had begun to send up the rockets, and cascades of coloured lights streamed in the sky and over the deeper violet of the hills. The thunder had been rolling about in the distance for the past hour, and at long intervals there were flashes of lightning, pale enough to make one imagine that they were reflections. These now came closer to the earth: the glitter of the fireworks against the sky became part of the uneasy crackling of the atmosphere, and all at once the darkness behind a fountain of golden sparks was split from side to side, as though it had been shrivelled, by a blinding flash. The thunder had completely stopped. Lightning came alone, with only a few seconds between one sheet of light and the next. A cold wind had sprung up and it whipped the trees with the noise of hail crackling against the leaves. Wave followed wave of light, turning the sky petunia colour, with forked lines of a sharper light running across it, now behind the trees, now tearing open a whole face of the sky.

"Your fireworks," Sarah said maliciously, "have been completely outclassed."

"It seems they are worth running against," Money answered, grinning.

Since they left the house Handel had felt out of place and more bored than before. He had had as much as he could stand of the company, and he thought they would only be relieved

when he went.   He spoke to Money, who was now so drunk that
he could only shake hands by pressing the other on Handel's
shoulder.   Lady Money did not ask him to stay.   She went with
him into the house in silence, and when he began to thank her
interrupted him with: "You promised to help me, remember."
He answered absent-mindedly.   ,

He was glad to find himself walking quickly towards the harbour.
An evening of that sort of thing is no good, he said to himself.
He felt very tired.   One thing is certain, he thought—society will
have to replace men such as Money by others with a sense of
responsibility.   There must be authority, order, degree, and it
must be honourable—decent, rational authority, and rational
obedience below it.

Near the harbour the people were still standing crowded together, watching the last of the fireworks.   Their upturned faces
appeared ghastly in the prolonged surges of lightning, but when
he turned from them to look at the water in the harbour he
saw that the colour actually flooded back to it with the light,
so that for minutes at a time it glowed with a peculiar hard
brilliance.

He crossed the bridge into Under Wik.   In the narrow dark
street the lightning came and went, throwing shadows across it
like knives slicing the houses in half, or like the up and down
beat of wings.   At first he was the only person in the length of
Harbour Street, but as he was passing one of the yards a child
ran out and stumbled dizzily against him.

He caught her.   She was half crying with sleep and excitement.
She stammered out that she was going to find Mrs. Waind for
her mother, and her mother was alone? there was scarcely a soul in
the yard but had gone off to see the fireworks.

"I'll go in and stay with your mother until you come back,"
Handel said.   "Be off, but don't hurt yourself."   She was bare-
footed, like every other Under Wik child in summer.

When he went into the bedroom he saw that it was almost
bare of things, except for the bed and a chair.   The heat was
stifling.   There was no window in this room, the bedroom, and in
the outer room the shutter was fastened over the little window.
When he wanted to open it, the woman said, "No, she was afraid of
the lightning."   He left it as it was.   There was one lamp for both
rooms, and it was standing on the floor near the bed.   Part of its
light fell over the bed, on the woman's hands gripping the single

N

blanket. Her body laboured under it, and its swollen shadow stood up on the wall at the other side. Looking at her, Handel saw that her face was wet. She was not young, but her eyes had the innocence of eyes which are no longer looking into life.

In the other room there was a grate with a little fire, and a kettle of water.

When he had been waiting for half an hour the little girl came back, rubbing her eyes, with the midwife—who took one look round the two rooms and sent her out again at once to borrow clothes "or any bit o' clean rag," and another chair, from any neighbour who was at home. She asked Handel if he minded waiting a little longer.

"I might want some help," she said, looking at him with a sort of angry energy.

She had become bent and smaller with age and the boldness had gone out of her face, which was dry and crumpled, almost childlike. It was as though at the end of her life she were getting ready to drop back into the cradle or into another womb.

Sitting in the other room, with his back to the door, Handel heard her talking to the woman and the woman's answers. She had never cried out, which was strange enough, since this was one of the few times when a woman might make as much noise as she liked without vexing her neighbours. "Is it all right?" she said, in a low voice.

There was a pause, then the midwife's grumbling reply. "Yes, it's all right. You've only to wait."

"I've been waiting since this morning."

"It's always longer at your age—you shouldn't have done it."

"Did I ask for it?" the woman sighed. There was silence, until she said once more: "Are you sure it's all right?"

When the child had been delivered at last, and washed, Handel stood looking at the mother again. Her face had become relaxed, but it was still without any sort of relief, and filled with a profound wretchedness.

"Can I do anything to help you before I go?" he said. "I'll come back."

After a moment the woman said: "My hands are cold."

He took one of them between his own and rubbed it. She held out the other; it was rough and dry, the hand of a poor woman. The ends of the fingers were covered across and across with deep black lines.

Going out, he was surprised to find that it was light. It was very early morning and the street was still as empty as it had been a few hours since. He walked slowly. When he reached the top of the Garth the freshness of the air struck on his eyelids, making them flutter once or twice; he closed them and leaned against the wall of his field. Now that he was not forcing himself to move, he heard on every side the fountain of bird-calls, the jets falling and rising, piercing the frail shell of time enclosing him, shattering it and his senses with their intimation of an eternity which has nothing to do with men.

CHAPTER XXIV

DURING the day Andrew Wikker stayed in his room in Herne Hill, and wrote. It is perhaps an exaggeration to say that he wrote, since the great part of the time was spent in scratching out what he had written or in pondering what he was going to write. He had a horror of inaccuracy and fluency. It was characteristic of him that at twenty he knew already that he would never be well known, since that was not what he wanted. He would be happy if he could spend two-thirds of his life exactly as he was spending these months. It must be supposed that he had chosen to begin by studying Baudelaire for no better reason than wanting to; since an editor to whom his father had given him an introduction held out no hope that he would be able to print any part of the work when it was finished: "Why don't you," he said genially, "write about Tolstoy? There's more of him, and people are going to be interested in the Russians. Mark my words." Andrew marked them, but that was as far as they went with him. Advice of any sort was generally wasted on him.

London, during August, quivered for him with a life that seemed more peculiarly its own than in earlier months. He had been here since April and he thought he was beginning to know certain parts well, but always until now their odours and emanations had been those of the people with whom he rubbed shoulders as he walked about the streets—alone.

Now, in the often sultry atmosphere, London itself seemed to come to life; he got an impression of languor and confusion, of a monstrous current of joy, despair, happiness, fear, satiety, which belonged rather to the stones of the pavement than to any of those who walked over them daily. The endless streets of shabby dusty houses gave out a haunting perfume, a nostalgia of the past which infected the present.

In the evening, when he went out, he searched for cheap eating-houses and ate meals that would have made him go hungry rather than touch them when he was living at home. He could have had no idea how difficult it is in London to find any cheap place where the meal offered will not disgust a palate which knows the difference between clean and tainted food. But since he was always hungry, he did not much mind being half poisoned.

One evening towards the end of the month he left his room about seven o'clock and walked over the hill, past Ruskin Park, into Camberwell, and along the Walworth Road. Passing cabs sent out an aroma of animal sweat and leather to meet the more pungent odours from the open front doors of houses and from shops crammed with cheap clothing, fried fish, meat, fly-blown pastries, and fruit that had been lying out all day in the hot sun on stalls on the pavement. Women sat staring listlessly in the open windows or leaned their elbows on the gates of soot-blackened gardens.

From one of the houses a woman came out clad from neck to toe in dark-red silk, a feather boa coiled round her plump shoulders, and a hat covered all over with flowers perched high on a mass of dark greasy hair. She minced along in front of Andrew on her high heels. Every step released a fresh wave of scent to join the other less overpowering evening smells.

He crossed Waterloo Bridge, his gaze turned to the violet and brown haze hanging over the buildings and the sluggish river; and plunged into the Strand with the sensation of diving into warm, thickish air. It was already darker here than on the bridge. The lights had been lit, and the tide of human beings swirled and eddied from light to darkness, was sucked into the doors of restaurants and hotels, and submerged in the shadows of side streets.

An intoxication which was partly hunger and partly excitement seized him. He looked about him eagerly, scarcely knowing what he wanted. Certainly not the invitation he now got from a woman younger and prettier, but of the same kind, as the woman in the Walworth Road. He walked on. But a new turn had been given to his thoughts. His body was suffused with a longing which was both definite and restlessly ambiguous. He felt dissatisfied, angry with himself because after so many months in London he was still alone, still unable to do anything to break down the invisible barrier between himself and these women he watched sauntering or hurrying through the streets every evening. He imagined himself speaking to one of them, a pretty shop assistant, one of the two walking past him with quick short steps, chattering like birds, or that other one who must—from the eager hostile glances she was sending everywhere—be, like himself, a stranger. A mixture of shyness and arrogance had so far kept him from trying to put into practice any of the plans he invented during these walks. Besides, he was too shrewd to have overlooked the fact that none of these young women would be content with the little he had to offer, supper in a cheap restaurant, and afterwards—let things take their way, arrange themselves as they would. They were all thinking of marriage. And he—he had planned a life in which marriage was less important than his effort, his fixed determination, not to grow tired of striving for the greatest rigour—in thought and word—even if he were never read, if the genial old editor had been right in warning him to "study the market first, and *then* to begin writing."

He was far from thinking that Tib would mind his living as best he could when she was not with him.

By the time he had reached Piccadilly Circus he was a young man in a rage. He walked straight ahead, not looking where he was going, choosing the streets at the back of Regent Street only because they were like himself, poor and shabby.

When he had been walking for a few minutes his shoe-lace came undone and he stopped to tie it. Lifting his head afterwards he saw a woman standing in an open doorway not more than a yard in front of him. The room or passage behind her was lighted, and since she was looking not at him but over her shoulder into the house, he could see her face plainly. He knew her. For a moment he could not remember who she was, but then the scene rushed into his mind: the low, dusty room, the blue and green beyond the window, and the four girls. She was Julia. It was how long since? eight years—her black curls were brushed closer to her head; she had still something of the air of an overgrown child, although the big white arms crossed over her breasts were those of a woman. She wore a black dress and black apron; if he had not known who she was he might have taken her for any poor Italian woman living in this quarter of London.

He realized that she had turned her head and was looking at him with annoyance. He blushed.

"It's me," he said. "Andrew, Andrew Wikker. You've forgotten."

She took a step forward, looking at him, then smiling joyously said: "Come in, come in and tell me what you are doing—tell me everything."

She took him into a kitchen, which was also a sitting-room,

with an armchair and a table with a red velvet cloth. It was warm and dark, and smelled of bread baking. Indeed, the first thing she did was to open the door of the oven and draw a loaf out, which she shook out of its tin and tapped with the knuckles of her left hand; he noticed the heavy wedding ring, and that she was pregnant.

She had made him sit in the armchair; she moved about the room quickly, as though her heavy body did not trouble her, and began to make coffee, talking the whole time in her strong lovely voice.

"As you see, I'm married. I came here, to London, as soon as I was twenty-one, with Lizzie—we were going to be teachers. Lizzie did teach, for years, but I married at once—I didn't go back to Wik until this February when mamma died . . . you must have heard about that . . . and what happened." Her eyes dilated for a moment. "And now my father—but she *drove* him mad . . . never mind, what was I saying to you? Yes, I married. My husband is a waiter, he works in the Café Royal— do you know it? You must have seen him."

"I have never had the money to go into the Café Royal," Andrew said, smiling. "What is he like?"

After a pause, as though she were looking at him in her mind, she said:

"He is not tall. He is pale, even his eyes—even his mouth, but it is beautiful, small, like a woman's—not like mine; you know we all, except Sarah, had too wide mouths. Still, you couldn't say we were plain—none of us were that." She looked at him with a smile. "I am strong and well, as you see, and happy; I have four children, you must see them, and Franz."

"And Lizzie?" Andrew said. He had been so soothed by the room and her voice that he was shocked when she struck the back of her hand against her mouth and cried:

"But you had to ask! You don't know that she killed herself, two months ago, in Vienna. She would have gone there sooner, a year ago, but for mamma. Then when mamma died there was nothing to stop her, and she went; she had been living in London with a man, a married man—we distrusted him; Franz can always tell whether a man is any good or not from the way he behaves eating and drinking, and this man behaved badly—he asked her to go to Vienna with him and she refused because of mamma knowing if she did that, but then she went. But it seems he was tired of her, and she jumped into a river there is in Vienna, I forget its name. . . . And since we have begun on the sad part of my life I may tell you that Sarah died a week after mamma, when something went wrong with her when her child was being born, but she saw mamma at the end of it. She spoke to her in such a voice I turned round, thinking she must be there, but of course I saw nothing since I wasn't dying. . . . That's all the misfortune, all the rest is good. Lucy is now married, last week, to a very rich man; a little old, but he will be all the kinder to her. . . ."

She laughed and poured out the coffee. She had been watching him while she talked, and what she saw made her smile and sigh. He is very good-looking, she thought; but he could do something foolish. It was natural for a young man to be tense and nervous—only ignorant and stupid people suppose that one is happy when one is young—but the coldness behind Andrew's nervous tension alarmed her. He is one who could die of anger or disappointment, she said to herself; if Franz were here he would know what to say to him.

"Are you in love?" she asked.

"Yes," Andrew said, in a voice so unfriendly that the woman felt embarrassed. "You may have seen her when she was a little girl. Her name is Mower. Isabel Mower. She is usually called Tib."

"Why don't you get married?" I may as well be hanged for a sheep, she thought recklessly.

This time the young man looked at her with his charming smile, without a trace of resentment or anger. "I have no money. Eighty pounds a year from my father—and I earn nothing."

"But what do you want?" Julia said, laughing. "A bed, a table, two chairs. A casserole."

"What's that?"

"What's what? A casserole? Earthly salvation for a woman —I do all my own work, and you can see it agrees with me."

"But you were always beautiful," Andrew said, smiling.

He told her where he was living, and about his work. He knew she did not understand a word he was saying about the last, but he felt that he must talk or choke. He was in such a state of excitement that if he could not talk to someone he was afraid of weeping with rage or happiness. When he saw her looking at the clock on the dresser and knew he ought to be going, he felt a sharp wish to take her in his arms. Rather, to feel her warm, beautiful arms round him, holding him close to her for a minute. The need became an agony, while he looked at her and told her that she had been kind, it was the best thing that had happened to him, and might he come to see her again?

No doubt she knew what was happening to him. She kissed him and held him tightly for a moment and, before he had time to speak, laughed and took him to the door.

"Come on Friday evening; it's Franz's night off."

He walked back past the side door of the Café Royal, thinking of her husband in there. He would come home tired, paler than ever, no doubt, and he would lie beside her big, white, charming body all night, knowing that it held his child, soothed and content. There was nothing over-familiar or sordid in a marriage in which children were made and bread baked; he could see the room, it would have a low ceiling, a small window with four panes and a large white-quilted bed between the wall and the iron fireplace. We shan't need a bed that size, he thought.

He felt exhausted with the satisfaction of having made a decision, his body empty. In his exaltation he noticed nothing, and people stepped out of his way to avoid being knocked down; the prostitute who spoke to him in the Strand thought he was drunk because he shook hands with her and apologized for not being able to do anything for her. If she had not been what she so plainly was it might have been different, but he did not like these women.

CHAPTER XXV

THE next evening, at the same hour as usually he left his room in London, Andrew walked up the Mowers' path and knocked at the side door. If he went to the front he could be seen from the windows of the next house. He had only just arrived. Uncertain whether to stay with his aunt, or to ask his father for a bed, he had left his bag at the station and come straight to find Tib.

Her mother opened the door.

Mrs. Mower had nothing to thank Andrew for; she disapproved of him, and she detested his aunt. None the less, when she saw him standing there she asked him in. It was partly to avoid speaking to him on the step, but partly because for a moment as she opened the door she had seen in his face some youthful bleakness which made her say to herself, After all, he's not much older than Tib. The corners of his mouth were turned up, but it was less a smile than a nervous fixity of attention to what she was saying. When he saw Tib his face took on a sober, drawn expression. He looked at her without speaking.

"Well, Andrew, we didn't know you were at home," Mrs. Mower said, in the hard Wik voice that covers any troublesome event, from birth to death.

He turned to her at once, this time with a smile of extreme sweetness.

"I've just come," he said. "I came here first, because I had to tell you how sorry I was for vexing you before I left. I was ashamed of myself. Don't you know your house is the one place where I felt happy? . . . I hope you'll forgive me."

She forgave him at once and even felt conscience-stricken for her past disapproval and distrust. She forgot that she had been vexed with him for thinking so little about her daughter that he went off without a word, and without trying to put things right. Her face reddened with the emotions of a woman whose life has been spent in a struggle with appearances—to make one "good" dress do for weddings, funerals, and Sundays, to smile when a better-off neighbour says, "I see you're having th' painters in *at last*," to watch a disappointing husband passed over for the better posts year after year, until it is too late to look forward to anything else. She put her hand to her mouth.

"I'm sure you've been welcome," she murmured.

Smiling, Andrew put his arm round her and kissed her. "Can I speak to Tib?" he said gently. "Alone, I mean. I owe her an apology, too."

Mrs. Mower hesitated, and said weakly: "Very well, Andrew. But you'll remember she's only a girl and not ask her to promise anything. I was going out for half an hour. I'll go now—and let you stay with her."

She looked at Tib, and felt vaguely irritated with her silence. She went out of the room, and after a minute she left the house. Leaning forward, Andrew could see her closing the gate, with a blind glance to right and left at her neighbours' windows.

It was only now when he was alone with Tib that he remembered he had not written to her since he went in April: four months. She must have wondered—suffered, perhaps. He thought of her for a moment, then he thought only of himself. His need to be close to her became a torture.

"Will you forgive me and let me stay with you?" he said. An effort to control his voice made it cold and severe.

"For how long?"

It was the first time he had heard her speak. He had forgotten what a deep sound—deep, rounded, almost a double note—came from her very slender throat. A little flute makes a lot of noise, Mower used to say.

His heart was pounding and he knew that he could not look at her much longer without losing his head.

"I don't have to tell you again that I love you," he said.

She lifted her hands in the gesture which said he needn't tell her anything if that was what he felt about speaking.

"Do you need me?" she asked.

"Yes. But do you know what I am? I haven't been with a woman in these months, but it was only because I didn't know anyone. Do you know what I mean? If I oughtn't to talk like this it's no use—I can't be careful. *Can* I talk to you as if you were my own mind? Your mother——"

"Never mind my mother," Tib said calmly. "She's only an old woman. You can talk as you like to me."

"Thank God that's all over. There's this other thing—very likely I shall never make any money. The sort of writing I do— the sort I want to do—probably no one wants to read it. I couldn't give it up simply to make money for us . . . I'm talking nonsense —I'll do anything. I'll find another kind of job."

"What a pity," Tib said, "that we can't live together first— to see whether you like it."

"That's your risk too. Can you stand being poor all your life?"

Tib shook her head. "The only risks for me are——" she paused, and the colour rushed to her face. "Never mind," she said, smiling. "You're too anxious, my dear love."

He walked across to her and took her in his arms, kissing her first on the cheek, and then only on her mouth. He was trembling violently and his hands on her neck seemed to him to have swollen to twice their size. Suddenly Tib moved her head back, and said in a quiet voice:

"Would you like . . . now . . . ?"

Later they were standing near the door, which Andrew had just opened. The room had become almost dark. Some children were playing outside, running, with shrill cries, into the yellow circle cast by the street lamp, and out of it again. Their voices seemed part of the noise of Andrew's heart beating, of the confusion in his mind. He looked at Tib, and saw that she was smiling a little. "Oh—mine," he said, stammering in a dry voice. When he put his arms round her again he felt only certainty and a deep, severe joy.

CHAPTER XXVI

HANDEL looked up when his friend came into the room. Mower had knocked, and called two or three times, without getting any answer. The door was open. After a minute—no one, not even a friend of thirty-years' standing, walks into a house in Wik un-invited—he went in. As soon as he saw that Handel was hard at work, he began apologizing.

"I thought you were out—or even that you were ill," he said.

"This house is as much yours as mine," Handel said simply.

"Is it? By God! I wish it was," sighed Mower. "You've no idea——" He broke off. One can't decently complain of a life which is no worse than that of a million other men who under-took to be someone, and ended by being nothing at all. Moreover, Handel knew what he would have said.

He sat down, closing his eyes, and passed his hand over his face. His hair had become almost white, except at the ends, where it was still the dark colour of rust. His face, sallow and dis-coloured, was as lean as a bone, a clown's face without the mock gravity. He was exactly Handel's age, fifty-six, but his appearance was that of an old man, defeated to his soul. Sometimes he wondered how he was going to endure the remaining years before he should have earned his pension as a headmaster and could retire.

He felt at ease in this room, relieved, comforted. If he had not been afraid of disturbing his friend in the few hours he kept to himself for his writing he would have come here every evening.

"Do you know why I've come?" he said, opening his eyes suddenly. "My wife has sent me to find out whether you knew that your son, that Andrew wants to marry Tib at once." He paused. "She's eighteen," he said sadly. Ever since his wife spoke to him he had been torn between satisfaction in being able in this way to pay, as it were, part of his debt to Handel, and a jealousy which was almost hatred, towards Andrew Wikker him-self. His love for Tib was all that remained to him of the passions of his flesh.

"You want to know about Andrew's prospects," Handel said calmly.

Mower nodded and blinked. He could without hardship have given Tib as much as thirty or forty pounds a year himself, but it never occurred to him to offer it. One does not, in Wik, reckon to support another man's wife for him—even when his wife is one's only and beloved daughter.

"We had better have supper first and discuss this afterwards," Handel said.

He went into the dark scullery and came back with their plates and the dish of rolled herrings that a woman in Under Wik had prepared and given to him that morning. He had forgotten to eat them at dinner-time.

"Did you roll these yourself?" asked Mower laughing.

"Not these. But I can. I prepared some yesterday when I expected King to supper."

"Oh! Did he come?"

"Yes."

"Weren't you working?"

"Yes, but I like to see my friends," said Handel with a quick gesture. He had been going to add: "You don't come often enough," but he saw his friend's face and said no more. "Do you add herbs to them in your kitchen?" he asked, lifting two of the rolled herrings on to a plate for Mower. "I always do. Then there's the question of using vinegar and meat gravy for baking them, or vinegar alone. A small tablespoonful of red bramble jelly——"

"Plum is better," said Mower with pretended ease.

"You're quite wrong. If you think that, you probably roll them up from the head, which is ridiculous; you should remove the head along with the backbone, and roll them from the tail. And always use black pepper, not cayenne."

Mower drank a little of the wine his friend poured out for him. He had once said to his wife that Handel must be better off than they supposed, since he drank wine: it had not occurred to him that Handel kept a few bottles in the house only for him, because a glass or two of wine was the surest and quickest way of freeing him from the constraint he brought with him. Presently his expression lost its defiant bitterness and he smiled warmly.

"I suppose," he said, "that poor women in Wik have been rolling herrings in the same way since, well, since the Danes landed and burned the town, and they'll be doing it in another five hundred years—when you and I are not even a puff of air."

"Andrew tells me that science will change everything, oh, in less than a hundred years. There'll be no Under Wik and no poor women. Every city will have become a sort of glass ant-house, the air will be clean because we shall extract our metals from the sea—I don't know what happens to inland nations—and no one will work. So presumably no one will roll herrings."

"All that and worse may be true," said Mower gaily, "but nothing they invent will be better than a book and a sheltered garden to read it in."

"But will there be any books? I think not. Literature, unlike music or architecture, doesn't give a voice to any secret of space or time. It simply fills in the gaps in our experience of men, things, solitary acts. For one sort of appearance it substitutes another, a little more or a little less lasting. And when we can move our-selves from place to place with the ease of gulls and when we are all rich, fluent, inquisitive, probably we shall have lost patience with this clumsy trickery. We may also be able to hear one another think, and what writer will be able to make us listen to him when he can change nothing? A building, on the other hand, creates a new form which, for as long as it lasts and is useful, is complete in itself. Have you ever imagined what that means? If it is so perfectly useful that it satisfies everything one asks of it, it has something of the miraculous precision of a Bach fugue. It is infinitely more precise than thought, which is always changing into itself. A book or a picture penetrates, perhaps deeply, perhaps only the skin, of a few moments in life, one faint quiver of the wings. Music does so much more. It replaces the bewildering succession of minutes, which may be full or seemingly empty, by the body itself of time. For exactly so long as we listen to a just piece of music, and each time we listen to it, we are living in a deliberately created universe which owes nothing to chance; it is no fortuitous flight of atoms, no collision in the darkness of space. This is the only universe we can possess. No mind will ever be able to contemplate the other one, except at the cost of ceasing to live in the body it has made for itself with such inconceivable trouble."

"Who wants to do that?" Mower cried. "If one could only go on living in it *at its best* forever."

"That happens only in music," said Handel. He stopped

short, frowning, and said quietly: "You went to see Vansittart last Monday. How is he?"

Mower drew a deep breath. "You know I always said that if you hadn't been away in London when his wife died—and that other woman and the talk and money trouble and the rest of it——"

"Yes, I know," Handel said. "What could I have done?"

"With you here he wouldn't have gone out of his mind. I did my best—so did Vawn—I'll say that for him," he added with a jeering smile—"but it was no use."

"Well?"

"He seems to me better than at any time since he was taken there in March."

"Did you speak to his doctor?"

"Yes."

"What did he tell you?"

"He says," Mower said slowly, "that if anyone would take the responsibility for him he could leave the asylum at once." He looked ashamed and harassed. "When you see him next month you will find him terribly changed. He's been ill. He's thinner than ever. When he makes a gesture it's as if he had to pull his body together, all the joints and muscles, to do it. Only his eyes are the same, and when I looked at them and thought what he must be going through, in that place—and since he could leave . . . It was all I could do not to say, Give him to me, I'll be responsible. One can't expect his daughters to take him—they're married, they have other people to think of."

Handel shook his head. He seemed scarcely to be listening.

"When I think that he tore up every piece of his music—all those hundreds of loose sheets," Mower exclaimed. "Some at least of it must have been worth hearing."

"It was. He was utterly truthful, precise, accurate. It may have been musicians' music—I don't know, I'm not a musician. I can only say I was impressed by anything I heard."

"But he got no reward," Mower said with fury.

"He never pitied himself."

The two men looked at one another for a minute. Then Mower set his glass down and stood up.

"I must go," he said with an evasive gesture. "It's late."

"I'll walk part of the way with you."

The night sky still glowed with a fine bronze dust floating over the darkness and the lights were lit in the town and in scattered farms along the coast. In the street by the harbour the air was heavy with the smells of water, of mud, of tired humanity. The yards on either side were still filled with a feverish murmur of human beings turning to sleep.

Suddenly Mower remembered his daughter. His wife's promptings, dinned into his ears, and his own jealous hesitations, had vanished from his mind. He stood still.

"Here, what about Andrew?" he said loudly.

"Oh, I can let him have a hundred and twenty pounds," Handel answered at once. "I've been doing rather better lately."

Mower affected to think. "Flora and I started with that," he said in a brusque voice. "That'll be all right."

"It's settled then," said Handel gently.

"Yes, it's settled."

CHAPTER XXVII

HANDEL had come to the closing phrases of his sermon. In a moment when he paused to draw a breath he became conscious of the ill-lit hall as a thing which had a life, almost a voice, of its own. The green paint on the walls, the big windows cut into a score of small dusty panes, the gas brackets set at intervals on the walls above the heads of people sitting below them on narrow hard benches, all had been here before he was born, had entered into the thoughts of men and women and shaped them.

". . . the freedom of which the apostle spoke is a spirit. It cannot be taken away. It can be lost. Freedom consists in an absolute refusal to surrender one's mind except into the hands of God. Our Lord Jesus Christ was a free man; He had no possessions and did not want them. He had no security. He had not insured His life. He had no rents, no mortgages, no bonds. He was not afraid of being robbed. He did not feel that His own people were destined to lord it over others. If He had been a shipowner He would have made His employees sit down to table with Him. If He had been an employee He would have been a faithful worker. None of us has any duty except to live like Christ—that is what is meant by the Kingdom of Heaven and by the Second Coming."

He saw, seated on one of the cross-benches in front, Sir Thomas Money and his wife. The shipowner's heavy face had as little expression as the top-hat he was nursing on his knee. His wife, leaning against the wooden support at her back, had lifted her eyes, so that only the clear whites showed under the lids; it gave her face a curiously ruthless, meditative look. From these two faces Handel's glance moved by an involuntary impulse to the back of the hall; here two or three of the benches were crowded with fishermen in jerseys and their women in black knitted shawls drawn tightly over their bare heads.

One woman, seated directly under a gas-lamp, had raised her head and was staring towards him. Her face was thin and fierce; she was black-haired and black-eyed; in the crude light her expression seemed to be one of shrewd, insolent curiosity. Her hand, holding the shawl at her throat, had a thick wedding-ring; it gave off a dull glint.

Something in the look of her hand, big, coarse, masculine, affected Handel unpleasantly. He could see it gutting fish on the quay, the knife held pressed against the palm. With a slight effort he turned away from it.

"The grace of our Lord Jesus Christ, and the love of God, and fellowship of the Holy Ghost, be with us all evermore. Amen."

Mower and the editor, King, were waiting for him when he came out of the room which was the vestry on Sunday nights and during the rest of the week the auctioneer's private office. They usually walked home with him—by an arrangement with each other to protect him from what Mower called the "fond, babbling women," who would have kept him standing about talking for an hour if he had been alone when he walked out of the place.

The three friends climbed the Garth slowly. They stopped when they had gone half-way and leaned against the loose stone wall, to look back, to rest. It was a warm night, with a light, warm wind. The September sky showed depth on depth of transparent colour and a light mist curled round the street lamp at the foot of the Garth so that its yellow flame sent out rays like a prism into the darkness.

"You are a curious fellow," Mower said dreamily. "I think I shall have to call you a Christian Anarchist."

"Why not call me a Christian and have done?" Handel said, smiling.

"Because your notion of freedom is that of an anarchist, and not, if one can judge by the available evidence, of any ordinary Christian." He threw his head back and laughed uproariously. "I would've given a pound to be sitting where I could see Money's face when you said that about shipowners."

"I wasn't thinking of him," said Handel drily.

"Everybody else was, you can be sure. Mind, I agree with you—but I'm not a Christian. My belief is that every man has the right to be himself, and if he had the chance as well, there'd be no more cruelty or unhappiness." He lowered his voice. "If I had only been brought up to want, before everything, to be what I am. Or was."

"To be only what you are? Are you sure that's what you want?" asked Handel.

"I've always known that *you* were an anarchist," King said slyly to Mower. "It's the sort of faith, if you can call it a faith, that appeals to a man of your type."

"What is my type?" Mower asked coldly.

"I should have said your class," King murmured, "if I hadn't been afraid of annoying you. And I belong to it myself. We are both, I think, the sons of clerks, we have both educated ourselves to a point where——"

"I'm self-educated above my intelligence," Mower broke in, with another heartless noisy laugh. "I've realized it in the last year."

King waved his hand. "In any case I don't agree with you. To tell the truth——"

"Why tell it?" asked Mower.

"I don't agree with either of you," King went on with a show of impatience. "Freedom is absolutely dependent on system and on authority. I could devise a system of society in which every man did as he was told in perfect freedom. But I haven't the authority to put it into practice."

"The only flaw in your perfect society would be that you don't know the difference between one kind of human being and another," Mower said in a jeering voice.

"Socially speaking, there is no difference," King retorted. "You're a schoolmaster and I'm an editor, and so long as we each stick to our jobs we are precisely equal."

"Oh! are we?" Mower said loudly. "That's what you say, and you're a good citizen. A citizen, moreover, who has just inherited a fortune. I hear you're moving to a house on the west cliff. I congratulate you. Equal, are we? Well, I say we're not. See?"

"Our house has been too small and cramped for us for years," King said. He blushed like a schoolboy. "You know perfectly well that I shan't—because I can afford, at last, to live comfortably—not like a rich man—my fortune, as you call it, brings me in eight hundred a year—I shan't give up working for justice, reform, a decent life for the people. . . ."

"My dear fellow, no one doubts your sincerity," said Mower calmly. The devil of it is that he *is* sincere, he thought with mild irritation and amusement. With his new house, his new

eight-hundred-a-year comfort, he'll still go on making himself
unpopular in the town by his radical principles, as he calls them.
Principles! They're nothing of the sort; they're sops to his vanity,
but he doesn't know it. Even that isn't true—he's sincere, and
he's vain. Upon my soul, I don't know which is the real man,
if either are.

"Now that I have a public ten times larger than it was when
I took over the paper," King said, as though following a train of
thought, "I can begin to do something. I know I'm not a brilliant
writer. But the fact that I needn't depend on the paper any
longer for my living means that I can be outspoken. You're going
to see things!" He gave a nervous, excited laugh. "One must
be sensible, of course. I shouldn't like to disgust my public, to
become a laughing-stock," he murmured. He was staring into
the darkness, overcome by emotion.

Mower could see that his hands were trembling as he held
them out wide open in front of him. He had been about to
growl:

"Your public! Hey, what do you think you are—an actor?"
He swallowed the words and his involuntary contempt with
them. There was something in the man beside him to be pitied.
His abysmal vanity and his nervousness; the yawning cavity
between his mind and his pretensions—such people become pitiful
when one is not disgusted by them. I do believe he sees himself
as the great radical editor, Mower thought, grinning. And, by
God! yes, he's already begun to dress the part. He noticed for
the first time that King was wearing a black soft tie, and with it
a hat he must have imported from London; no such wide-brimmed,
rakish article could conceivably have been bought in the town.
He felt irritated again.

"Thank God," he said in biting tones, "your public isn't large
enough to matter. Otherwise we might find ourselves trapped,
with our backs broken, inside your precious system. Freedom!
You, you know as much about it as an old maid."

"That will do, John," Handel said sternly and tenderly. He
paused and went on in a different voice: "Every man believes that
he is free if he is not forbidden to do certain things, and if he has
money. But no one is free who is afraid. It doesn't matter
whether one is afraid of death, or afraid that a child or a lover
will die. Die—so that one never sees them again. Or afraid of
failing, or of not earning enough money. Or of being tortured.

Or laughed at. Men who are brave for themselves are afraid for someone at their side. So you see—none of us is free, because none of us can bear life unless he feels secure."

"But you—you're not afraid of anything," King said. He added timidly: "That's why I admire you." It was the darkness which gave him courage to say it. There was a minute during which he felt very uncomfortable, then Handel said drily:

"Oh, yes, I am not different from other men."

After a moment Mower said: "If one could take away from men the mean fear of poverty—how much braver most of them would be."

"It will come," said King.

"Yes, I believe that," Handel said. "A wave is forming, out there in the darkness, which will throw us beyond that."

The dark North Sea stretched before their eyes, a great bowl of black water. They glanced at it. As they began to walk again towards the top of the Garth, Mower thought of a man standing on this same stony piece of ground, looking out at the sea, and before he had reached his hovel down there by the harbour the long black-keeled ships were running against the land, and women—his woman among them—were stumbling with their children towards the hills, to die of cold or hunger, those who escaped the knives of the Danes. He felt in his body the other man's rage, hating and dying in the same moment.

"Do you never have bad dreams now?" he asked Handel.

"No," Handel said, as though he were ashamed and surprised. "I sleep well."

"Anything one dreams is in the past," King said.

"Why not the future?" said Mower offensively.

"I used to think I was feeling my way forward," Handel said. "I am still certain that some change, some extraordinary change, is coming over the world, but where I used to think it was evil I'm now perfectly content. I shan't see it; I shan't suffer and I shan't rejoice. Those after me will suffer or rejoice, without my knowing. I don't want to live too long, but I should like to live, say, another thirty years, to know what's going to happen to Andrew and his wife and their children."

"You could easily live that long," laughed Mower. "You'd be—what?—in 1933? Eighty-six. Good God, Wik is full of people over ninety."

They had reached his house, and King and Mower turned to

go back. They never went in with him on Sunday night. He had walked slowly and Mower thought he was tired.

Just as they were going a woman came in at the gate and hurried towards them, moving clumsily, as though she were very awkward or as though her legs were bent. Handel had lighted the lamp inside the kitchen and a little light from it fell on her face. She was bundled into her clothes like a countrywoman: she spoke like one. She might have been any age. Mower noticed these things about her while he stood listening.

She was asking Handel breathlessly to come and see her son. "He used to come to your class on Tuesday night," she repeated, as if this were the reason. "Now he can't come," she said. Her voice went away from her. "Now he can't come. . . ."

"My good woman, won't the morning do?" King said in his editorial voice.

The woman looked at him, and looked back towards Handel, pulling at her mouth with her hand.

"Of course I'll come," Handel said, sighing. "Where is it?"

"It's th' other side of Upsal Wood," she said with sudden energy.

Handel went inside to get his overcoat. Mower asked:

"How far is it you want him to go then?"

"It's five miles," she said, looking at him with a mixture of timidity and defiance.

They walked as far as the bottom of the Garth together, Handel and the woman in front. He was questioning her about her son, but the other two did not hear her answers. She seemed afraid to speak above a whisper, and kept glancing about her, as though she thought someone might be watching her from the wall. Her shoulders, bent forward, were as full of suspicion as her sharp, rapidly moving eyes.

It was not until she and Handel had walked two miles beyond Wik, and when she felt they were alone, that she began to talk, and to praise her son. He was a fine lad, she said: he was that sharp, too; when he went to school he learned quicker than bairns twice his age. At that time the doctor had said to get him out of their cottage, because it was damp where it was, fast, as you might say, between the stream and the rigg—but where else could they have gone with him? Nowhere. There was nowhere, if you left th' cottage you left th' job and then—— Nor he didn't want to leave off learning either, but what could you do? He worked

hard, helping his father, and th' master paid him a boy's wage.
"And we were glad of it," the mother said, with a sound almost
like a laugh. "When he heard of your class he was all for going.
But you know," she said, looking at him with her hard, sharp,
unchanging eyes, "it was too far at night. Five miles there and
five back. But he would go." He used to talk to two other
men in th' village about it th' next day. Th' master didn't like
it, it would spoil them for work, he said, and after that they used
to meet on the quiet; it was then he got cold.

Handel had been trying to remember her son among the score
of boys and older men he had been teaching for eight or nine
months. He saw him suddenly, a thin, energetic, dark-skinned
young man, with a long smooth face and sharp eyes. He slipped
in and out of the room like an animal diving out of sight through
leaves: there was something hard, yet alive and supple about
him.

The cottage lay between two steeply sloping fields, squeezed
between them, with a stream running against the wall. The path
to it led downwards through the field from the road. The young
man's father was standing at the side of the road with a lamp
that looked like an old carriage-lamp: a stump of candle was
burning in it behind the thick glass. He held it up in the darkness, and Handel saw that his hand was shaking.

His wife spoke to him sharply. "Whatever have you come out
here for?" she said. "We could ha' found the road without you
coming, and leaving th' lad in alone."

The father did not answer. He lowered the lamp so that its
light fell on the gate and the path leading from it across the wet
grass. "You must mind not to slip," he said in a low voice to
Handel. "It's a bit mucky." He kept stopping so that Handel
could see a wet place in the path in time to avoid stepping in it.

When he opened the door of the cottage they stepped straight
into the kitchen. It was a small room, with a stone-tiled floor.
The first thing Handel noticed was the handful of smoky fire in
the fireplace, and then the bed between it and the staircase. The
young man was lying in the bed, his arm hanging, knuckles touching
the floor. He did not look up when they came in.

His mother went over to him, her lips pursed into a smile.
When she bent over him it died, leaving her mouth open and
contorted, her eyes gone in her face. She passed the back of her
hand across her mouth, whimpering. Handel went across to her.

There the young man was, with the scarlet thread of his life hanging from his lips: he was dead.

After a few minutes the woman began to move about the room, fetching out a loaf and a little cheese and milk. It was for Handel, and he let her get it ready, although he did not want it. He thought it would soothe her.

"This is his bread I'm giving you," she said. "Last Friday when he was too weak to go out he helped me to set it. He marked this loaf, look, with the cross. 'That's mine, our mother,' he said. It was a joke. 'That's mine: see,' he said, 'I've marked it.'"

Without turning round, the father said to Handel:

"He worked hard; he worked as hard as a man."

"He helped with th' bread when he was a little boy," said his mother. "He used to carry th' tins for me, and I let him mark one of th' loaves for himself. That's what he was doing on Friday." She cut a slice and gave it to Handel. "Take it," she said.

After they had eaten, he helped her to wash the young man, her son. His body was so thin that she could lift him and turn him over almost as easily as when he was born, but it was a man's body, and the feet and hands were those of a man.

It was beginning to be true daylight when Handel left the cottage. The woman went with him to the door and threw a little water away from a chipped bowl on to the ground. A fire of leaves and wet wood and rubbish was smoking weakly at the edge of the stream, started up by the light rain; a thin, searching smell came from it. Now in the growing light Handel could see the poverty of the place where the young man had lived his twenty years, the stones of the walls blackened with trickling moisture, the poor clayey earth, a few yards fenced from the field.

"Is that all you have?" he asked.

"As much as goes with th' cottage," she said, looking at it. "Th' fields aren't ours, of course."

"No one ought to live down here," said Handel. The fields pressed against it on both sides; the water from the earth must have soaked into the house for years. "Who employs your husband?"

The woman gave him a sly, half-embarrassed look. "I thought you'd know," she murmured. "It's Mr. Wikker. Ezekiel Wikker."

"Ah, my brother," Handel said.

He looked once more at the house, and moved away, walking

slowly and heavily; he was stiff with fatigue and another weariness. As he went he saw the young man for a moment, standing at one side of the path. Handel looked at him, forming without realizing it the one word: "Forgive." During the instant he remained the young man looked back sharply, with love, with deep anger and gentleness.

The same day Handel went to see Thomas Money. A few days before, he had had a visit from the union secretary. Lamb was indignant and baffled, ashamed that he had not been able to do anything himself, and angry with the weak sour anger of an inferior. For weeks he had been trying to see the shipowner, but Money put him off with excuses which were so openly lies that they were insulting. In the meantime discontent in the yards became sharper and Lamb feared what to him was the worst trouble—a strike which the union would refuse to take up. "If it comes to that I'm done for," he said bitterly.

It was easy for Handel to see Money, but he felt that he was acting as errand boy and this forced him to speak in an overbearing way. He stood in front of the fire in Money's room and told him with bland arrogance that he was one of the worst types of employer and ought to be punished as much as any agitator. Money stared at him in astonishment, at his dirty shabby clothes—Handel had hitherto put on his one tidy suit when he came to see him—and sarcastic smile.

He ought to have felt angry, but in fact he felt only a passionate curiosity about the motives which moved a man like Handel to mix himself with scum, discontented workmen, and the rest of it.

"I'll be damned if I understand you," he burst out. "Anyone would think I wanted, yes, wanted to employ these men. If I could find a machine to build ships for me, and sail them, I'd undertake never to employ a man again. They get married, drink, break their legs, and God knows what, and I'm expected to pay them wages for doing it. They ought to be on their knees to me begging me to forget they're made of flesh and rags instead of boasting about it. I'd a damn sight sooner employ steel."

"And you'd have to employ men to make the steel for you," Handel said with contempt.

"The fewer of the brutes the better," laughed Money. He had not lost his good temper. "You don't expect me to treat them as my equals. If they were, they'd be sitting in this room. They're either animals or faulty machines, whichever end of them you're looking at. The trouble starts when someone puts an idea into their thick heads. They ought to be kept half-starved—hungry men don't make trouble. A little simple fact which is often overlooked."

Handel's face had become like a stone with his contempt and anger.

"You're talking to amuse yourself," he said, icily. "I happen to be in earnest about these men. I'm not threatening you, I'm only saying that if it comes to a strike in your yards I shall try to show you up. You don't know whether the men's grievances are genuine, you won't see Lamb—how do you expect to have the support of decent people for your attitude?"

"I didn't ask for support," Money drawled. He let his big head sink forward on his chest for a minute. He was wondering why he still liked the man in front of him. An ironical gleam came into his eyes. He had long since decided that he would compromise with the men: he would give them half the rise they were asking, which he knew from his ears in the yard was all they expected. Times were good with him at the moment; he could afford it. Only dislike of Lamb had kept him from giving way before, and it amused him to seem to do for Handel what he had refused to the men's leader. He looked up with a sharp smile.

"Very well," he said, trying to look like a clown. "I'll do as you advise. I'll meet the men half-way. You can tell Lamb. I'll even see him if you insist."

This unexpected victory gave Handel a start almost of annoyance. In the same moment he thought of the young Jewish agitator he had sheltered for a night. What he was not able to do by violence I have done in half an hour, he thought, by reasoning. His momentary annoyance vanished, but without softening the contempt he had felt for Money when the other was speaking about his workmen as animals. He believed Money was showing off, and despised him for it.

He had just summoned up all his urbanity to thank him, when the door opened and Lady Money came into the room. Although it was the middle of the morning, she was wearing a loose fur-trimmed wrap more suitable to her bedroom than her husband's study. It had wide sleeves which fell back, showing her arm, thin, with a blue vein running from the inside of her elbow towards the shoulder. She walked across the room with her long rapid stride, and smiled at Handel.

"I didn't know you had anyone here," she said to her husband. He looked at her drily, without answering. She sat down, drew the wrap closer over her shoulders, and relaxed, into her chair. Crossing her feet in soft slippers, she looked from one to the other of the two men with an inviting smile. "What is the matter with you?" she demanded. "Am I really in the way?"

"We were discussing a business matter," Money said in a curt voice.

"But it's settled now," she laughed. "I'm sure of that. Mr. Wikker had begun to go away. Now he can stay a minute longer and be the judge in a really serious business. But first let me tell you that the fur coat I put away in the camphor chest you gave me has been spoiled by moths. We have just taken it out to look at it. I shall need a new sable cape and muff."

"And the serious business?" asked her husband ironically.

She made an extraordinary grimace. "Listen," she said to Handel, looking at him between her eyelashes, "two months ago my thoughtful husband allowed his second cousin, a sour, bad-tempered old woman, to establish herself here, apparently for life. Since when she has not only made my life a burden to me, but the servants are threatening to leave because she spies on and inter-feres with them. It seems she was kind to Thomas when he was a boy—and is that, I ask you, a sufficient reason for keeping her here to make trouble?"

"If you send her packing she has nowhere to go," said Money frowning. "You could keep the servants quiet if you chose."

"But why not take a room for her somewhere else?"

"Because I offered her a home," her husband said violently. "This is my house and I say who is to live in it." He made a great effort to control himself. "I have promised our friend," he said, staring at her with a malignant expression, "to settle the trouble in the yards. I hope you're satisfied as well—since, for heaven knows what reason, you've been taking an interest in it lately."

"You ought to have done it long ago," Sarah murmured, her two hands at her white long throat. She glanced at Handel, expecting a look if not words of praise for her virtuous interest in underpaid workmen—but he took it for granted. She blushed and dropped her head.

At this moment Money was called into the next room by his

secretary, and Handel prepared to leave. Sarah stood up. Resting her hand on his arm, she said in a pleading voice:

"You agreed to help me. I have been trying by myself to do something—and I've failed."

"To do what?" Handel asked.

"To change myself—to be less restless, futile."

The shadow of impatience crossing Handel's face was not noticeable in his voice: he said calmly:

"I don't think I can help you. You're a clever woman; you could do more than you do, if you chose to do it."

Sarah took her hand from his arm and looked at him with a slyly mocking smile. "You won't take responsibility? Well, will you give me a discipline—something I can practise?"

"Yes, I can do that," he said ironically. "But I'll give you a secret one. I suggest you go out of your way to be kind to this tiresome old woman in your house."

"Is that all?" she said, biting her lip.

"What sort of a discipline did you expect? I daresay you'll find it hard enough. But there's one other thing. Avoid, like a plague, thinking of yourself and your sins and needs——"

When he left the house he walked a short distance to the Piece. The schools had not yet started, and bare-footed children were everywhere in the streets, on the wharves, the shore; at high tide the waves drove them to the foot of the cliff, and then to scramble up the dry red clay of the face to the Piece itself. The ruddy-faced little boys lumbered about in jerseys and cut-down breeches, women of nine and ten shrilly admonished a crew of infants and carried a bundle of dirty cloths that whimpered when they forgot it for a minute, the young vixens of six bullied their brothers and stood about with hands on their hips to look as like their mothers as possible. It was a warm close day, but the air here was cool.

As Handel looked at them he thought he had never seen so many heads of red or yellow curls or such ruddy limbs. They seemed to him taller and better-looking than other children. They had the strong piercing voices of sea-birds and ran and leaped like young and thoughtless animals. How many generations of them, he thought, issuing from the hand of God, have played here on this piece of ground, which belongs to them so firmly that one can think it and them immortal, as though the grass came up and the sea fountained with light only for them.

One of the immortals ran past him, screeching "Awa, awa" to his fellows. Handel listened for a moment, with a curious intensity of happiness, then went home.

Early the next morning he took the train to the town where Vansittart had been sent when he was pronounced insane. He was in a private asylum, paid for at first by his friends, during the last month by his youngest daughter. After a few days he realized where he was, and his anguish was unspeakable. It was lessened in time by the tact and gentleness of the doctor in charge. Dr. John Faber was a man of fifty-five, partly Jewish, suffering from a slight stammer which made him speak in as few words as possible. A beard hid his long, womanish, compassionate mouth.

He rose when Handel was shown into his room and shook hands in silence, looking at him attentively. Then he seemed to relax, and said:

"Your friend is prepared for you, Mr. Wikker."

"I can take him home?"

"You are quite sure you know what you are doing?"

"You have read my letters," Handel said quietly. "I have told you he will live with me alone. I have no servants. The house is quiet, and it's familiar to him. He has often been in it."

"Yes, I understand," Faber said.

"Have you anything to tell me about him? Do you want to give me instructions?"

Faber shook his head. "You will not make any mistakes," he said slowly, as if choosing his words. "He is good, patient; his mind is clear—except very rarely, as I told you in my letter, when he becomes excited. He could do himself harm then—but you will know beforehand, and you will give him a s-sedative I shall give you. He'll sleep it off." He paused. "And since you're not afraid——"

"There's no other way of calming him?"

"Yes. The last time it happened—a month since—I was able to calm him by talking. That's better. It will help his cure. I should warn you that he has the—the astonishing alertness of a child in reading motives. If I were impatient he would know at once, however gently I spoke to him."

In another room Vansittart was waiting, dressed for the journey.

He sat on the edge of his chair, clasping and unclasping his hands. When Handel and the doctor came in, he jumped up and stood looking eagerly and nervously from one to the other. He was, as Mower had said, extraordinarily thin and bent. His arms hung limp, and his features looked as though they had been worn down by a file working on them. His body was lit by his eyes, which were bright and very clear, almost sparkling.

"You're ready to leave us," said Faber, gently.

Vansittart looked anxiously at Handel. "Yes; I'm ready," he said in a timid voice.

"Then we'll start," Handel said.

In the train, Vansittart asked: "Where are we going?"

"Home, of course," Handel answered. "We're going to my house."

"Are you sure you want me?"

Handel felt himself almost crushed by the pity he felt for his friend.

"Certainly I want you," he exclaimed. "I've lived alone long enough. There'll be the two of us now in the house."

When they reached Wik and were driving away from the station in a broken-down cab, he tried to distract Vansittart's attention from the too-familiar streets by speaking to him about his music. But Vansittart's face showed such distress that he stopped at once.

He had asked a woman to come in and light the fires before they arrived, so that not only a fire but a lamp was burning in the house when they went in. The woman had stayed, to see whether she was needed and to have a glimpse of "the softie." Handel sent her away. Turning to Vansittart, he said cheerfully:

"I've given you the room at the other side of the passage, the one I used as a study. It's small, but you'll have it to yourself when you want to be alone, where this room has to be dining-room, living-room and kitchen, all in one."

"Where will you work?" asked Vansittart in a subdued voice.

"Upstairs—in my bedroom."

He could not help a sigh after he had closed the door of the little room on Vansittart. It had not been easy to find a place upstairs for all the books, papers, and instruments he kept scattered about the other room, and as he moved about preparing a meal for the two of them he struggled with a feeling of boredom and irritation. He had subdued it when Vansittart came out of his room, and he was able to speak to him calmly and gaily. Vansittart watched him silently for a moment.

"You didn't want me here," he said calmly.

Handel was not in the least put out. He seemed to reflect for a moment before he said:

"It's quite true that I'm used to living alone, considering no one but myself, eating and sleeping when I felt like it, and dropping books, papers, and boots all over the house." He laughed quietly. "You wouldn't believe the junk I found in your room when I was clearing it out for you. Now you're here I shall have to lead a reasonable life—at least, so far as meals and boots are concerned. It's a very good thing."

"I'm glad you feel like that," Vansittart said, smiling. He added dreamily: "I shouldn't like to be the stone of offence—you know what I mean—to break down your pride."

"I? Proud?" Handel said testily. "Why do you think that?"

"Oh, I don't think it, I feel it," Vansittart answered. He watched Handel lifting a pan from the fire. "You must let me do that," he said eagerly. "I used to help—in the old days."

CHAPTER XXVIII

WILLIAM WELLHEM, dying, lay in one of the smallest of the spare bedrooms of Soureby Bog Hall. He watched the September sunlight creep along the wall at the end of his bed. All round him, in the narrow low room, was a silence which seemed to come into the house from without, from the marsh. He had the feeling that this silence spread across the marsh, across the North Sea, to the end of the world, and he lay on the edge of it as though he were lying on the edge of his life: the two were in some inexplicable way the same. The only sounds he heard were bird-notes; these, too, seemed to him to have been going on all his life, and in other lives, in countries he had never seen. It no longer seemed strange to him that these countries existed.

Lying here, his pale eyes turned to the wall, he was filled as with happiness by his sense of the mystery surrounding him. Some impulse stirred in him, blindly and feebly, as though it had just been born. Moving in the helpless cocoon of his body under the clothes, it stretched itself delicately, reaching towards an unseizable good.

The door of the room opened and his daughter Lily came in and walked slowly over to the bed. William closed his eyes until he realized by her silence that whoever had come in was not his wife; then he opened them and looked up timidly.

Lily was settling herself in a small chair placed close to the bed where she could see him. She had come to carry out the task known as "sitting with your poor father"; she came two or three times a day and sat with her hands folded in her lap; she never spoke and she did not expect the man in the bed to speak. When, after a moment, he began to talk in a monotonous voice she gave a slight start, but composed herself at once.

He was talking, she realized, when she began to distinguish a few words in the trickle of unintelligible sound, about the weather. You could really think that all these years he had been noticing nothing else.

". . . little rain but good sunshine . . . showers of misty

rain from the sea . . . brambles as large as grapes . . . it's
not cold and the air is pure and sweet. The sun shines in
long intervals . . . the temperature fifty-four degrees in the
shade. . . ."

She listened to him in her usual silence. Her quite colourless
face and pale eyes conveyed no expression: when he stopped talking and closed his eyes again she leaned forward a little and stared
at his face, the skin shiny and puckered, the thin white beard.
He is like a wizened foolish old goat, she thought. He seemed to
have fallen asleep and she left him.

In the afternoon Semiramis Jordan came to the house.

She walked in at the back door, which was ajar, and finding no
one downstairs, not even Horn, she began a thorough search of the
sitting-room. She emptied every drawer, turning the contents
over and over and tumbling them back anyhow with no attempt
to conceal the traces of her work. There was a china cabinet, in
the lower half of which Ann kept various precious articles of food,
a cake, a little cream in a jug, a dish of custard. Semiramis broke
a piece off the cake, cramming it into her mouth, and thrust her
rather dirty fingers into the custard and licked them. She
was looking under the sofa cushions when she heard a sound
behind her and turned her head to find Lily watching her with
a sarcastic smile.

Semiramis was not abashed. "I left a good handkerchief
in your house on Monday," she said boldly; "I'm looking
for it."

"You'll not find it under those cushions," said Lily
drily. "Mother says will you come to her room? She's lying
down."

"What's the matter with her?" demanded Semiramis. "Is
she poorly, or dwammish or summat?"

"No," Lily said; "she's resting. She's not tired, but Mr.
Wellhem died this morning and the widow usually rests a little
after it."

Semiramis stood still with her hand on the banister. "Mr.
Wellhem!" she said, stupefied. "You mean your father."

"Yes—isn't he Mr. Wellhem?" said Lily with an air of innocence.

Ann was lying down on the bed, fully dressed except for her
wig. She snatched it up when her sister came in and clapped it
on her head with energy and dexterity.

"Well, William's gone," she said in a complaining voice. "He's cost me five pounds this week. But I told him before he went. I said to him this morning, You've cost me five pounds this week, *so far*. Th' worst of it is I wasted a chicken on him yesterday. If I'd known he was going to die so soon I'd never have gi'n it to him."

"You ha' plenty of chickens," said Semiramis.

"Well, you needn't think *you'll* get one of them when you're ill——" She broke off suddenly to listen. "Is Ezekiel down there?" she asked.

"He wasn't when I came through t'kitchens."

Ann leaned back on her pillows. "You'll let me ha' Skelton to help with th' tea, sister, won't you? And I suppose you bowt black kid gloves for th' mourners when you lost Merry—though it's a fact I didn't get a pair gi'n to me. It's a queer notion to give away good pairs o' gloves to strangers and grudge them to your own flesh and blood. If you've any on 'em left over I'd be glad o' them for William's relations. They'll troop to th' funeral and rap and ree all they can lay their hands on—but they needn't think I s'll run to a flesh funeral. He's not worth it. They shan't have much—I'll see to that."

"I hear someone downstairs now," Lily said with her uncomfortable smile.

Ann started up. "It's Ezekiel, I'll be bound! He's been here at all shoorts and owers. He's got among the food—I won't have it—he shan't have a bite."

She got off the bed and hurried out of the room. Ezekiel was standing in the hall, looking about him with an air of vigorous cunning like a fox. He had kept his hat on.

"Take your hat off in th' house," Ann shouted. "Don't you know William's gone? And after I gave him a chicken for his dinner yesterday." She lowered her voice as she came closer to him. "You'll give me three or four hams for t' funeral, won't you?" she wheedled him. "I'm bound to have all them Wellhems and Piersons flocking to it to see what they can dredge up. You ha' a good few hams in your loft; you won't miss three or four."

Ezekiel thrust his lips forward—it was the gesture he had made as a little boy when he tried to haggle with his sisters for a bigger share of the meal they were eating alone.

"But you shan't flatch them out o' me, you must give me something," he said slowly, winking at her. "I could do with a glass o' some sort—what about yon glass in the bedroom over the front door? You let me have that and I'll bring you four, no, three splendid hams."

"It's only a small glass and it's spotted with damp," Lily said. She had come downstairs noiselessly and was standing listening.

"Mind your own business," her mother said angrily. She was reluctant to give away anything, but the glass was really worthless. She told Ezekiel he could take it, and hurried along to the kitchens to see whether he had taken anything there.

Ezekiel opened the door of the bedroom where William was lying, alone now. This room was—if you liked to put it that way —over the front door, in the sense that it was on the first floor at the front of the house, and it, too, contained a mirror. This one had belonged to their father: at his death Ezekiel was revolted to learn that the furniture was to be divided between Ann and Semiramis, leaving him only the land and the house. Handel was left a sum of money, and little as Ezekiel relished giving it to him from the estate he would have paid twice as much to keep in his own hands a big handsome cheval-glass which, for some reason or other, had seemed to him since he was a child the most magnificent thing in the house. When their father died, and it was covered with a dust-sheet in the room, he could not resist lifting a corner of the sheet to make certain that the glass was still there when it could no longer reflect the figure of the tyrannical old man who had got children on a wife he never allowed to eat at the table with him or sit down when he was speaking.

Ann had not taken the trouble to cover it—why imagine that William would come back? It reflected nothing of him except his long feet, poked up under the quilt, and Ezekiel moved it slightly so that not even these came between him and his own reflection while he preened himself in front of it, smiling and mouthing silently in ecstasy. He glanced once at William, to whom death had not given any dignity; he looked as nothing as ever.

After a minute, Ezekiel crept from the room and listened over the banisters to his sisters talking at each other. They were at the back of the house. He went into the room, lifted the heavy glass, and began to carry it downstairs. Sweat was running from him when he opened the front door.

Now he had only to reach his horse and trap. He had left it in the lane at the side. He held the mirror in front of him, peering round it to see where he was walking; at last he shut the door of the walled garden behind him and set the mirror down in the lane to get his breath before hoisting it on to the floor of the trap.

The sun had gone in; the air was extraordinarily close and heavy. A wave of heat seemed to roll towards him from the marsh. He could feel his heart pounding; his head throbbed and his flesh stuck to his clothes. As he climbed into the trap he thought, It's going to rain or thunder. He drove as quickly as he dared in fear of shaking the mirror; before he reached the road the sun came out again with a rush, and he had to avoid looking at the glass which flung up from one corner an intolerably sharp blade of light.

It was going on for five o'clock when he reached Upgang House. He carried the glass up to his room and came out again, locking the door and putting the key in his pocket. He was now thoroughly restless and bad-tempered. As he crossed the landing he heard the murmur of voices in his daughter's room. He stopped to listen at the door. With a pang of fury he realized that she was giving someone tea in there. He opened the door at once and marched in.

There were three women in the room beside his daughter. All four started up when he came in and stood looking at him with surprise and embarrassment.

He felt himself growing hot again, and his head seemed to swell with the blood which rushed into it. He could scarcely control himself when he looked at their silly women's faces; his hand itched to set its mark on them, as he marked the flour to keep Soal from stealing it. He looked at the table. *My* food, he thought. Invited here to stuff themselves with *my* food.

"How charming you all look," he said. "Charming, charming. What a pity you can't stay a minute longer. Nothing would please me better than to see you enjoying *my* food—have you had enough?—are you crammed to bursting your seams with it?" He seized a plate from the table and held it out to the woman nearest him. "Help yourself. What, you won't have any more? I see what's wrong—it's not fine enough for you." He turned to his daughter and said grinning: "Tell me why you offered your friends such wretched food? Why *only* thick good cream, honey, butter cakes? It's disgraceful! Wouldn't you like to give them the silver off the table to make up?"

He lifted the heavy silver teapot and bowed with it before the four women. "One of you take it," he said.

"Father!" Bessie said. Her face was crimson, and his voice made her feel sick and weak. Her guests hurried towards the door. Ezekiel held it open for them, smiling effusively, and when the last had gone he turned to her and said: "I've a good mind to tie you up, my girl." She was crying with mortification and bitterness and did not answer.

He watched her for a minute with a curious expression on his face, neither wholly cruel nor wholly inquisitive. Then, sighing, he went away. He went downstairs and out of the house. He felt a little better.

He had a hot walk to the fields, the air stifling and the sun, although it was wheeling down, merciless. The sky seemed to be throbbing with heat. There were no clouds, the distance was clear and blue, but Ezekiel could feel the thunder. It made him miserable; his head ached and felt empty, his tongue was dry at the roots. The ground gave off a curious smell which he had recognized all his life as the smell of thunder—it was dry and yeasty, as if some change were taking place in the earth.

He told his men that they must finish carrying the barley before they knocked off, and he drove them at it furiously until nine. Seeing his enemy and neighbour, Scoresby, watching him, he shouted: "You'd better keep at it and clear yon field before it rains."

"Rain?" drawled Scoresby, squinting up at the brazen sky. "That's not going to come down for a week yet."

"Don't say I didn't tell you," Ezekiel shouted back. He was holding his head and his eyes were bloodshot. The men grinned at each other behind his back. "Up he comes, drunk and roaring of judgment," the foreman said.

He went back to the house with the last load. As he came into the hall from the kitchen passage he heard Ann gabbling excitedly in the sitting-room. She darted out, saying:

"Here comes t'thief," and shook her fist at him. "I've come for that chevvel-glass you stole from me," she said.

He pretended not to understand her. "A glass? Stole from

you? . . . Who has been stealing? Why don't you tell the police? And you a newly-made widow. Why, it's shameful!"

"You'll give it back to me, Ezekiel, or I'll county court you, I'll skin you . . . you shan't get round me with your sins. . . ."

He forgot his headache in his enjoyment of her helpless fury. He knew she had such a horror of lawyers that she would never go to the length of calling one in. "You," he said, reproachfully, "an old woman with one foot in the grave, to be making so much fuss about a trifle."

The hall was quite dark. Bessie came out of the room behind them and lit one candle on the swinging brass chandelier over their heads; shadows swooped round it, and the faces of both, Ann and Ezekiel, were livid and distorted with energy in the fitful light. Ezekiel was ruddy and Ann thin and without a trace of colour, but the old man's arched nose and rapacious mouth and hands were reflected in his sister's. Bessie looked at them with a sense of despair and bitterness. They'll live for ever, she thought, and her heart sank as though she were going to be imprisoned in this hell, with its one feeble light under a canopy of darkness, for the rest of her life.

Ezekiel had begun to soothe and flatter his sister. When that had no effect he told her that he was going to stand for the District Council at the coming election. He would be returned in the Upsal ward unopposed: more than three-quarters of the voters in this ward were his tenants, and since he had put it about as a secret that he would lower rents when he got in, the local butcher, who as a liberal had been going to oppose him, had withdrawn already. He promised Ann "faithfully" (as when they were children) that he would persuade the Council to buy a worthless piece of property she had in Wik: it was a rat-infested warehouse near the harbour, and the site would do as well as another for the new school. There were ways and means. Why, one councillor would have a brother-in-law tendering for the building of the school, and another would need something else, some family business; it was give and take all round (you may say)—"A happy band of brothers," he exclaimed, looking at her slyly. Raising his voice, he sang:

> "Oh happy band of pilgrims,
> Look upward to the skies;
> Where such a slight endeavour
> Shall win so rich a prize."

"If you can't do your own sister a good turn, what's the use of going on the Council?" Ann exclaimed. She rolled her eyes up and put her head on one side. "It's my chevvel-glass you've stolen," she said softly, "but if you can—mark you, if you can—get them sheds off my hands I'll overlook it."

When she had gone Ezekiel went into the dining-room, and began to drink burgundy to relieve his headache. He now felt that a heavy ball was hanging between his eyes, dragging at them whenever he moved his head. When he was almost stupefied by the wine he had drunk he fell asleep with his head in his arms. At once he was a child in this room; he had on a red dress and petticoats and he was crouching under the table: there were tears on his cheeks—he was afraid, and still weeping because he had been beaten. Why had he been beaten? It was something he had said that annoyed his father—he felt the rough surface of the carpet on his bottom, which was bare and still sore.

He woke up with a start. Lifting his head, he saw that the blackness of the window was splintered with rain; it flew past in the yellow light from the lamp on the table between the bottles and his empty glass. His headache had gone. He stood up and went into the kitchen where Soal was squatting in front of the fire laboriously matching rags.

"It's raining, woman, raining," he shouted.

"Yi, I hear," she said drily.

In his excitement he ran out into the yard; pulling off his clothes, he leaped about like a savage in the icy rain until he was exhausted. He was still drunk when he came in, and the old woman helped him up to his room and stood looking at him for a time with an expression between jealousy and contempt. When she saw that he was soundly asleep she took the lamp and the matches away, for fear that if he woke up he would set the house on fire.

When her aunt left the house Bessie went slowly upstairs to her room. She lit the lamp and looked round it with a bitter smile. The tea-things were still on the table she had placed near the window—she had felt too humiliated to look at them or touch them after her father went. It was the first time for a year she had ventured to ask anyone to the house, and it had taken her and the old woman a fortnight to save up the butter, eggs, and sugar for the cakes. She had brought in chairs from downstairs and placed them over the worst places in the carpet, and had filled jugs and vases with marguerites to give the big ugly room gaiety. It was wasted, she thought; I shall be the laughing-stock of the town.

Setting the lamp down on the dressing-table, she avoided looking at her face in the glass. The sight could not give her pleasure.

The window was open. She went over to it to pull the blind down. Her weariness—of spirit rather than body—was so great that instead of drawing the blind she seated herself listlessly on the narrow seat and, resting both hands on the sill, leaned her head and shoulders out of the window. The night was no cooler outside than in the room. Mingled scents of roses and of dry dusty earth came up to her, with a puff of warm air. She thought, It will be autumn, then winter, and then another year of my life will be over with nothing happening. She meant, Without any man falling in love with me and taking me away from here.

When her eyes were accustomed to the darkness she could see as far as the hedge at the farther side of the road. A gate in it led into the rick-yard, and a man was leaning on this gate. If he had moved she would have seen him earlier, but he was standing still, apparently looking up at her. His face was only a lightish blur, but she knew him at once. It was Charles Mower.

For a moment she did not move. Her heart had jumped in a way that made her dizzy and sick. Then, almost calmly, she moved away from the window, turned the lamp out, and stood in the darkness with her hands pressed to her throat.

Charles had moved during these few moments. He sauntered into the middle of the road and looked about him as though he were wondering what to do.

The fear that he would go away roused her to act at once. She opened the door of her room quickly and stealthily and went downstairs. Listening at the dining-room door she could not hear a sound. Now she was so terrified that Charles would have gone that she risked everything. She unbolted the front door, ran across the lawn to the door in the wall between garden and road, opened it as noiselessly as she could and stepped out, almost into Charles's arms.

Her heart was beating so that she was out of breath. She listened without understanding them to the young man's ingenious reasons for being here at ten o'clock. The truth was that he had been dining at a house in the village and he thought it would do him good to walk home—he was passing Upgang House when she lit her lamp.

"Have you been here long?" she asked him in a nervous whisper.

"An hour," he said.

Bessie trembled with joy. "But you didn't know my room was on this side of the house. You might have waited for nothing."

As she was speaking she felt a drop of rain on her cheek, and brushed it off. No, it can't rain now, she thought desperately, with the feeling that he would turn against her and dislike her if he were drenched with rain.

In a minute or two the rain came faster, big heavy threatening drops. There was no hope—it was going to be a downpour. She seized his arm.

"You must get out of this," she said feverishly.

She had a half-formed idea of asking Soal to let him wait in the kitchen, but when they were standing together in the hall, in complete darkness, another impulse made her open the door of the drawing-room and push him in there. She had snatched up a candlestick from the chest in the hall, where two or three always stood, and now with shaking fingers she lit it. As she held it up she saw that Charles was smiling slightly.

This glimpse of him was almost too much for her courage. She wanted to cry, I love you—you are the only splendid and beautiful creature I have ever known. Her hands were shaking violently and she put the candle down on the nearest chair.

"We mustn't talk aloud," she murmured. "My father never comes into these rooms at night, but if he heard voices. . . ."

In spite of her fear of her father she could not think about the risk she was running. Her whole being was concentrated on the mingled joy and anguish it felt in watching the young man as, without answering her, he began to examine the room.

He had taken the candle and was holding it to mirrors and

china cabinets, and carved secretaires. As he moved slowly down
the room she saw the tiny flame reflected in the mildewed glass of
the four tall gilt-framed mirrors, in the glass fronts of the cupboards, and then, when he held it over his head, in the drops of
the elaborate crystal chandelier. He lowered it next to look at
an arm-chair against which he had stumbled; if you did not look
at it closely, it like the mirrors had still an air of luxury, almost
of splendour; but the faded silk tapestry had rotted over the
arms and back, and the stuffing burst through. There were five
others, and a couch, all covered with the same spoiled red silk.
The gilt of the mirrors had turned black. The carpet, still thick
and soft to the foot, was covered with stains and with plaster
from the ceiling. Strips of the wallpaper hung down beneath
the windows and behind the cabinets.

The room was so large that the candle made only a poor show;
it revealed as much of the room as a street lamp does of the harbour
in which it is reflected. When Charles came back to the end
near the door where Bessie, feeling that her legs would not support
her much longer, had let herself drop on to a couch, he lifted his
candle to look at the second enormous chandelier. A score of
tiny flames winked back at him from the crystals as though frozen
there.

"Another one," he murmured.

"Soal calls them candeleres," Bessie said. She tried to
smile.

She would not look at the anguish she felt in seeing him so
impressed by this tarnished wealth. An obscure instinct warned
her that if she let herself think clearly about it she would not
be able to keep up the fantasy she had woven round their few
meetings. The imaginary life she was living with him would
collapse.

Charles set the candlestick down on the edge of the table nearest
the couch and seated himself close to her. He was silent for a
minute, his head turned slightly away, so that she thought she
could look at him without being seen. Her gaze fastened on
the line of his cheek from temple to cheek-bone with as desperate an eagerness as if she were looking at it for the last time.
Suddenly he lifted his head and looked at her with a soft, insolent
smile.

She felt the blood run into her face. It was as though he had
told her that she appeared to him immodest and ridiculous. She

made a movement to get up and rush away, but as she pressed her hands on the couch to help herself up Charles placed his own over them and thrust his face against hers, so that she could see nothing except the upper part of his head and his eyes. Her head forced on to the back of the couch by his pressure on her lips, she struggled to breathe, then relaxed and let herself fall limply sideways. Now he was able to put his arms under her and lie over her. For a moment she thought she was going to lose consciousness; the feeble circle of light behind his shoulders was sucked under by a black wave, and with it she lost all sense that she was lying on a solid piece of furniture. She felt herself falling giddily backwards. Charles released her for a moment. She opened her eyes to look at him; her mind steadied itself and she felt an anonymous joy in the weight of his limbs on hers. She seemed never to have had any other existence than this.

He left her abruptly. He put the candle out and stood beside her for a minute; she did not know what he was doing, and the shock of being abandoned like this was too much for her. She gave a choked cry and stretched her arm out. It was seized by the young man, who said in a low rapid voice:

"You do want me, do you?"

She could not answer. For a few minutes he was very gentle with her; a delicious sense of warmth and happiness succeeded to her momentary dismay. Suddenly he did something so atrocious and unexpected that if her mouth had been free she would certainly have groaned. She dared not move, and her body was shaken by a fit of shivering that lasted fully a minute.

She felt the warmth coming back into her body and with it such a feeling of being soothed and comforted as she had never known. Charles re-lit the candle. He seated himself on the edge of the couch and began to stroke her forehead. Seeing him like this, smiling and calm, she was pierced with happiness.

Suddenly a door opened at the farther side of the hall. Footsteps, her father's, crossed the hall quickly and heavily; he stumbled against the baize door leading to the kitchens.

Bessie had started up. Her hair, her dress, were disordered, and she could scarcely stand. The young man put his arm under hers to steady her.

"Don't be frightened," he murmured. "I can slip away now. It's all right, you needn't worry about anything."

"It's still raining," Bessie said.

She was surprised. She thought they had been in this room for hours. Even now she did not realize that it was less than half an hour. Her mind was stupid with joy.

When she had bolted the front door behind Charles she walked upstairs to her room and let herself fall on her bed. She tried to think about what had been happening, but she felt herself rushing towards sleep; before she could force herself to stand up again her body relaxed, her head fell sideways, and she was asleep.

IV

CHAPTER XXIX

ONE mild day in March—it was in the very early morning—Handel came downstairs to find the door open and Vansittart gone.

His restlessness had been growing for days. It happened every spring that he left the house, usually before daylight, and wandered about in the country until Handel found him and brought him back. During the rest of the year he was docile and obedient, and seemed happy. But his doctor had been too optimistic in believing that he could be completely cured—he had been living with Handel now for five years and he seemed settled in a state which was certainly not insanity, but neither was it sanity as other men understand the words.

During this five years he had become stronger in body, but he was still so thin that his wrists seemed transparent when he held them up to the light, and the skin of his temples appeared to be stretched over a void.

When he had drunk some coffee and eaten a mouthful of bread Handel went out to look for him. The winter had been soft, and already spring was stirring, with showers of warm rain at the roots, the clear glistening pink and brown of sycamore buds, coltsfoot burning in the hedges. It is very strange, an early spring, as though a tired woman, dreaming that she is young and glowing, were to wake and find it the truth and all those years of child-minding and the shedding of hopes and confidence so much clutter of winter sleep, to be swept off with a feather.

Climbing the slope of the moor where he expected to find Vansittart, Handel stooped to pick up the pale downy feather of a young curlew lying on the black earth. Its softness entranced him. He could not bear to throw it away again and he thrust it into his pocket. He heard above his head the long, liquid bubbling call, so unlike its ordinary piercing cry, which the curlew will keep up hour after hour on the moors. It sounds like a ritual chant, but the rite is a joyous and familiar one; it might be a kind of audible meditation on the pleasure of thrusting against the wind, or on the scents which in this thin air take the place of landmarks.

During the afternoon, when he had been walking and searching for several hours, he found Vansittart lying on the edge of a bog. He was lying face downwards, staring at the red trumpet moss and at a bright thread of water running soundlessly and swiftly through the coarse reeds. His clothes were mud-stained and wet, as though he had fallen more than once. He saw Handel coming and dragged himself up. He was obviously exhausted.

"Have you had a good day?" Handel asked gently.

"You had to come and look for me—I'm nothing but a nuisance," said Vansittart. His forehead was covered with sweat and he could scarcely stand. "I'm ashamed of myself," he went on with effort.

"You have a perfect right to go where you like and when you like," Handel said tranquilly, "and if I choose to make it an excuse for coming out instead of working indoors that is my affair."

Vansittart had come up to him and was resting his hand, which was torn and bleeding from five or six deep scratches, on his arm. "I couldn't stay at home."

"It's the first day of real spring," Handel said. "You were right to come out here."

"Do you think I came for that!" said Vansittart bitterly. "I detest spring. It's an old pain that returns every year. I should be glad if I were told one year that winter had come for good, never to retreat again leaving us to suffer another spring and another memory. How can an old man endure his life in spring?"

"You should cultivate a memory of the future," Handel retorted, "or grow herbs. If you weren't afraid of spoiling your hands with digging you could have taken over the herb patch and then you'd count the days to spring and the end of winter."

Vansittart gave a little wheezy laugh and for a few minutes he stepped along almost gaily. But he was really at the end of his strength and when they reached home Handel made him lie down on the sofa in the living-room and covered him with a blanket. He put their soup on the stove to heat through and went upstairs to his room. His boots were wet and caked with mud, which had even gone through to his socks. He began to pull them off.

Although he had almost carried Vansittart for the last three or four miles he was not tired. There were days in which he seemed to himself to have the strength of a young man. He was

as upright as a young man. Yet he looked now what he was,
a man of sixty and over. He was sixty-one. His features were
still sharp and delicate, and his grey eyes as piercing as in youth.
But they had that remoteness which visits the eyes even of children
and becomes proper when one has three-score years and no to-
morrow. His hair was white; it stood up over his head like
wool.

When he was in his room he heard someone come into the
house and opened his door to listen. It was Mower. He heard
him speaking in his loud resonant voice to Vansittart, and when
he went downstairs he found that they were talking about music.
These conversations were always begun by Vansittart himself;
his friends avoided talking to him of music because it distressed
and excited him.

Lying on the sofa, his shrunken head and sharp pallid nose
turning from side to side to follow what they were doing, he said
in an undertone:

"I find it easy to believe that Satan, as naturally as God, is
a musician; but an unscrupulous one, dishonest, condescending
to all kinds of tricks. I mean that music is the thought of God,
but the vanity of the Devil. It was no surprise to me to hear
that God has been wounded, and that life will dry up at its source;
there will be no births. A musician will be ashamed if more than
two or three people listen to him; when that happens he'll know
that he has betrayed his Master and taken the Devil's wages."

"Ho! that's the *Parsifal* story," Mower said, laughing. His
gaunt, ugly face was distorted by anxiety and a sly compassion.

"Don't talk about Wagner," Vansittart said sternly. He
broke into harsh abuse of Wagner; sometimes he seemed not to
know whether he was talking about Wagner or Satan, or perhaps
he really confused them in his mind. After a time he grew quieter.
Handel brought the cheese and the bread from the pantry and
poured out soup. He lifted Vansittart against the dirty shabby
cushions of the couch and tied a napkin round his neck before
giving him his bowl of soup. What with carelessness and the
feeble shaking of his hands, he spilled a great part of it between the
bowl and his mouth.

During supper Mower told Handel that the Council had sold
the Piece to Sir Thomas Money, who was going to enclose it and
put up a band-stand and a theatre to take the place of the old
theatre in Cliff Street which had burned down in January.

"Are you certain?" asked Handel.

"Of course I'm certain. Do you think I'd come up here to tell you if I weren't? A damned disgraceful thing to do, I call it."

"But have they the right to sell?"

Mower shrugged his shoulders vigorously. "I don't know. It's always been common land. I believe it's mentioned as common land in a document of Edward Third's reign—but who takes any notice of that sort of thing?"

"Every decent man," answered Handel shortly. He sat frowning, staring in front of him, while his friend watched him eagerly. "I'll go and see Money himself about it," he said.

He seemed to put it out of his mind as he cleared the table, and fetched coal from the tiny outhouse with the air of a man who has nothing to do but build the fire up and talk to his friends. To one of them. Vansittart was sleeping off his excitement; he had dropped asleep with the suddenness of an infant. His mouth, tightly closed, seemed lifeless, his lids barely covered his eyes—it was a death-mask. Handel and Mower talked in undertones. This evening was like other evenings.

The next day he went to see Money. He was shown into the room which no airing would ever clear of the smell of cigars—it had impregnated the leather of the chairs and the walls themselves. Money was writing, but he stretched his hand out with a pleased smile.

"Sit down and wait one minute," he said amiably. "I want to finish this."

Handel remained standing. He walked over to the window and looked out at a segment of the harbour, green-grey, smooth, backed by the old houses leaning crazily one above the other to the smooth grey-green of the field. Turning, he saw Money's back reflected in a wall mirror, the thick neck webbed with black veins, the thick shoulders, strong buttocks thrusting down and back into the chair. All that was genial, even polite, in the man withdrew with his face.

Handel turned away. At that moment Money opened a drawer of his desk, closed it again and looked up at him with a smile.

"Did you come because you knew I should be glad to see you, or to ask for something?"

Handel did not smile. "I came to talk to you about enclosing the Piece," he said quietly. "Is it true you're going to put railings round it and charge for admission?"

"I hope I'm going to do better than that," Money said. "I'm going to lay the place out, build a theatre, have a band playing in summer. It's time we civilized Wik a little. It'll bring visitors to the town. Don't you like the idea?"

"I can't say I do," Handel said drily. "It's not my idea of civilization to turn a pleasant piece of common land into a parade ground for rich women."

"Damned nonsense! Half its time the place is overrun with screaming children from the east side. Nothing pleasant about that. Time it was stopped."

Handel felt a sudden anger against him, and an astonishing contempt. "What you're doing," he said coolly, "is so infernally vulgar that it's worse than a mere theft."

Money understood for the first time that he was being attacked. His face hardened. "What do you mean by talking to me about theft?"

"You may have paid for the land, but from any intelligent point of view you have stolen it," Handel said in the same quietly ironical voice. He was not conscious that it was maddening.

Hot with resentment, Money said: "You're talking to me like a filthy Socialist."

"As a matter of fact I'm not a Socialist," Handel said calmly. "I've never altered my opinions—and I've never hidden them from you. I consider that to take money from slum property— you own almost the whole of Under Wik and it's certainly a slum —is a piece of sheer impudent vulgarity. I've always thought so."

Money started up, but dropped back into his chair at once: he was making a severe effort to control himself. He stared at Handel with reproach and fury.

"It's useless to talk as if these people were being injured in some way," he said. "They have their own lives—the sort of lives they're fitted for. I'm not speaking for myself, you understand, but you must admit that a man of character, will, intelligence, force—whatever you like—is naturally superior. I have the right to think myself different from these people—simply because I am different. I take what I want and they take what I give them. That's exactly the difference between us. If you and others like you commit the criminal folly of informing them that I'm stealing from them they may come in time to believe it, and try to give trouble. And then what happens to them is more your fault than theirs. If I gave way to them it would be proof that I was losing my superiority. Do you suppose there's one of them that wouldn't be in my shoes if he was big enough, trampling on the others—and on me, too, if he got the chance?"

He thrust his lips out. "Have you anything else to say to me?"

"Nothing you would listen to," Handel said with unemphasized contempt. "You're less impressive than you imagine. What is more," he added indifferently, "I believe that you and your sort are less secure than you imagine. A society dependent on poverty and injustice must be unsafe, it will either be destroyed or destroy itself."

Money lifted his hands and let them fall again on his desk.

"If I knew what you were talking about I might be able to argue with you. There's no injustice—my grandfather was brought up in a small dirty bake-shop in Under Wik, but he had the spirit to get out of it into a shipping office, and his son owned ships, and I own them and build 'em. If we hadn't been bigger than other men we'd still be living and eating in that back room. . . . Injustice my—— Talk to me of injustice! You might be that hulking fool, Lamb. Well, trade's damned bad—I'm laying up half my ships. That'll teach the other fools a lesson. It might teach you—if you weren't naturally unteachable."

Handel walked over to the door. "The school in which hardness and dullness of heart learns its lessons is usually a bloody one," he said mildly.

He went to see his friend King at the offices of the *Wik Times*. Five years of prosperity had changed King less than he hoped. He was still afraid of failure, afraid that he was being laughed at, of slights. He lay awake as many nights, turning over in his mind an encounter with another man to see where he had laid himself open to being mocked and ignored. He was happy when he was writing. The words rushed to his mind, stinging powerful words—they seemed all that to him as he wrote then—how was it they made so little noise? In strict secrecy he practised speaking before a mirror, smiling, advancing, raising his hand—so—mouthing the words. One of these days he would astonish the town. What, you didn't hear him? But he was magnificent—

oh, he had them all right. The other speakers fell flat after him, I can tell you.

His wife felt no interest in his ambitions. She complained that in the new house she could see nothing from the windows except the hills and the sea—no life, nothing. He suspected her of complaining about him behind his back. But he suspected everyone; words, looks, pricked his quivering skin like arrows.

When he heard Handel's voice in the outer office he relaxed, smiling, drawing down the corners of his mouth. He stood up as Handel came in.

"I thought you were someone else," he said eagerly. "They sent up the wrong name. Sit down. I haven't seen you for a fortnight—I'm getting too stiff to climb up to you, but you're the only man in this place I shall ever want to see."

"That's very kind of you," Handel said. He looked at King drily, almost coldly.

Sitting down very much at his ease, he told King that he wanted his help to prevent Thomas Money from enclosing the Piece. The Council had no right to sell it, since it belonged not to them but to the whole town: it meant turning the children from their only playground except the shore, wind-bitten and icy cold for half the year. He was going on, but his friend interrupted him eagerly, stuttering.

"I'll write a strong article," he exclaimed. "That damned bullying loud-mouthed devil! I shouldn't be sorry to pull him down a peg."

"It's a question of justice—not of attacking Money," Handel said quietly, looking at him.

He may be thinking of her ladyship, King thought angrily. She goes to see him. They talk. What takes her up there when she hasn't seen fit to call on Mary, when she wouldn't see me when I wanted to interview her? His stomach felt mortified.

"You don't suspect me of personal motives?"

"My dear fellow, of course not," Handel said serenely.

He stayed a few minutes, to allow King to soothe himself with words. Walking home, he felt calmly happy. The light was just leaving the water in the harbour, ebbing back over the hills; it was the moment of that strange clarity which comes before dusk when with the colour going the hard skeleton of the earth sharpens under the skin. He was watching it, his glance wavering to the half-empty shipyards—years now since Money carried his

main yards and works farther south, away from the dying town—
and almost walked over a child standing in his way. He looked
down and saw a stout red-faced scowling infant, three or four years
old, a boy. "You gimme a penny," it said; "you ought to gimme
a penny."

"I don't know why I should," said Handel. He found two
ha'pennies in a pocket and held them out. The child snatched
them without thanking him and swaggered off.

The protest meeting held on Friday in the Temperance Hall was
crowded to the sills, men sitting on them and standing up at the
back, the door opening long after the room was full to edge in
another and another. King, in his place as chairman, looked at
his audience with satisfaction. There were many more decent
people—householders, shop-people—than the others.

He noticed that two of the doctors had come with their wives.
The Under Wik lot were squeezed in at the back and along the sides;
they knew better than to come to the front.

He had dressed carefully, choosing a dark suit and paying
careful attention to his shoes: they would show under the table
at which he sat. He was austere, but not too austere. His speech
went well, and for a time afterwards he sat in a trance of excitement, feeling his body glowing with energy as though he were a
young man. After a time he began to listen to Handel's voice.
Handel had begun by talking about the Piece, the dubious legal
position, and the children, but slowly he widened what he was
saying until it became an indictment of privilege and poverty.

King felt uneasy, then excited, then seized and swept up by
love and admiration and loyalty. Glancing sideways at Handel,
he's splendid, he thought; he'd let them kill him for what he
believes in, and so would I now. I believe in him, I believe what
he says; all this is bigger than one man, it's the new age, a new
spirit—take me, use me; here I am, send me.

Reminded by Vansittart, Handel had put on his good suit, but
it was now shapeless and hung on him like a sack. He rocked
on his heels and toes sometimes as he spoke. His voice was quietly
slow at first, but before long it quickened to the familiar authority,
with the coldness and harshness of a trumpet.

". . . . what goes on in the minds, or what passes for mind,
of a rich woman who accepts the poverty of other women as natural

and endurable. It passes my understanding. Why is it that rich women are not ashamed? Why, if they must clothe their bodies with what would warm and feed half-hungry children, don't they perform this disgusting act in secret? We all know that children, born healthy, sicken and die in slum streets and in rooms without air, light or warmth, yet in polite society no one objects to meeting the man who owns these rooms and draws a rent from them, though in effect he is the murderer of these children. . . ."

King noticed a woman in the front row drawing the collar of her fur coat round her. He thought she was preparing to walk out of the meeting, and at once his uneasiness returned. Looking from face to face he saw curiosity, furtive smiles, cold queasy reproof. The women's faces were calm enough, but in the eyes of their husbands he saw a ripple of the shrewd, cold, ironic laughter he dreaded. He saw his own wife seated, with a very red face, looking anywhere but at the platform, uncertain whether to hurry off or to let the hall empty first.

"I think it went off very well," Handel said with a strangely innocent smile.

"Are you sure that most of them didn't come from curiosity and nothing else?" King said.

"I daresay they did," Handel said calmly. "But does it matter?"

He turned away and left King. He was tired—the speech had taken it out of him. Virtue has gone out of me, he thought, half ashamed. His weariness was more of mind than of flesh. The clear night, windy, starlit, tempted him to do as he had often done in the past, walk into the country instead of going home to sleep.

He took the road out of Wik to Upsal Wood. A clearing west wind had set the heavens further back. Stars rippled behind stars, streaming away out of sight. The earth smelled moist and fresh but not cold, as though the new life stirring in it kept it as warm, say, as new milk. In the wood the bare trees were making a tremendous noise with their branches, rising and falling against the sky with the hissing clatter of waves. For a long time Handel listened to it with a sense of pleasure, then slowly he ceased to hear it or to be conscious of it except as the regular sound of a breath drawn and released or as the alternate beating and stillness of a wing covering the earth. When he rested his hand on the Stone he felt it beating in that, too, as distinctly as he could feel the pulse in his own wrist.   He put his ear to the Stone and heard it.   The sense of pleasure faded, but so did his weariness; he could no longer feel any distinction between the skin of his finger-ends and of the Stone, or between his body and the darkness.

He did not know how long he had been standing there, but at first his eyelids, and then the eyes, then finally his mind became aware of a change in the sky.   The stars were disappearing as water sinks into the sand.

Veil after veil was lifted before his eyes until light sprang in a fountain, spurting quickly up, still without warmth, spreading, rippling out farther until it had eddied round every blade of grass on the ground near him.   His feeling of peace narrowed into happiness.   *"This queen of colours, the light,"* he remembered.   But the sky was already changing, taking on the colours of sunrise, and he turned to walk home.   The wind had dropped.   The branches of the trees stretched out in the air, like seaweed in a current which is moving so fast that it seems not to move at all.

Late in the afternoon of that day he went to see Vawn, to ask him to sign the petition to the council.   He did not suppose for a moment that Vawn would do it, but it was necessary to ask him.

Charles Vawn had grown, not less suave, but less generous and less acute with the years.   His delicacy of manner had stiffened into a rigidity which was almost pompous.   He seemed to think of himself less as a priest than as a senior civil servant in some Ministry of Religion, and one would have hesitated to remind him that the permanent head of his department had been executed for sedition.

One might have expected Handel to dislike him, or at least to cease to feel intimate with him.   In fact, he liked him as well as ever.   The truth is that Handel was, in his way, as ruthless an authoritarian as any church ever nursed.   But for that flaw in his life, which had thrown him out of the Church, he might never have become a rebel, a "filthy Socialist," a stone of offence to his own kind.   He understood Vawn.

As soon as Vawn had refused, which he did at once, to have anything to do with the petition, Handel's eyes lit up and he smiled warmly.   He stretched his legs out without noticing that he had dropped flakes of mud off his boots on Vawn's thin and beautiful rugs, and said genially:

"How you detest anything that savours of humanity, my dear

fellow! I don't believe you'd lift a finger to save me from being beheaded or broken on the wheel, if such punishments for thinking unorthodox thoughts ever become fashionable again."

Vawn smiled coldly—it was less a smile than a twitching of one side of his nearly colourless face, and it was not disagreeable. "I don't approve of violence."

"There's nothing violent in the method of a petition," exclaimed Handel. "It's a form of protest as old as writing, probably older."

"The violence is implied," Vawn said coldly and drily. "If protests against perfectly lawful expedients are made—oh, in the name of justice—and supported by educated people—and then defeated—what is the next step? *You* may be willing to submit, but what about the other less responsible, less decent— to put it frankly, the hooligan elements you will have roused?"

Handel looked into his face with an impersonal curiosity, much as he might have examined a strange new animal.

"So you regard robbery—the removal from poor children of one of their few rights in this town—as a lawful expedient?"

"Nonsense! Children have no right to it, none at all. Once sold to him, the land becomes Sir Thomas Money's property—and he can do as he wishes with it."

"In fact," Handel said mildly, "you find yourself with tenderer feelings towards Money than towards children from the east side, who make a devil of a noise and don't rent a pew."

Vawn made an impatient gesture. "Not at all. I refuse to throw away everything I believe in for a noisy sentiment."

"What do you believe in?" Handel asked in a mild voice.

"I believe that one should support tradition—the security and decency that are worth all the sentiment in the world."

"But which tradition, my dear Charles?" He shook with his soft chuckling laugh. "You can't support all of them, you know. The tradition of the Church before it surrendered itself bodily and spiritually to the State was, well, bitterly critical of the Thomas Moneys and their habits."

Vawn stood up and walked stiffly—he was becoming slightly arthritic—to one of his bookcases, and took down a book of which he turned the leaves, frowning and tightening his lips. At last he found the passage he was looking for.

"I'm going to read you three sentences from this book," he said, lifting his pale eyes to Handel's face for an instant.

"One moment. What is the book?" demanded Handel.

"It is *The Gifts of Civilization*—by Dean Church."

"You may go on. I haven't read it."

"With your permission," Vawn said sarcastically. "'It seems impossible to conceive three things more opposite at first sight to the Sermon on the Mount than War, Law and Trade; yet Christian society has long since made up its mind about them, and we all accept them as among the necessities or occupations of human society. Christ has sanctified, He has in many ways transformed, that society which is only for this time and life; and while calling and guiding souls one by one to the Father, He has made His gracious influence felt where it could least be expected. Even war and riches, even the Babel life of our great cities, even the high places of ambition and earthly honour have been touched by His spirit, have found how to be Christian.'" He put the book back on the shelf and said drily: "Apart from the note of enthusiasm, which personally I find distasteful, I should say that it answers your question."

He walked carefully back to his chair.

"A singularly indifferent piety," Handel said yawning. "I should say that it was the utter abandonment of peculiarly Christian standards of conduct or economics."

"What on earth has the Church to do with economics?" Vawn said irritably.

Handel pursed his lips into the slyly contemptuous smile that made Vawn quiver with dislike. "It has to draw its rents from abominable slums, and keep on good terms with the Thomas Moneys."

"Its concern is with the soul of any man or woman," said Vawn; he was controlling himself with effort. "You haven't forgotten the command to render unto Cæsar. . . ."

"I should admire, if I were not a Christian," Handel said placidly, "the tact with which you have seen to it that no one is inconvenienced by your rendering unto God the things which are God's."

Blotches of colour crept under Vawn's thin, poor skin; his delicate nostrils were pinched and quivering. "You're an enemy of society, Handel, a man of bad will," he said quietly. "I like you as a man"— he forced a smile—"but neither as your friend nor as a priest. . . . I won't have anything to do with your petition. . . . The Church isn't looking for allies among radicals and upsetters. It sees far too clearly the folly of trying to force

improvements.   To be of any value they must spring from conviction—and convictions change slowly, very slowly, in this country.
Thank God."

"You should certainly thank someone," Handel said softly;
"but I'm not sure that your thanks are directed to the right quarter
—for a doctrine so—yes—so extraordinarily convenient to a
Church supported by the State, in effect by Thomas Money.   Just
imagine what would happen if the Church decided to apply Christian
doctrines to the accumulation of wealth, or to profit-taking, or to
poverty—or war. . . .   The loss of Money's approval would be
the least shock you would have to face."

"You're becoming a Socialist," Vawn said, smiling palely.

"I?   Dear me, no.   Not at all," Handel said vigorously.

"Oh.   It would have accounted for the deplorable spectacle—
I didn't attend your meeting last night, but I'm told you had the
bad taste to make a speech against Money in front of his own
workmen."

"My dear Charles," Handel said, chuckling again, "I'm in the
fortunate position of being able to speak against cruelty and
avarice even, as your friend would put it, even in the high places
of ambition and earthly honour.   Unlike—unlike Erastian clerics
—I'm not forced to serve Christ and the State from the same dish."
Still laughing, and shaking his body inside its slovenly clothes,
he quoted with rich joy: "'Think not that Mankind liveth but
for a few, and that the rest are born but to serve the Ambition of
those who make but Flies of men, and Wildernesses of whole
Nations.'   Not only the style but the sentiment is infinitely more
admirable than your muffineer, Charles."

"What did you call him?"

"A muffineer . . . an eater of spiritual muffins, my dear
fellow, a clerical cake-eater."

He stood up, shook himself, and brushed off his jacket the
tobacco ash that was still clinging to it.   The rug under his chair
had been creased and muddied by his boots, but he would never
give Vawn credit for the self-restraint which forbade him to look
at it.

Vawn went down the stairs with him to see him out, walking stiffly and painfully.

In the hall he rather hesitatingly opened a door and showed
Handel a painting he had just bought in Paris.   He divided his
private fortune in half: one half he gave away, and with the other

he allowed himself to indulge a taste for modern painting. He
bought with extreme shrewdness, and his collection had already
trebled its value.

"What do you think of it?" he asked.

"Who is the artist?"

"Vincent Van Gogh."

"I have never heard of him," Handel said slowly.

He stared at the painting in silence, and finally at one figure
in it, a young man, gaunt, bony, with the face, hands, and clothes
of a labourer. Shocked and repelled by its violence, he felt, after
the shock, that this artist of whom he had never heard had wanted
to paint a crucifixion, and unable to imagine it had resigned himself to seeking his models in the streets.

"I don't know anything about painting—it seems to me very
fine," he said.

He looked serenely from the young man to Vawn. Vawn
met his eye. Something trembled in the air between them, an
unresolved question. Handel hunched his shoulders together,
mumbled, "Good-bye, good-bye," and marched out.

Late at night he was writing an article for the *Wik Times*.
He wrote in the living-room, because of the cold of his bedroom.
The room was cleaner and neater than before Vansittart came,
but scarcely an article in it, except the stove and the table, was
better than very shaky. The sofa was covered with a cushion
of which the colours had long since run into an indeterminate brown
with dust and wear. The walls were stained and the canvas on
the floor was in holes everywhere.

To Vansittart the room was a warm refuge; the walls seemed
to him to breathe gently and he knew the feeling of everything,
every chair and cracked saucer, as intimately as if they were the
fingers of a hand which touched him.

He watched Handel writing. He wrote very quickly, in an
almost indecipherable hand, with long pauses between the sentences.
After an hour of watching in silence Vansittart began to feel fear.
He had no idea where it came from. It rose like a vapour through
his senses and possessed him. His teeth chattered.

"Why don't you go to bed?" Handel said, without turning
round.

"I'm all right."

"Don't you sleep?"

"Yes."

"Then why sit up any longer? I may be an hour finishing this or more."

"I'm not sitting up because of you," said Vansittart gently.

Handel turned his head, scratching his cheek with the penholder. "You're losing weight," he said testily; "you eat nothing and then you feel cold at night."

"I'll pull the rug over my legs," murmured Vansittart.

Handel turned back to the table.

After a silence which had lasted almost half an hour, Vansittart cried suddenly:

"Don't stir up against yourself the malice of stupid people."

"Now how did you know," Handel said, with his soft laugh, "that I was only this minute thinking that the most guilty and cruel people in the world are the stupid people—who don't know, and don't want to know, what is happening to anyone except themselves?"

Vansittart got up; he came closer to Handel and said confidentially:

"I listen with my ears. I don't let my mind choke them."

"Perhaps all cruelty is only a matter of stupidity."

Vansittart was making up the fire with logs and cinders. He swept the hearth carefully, hung the worn, singed brush back on its nail, and straightened himself with a very red face.

"No, no!" he stammered. "You're quite wrong. It's a matter of—don't you see?—lust. Lust and cruelty are the same thing. A man like Money craves for power, and the more he gets the more he thinks he has a right to it, and the right to force other men to do things for him and for their own good—it's the same in his eyes. And the right to inflict any cruelty on them to make them do what he thinks is necessary. It is power that allows statesmen to think of war as something they can use in the last resort. It allows generals to give their orders without going mad with horror at the meaning of what they're doing, it lets Money think of babies lying in their mothers' wombs as being born simply to work for him."

"I wanted to tell every man and woman," Handel said, as if he were talking to himself. He sighed. "I've become an old man. Still," he added with an energy that made Vansittart start and begin trembling, "there may be someone in this town, a young man, a boy, even a young girl, who will do more than I have."

"This—this trouble about enclosing the Piece," Vansittart said timidly. "Who is going to help you with it?"

"Every man and woman in Under Wik," Handel answered, writing. "And every liberal-minded man in the town. All decent people."

"A great many people dislike things as they are," Vansittart said dreamily, "but they'll endure misery rather than alter them. And they'll hate you if you upset them."

He waited in vain for an answer. Handel had become absorbed again in his work, and Vansittart sat, almost without breathing, at the end of the sofa; he was afraid to move even his arms, lest the creaking of the many broken springs should disturb the writer. The fire burned low again, and Vansittart did not get up to mend it. He had been watching Handel with tenderness darkened by his fears. At one moment his face turned very white and he placed a hand over his heart, in which he felt a pain as sharp as though a sword pierced it. This was the moment when he had realized that they would kill his friend.

CHAPTER XXX

ONE afternoon early in July Andrew Wikker waited for Tib on the platform at King's Cross. Her train was due in at four and it was late. The young man walked up and down the long platform, scarcely breathing the exhausted air, thick with dust, under the roof. When he came into the hot sun outside he stood still a minute, gazing along the lines. He was enduring a nervous tension which would have been less surprising if Tib had been away a year instead of the five weeks she actually had stayed in Wik with her parents. His mouth felt dry, the nerves of his chest appeared to be drawn up and knotted into a hard ball which he would have been glad to spit out.

When the train came in, three-quarters of an hour after its time, he did not see Tib in the hurrying jerking current of travellers towards the barrier. Now he became simply anxious: he might have missed her in the crowd; he turned his head, trying to look in both directions at once. In this way he did not see her until she was close to him. She looked at him with a smile and said: "Hullo, darling."

He took her suitcase. He avoided touching her and said coolly:

"Oh, you've come, have you?"

He walked off quickly, so quickly that she had to run to keep up with him. She soon dropped behind, smiling a little. He was making for the entrance to the tube station. He looked round for her, and waited. A little reproachfully she said:

"Can't we take a cab, Andrew?"

His anger exploded at once. "Certainly we can't," he said drily. "We can't afford it, you know that. You always want the most senseless extravagances. Can't you remember for once that you've married a poor man? Come on, we're going by tube."

"All right, all right," Tib said; "but don't say anything more about it."

It was only one station, but they had to walk a short distance at the other end. Tib felt confused. Until this moment she had still felt herself living in the air, clear, and splintered sharply with light, of Wik: now suddenly she felt herself plunged into another world and neither her lungs nor her mind were able to adapt themselves at once. She tried not to cough with the dust irritating her throat. The people passing her in the street were still insubstantial—the vague, unfocused attempts at a human being sketched by the eyes of a patient recovering from an anæsthetic. She could believe more readily in the humanity of the porter who had lifted her bag into the train at Wik, a thin dejected fellow with a sharp nose whom she had known all her life, than in the people jostling her in the street as she walked beside Andrew to their rooms.

They lived in Guilford Street, in two rooms at the top of one of the shabbier houses. It was the attic floor of the house, and its charm, if you can speak of charm, was that a door and a staircase shut it off from the rest of the house. A kitchen had been contrived by dividing one of the rooms in half, and there was a bath in the kitchen, of which the geyser provided hot water for washing up. There was some slight excuse for calling it a flat.

Tib looked round her when she came in, seeing it for a minute without the gloze of familiarity, so that it seemed cramped and ugly. But during the five years they had lived here she had learned so well to hide even from herself her thoughts about it that already she was seeing it as an intimate, whose faults one excuses because they have ceased to count. The kitchen door stood open. She saw that it was remarkably clean and neat, not a cup out of place.

"But it looks splendid, my dear. How did you manage to keep it like this?"

"Oh, I didn't," Andrew said. "Don't you think it. I had a woman come in yesterday and clean it out. It was awful."

She went into her room, the larger of the two. It was their living-room as well. Andrew followed her in. He put his arms round her and kissed her, holding her so closely that she seemed to be bearing the weight of his body. He was so unconscious of her that he was brutal.

"Must you—now, Andrew?" his wife said with her quick smile.

"No," he said. He released her and went into his own room.

When she had unpacked the suitcase and put her things away

in the wardrobe she opened his door. He was, or he was pretending to be hard at work, at his desk, and did not look round.

He now worked regularly as a reviewer for a weekly journal. In his spare time he had begun to write, slowly and painfully, yet with a peculiar dispassionate eagerness, a novel in which the only character of importance was London itself. He worked for long hours, and he had written actually some thousands of disconnected passages, a few very long, others containing a few lines, even only a few words; he had still not succeeded in finding a form which would convey adequately what he had seen when one evening during his first weeks in London he remembered: "Thou art full of stirs, a tumultuous city, a joyous city." In the meantime he made his notes, cartoons for a painting; a street-walker waiting beside an eighteenth-century building, half-demolished, its hoardings covered with posters advertising a circus against which, framed by lionesses, she posed her magnificent body in its tight velvet jacket, a buttonhole of parma violets poked between large insolent breasts, long white kid gloves, one bare hand, the glove dangling from it at the wrist, held to a mouth dark-red, wet, defiant, and as round as an O: the face of an old woman sleeping in a doorway in Leicester Square, so withered a piece of flesh that it must have been created as it was; no woman ever bore this woman, no infancy, no childhood, no youth lay hidden in this husk, no seed either. He had tried to describe the sense of an absolute division between the river running below his feet when he was standing looking at it from the embankment and the torrent of humanity at his back, this so strange frontier in time and space, across which no smuggling takes place. The two currents, filling the whole of space without once meeting, create London, the image of London in the mind of the writer.

Andrew's difficulty, when he had assembled so many details that together they included the widest conceivable range of excitement, suffering, despair, joy, disgust, exaltation, would be to arrange these so that the two currents flowed side by side on his pages, so that they were seen *in themselves* and not only as a whirl, a rain, of fortuitous drops. He tore up three-quarters of everything he wrote. He was not merely self-critical, but he had set himself an almost impossible task—to deal only in words which are precise and yet suggestive, extreme precision with extreme evocation—so that the fewest words descend to the greatest depths and carry the heaviest burdens.

He was not writing at this moment, although he had opened the notebook. Tib watched him for less than a minute and said:

"How have you got on, my darling?"

He put his pen down and sat with his arms laid across the desk. "I've been too busy to write at all," he said, without looking at her.

She shrugged. It meant that as always when she was away he had wasted his time. He had done his office work, written the weekly review, and the rest of the time he had slept, talked, or run about to find somebody willing to be amused by him.

"By the way, Julia said she'd give us supper if you weren't too tired to go there."

"I think we'd better go," she said, after a moment. It is easier to go out to someone's house with him, she thought, than staying here while he is still angry with me because without me he is bored and can't work. They had this trouble each time she came home after she had been away for several weeks.

She found that Julia's sister-in-law was staying with her in the house. She was a young, quiet, handsome woman. Andrew clearly knew her very well. He began teasing her at once about something that had happened the evening before, when he took her to the theatre.

Tib had the impression that he had spent a number of his evenings taking Agnes Broek to the theatre and on the river. I don't mind, she thought; she is a nice girl, I like her. She felt almost, but not quite, certain that the other young woman was sensible.

Franz, Julia said, had brought home that afternoon a bottle of white burgundy for Andrew. "He says it is very good. He says you will know, Andrew, that it is good. It is for you. We shall drink some of it, but it is from Franz to you."

"And I'm certainly going to drink it," said Andrew. "You and my wife may taste it if you like, but that's all." He looked at Agnes. "You don't want any, I know. You can't tell the difference between claret and stone ginger. Never mind, I adore you, anyway."

During supper he talked with a gaiety that would have jarred on even a stupid person. It was as if he had been wound up to deliver so many jokes. He had an ear-splitting laugh. With Agnes he was shamelessly loving, and she allowed him to say what he pleased, and smiled at him. He finished the bottle of *Meursault*, drinking almost all of it himself.

Julia had made soup, an omelette, and Viennese coffee. When they finished the meal Agnes began to clear the things away into the little scullery, and Andrew helped her; he insisted that he was going to dry the plates for her. She accepted the offer calmly, but when Julia was about to follow them into the scullery Tib stopped her.

"What is this?" she asked quietly, glancing towards the other room.

"Nothing at all," Julia said, biting her lip. She seemed vexed. "You can be sure that Agnes does not take him seriously—not for a minute. She is not Franz's sister for nothing. And she is engaged to be married." She added: "It's not always Agnes. He has sometimes been like this with me. It doesn't mean anything."

Tib lifted her hands. "Andrew is never serious, not with any of the women he flirts with," she smiled. "But if they think so—it is a pity."

Julia's face cleared. "All the same, my dear, I'm glad you have come back. Andrew is impossible when you are away. *I* know—Franz said so—that he is sane and rather hard, but he does not behave as if he were. When you have been away a week he is as nervous as a cat. . . . But now, what's the matter with him? Have you quarrelled?"

"No; not yet. He's still angry because he has found out he doesn't like living without me."

"Is he mad?"

"Not in the least—but he can't forgive me for it, for being necessary to him."

"But, my poor Tib!"

"It was his aunt's fault," Tib said, shrugging her shoulders. "She wanted to swallow him alive, as if he had been her son, and he had to defend himself against her. He defends himself against me, poor boy. It's stupid, but I can stand it."

The washing-up had been finished, and Agnes came back into the room, taking off her apron. She walked directly over to Tib and talked to her in her quiet halting voice until Tib said she was going home.

"I am tired," she said to Agnes; "we must go home now, but I hope you will come to see me."

"Thank you," the other girl said, smiling. "I shall come."

It was cooler in the street than in Julia's small room, which smelled of sour milk, ironing, and *pot-au-feu*. Andrew and Tib walked in silence for a short distance. Suddenly Andrew raised his hand and stopped a cab which was passing them: he hurried Tib in, and when she protested that they ought not to spend their money in this way he said:

"Never mind. Don't let's talk about it."

He sat with a fixed smile on his lips—less a smile than an unconscious tension of the muscles of his face—humming, and beating time to the tune on his knees. As soon as they were in the flat he went over to his desk and began to work without taking any notice of her.

"Have you some work to finish?" Tib asked him.

Turning, looking into her face, he retorted: "Don't begin now to interfere with my habits. When you were away I got through twice as much work—and it was better work."

"No, this is too much," she exclaimed.

"What did you say?" he asked, smiling.

"That's enough, my dear boy," Tib said with energy. "Either you begin now to behave reasonably, or I go and live with Julia until you become sensible. One thing or the other. At present you are only boring and tiresome, and I can't stand it. You are making our lives impossible."

She went into her own room. Andrew watched her go, without speaking. Her indignation was half serious, but she had spoken because it was time to speak. When she was brushing her hair he came in and knelt beside her, with his hands clasped behind her shoulder-blades, as hard and firm under her skin as the little horns of a kid.

"Now forgive me," he said gently. "I don't know what has been the matter with me since this afternoon . . . I was crazy to have you home, and yet when you came I wasn't happy—not until now . . . the truth is, I'm restless and lost when you're away—I haven't done a stroke of work for a month——"

"I always come back."

"I know—it's not that."

Tib did not answer.

"You're the only woman I could live with . . . or would live with me . . . and the only person I love."

"Then don't let's torment ourselves any longer," his wife said.

She threw the hair-brush down and let him carry her across the room. In her arms Andrew felt not simply the most cruel joy but an exquisite relaxing of his body so that he could sleep, and a comfort that was more than the satisfaction of an urgent physical desire. It was not only his body which satisfied itself by touching her small, sharp-nippled breasts and her legs and arms, thin, young, flexile.

They fell asleep together and when Tib awoke after an hour she was horrified because the electric light had been left burning in both rooms. It was a waste! Slipping from the bed she woke Andrew by shaking him gently.

"Andrew, you must go to bed. Wake up, please, darling. And we left the light on—there will be such a bill."

Yawning, and staggering on his legs like a colt, Andrew went off to his room.

Tib was up first in the morning. She was making the coffee when Andrew came into the kitchen in his pyjamas, his hair standing out round his head. He told her that he had been offered the post of literary editor on his paper. The salary was three hundred pounds. At present he earned only seventy-five.

"Does it mean a great deal more work?" asked Tib anxiously.

"About twice as much—and I'm going to jump at it. The only question we still have to decide is whether I start in August—that is in three weeks' time—or next January. The present man will stay until January, or go now—I can please myself."

"Why not wait for January and finish your novel?"

He frowned. "No. I should give it up if I had to finish it in a fixed time. Writing as a profession—hideous! I don't think I'll start it, thank you."

"But what are you doing now?" asked Tib. When she smiled her eyes became a bright line, hidden by her lashes.

"Reviewing, my dear girl, is a skilled trade—not an art. You need never respect a reviewer who calls himself an artist. What it means is that he's an amateur. . . . I've forgotten something. . . ."

He hurried into his room and came back carrying a box from a Bond Street shop. From layers of tissue paper Tib shook out a blouse made of sprigged silk. It was the one she had admired in the window when she and Andrew were walking through Bond Street on their way home the day before she went away, but she would as soon have jumped over the house as put her nose into one of these shops. Looking at it with a guilty happiness, she said:

"My darling, why have you spent so much money on a present? We can't afford to buy these things."

Andrew looked at her with a smile, and laid his fingers on her breast for a moment in a touch as light and brief as it was, in spite of his smile, serious.

CHAPTER XXXI

DURING these five years Wik has changed. Two or three years after the turn of the century it was still very much the town, small, compact, lively, above all, built to last, that it had been in Semiramis Jordan's childhood. The tide of extravagance and vulgarity sweeping over England during the 'nineties retreated without touching it. For how many centuries it had lived to and for itself, a port rather than a town. Because it turned its back to the rest of England and its face to the sea and to the coasts and harbours of strange lands there was in its life, at the very quick of its life, the impulse of a poet. Yes, during these centuries it lived easily in its imagination.

The change begins when first one and then the other shipyards shut down or were moved away from Wik. There is at first no outward mark. So that it seems that only five years have been needed to bring about changes as subtle, as irrevocable and complete as those which take place in a boy's life between fifteen and twenty.

It was these changes, and her almost animal fear of them and not her age—she was sixty-eight this July—which had put a stop to Ann Wellhem's journeys. She could no longer cadge about. Houses where she had stayed belonged now to younger third and fourth cousins who would not allow her to quarter herself on them for as much as a night. There was no picking up of bargains to be done. Now that in spring and summer Wik was overrun with visitors from softer parts of the country even a labourer's wife knew the value of her old chairs and paintings on glass.

When she went no farther than into Wik, to shop, it was with less than her former assurance. With the death, exactly five years since, of old Mr. Charlton, it was as though a change came over every shop in the town at the very moment when his coffin was being lowered into its grave neatly on top of the coffins of two of his three wives. A new generation of shop assistants stepped forward, pretending civility, but unable to tell the difference between an old customer and any jumped-up visitor—even laughing behind their hands. Ann formed the habit, when she went into Wik, of going directly to her sister's house and asking her to send Skelton to the shops to buy, perhaps, a quarter of cooked ham and a reel of thread.

Semiramis herself rarely went out. But it was not want of self-assurance that kept her sitting day after day, winter and summer, in the house. It was that she hated to see walking about the streets smiling young matrons who did not even know who she was, and girls whose thin frocks were more shameless than their faces, whipped by the salt wind and rosy with happiness. Nothing inside her house had changed: not even its smell of food, dust trodden into old carpets, and dry, ageing flesh. Anyone coming from outside into her room made a journey of at least forty years in time—it was as long as that since anything had been moved in the house or the air admitted to any room.

She went out occasionally, and then it was almost as though the past of the town, its unacknowledged dreams, the cruelties carried out behind the doors of dignified stone houses, the tears flowing unseen, had taken the shape of an old woman in a seal-skin jacket, fitted tightly to her waist, and a black flower-trimmed toque.

There were more lines on her face than veins in a leaf. Her hair was still black, in spite of her age. Her small black eyes spied out every blemish in a face or a street, feeding her unsleeping curiosity. Perhaps she was more like one of those fetishes, innocent in themselves, into which savages cast the monstrous activity of their dreams and so escape from it.

For many years she had never been into any house except— three or four times a year at the most—into Ann's. Soureby Bog Hall was too far for her to walk, and she had herself driven there in a carriage from the livery stables in Over Wik. The proprietor drove her himself. He was years older than she was: his sons now ran the business and they allowed him to hang about the place and attend to such relics as Mrs. Jordan. He was deaf and very dirty. Probably he was no dirtier than Semiramis herself.

She sent for the carriage on Ann's birthday. By an oversight it was sent out with the hood folded down, and the old man quite unable to close it. So for the first time for years she was forced to sit in an open carriage, where she could be seen as well as see.

The day was very hot. The sun burned in a sky without a cloud and without wind. It drew out of the carriage the pungent scent of dust and old leather: the seat on either side of her became so hot that she could not rest her hand on it. She seemed to feel the heat on her legs through all the layers of the clothes she was wearing, and her hand holding an umbrella over her head trembled.

When they were driving past the marsh she stared, almost blinded, at the burning yellow of bog buttercups. The ditch to the left of the track was filled with meadow-sweet, its dry sickly scent poured into the carriage minute after minute. The whole surface of the marsh seemed to be alive and running with light. A streaming warmth rose from it, and where the sea crept towards it an unseen ripple broke off splinters of light and tossed them into the air.

A profound feeling of discomfort filled the old woman's body; she was itching in the sun, her skin creeping, and itching to get out of it. With a groan of relief she found herself at the side door of the house. She felt better the moment she stepped into the narrow passage which led to the hall, and stood blinking until her eyes became used to the semi-darkness of the house with the blinds dropped to keep out the sun.

Ann's drawing-room was crowded with heavy pieces of furniture so that there was scarcely room between them for the strips of oilcloth she put down to protect the carpet. Its three windows were covered with linen blinds and curtains through which the light filtered in a strange yellow fog. There was a chiffonier laden with a great deal of tarnished silver, shelves full of painted ostrich eggs, fans, *papier-mâché* trays, vases filled with dried grasses, photographs.

In the centre of the large room a table held three cups and saucers, and a plate of bread-and-butter.

When Semiramis came into the room she thought at first that it was empty, and she was hurrying towards a cupboard which was usually locked but in which the key had been left, when to her extreme annoyance she saw her niece Lily peering at her from its far side.

"Oh, you're there, are you?" exclaimed Semiramis.

Lily had become very queer during the past year or two, but Semiramis believed that she put it on. It's her badness, she thought; she's not queer at all, she's bad and spiteful.

Although she was thirty-five, Lily dressed in the skirts and blouses she had had when she was a girl and she wore her hair in a plait. Her mother had talked to her about it, but Lily said drily and obstinately that since she was three months younger than her cousin Bessie it would not be suitable for her to alter her style of dressing until Bessie married.

"She's the elder, let her dress as she pleases," she said. "If it gives her a better chance of marriage I shall be doing my duty; it will be time when she's safely married for me to put myself forward."

In her ridiculous clothes she had an extraordinary air of dignity. People had become accustomed to them, and although they talked about her no one laughed.

"Yes, I'm here," said Lily calmly; "so you won't be able to stick your fingers in the cupboard after all."

Semiramis looked at her furiously. She was going to retort, but the door opened again, Ann came in, and she had to swallow her rage.

"Well, H'Ann, it's your birthday," she said, "it's your sixty-eighth—you should make t'most of it, as you'll not have many more."

Ann's pale eyes sparkled with irony and happiness. It was too easy simply to point out that since she was three years younger than her sister she ought to outlive her. Instead, she said in a mild voice:

"It's queer no one writes to you for your birthday. I've had ovver thirty letters and presents."

Lily was pouring out the tea. She looked up and exclaimed: "You haven't had a letter."

Ignoring her as easily as if she had not been in the room, Ann went on to say:

"Ay, and at church yesterday everybody I met asked me to be sure to come in to tea."

"No, they didn't," her daughter said.

She contradicted her mother in the same curt emphatic voice several times during tea. Ann took no notice of her, neither did Semiramis. It was as though the two old women were silently resolved not to be embarrassed by her, whatever she said. Lily's likeness to her father had become more pronounced, but there was nothing of William's melancholy timidity in her voice. She had begun to say exactly what she was thinking, and the only way her mother could defend herself was by pretending not to hear. Even Semiramis understood this. Something that was almost sympathy for her sister woke in her. She heartily disliked Lily.

After tea, Ann asked Semiramis to help her to sort out one or two garments to send to a Jumble Sale at the Congregational church.

"You mean t'chapel," Semiramis could not help saying.

Ann did not answer and the sisters went into her bedroom where, spread out now on the bed, were clothes in every stage of decay and shabbiness. Not one of those she had turned out was less than thirty years old. An indescribable aroma—of life itself —rose from the heap, more pungent than memory, a welter of images. There was the cashmere shawl in which a baby's weak head had been wrapped; a yellowed nightgown from which strenuous rubbing and soda had not been able to wash out every trace of the birth-labour; the torn, coffee-coloured silk of a small parasol clinging to its ivory handle. As they touched the clothes, both old women felt moved and excited: their minds were clouded by the odour of meals, fuller's earth, beds, every variety of calico or woollen material, unwashed, into which Ann's body had breathed out secretly its hungers, fears, pleasures. They clawed over the garments, holding them to the light so that each in turn reflected on to the dulled retina of their eyes the image in their minds: a torn discoloured bodice became a child's illness, or the moment of tenderness felt, one evening, of which nothing remained except the smell of autumn.

Ann began laying aside all the garments she couldn't, now that it came to the point, give away. She found the most unlikely reasons for keeping them, and the more worn and hideous a garment the less willing she was to part with it. Even a moth-eaten scrap of fur seemed infinitely valuable when she had it in her hands.

Lily came into the room without speaking and stood watching them. Ann was left at last with a thin yellowed square of blanket which used to cover the mattress in Lily's cot when she was a year old. It was full of holes.

"I shan't send it, it might come in useful," she muttered. Her face relaxed into a sly, pitiful smile.

"Ay, it might," Semiramis agreed.

"Our minister, Mr. Sele, was only saying this week that I gave more to t'church than anyone," Ann said, tossing her head. "I shan't expect anything from you for th' sale, he says; you do far too much."

Lily had turned her back and was walking out of the room. She looked over her shoulder and said:

"That's a lie!"

The two old women looked at each other without speaking. They went back to the drawing-room, relieved to find that they were alone. Ann pushed her wig to one side, in order to scratch her scalp, and her sister said calmly:

"I should ha' thought you'd give up wearing that article now you're a'most seventy. It's no credit to you."

"I've onny such a scrap of hair. I ha' to wear it for decency's sake."

"I suppose you'll be having yourself buried in it," Semiramis said.

"What I'm buried in is my business," said Ann drily and coldly. "I've prayed about it and received guidance. You don't ha' guidance in th' Church of England, I know, but you'll not tell me to m' face that I haven't had it. I'm a good prayer. I may say that I pray for you every night. I pray you may come to think less of food."

An hour was as long as Semiramis could stay in anyone's house. When she went out, she found that with Horn's help, the old man had managed to get the hood up, and she drove back in peace of mind.

She opened her front door to find Handel resting on a chair in the hall. Skelton, with an anxious foolish face, was standing beside him holding a glass of water.

"Now what's going on?" she said sharply. "You'd better let me send after t'carriage if you're poorly—we can't do with it here."

Handel's eyes, pale, clear, had a look of vacant anxiety. Lifting his head, he made a visible effort to bring his mind back from some inward preoccupation. It might have been listening to something that was taking place in his body, or counting the beating of his heart. He even smiled. At this moment he looked less like himself than like any of the Wikkers, men and women in whom a dry and sarcastic spirit lived in the same room with senses of an intolerable quickness. He looked like his own father and like his brother. Semiramis noticed it; she was afraid and startled.

"You can stay t'night," she said grudgingly.

Handel shook his head. "I'm obliged to you," he said firmly. "But the pain's gone—I must get home." He told her that he had felt giddy and breathless in the street, the pain over his heart

became so severe that he was only able to drag himself as far as
her house, and there he collapsed. It was not the first attack he
had had.

"You should see Nock, or whatever he calls himself. That's
if you can find a time when he's sober."

"I'll see no one," Handel said with impatience.

He drank a little brandy and water and prepared to go away,
but he was forced to stay several minutes while Semiramis scolded
him. It annoyed him, but he felt as though he were a little boy
again, being bullied and ordered about by her as the eldest sister.

"No wonder you've attacks, the life you're leading," she said.
"You were always a blockhead, brother Handel. You've mebbe
forgotten getting yourself thrashed eight times in as many minutes
before you were a year old, trying to climb t'stairs. But you
haven't forgotten spending a week in jail in Cronstadt for answering
back t'master of t'ship you were apprentice in—nor you ha'n't
forgotten how you got yourself kicked out of t'Church ovver th'
trouble with yon gel. And now all this blethering against Thomas
Money. Fond talk. . . ."

Handel was scarcely listening to her, but as though some part
of his mind were attending to it he saw, as sharply as if he were
there, the grey walls of the street in Cronstadt near the quay,
and a bearded ruddy-faced giant, the Russian warder. The man's
face vanished toppling back. He saw Kezia, her large black eyes
under their thick brows squinting slightly, in the intense effort
to understand what he had been saying to her. It was long since
he had recalled her with so little effort. He almost cried out.

"Hold your tongue," he said to Semiramis. He went away.

When he had gone, she sent Skelton into the shops, shouting
after her: "You'll bring in som'ut decent for m'supper, mind."

She sat in the window of her room and watched the servant
hurrying out of sight round the corner, and thought cruelly, She's
not right in the head. A young woman came out of the next house
and walked briskly along the road, swinging her arms. Semiramis
eased her chair nearer the window. That'll be Mrs. Sanderson's
eldest, she murmured: ay, I remember now, she married an engineer,
they gave out he was an engineer, he was mebbe nothing of t'kind;
whatever he was he left her wi' two bairns and she's had to come
crawling back to her mother's with them—serve her right. There
goes that Tylney after t'barmaid at *The Swan;* he goes there every
night, and his wife daren't turn him off for it, he knows too much

about her and her goings-on before ever they were married. And yon's that Thomas Henry—they say he's dead drunk every afternoon—why, it serves his wife right, for she has a tongue like a saw.

She could see Skelton coming back, and she went downstairs into the dining-room and called to her as she came in.

"What ha' you got for me?"

Skelton came into the room, folding back the outer wrapping from the slices of cooked ham. They showed faintly pink through the grease-paper inside.

"You may put it down here—and bring t'plates in."

The moment she was alone, she snatched off the paper and began to turn over the thin moist slices, tearing off pieces of the fat and cramming them into her mouth. Skelton came back to set the table, and Semiramis wiped her fingers on her sleeve before going to the sideboard to take out a bottle of port and open it. She ate the ham with sharp pleasure, folding each mouthful on to a piece of bread, and moving her lips round it. At the end she was able to find a few morsels clinging to her gums as she explored her mouth with tongue and forefinger. She belched joyously. Her face slowly became crimson.

When she had emptied the bottle she tried to stand up, but the room swayed about her; she sat down again quickly, rubbing her face with her doubled hands—gesture of a sleepy child.

Skelton came in and helped her upstairs to her room, coaxing and encouraging her. She drew off as many of the old woman's clothes as she would allow her to take and lifted her into bed, attending to her like a baby. Semiramis did not speak. She lay on her back, staring forbiddingly with her small black dull eyes at the ceiling.

CHAPTER XXXII

HANDEL had first tried to get an injunction hindering the Council from selling the Piece. He lost the case, and it cost him the little he had in the bank and a hundred pounds he borrowed from his publisher.

He had to decide what to do next. Was there enough indignation in the town, among respectable people, to force the Council to withdraw? It was said that the money had not yet been paid. The Piece was still as common to all, and the children played on it at high tide and after dusk, waiting for the cool of night. There is no air, in summer, in the yards sunk into the cliff or squeezed between cliff and harbour.

Handel's will was clenched on his wish to save the Piece for them.

When he left Semiramis's house he walked quickly, his eyes staring and remote. He passed people without seeing them. His mind was sunk in a past so distant, now so strange, that he was, truly, *not all there.* He had forgotten the prison at Cronstadt, forgotten everything—now he saw the stones on which he placed his feet on the way to it, a nail driven into the wall of his cell, the hand, as hairy as a monkey's, of the warder. And this man, who had picked up a little English in the port, said to him over and over again: "You—are—soon—free." It was said to comfort him. He remembered it with an astonishing gratitude.

When he reached the bridge he saw that it was open. A sailing-ship, the handsome Norwegian barque that had been lying in the upper harbour for a week, was going out. He watched the masts sliding across the grey houses.

Two or three country carts were waiting at this side for the bridge to be closed. A man walked behind them and came towards him. Thomas Money. He stepped close to Handel and said abruptly:

"Wikker, this business has gone on long enough. I find it unpleasant and awkward."

Handel turned his head slowly. He gave the other man a
piercing glance from eyes which seemed to have difficulty in focusing
him.

"I'm glad to hear it," he said.

"Come back with me to my office now," Money said eagerly,
"I'll show you the plans we've drawn up for the theatre and the
rest. You'll see they're not bad. After all, it's the best part of
the west cliff—we're going to lay it out with beds and shrubs
and call it the Spa Gardens. . . . We must civilize ourselves—
visitors nowadays expect that sort of thing. . . . I've given
the job to a young architect, a cousin of my wife's—he's up to all
the newest dodges, he'll make a good thing of it. . . . I can con-
vince you in ten minutes that we're not spoiling anything."

Handel spoke so carelessly that he almost mumbled his
words. "So far as I'm concerned," he said calmly, "you may be
building a cathedral, but I should still consider it an outrageous
act."

Money's face darkened. He forced himself to smile and said:
"Come, you're exaggerating."

"Not at all," said Handel. He had not raised his voice, and
he was completely unconscious that the dislike he felt for Money
at this moment was showing itself in an unbearable insolence of
tone. "You have chosen to rob a number of poor children of
their playground—why not say so? Why talk about civilization
—about which you know nothing. Nothing at all. There are
other sites in the town for a theatre. What you're actually doing
is to vulgarize the town in the hope of attracting a different sort of
visitor, people who share your tastes." He watched the halves
of the bridge swinging back very slowly into place. "I don't
know why you should call that civilization," he added indifferently.

Money's face had become distorted with his rage. His eyes
were bloodshot. A violent man, he had made a sacrifice of his
pride and temper to try to mend the quarrel. He was carrying
a walking-stick and he swung it up as though he were going
to strike Handel. "You—fellow——" he shouted. He realized
that people were standing about to listen. Lowering his arm,
he turned and went away. Handel walked off across the
bridge, holding himself stiffly as always. His face was pale
and the lines in his cheeks seemed to be sucked in by his
breath.

The offices of the *Wik Times* were near the bridge, on the west side. He turned before he had gone far, walked back over the bridge, and went in to talk to King.

"I was coming up this evening to see you," King said. "I wanted to talk over things."

Without waiting to hear what he had to say, Handel said, slowly: "There's only one thing to do now . . . we must go on with the protests. A petition may be some use——"

King's face took on the stubborn, defiant expression it could wear when he was forcing himself to overcome a fit of shyness. "I've been thinking it over, Handel," he said loudly, "and I think it's no good having trouble. We'd better try to get the Council to give us a playground somewhere else for the children. It's the most sensible way out."

Handel looked at him. "It has become a question of social justice," he said, in a dry mumbling voice.

"But if we go on we shall come into conflict with the law," King said. He kept his head down. His hands stroked the fine broadcloth over his knees.

"I'm afraid," Handel said, with a laugh that was half tender and half an apology, "that I'm prepared to behave thoroughly illegally—if it's the only way to get justice done. There are one or two things I'd still go to prison for. Social justice is one of them."

He was tempted to tell King the story of Cronstadt—and of the incidents that had forced him to disobey orders on the voyage out, the mad bullying master, the boy kicked senseless every day, the warder—*You are soon safe.* He shook his head. Better leave the past where it is. Why try to share it?—at sixty-one a man is alone and had better not try introducing his friends to the boy he was.

King was stuttering. "Yes, but it might come to violence —are you prepared for that?"

"Nonsense," Handel said. "I don't object to violence unless it's inflicted on defenceless people—I shouldn't object to being killed if I had persuaded myself that it was going to prevent an injustice."

He laughed softly again.

"You always defeat me," groaned King. He felt himself trembling with love for the man sitting in front of him. His caution and his suspicions vanished together. "Look here, I'll do anything you tell me."

"Oh, don't obey me," Handel said coldly. "Obey your own judgment."

King was in such a state of distress and generous emotion that he was almost weeping. "No, no," he stammered. "I believe you're right. Don't misunderstand me, I'll do anything possible. Of course you're right—we must keep up the protest—we—— Are you going?"

Handel had risen. He looked down at his friend with an embarrassed and good-humoured smile. "Thanks," he said gently. "I can't think what we'd do without you, you know." He blundered into things on his way to the door as though he were very tired.

A week later Money had the railings put round the Piece—high pointed iron rails, hideous. They enclosed all the grass along the cliff top, except for a patch at the end nearest the harbour. Here the children gathered the first evening—there was not even room to quarrel, and most of them wandered back to Under Wik and the yards. "How peaceful!" one visitor said vivaciously. It was. Her fat friend nodded and agreed: "It will be even nicer when we get the band."

As soon as Handel heard about the railings he made up his mind. Taking with him two or three shamefaced men—his deacons, as they had liked to call themselves when they met to discuss the notices for his Sunday night addresses, coal for warming the hall, and the rest—he went on to the unenclosed ground and began to make a speech. In a few minutes he had a small crowd —fishermen and their women from Under Wik in front and at the back a few visitors and decent people. The windows of the houses looking on to the Piece opened, so that women "sitting in the window" could see, although they couldn't hear what was going on. The news ran through the town. Soon there must have been a couple of hundred people squeezed between the railings and the edge of the cliff. Women began yelling at their children to keep back.

Handel raised his voice. It vibrated with his passion and a hard bitter joy. He threw his arm out behind him and grasped one of the rails. "This land has been stolen. These railings are illegal, the property of impudent robbers. We must throw them down—now!"

His voice changed. "Put that stick down," he roared at a man near him. "No sticks! Use your bare hands. . . . Watch me."

His "deacons" had drawn back in alarm and annoyance. This was not what they came out to see. Two of them walked off, pushing their way through the crowd; the third stood regarding Handel with a discomfort which quickly became fear. "He's possessed," he said aloud in an anguished voice.

A dozen men and boys were tugging and pushing against the railings. They gave way in one place, in another, in a third. The deacon saw that no one except Handel did it seriously. The others were laughing and struggling—it was a lark.

"T'bobbies is coming!"

The scuffling and swaying turned outwards. Men began running away. A stone flew up. Then a shower of stones. One caught a policeman on the cheek and drew blood. It happened in less than two minutes—the time the third deacon needed to push his way to the other side of the crowd. Standing on the edge of the pavement, he saw three policemen dragging Handel across the road. They wrenched his arms back, and one of them in a nervous temper kicked him brutally in the side.

"What a disgrace!"

The deacon turned his head. Who spoke? He was standing in front of the wife of one of the doctors. "A most disgraceful and shocking business," she repeated. "He ought to be locked up—and fined."

"He?—who?" stammered the man.

"Why, Handel Wikker, of course."

"Yes, of course, of course," he answered.

He waited a minute, then followed the people running behind the policeman and Handel to see the end. He was afraid to come too close to him. Someone might have seen him with Handel before the speech. He saw him taken into the police-station, and for a time he tried to make up his mind to go in. In the end—and afraid Handel should somehow see him—he went home.

The police kept Handel at the station for an hour, and released him. He was followed on his way home by a rabble of youths and children.

Some wag in Over Wik stumbled on a joke; that evening he spread it joyously. "He was taken off without ceremony." "Without what?" "You 'eard. Without Sarah Money."

Semiramis had written to Andrew and told him that his father was off his head and in jail. He came up at once. Walking to his aunt's house from the station, he felt diminished and harder; it was as though he had thrust back into his body, into the shelter created by his skeleton for it, a vaguer and less defenceless self which could show itself without fear in any place in the world except Wik. Here nothing must live except the hard core. The thought must be wiped from the face, the spirit hardened, the eyes must suspect. "I don't like to go back to Wik with Andrew," Tib said once; "in Wik he's not himself." Yet here, where he was *not himself*, he felt safe. Here and nowhere else in the world. A seed if it could remain in the earth and yet live, or a man if he could return to the first moment of pure happiness in his life, would know the same pleasure, as sharp and bitter as a bitter fruit.

I ought not to come back here, he thought.

He had been certain that Semiramis was lying when she said his father was in jail. All the same he was relieved by her first words.

"Well, they've let him out, it seems. T'magistrates bound him over—he had to show himself in court this morning with th' other riff-raff."

"Why not tell me what's been happening?" Andrew said coolly.

He listened, trying to disentangle truth and lies.

". . . marched to t'Piece with clavvers of people at his tail . . . he calls himself religious. This isn't religion, it's downright badness . . . leading poor men astray as well."

She seemed smaller and shrunken. She sat in her chair in the window, clawing at her dress, bad-tempered, malicious, dirty —yet he felt a pang of liking for her. She has never, he thought, pretended to be anything but herself. He was beginning to think this a great virtue, perhaps the greatest of all.

"You'll speak to him, won't you?" she said, with a sharp glance.

"I'll do anything I can," he said in a doubtful voice. He had a feeling of resentment and weariness. How could he argue with his father? It's not my business, he thought, and I have my work to do.

"You'd better stop here a few weeks," she went on energetically. "You can have t'back bedroom. Your wife can stop here as well—you'd better send for her, you don't want to leave her to traipse about London by herself; it's not right."

He thanked her. "I'll stay a day or two, and see," he said evasively.

He went off as soon as he had drunk a cup of strong tea, the colour of mahogany, brought to him by Skelton. It was a good way to his father's house, down the long steep hill to the harbour, across the bridge, through Under Wik. He avoided the inquisitive smiles of people who knew who he was. By the time he reached the Garth he was eager for some way to prove to his father that he loved and admired him. An excited amusement seized him. He felt growing up in himself the indulgent son of a lovable, eccentric old man. It was not until he halted at the top of the hill that he began to be uneasy. Was it actually so simple as that?

Handel was gardening. He waved his arm when he caught sight of Andrew, and at this moment the young man felt ashamed and uncertain—and then certain. There's nothing I can say to him, he thought.

His father looked at him with a smile. "I suppose you've heard the story?" he said. He was brushing the earth off his hands.

"Yes," Andrew muttered, "but I came up to ask you about it."

Handel stood for a moment as if sunk in thought. "There's very little to say," he said at last. "It's simply an act of injustice. And a protest must be made against it—that's all."

"Is this the best way?" his son stammered.

"Really I don't know," Handel said simply. "It's the only way. We've been holding meetings and writing letters about it since March. And I tried and failed to get an injunction. I'm afraid the only thing now is just to refuse to submit."

"To refuse to submit?" Andrew repeated. He hesitated, feeling ashamed of what he wanted to say: he did not believe it himself, but it seemed to him that his father, of all men on earth, ought to believe it. "Isn't submission—forgive me, but isn't it a Christian duty to submit? I'm not a Christian," he added hurriedly, "but I've always supposed——" He broke off and looked, frowning, at his father.

Handel shrugged his shoulders almost as though he were indifferent or, which was even more disconcerting, bored.

"It's astonishingly difficult to know what one has the right to call Christian," he said slowly. "I'm only certain of one thing nowadays. We must not accept injustice. Even if we can do nothing, if the force against us is too great, we must rebel. I have no quarrel with Money himself. I don't want him to be kicked and humiliated. But if he puts railings round common land which has always belonged to the Under Wik children I shall go on pulling them down. At the same time I shall talk to people and explain to them why I'm doing it . . . I don't see what else one can do."

Andrew felt a sudden excitement. No, I can't leave him, he thought sharply; I'll stay here and look after him.

"If it involves brawling and violence," he asked drily, "are you certain it's justifiable?"

Handel looked at him with an impervious sly smile. "They won't arrest anyone except me. I don't like it. In fact, I dislike extremely being mauled. But one can't swallow an injustice merely because one dislikes violence used on oneself, any more than one can hold one's tongue about an injustice. To say nothing, to submit, is shocking. It shocks me. I couldn't do it."

"Very well——" his son began impulsively.

"There is actually one thing that makes me anxious," Handel interrupted. "That's your allowance. Shall I be able to pay it next year?" He explained that he was in debt to his publisher already. "And I have two mouths to feed here," he added, nodding towards the house.

"How is he?"

"Still the same."

"One of the things I came to tell you," said Andrew, "was that I needn't take any money from you after this. I've been offered a job, which I can start next month or in January. At a good salary." He thought of saying: I could help you—but he felt embarrassed.

"Oh, I suppose you'll start at once," his father said. He turned and began to walk towards the house.

Andrew pressed his lips together. "No, I want to know what's going to happen here," he drawled. "I shan't go back to London yet. I can start in January."

Handel stood still. "You're staying here because of me?"

The nervous tension in Andrew's body went off in his sudden piercing laugh. "Must you make that really terrible noise?" his father said testily.

His annoyance sobered Andrew. "I'm sorry," he said smiling, "but if you're going to begin a crusade you'll need a disciple or two."

"Heaven forbid!" Handel said with energy. "Neighbours to join with neighbours is what is wanted. I'm not a leader. In any case I'm too old to do anything except talk to people . . . and try to make them less afraid and anxious about their own happiness and respectability."

They went in and ate the meal Vansittart had prepared—it was only bread and salad, but Handel still kept a bottle or two of wine for his friends and he now opened one of them.

"I was expecting Mower this evening," he said. "I daresay he's forgotten."

"Is he one of your—neighbours?" asked Andrew.

"Oh, yes. He's been writing articles and letters to the *Wik Times*. He can't sign them, you know, he'd lose his headmastership." He began laughing to himself in the way which shook his whole body. "I was thinking I might write on walls. *Keep the Piece*—or, *Suffer little children*. What do you think? *Suffer little children* is probably too idyllic to write about Under Wik; they're less children than young devils. But I got the idea of writing on walls from a young man who stayed here one night about five years ago."

Vansittart had dropped his knife on the floor. He stretched out towards it an arm so thin that it seemed made of a more brittle ivory.

"What happened to him?" he asked.

"Oh, some scoundrels tried to drown him at the Dock End."

"Take care," Vansittart said.

"What about your other friends? What about Vawn?" asked Andrew. He was intensely curious to know what attitude his father's old friends had put on. Which of them would leave him?

"Charles is so anxious to remain unspotted from the world,"

Handel said drily and impatiently, "he forgets that his club was founded by a fearless and penniless revolutionary."

Andrew stayed until it was beginning to be dark.   In the gully of the street by the harbour his eyes, ears, and nose brought him the rumour of a life as strong and unabated as when the Saxon huts leaned over this grey mud.   His own roots were sunk into it.   The tide as it drew slowly sucked at them; he felt the weak nostalgia of childhood, the sickness of the north

Suddenly he reflected that he would have to write to Tib and break it to her that he wanted to stay on here.   His expression became uneasy and stubborn.   Well, she must put up with it, he said to himself.

CHAPTER XXXIII

HE wrote to Tib that night. He said that if she could not bear the thought of living in his aunt's house she must go to her parents'. He knew, as he wrote it, that she wouldn't do that. Even if she had wanted to live apart from him her mother would never dream of going against the Wik law which says that a wife must live with her husband. Within an hour of her reaching her mother's house it would have been known over the town that although Andrew Wikker was staying with his aunt his wife had gone to her parents. There must be something wrong. "If you see Mrs. Mower after church in the morning you may hear."

Tib came up to Wik at once. Semiramis was out when she arrived and Andrew was able to take her directly to their room. From the windows of the back room you saw a long way, across the marsh, to the hill beyond, and to the hills beyond that, line bounding behind line with the strength of lions. On the right the July sea thrust its sleek tongue between cliff and sky.

Tib walked straight to the windows. There is the map of my heart, she thought, looking. The road climbing from the marsh towards Upsal was indistinguishable at this distance except for a thin mark—a vein.

Andrew had remained standing in the middle of the room. "Is the rest of your luggage coming?" he asked.

"What rest?" she said, gently, turning round.

"This suitcase isn't all, is it?"

"How long are we staying, Andrew?"

"For some time, I hope," he said with the energy of guilt. "I want to know what my father is going to do. I can't just leave him to quarrel with the police—they treated him badly last time." He explained to her what had happened.

Tib did not interrupt him until he had told her the whole story. She felt angry with him for bringing her up here without any warning of what he was letting her in for, and in the same moment touched. He will always do these things, and always expect me to come and help him, she thought.   She stood with her head a little on one side, watching him.

"What else could I do?" he asked, glaring at her.

"You could have waited to think it over," his wife said drily. "You know you can't live with your aunt, she drives you quite mad. And as for your father—I like him very much, I admire him, but we can't give up everything, your work—you won't be able to write here—our lives, to look after him.   It's quite foolish.   People of your father's age have their own lives—you have no right to sacrifice ours to them.   You're behaving badly, my darling."

Andrew listened to her with the nervous contraction of his face which might be a smile.   He came over to her and held her against his body so closely that she no longer felt or saw anything else; he came between her and the light.   She was soothed and at peace, aware of the beating of his heart in her own body.   With a sigh, she lifted her arms so that she could feel herself even closer to him.

"After all, you've come," Andrew said inaudibly.

"What did you say, my darling?"

"Nothing, nothing."

"Is this nothing?". . .

Semiramis had begun by trying to overbear Tib.   But the young woman had a calmness which turned aside the rudest remark as easily as it baffled Semiramis's curiosity.   Semiramis suffered agonies of unsatisfied curiosity.   If Tib had told her everything she was thinking, everything about her life with Andrew in London, whom they saw, what they ate, what time they got up, she would still have believed that Tib was keeping things from her, incredible things.   She sat drawn together in her chair, in the drawing-room which was never aired, and watched Tib as she sewed at a dress she was making, with black dulled eyes, unrelenting in their malice. Th' gel's bad, she thought, it's written on her; she'll spend th' boy's bit of money on herself and pull him down.

"What was it you told me you paid for that dress you're wearing?"

The young woman answered her gently, and yet coldly and sternly.   "I didn't tell you."

A beam of sunlight came into the room between the slats of the blind.   It bothered Semiramis and she shuffled across the room to close the blind.   She felt its fierce warmth on her face for a second.

An extraordinary languor overcame her. Going back to her chair she forgot how many years it was since another girl, younger than Tib, stood leaning against the crimson curtains. So it's you, is it? she thought; you, Kezia. Her throat felt dry and constricted, her limbs heavy. She thought that her brother Handel had come into the room and was embracing his wife before her eyes. A pang she did not recognize as jealousy shot through her; she trembled with grief. What they'll do together when they're alone, it's shameless, it's what no one can forgive—she's ruined him with her badness.

The corner of the rug caught her foot; she stumbled—and saved herself by seizing an edge of the marble shelf over the fire-place.

Tib had jumped up. "Are you all right, Mrs. Jordan?"

"Where's the other?"

"There's no one else here," the girl said after a moment.

Semiramis sat down, leaning forward. She took up a corner of the dirty lace at her neck and wiped her lips with it. "Are you going to ha' a bairn soon?" she asked.

"If I were I shouldn't think of telling you," Tib said in a calm voice.

Without moving, the old woman gripped the sides of her chair to restrain herself from calling out. Even she was afraid of the hatred she felt going out of her, leaving her weak, assuaged. Her tongue moved in her mouth like something which had withered there.

Without looking up from the dress, Tib said quietly: "You opened a letter of mine this morning."

Semiramis tried to brazen it out. "Well, what if I did?" she said sharply. "It was onny a mistake—you shouldn't ha' letters sent to you; I'm sure I didn't when I was living with m' husband."

"You did it purposely," Tib said. "Don't do it again, please."

If Semiramis had not been anxious to keep Andrew as long as he would stay she would joyously have poured out all the spiteful angry things that rushed into her mind. The brightness of Tib's eyes, the half-ironic, half-mischievous smile which was never far from their surface, annoyed her so much that she was always hoping that something would occur to disfigure them. She thought that Tib spent too much time on her clothes, and whenever the young woman went out she hurried into her bedroom and turned over all her things. She did this not once but every time Tib left the house. Her dry, bony fingers, far from clean, caught on the thin garments and sometimes tore one.   She played with the idea of destroying them.

One day, half because she coveted it and half to vex Tib, she took a silk scarf.   Instead of hiding it in her own bedroom she carried it downstairs, and when Tib came in from her walk she saw her pushing it out of sight under the cushion of her chair.   She recognized it at once.

"What are you doing with my scarf, Mrs. Jordan?" she said quickly.

"It's not your scarf," snapped Semiramis.

Tib moved so suddenly that the old woman blinked.   She pulled the scarf from beneath Semiramis and held it up.   It was unpleasantly warm and creased.   Tib was not able to recover her serenity, the kindly disgust she felt for the old woman, and tried deliberately to hurt her.

"If you want any of my things I'll give them to you.   But please don't take them or pry into my room."

She went out.

"I've had that scarf for years," Semiramis shouted after her. "If it was among your clothes you must ha' taken it from me."

She waited, trembling, for the answer to this.   None came.   She heard Tib cross the hall to the front door and go out.   Moving as nimbly as she could, the old woman went upstairs to her bedroom, from the window of which she could see the road.   She watched Tib out of sight, and sat down in the window with a sense of soothed, triumphant satisfaction.   The sun was at the other side of the house now, so that she could open the blinds and look across at the strident sunlight beyond the shadow of the house.   In an hour's time she saw Andrew coming.   He came in, and she heard him go into his bedroom at the other side of the landing.   He was there less than a minute before she heard him open his door again.   She called him.

He stood smiling in the doorway of her room and asked with apparent indifference: "Where is Tib?"

"You may well ask," Semiramis said excitedly.   "She went off with a young fellow—I'm sure I don't know who he is, then—he's been hanging about in t'street on and off for days.   She's coming back now, look—by herself."

Andrew looked at her queerly and did not speak.   He went back into his room, and when Tib came he asked her who it was she had met and gone out with.

"What are you talking about?" she smiled. "I went alone, of course."

Andrew burst out laughing. "Oh, that's good," he said, "that's really marvellous. She's an old devil." He told her, still laughing, what Semiramis had said.

His wife frowned. "Don't laugh, Andrew," she said seriously and energetically. "That woman is thoroughly bad and heartless, and not in the least amusing."

"She's a good hater," Andrew said, smiling.

"Listen, my dear. If she says such a thing again I'm going back to London—I don't care what anyone says—and you can do as you like."

"All right, all right," Andrew said.

A curious shadow crossed his face, as though he regretted something he had said. He felt a twinge of compunction for having given the old woman away. For less than an instant he was on her side, against Tib, against himself, with a speechless and shame-faced loyalty, a sympathy in which his mind had no part.

The incredible heat of that July lasted well into August, until it was broken by a day of torrential rain and thunder. Semiramis disliked thunder. She shut herself in her bedroom with cotton-wool twisted into her ears, the blinds close, and a night lamp burning on the marble-topped commode. This room, like the sitting-room and the passages of the house, was pervaded with a dry acrid smell, the exhalations of her slowly withering body. Now that she had almost ceased to go out she might have found difficulty in breathing in any other air.

None of the coolness of the rain-beaten earth in the garden had yet found its way into the room. It was stifling. Huddled in her chair, Semiramis yawned, scratched, and began to talk to herself in the voice of a tired woman. She felt drowsy. Memories of the remote past mingled with words she had heard spoken less than an hour ago. Now Skelton was telling her that a gentleman wished to speak to her downstairs. With a cool excitement she looked at herself in the glass, at her black eyes and firm cheeks, at the thick black curls rioting over her forehead. She ran down boldly, forgetting in her excitement that a young married woman should walk, holding to the banisters. The haggard embarrassed face of her husband's friend turned slowly as she came into the room; she had to hide her smiles. An hour afterwards she was unable to remember what he had said when at last he came to the point; she had been too anxious that no one should see what she was feeling. But what did I feel? the old woman said to herself. She stood watching from behind the blinds when the coffin was carried out of the house. She was alone in the room. The ladies who came to sit with her had left, hurt by her manner to them. She felt a movement in her body, piercing her with joy and stupefaction. In her sleep her limbs twitched and joy flooded through her. That was the child, she said. The child—I am going to have a son now, I am a young woman, my life is warm and perfect. For five months longer she lived with her son, and when the pain broke she endured it with set teeth, still certain, impatient, racked with joy. My son, my son. "Well, Mrs. Jordan, it's a fine girl; you've done well." Struggling to speak, she felt her tongue caught down in her mouth. Trapped, I'm trapped, she thought. Her whole life ran backwards like water pouring out of sight into a hole. She laughed.

The sleeper's mouth opened. Incoherent sounds escaped from it, and the strings of her throat quivered. Her head fell to one side. She saw a child in a dark dress and pantalettes standing close to the bed curtains of her mother's bed. The stuff of the curtains felt rough. She looked at the face on the pillow and knew that her mother was going through some strange and horrible transformation, but the light from the lamp showed only one side of it. The other was a black shadow. She slipped away from the room and ran downstairs into the kitchen where she walked about grotesquely on her hands and toes in front of the servants, clowning desperately—"Don't you know that your poor mother is passing away?"—the child put her tongue out at the speaker and waggled her body: "Look at me," she said anxiously. She smiled like an idiot. Who had told her that she must never seem to care? No one. She had known it before she was born.

The night lamp smoked. Rain beat thickly on the windows, spurted up under the sills. A current of cold air forced its way in and stirred the valances of the bed. It struck on the sleeper's body, she tried to move to avoid it, but her body was stretched stiffly in the bed, unable to move even its tongue—it lay in her mouth like a snake paralysed by the cold and when she thought she was speaking only senseless noises came between her lips. She felt no fear, only furious anger against whatever was holding her in the bed, helpless. Now the dark underground flood of her life began to move towards an outlet. In her sleep the old woman knew that the helpless creature in the bed was waiting somewhere in her body. It was in the body of the clowning desperate child. The child I am, she thought, feeling again the stuff of the curtains and the lightness of her limbs. All that seemed close to her.

She saw Kezia taking the things out of her wardrobe, folding some up and destroying others; she tried to speak to her, to stop her: imploring, cursing, her eyes alone moved, and Kezia looked at her with calm cool pity and, speaking in Tib's voice to someone indistinct, said: "Poor old woman—it's awful, but she can't feel anything."

She opened her eyes. In the instant between her dream and the lifting of her dry, almost lashless lids, time, the inward time, shrivelled in her mind to a worm-like thread, the present.

She started up. Stiff and uncertain, she fumbled at the cord of one of the blinds and opened it cautiously. Rain was still hissing outside from a sky which was lighter than when she put the cotton-wool in her ears. She looked at the clock and saw that less than ten minutes had passed. Her mind was still confused and heavy.

She felt that someone was in the room. Turning round, she saw Andrew coming in at the door; he was speaking, but she did not hear what he said. Something exploded soundlessly in her brain behind her eyes; she tore the cotton-wool out of one ear and said instantly:

"That wife o' yours is a lying thief. I saw her take th' things. She's a thief."

Andrew stood suddenly still. She thought joyously that he believed her, he believed, he knew at last what his wife was. "She's worse than a thief," she cried. "Anybody in t'town can tell you of her goings-on before she was married. Every man as spoke to her could have her, she went with all sorts——"

She actually believes what she's saying, Andrew thought. His sudden understanding of her only filled him with a sharper horror and detestation. He could have no mercy on her. He must kill her, strangle her; he took a step forward.

Tib, who had followed him into the room—they had been knocking at the door for three minutes without getting any answer—stepped between him and the old woman and took hold of him so that her arms were lying on his. "That's enough, my darling," she said gently.

T

He let her push him out of the room. When they reached the
door Semiramis shouted out in a harsh, jeering voice, which quivered
as though she were going to burst into tears:

"Look at the two of them! The love-birds. My word, he
does as he's told, the soft, shabby fellow."

As the door closed she actually had the impulse to open a window
and stretch her head and neck out into the rain. But the strange-
ness of feeling it on her scalp among the thin hairs made her draw
back quickly. She hardly knew what had happened during the last
few minutes; the ragged edges of her dream were still in her mind.
Looking at the bed she would not have been surprised to see that
someone was lying there.

Handel Wikker was writing; so sunk in what he was trying to
make clear that he did not notice when Vansittart crossed the room
to open the outer door. He glanced up, surprised to see Andrew.
The young man said with shamefaced abruptness:

"I came up to see you this evening because I have to go back
to London to-morrow. It's no use, I can't work here. I thought
I could, but it's impossible."

"Don't go," Vansittart said in a low voice.

Handel passed his hand over his face in a confused gesture.
"I shall be sorry when you go," he said quickly, "but you must
do what you think best. If you can't write here you ought to go."

"My aunt has been making Tib's life impossible."

"It takes a lot to make life impossible," Handel said with a
gleam of irony. His sunken eyes, as lifeless as frozen water,
looked through Andrew without interest or pity. He seemed to
come to himself, and laughed. "You'll be better off in London,"
he said kindly. "It's always a mistake to come back. To try
to force oneself into an old skin."

The young man glanced at him. His face was pale and he
was making an effort not to break down into childish excuses.
"Perhaps I can interest people in London in what you're doing,"
he stammered.

"It's a very insignificant affair after all," Handel said re-
flectively.

Andrew answered this with a feeling of anguish. "You don't
think it's insignificant."

"The important thing," Handel said, frowning, "is to keep a

tight hold of principles without losing one's sense of proportion. First and last, nothing is more terrible or more urgent than an injustice to one poor woman's child. But it will simply be a proof that I am losing my senses if I begin imagining that other people —people in London, for instance—will think so."

He got up and lumbered about the room for a few minutes, talking of Andrew's writing, in which the day before he had been interested enough to ask questions. Andrew listened to him, speechless in front of this apparent serenity. He suspected the existence of a sadness and a distance he was incapable of feeling in himself. I could not watch one hour, he thought. He was wretched, yet his impatience and uneasiness grew every minute.

He was longing to get away. The thought that to-morrow night he and Tib would be back in their two rooms in Guilford Street intoxicated him with happiness.

CHAPTER XXXIV

EZEKIEL was talking to Bessie and Soal after breakfast, in the kitchen. It was the day after the thunderstorm; a fine vapour, drawn out of the drenched earth by the sun, clung to the tops of the trees. It was already intensely hot, the sky clear and burning, and no wind.

He was happy. All his hay had been carried before the rain, and he had not begun reaping. He boasted that he had known the thunder was coming for three days before it came. Strutting between the door and the table, his sagging cheeks crimson after the meal, he told the two women how he had impressed a lawyer in *The Swan* by his shrewdness.

". . . he said, 'You're not going to tell me, Mr. Wikker, that you didn't inherit above five hundred acres.' I can show you the deeds of th' farm, I said; it was five hundred acres all told, and strummocking all over th' place. Now if that beast Scoresby would part, I said, you could offer me life everlasting and the rest of it, and I wouldn't take it. When I'm in my own dining-room, I said, or standing in my own fields, I don't envy even the devil himself. I'm sixty-six, nearly sixty-seven, but it doesn't show, I'm not dry yet. I've pleased m'self all m' life—I've done as I wanted—and by God I shan't change now. Anyone who wants my advice on living can have it in two words . . . well, perhaps I won't . . . better not, but you know what I mean."

"Are you going to give me some tea before you go out, father?" Bessie said drily.

"You must blash in tea all day," he grumbled. Since he was in a good temper he measured her out several spoonfuls before putting on his jacket to go out. He met the postman in the yard and took the single letter the man gave him. To his disgust he saw that it was from his sister Semiramis. What does she want? he wondered. He pushed it into his pocket unread.

He went straight to look whether the barley had suffered from yesterday's storm. For some reason he thought more of it than of the magnificent fields of wheat. It had an airy grace he recognized very well, and in a wind it hissed like the sea, or like the petticoats of a woman—a sound quite different from the dry brushing of ears of wheat. To his relief it was undamaged. The light quivered over it as though broken into atoms by the tiny spears guarding each ear. He looked from it to the August sun passing across the sky like a bright bird. His heart quickened in his side until he felt suffocated.

A shadow fell over his happiness. For less than a second he felt angry because he had no son to inherit his fields. It never occurred to him to wonder whether he would not have hated his successor so much that he would have driven him out of the place. Why, for that matter, had he looked on Soal's boy not as his son, but as something which belonged to him, to be fed and worked, as he would have worked a foal dropped by one of his mares? It might have been the only way in which he could endure him about the place.

The shadow had gone. Unless he died, the land needed no one except him. He refused absolutely to think of his own death. When he looked at his fields he felt the utter impossibility of dying. The warmth of the earth, which had swallowed all that rain at one gulp and looked as dry as ever, mounted to his head. He knelt down and almost rolled on the ground, embracing it with both arms flung out.

He remained in the fields all day. He took his share of the binding for an hour or two, but he had to give it up when the blood rushed to his head and made him dizzy. After that, he lent a hand once or twice; he watched; he walked over to look at Scoresby's Field, which had been sown with oats, and drew a sour pleasure from the fact that it was a poor crop.

"You're starving your land," he yelled at Scoresby. "You ought to be ashamed of yourself."

Scoresby blinked palely in the sunlight, which oppressed him, drawing the pain in his joints to the surface so that his skin seemed to fit him badly and if he rolled on the ground it would not be to embrace it.

"It's my field and I'll do what I like with it," he retorted.

This answer infuriated Ezekiel, because it was precisely what he would have said himself. "You're a murderer," he said in a stifled voice; "you ought to hang for it. When you're dead and I've bought the field from your nephew I'll—I'll rename it."

He walked off. During the evening a coolness rose from the

ground, yesterday's rain finding its way up through the soil.
Ezekiel took his place with the binders and worked for two hours
until he was in a muck of sweat: then, highly pleased with himself,
he went home to the cold supper Soal and Bessie had laid ready
for him.   He ate cold game pie, jellied lamb cutlets, cold salmon
trout, the first grouse of the season, and drank a bottle and a half
of claret.   The windows were open, and a timid fragrance of
southernwood mingled with the odours of food and wine.   Towards
the end of this meal he remembered Semiramis's letter and drew
it out of his pocket.   Better read it and know what she's up to,
he said to himself.

The letter—which began "Dear brother Ezekiel"—was less
than a page of Semiramis's cramped writing, and as he read it
his face, crimson already, became so congested that it was almost
black; its air of amazement was followed by an incredulous dismay and rage.   His hand shook: he poured out a glass of the claret
and swallowed it without tasting it.   The words of the last sentence caught his eye—"If you can't stop that girl of yours making
a show of herself with a fellow eight or ten years younger, and a
solicitor at that, he's after her money whatever else, you're more
of a fool than she is——"

He put the letter in his pocket and stared fixedly at the dishes
and at a stain spreading on the white cloth where he had upset
his glass.   He felt as much bewilderment as anger.   "They're all
the same," he said to himself; "run after any man, disgrace themselves . . . no morals, no decency."

The thought that Charles Mower was after *his* money almost
choked him.   His neck swelled and he began to beat his hands
on the table.   In the middle of it all he felt hurt that his daughter
had thought so little about him that she was willing to give away
his money to a rascally solicitor, a young man who had never
worked.   The sin of it, he thought, the sin.

He rose from the table with difficulty and went upstairs, to
confront his daughter.

She was sitting in the window in her own room.   She had grown
heavier during the five years in which she had seen Charles not
less than three or four times a month, heavier in body and almost
lethargic in mind.   Her dark hair had even a streak or two of
grey, but she was able to hide these since it was as thick as ever.
In spite of this, and in spite of the anxiety she suffered when she
thought that Charles must be growing tired of her, she looked

younger than her thirty-five years. Her face had something childish and unreflecting in it. In her eyes the brilliance of youth had been exchanged for an ambiguous depth, troubled and lively. It was as though her thoughts had centred in them, afraid of any effort but that of looking at a world about which, in spite of apathy and disappointment, she was still burningly curious.

As soon as her father came into her room she saw that he had found out. Her heart moved in a sickening way. She wondered how much he knew. She had just sense enough to wait.

"So you've been figging yourself out and running from house to house after this Mower. What is he? Clerk to a solicitor! A splendid life!—And he's years younger than you are—I don't know how many years—enough to make you a laughing-stock. Splendid! It's splendid. Why haven't I been informed; why keep such a triumph from me? Come, 'liver it up now. Tell me."

Bessie realized that he knew scarcely anything. He did not know of Charles's visits to her at night; in her relief she almost laughed at him.

"I shall do as I like," she said roughly. "I'm thirty-five, old enough to marry."

Her father's eyes sparkled maliciously. "And has he offered to marry you?"

The poor woman's defiance dried up; she recalled too clearly Charles's manner when she had forced herself to explain to him that she had no money of her own, it was all her father's, and she was afraid—no, certain—that he would never hand over a penny to help her to marry a man who had no money himself. And a young man, eight years younger than I am, her thoughts added painfully.

Making an effort to seem calm, she said:

"Yes."

"Then why didn't the pair of you come to speak to me about it?" said Ezekiel.

He did not believe her and he despised her now as a woman whom no man had ever wanted to marry.

Bessie felt herself trembling. "Very well, I'm speaking to you about it now," she said coldly. "I want to marry Charles Mower. Do you object to it?"

Ezekiel looked at her spitefully, but with a feeling almost of anguish. He felt very much as he had felt when a clumsy stable-boy lamed a valuable horse so that it had to be destroyed; but his daughter was less valuable to him than a good horse. "Giddy *fool*," he said heartlessly. "Giddy *old* fool. You—at your age —not to know when a tricky fellow is after your money."

"It's not true," Bessie said, trembling.

Her father turned to go out of the room. "Tell him you'll marry him, then, but you haven't a penny and won't have—and see what he does." Turning with his hand on the door, he looked at her with an expression of surprised, sullen grief. "And mind you, if you make a fool of yourself, you'll get nothing when I'm dead. I'm not going yet, either!"

As soon as she was alone Bessie walked over to her dressing-table and sat down in front of the glass. Her face was blotched with colour. She turned her head from side to side, trying to see every mark of age, the lines under her chin and at the corners of her mouth, the dullness of her hair where it touched the skin of her forehead. She closed her eyes, trying to rouse in herself the excitement of Charles's love-making, of his hands on her; she repeated words he had used: she had repeated them so often that they were losing their power to stir her blood.

With a sudden cruelty towards herself she said aloud: "He's waiting for my father to die, so that we can be married, then he'll live on my money."

But at once she turned away and went to sit in the window. Her mind had simply refused to think any more about her life. She sat a long time. Her father came up to bed; she knew by his footsteps that he was drunk. Outside, the brief darkness passed imperceptibly into a white opaque light; the moon had floated above the clouds. It was a deceptive light. The distant gap in the hedge towards which Bessie strained her eyes was less distinct than a much smaller gap in the trees many miles farther off.

She did not expect her lover this week. But when she saw, or imagined, that a man had walked quickly past the place at which she was looking so hard that her eyes felt swollen, she was certain that it was Charles. She started up. The joy that had seized her was unbearable, atrocious.

CHAPTER XXXV

HAPPINESS is tempered to age. An old man, an old woman, cannot bear the absurd, exaggerated, terrible emotions of the young, or the more poignant because less exaggerated feelings of middle-age. When Handel Wikker said that he was happier now than he had ever been in his life, he meant that his happiness was free from pain—that is, from everything which in other years would have made it different from mere tranquil living.

During that September he walked many miles every day, taking in the scattered houses and villages behind Wik, to get people to sign his protest against enclosing the Piece. He wrote to friends in London, to well-known artists who came to Wik every summer, to men whom he knew in the Royal Society. He still preached on Sunday evening in the Temperance Hall, and if he did not allude to the dispute he never forgot to remind his hearers that the protest lay open on a table in the entrance, to be signed.

He began to write a history of common law. As he planned it, it was to show how in the guise of protecting him the law binds the limbs of the common man from his cradle to his grave.

He had no doubts. And no regrets. When his friend Mower begged him, if he must write all night, at least to save himself these exhausting walks, he said in astonishment:

"But I have never felt stronger than I do now. I feel that I can do anything."

Mower held his tongue. He saw that it was useless to tell Handel that he felt strong because he had narrowed his life to one point. It had not occurred to him that he was old. And he was not alarmed by his poverty. He had no time to earn money. He refused to lecture and excused himself from writing the articles he had already promised.

He allowed Andrew to think that he had given up his "crusade." It was quite simple. All he had to do was to avoid writing about it in his letters.

One thing encouraged him during this month. It was that

the railings he had thrown down had not been replaced. The bolder Under Wik children ran in and out of the gaps. Mower had not the heart to tell him the truth—that they were being left until the end of the season. When the visitors had left the town they would go up again.

He was so far sunk in his effort that he almost forgot that Vansittart was in the house. During the day he went in and out without noticing him, his mind turned inward, grudging the energy wasted in speech. He would work the whole evening, reading and making notes for his book, without speaking to him. Without hearing him when he spoke. When Vansittart had prepared a meal for him he ate it. If there was no food he did not ask what had happened.

Vansittart tried, like a child, to get attention. He served up badly burned potatoes. But although Handel made a wry mouth he ate them without complaint. So Vansittart began a cough. He sat on the sofa coughing fit to burst his lungs. Once during the evening, Handel glanced up and said sternly:

"You'll see Nock to-morrow. I suppose you've caught cold."

The next morning Vansittart ran away. Handel looked for him all morning, found him and brought him home. He did not scold him. After two days he ran away again.

This time he was not found until late at night. He had been lying on the dry iron-stained bed of a moor stream. His thin body was screened by the heather growing above it; Handel had passed it during his search more than once. He collapsed before they reached the house, and Handel carried him to his room. Vansittart clung to him in fear. His body was so limp that it seemed disjointed, and he was very cold.

Handel laid him on the bed, took his clothes off, and pulled the blankets and quilt round him. He did it all very gently, in silence. Inwardly he was wondering how long this was going on. The waste of his time vexed him and he was impatient to begin work.

The sick man had seemed to be unconscious. His eyes were closed. He opened them when Handel was stooping over the bed and looked at him with an intent scrutiny.

"You're tired of me," he said distinctly.

"No," Handel said. He added quietly: "But need you exhaust yourself by these long walks? You'll end by killing yourself."

Vansittart closed his eyes again and said nothing.

Handel went away into the next room and set about preparing supper for them. The fire had gone out. He crouched on the floor and began to break a piece of wood over his knee. He did not hear any other sound, but he heard what can only be described as not-sound, a withdrawal, a disturbance of the air close to him. He sprang up scarcely in time to throw Vansittart off his balance. The sharp-edged bread knife jerked out of his hand and Handel caught him before he fell. He thought instantly, After all these years this is the first time it has happened.

Vansittart's face wore a look of horror, as though he had all along been horrified by what he was doing.

His teeth chattered. "You're not angry?"

"No."

"You weren't afraid?"

"Of course not," Handel said brusquely.

Vansittart began to cry with a despair that was terrible to listen to, while he never stopped trembling. Handel carried him back to bed and went back to light the fire. As soon as he had heated some milk he took it into the other room. Vansittart looked at him and said coldly and lucidly:

"You must take me back to that place."

"Never," Handel said. "No, certainly I won't."

"But how can either of us know I shan't do that again?"

Handel did not smile. "We must risk it," he said drily. With an air of plainness he added: "I don't believe you'll try to injure me, nor am I afraid of it."

He took the empty cup away from Vansittart and left him. Vansittart fell asleep after a time and woke up thinking, I was asleep. He felt afraid. But he felt too that he had been dreaming and had not finished his dream. He lifted his head a little from the pillow and looked about him; there was nothing to explain his fear. From the quality of the silence he knew that he was the only person awake in the house.

The curtains had not been drawn over his window and he could look at the sky. It was scarcely dark, covered with soft fleecy clouds as closely as frost lies on the grass. He could see the tree, its leaves dry and unmoving. There no longer in them the watery flow of a tree in summer; they were stiffening to their wintry deaths.

He realized that it was only himself frightening him. In his sleep he had learned something about himself which placed him outside the pale of a safe life. It was as if he stood aside and looked at himself, and condemned himself. He would like to be rid of me, he thought. This was the first time he had dared to think it. After a long time he thought, If I stay here I shall kill him.

He knew that Handel would never send him away.

"He took me out of that place and brought me here," he whispered.

His eyes closed again almost against his will. He was very tired. In a short time he fell asleep.

He got up as early as usual and prepared the porridge and coffee for breakfast. After breakfast he began to clean the three rooms and the staircase. He had not bothered much lately and there was a great deal that needed doing. He moved quietly. Handel was writing at the table in the living-room and he was anxious not to disturb him.

Towards noon Handel pushed his papers away and stood up. Vansittart had come into the room with his almost noiseless step and was watching his movements. He forced a timid smile and said:

"Are you going out?"

"I'm going to the offices of the *Times*, to see King. Do you want anything?"

"He's no good to you," said Vansittart in a dreamy voice.

Handel laughed. "What do you know about him?" he exclaimed.

"As much as I know about myself," Vansittart said tranquilly. He went on in the same voice: "The coffee is finished."

"I'll bring some back," Handel said.

He went off at once.

Vansittart stood in the doorway, with a brush in one hand, and watched him go.

Handel was shown into King's room. The editor of the *Wik Times* greeted him absent-mindedly, or as though he had a great deal on his mind, and added:

"Would you mind waiting one minute while I finish looking through this proof of an article?"

He bent his head, pretending to read. He made marks at

random with the pencil he had snatched into his hand as the door opened. Even the back of his neck was eloquent.

He was thinking with a confused desperate energy. How shabby he is; is there any need for him to neglect his clothes, his hair, to look, yes, like a tramp? You'd expect him to spit tobacco. That's not true—I'm lying to myself, he doesn't look like any sort of a tramp; his eyes look clean through me. He overbears everything I say. There's no kindness in him; it's all a disdainful cruel hoax. Even that's not true—perhaps I can't tell the truth about this man, I'm too close to him; for years and years I've let him know too much about me. What's the matter? I don't deny he's killing himself with work, obscure work for common men, with no fame attached to it—why is it only I who notice that he is cold and implacable? It's not fair! How he stands there, so that I can't see anything else. Do I resent him because he's the only great man I know, because he expects calmly that other people—me!—that I'll ruin myself for his ideas? Why should I? Why should any man do that for another?

In the desk below his hand he had a pile of letters which made it shockingly clear that in the eyes of many respected men he had become a suspicious, ill-advised person. His reputation was in the gravest danger. Every day now when he went home his wife had a fresh complaint to make. So-and-so had snubbed her; Lady Money had cut her at the Conservative whist drive; another woman had dropped acid into the wound. She made his life wretched to him with her hysterical anger.

Suddenly, squinting sideways, he caught sight of his friend's hand, a hand roughed and thickened by hard work. It hung loosely at his side. Without knowing why, he felt as ashamed as though he had spat on this living flesh. It came to him as a shock that it was living. He had actually forgotten that Handel could feel. A shamefaced love possessed him. Tell me what to do and I'll do it, he cried dumbly, his heart pounding.

Again, instantly, he grew cold with fear. The fear of being cut off. The fear that he was making a fool of himself, throwing away his reputation for nothing. Nothing at all.

He put his pencil down and turned to Handel with a nervous smile.

"What did you come to tell me?" he asked amiably.

Handel turned round. His movements had become slower

lately, as though his body were feeling its way. "I'm going to speak at the Dock End on Saturday evening. Will you put a notice in the paper?"

King stood up and took a few steps across the room.

"Certain people have been to see me," he said presently, "important people. They've hinted pretty broadly that an opposition paper to the *Times* may be started."

"May be started?"

King smiled sourly. "Will be started," he said softly. "If—as they put it—I persist in making the *Wik Times* an organ of radicalism and revolution."

Handel looked at him in his piercing arrogant way and said calmly: "Well, do you mind?"

King felt that he might scream with irritation. His life had been given to the paper; he had made it what it was by giving his blood to it. And now that it was threatened, now that his life was being wasted, Handel asked him: Do you mind?

His knees were shaking and he sat down and braced them against the side of his desk. Controlling his voice carefully he said:

"There's an idea—a suggestion—that the sensible course would be to stop arguing about the Piece. It can't be saved now, so what's the use? No one wants to waste energy quarrelling—apart from the bad impression it gives visitors. If we do this Sir Thomas Money will give to the town the strip of ground at the end of the Piece. The edge near the harbour. It could be made into a little garden with a seat or two. Quite pleasant, in fact. . . . Nothing can be done. Don't you think, Handel, that we ought to face the facts? And take what we're being offered."

"Who suggested it?"

"I've been asked not to say." King was sweating great drops and he locked his hands together. "Can't you see that you're expecting too much of me?" he cried.

Handel had been watching him with an indescribable expression. It was not unkind—neither kind nor unkind—but King felt himself shrivelling under it.

"You know that that strip of ground is crumbling into the harbour," Handel said presently in a detached, icy voice. "It's no use to anyone, not even to Money."

He turned away and walked to the window. King looked

at his back with a sullen, imploring grief. If he asks, yes, asks me to go on with him, I shall, he thought. His imagination swung him to a giddy height and dropped him. He felt a sickening qualm. It means throwing everything away, he thought. He was excited and then very much afraid.

Handel turned his head, showing an expression so contemptuous and indifferent that the other man could scarcely sit still.

"Nothing has changed during the past months," he said quietly. "You say we ought to face the facts. Facing the facts is a well-tried method of saving oneself from trouble or disgrace. Quite clearly, if Socrates had faced the facts he would have held his tongue. And if Jesus had faced them He would have taken good care not to come near Jerusalem. The man who faced them on that occasion was Pontius Pilate. Like you, he was *willing to content the people.* You're clear-sighted enough—you know what's been happening. You've always run the *Times* as a radical paper and no one objected to it, because things were going well and smoothly in the town—so why shouldn't you have your fling? As soon as things begin to be serious—as soon, that is, as you begin to touch the property rights of a Thomas Money, your clown's licence is withdrawn and you're warned; certain important people come to see you, as you put it, you're told that you'll have to pay for your fling in loss of reputation. You might, if you were a poor man, pay in actual hunger. In certain circumstances, in loss of liberty. In imprisonment or in a crucifixion. When this point has been reached, the offender, the rebel, can decide whether to ignore the facts or, as you say, face them. You must do as you please."

"You might put yourself in my place," said King.

He was humiliated, crushed. He felt that he was behaving so shamefully that he would never be able to endure himself again. His legs were weak, his throat ached and, worst of all, to his dismay and stupefaction tears came into his eyes and ran over his cheeks. His body seemed full of them. He turned his face a little to hide it from Handel.

"Should I be able to sit in it?"

"You forget that other men have lives of their own," King said in a choking voice. "Can't you see how unhappy I am?"

"I'll go. I'll leave you," Handel said coldly.

He went out. On the worn stairs going down he felt everything go from him, an awful sensation of weakness and fear. Pressing his hands against the wall on either side he mastered the weakness and forced himself to stand upright. He walked out into the street. His eyelids flickered for a minute in the water-bright sunshine. Then he was able to see clearly and walked on, his hands laid behind his back. He was not thinking of the man he had just left. He had decided that there was nothing he could do for him. He must be left alone.

CHAPTER XXXVI

VANSITTART must have thought carefully about what he was going to do. He had gone across the moor by a road which passed three farmhouses, and at each one he asked for a drink of water. From the last house he turned with the woman watching him and scrambled back over a dyke on to the moor and walked on steadily. It was this woman who sent the searchers farther across the moor on the second day.

When Handel came home after seeing King, he found Vansittart gone. Except when he was running away he did not leave the garden. Handel looked for him until dark. He started out again in the early morning with two men from Under Wik helping him. On the third day there were the police and men and boys from the moor farms.

That evening a boy who was gathering seaweed on the rocks below the east cliff found Vansittart wedged tightly between two rocks. As a gull flies, it was not a quarter of an hour from the house. How had he kept going long enough to trace that wide circle across the moor? And then scrambled without breaking his neck down the precipitous cliff to the rocks. The place where he lay was covered at high tide, and five tides had washed over him. Death had found him as exhausted and helpless as a child, his mouth hanging open. He did not look younger or startled.

When he was left alone Handel looked at him with a half impatient pity and grief. If he could he would have brought him back to life. And yet there was the impatience.

"Why were you so impossible?" he said gently.

Vansittart had only one possession except his clothes. That was a signet ring which had become too loose for his fingers, and he did not wear it. Handel found it in a drawer in his room and sent it to his daughter Julia. There was nothing left of Vansittart in the house he had lived and worked in for five years. Not a single trace.

Handel took the bed out of his room, put the table back, and brought his books and papers downstairs. He was scarcely conscious of the relief he felt in having a room to work in again. For a day or two he expected to hear Vansittart speaking when he opened the door and then he forgot that he had not always been alone in the house.

On Saturday the *Wik Times* had an editorial article making somewhat brutal fun of him. He read it, and put it out of his mind at once. His conscious feeling was of anger.

Mower had been going to call for him to go to the meeting at the Dock End. When he did not come at the time arranged Handel set off alone. It was dusk now soon after eight o'clock. The harbour seemed to swallow up most of the light, and all round it the air was dry and heavy. There was a little wind blowing the dust.

He climbed on to the cart and began to speak. The greater part of his crowd had followed him across the bridge from Under Wik and some rough half-grown lads pushed round the cart and stood grinning at him. They were hoping for trouble. It came almost at once. The police had had orders to stop any trouble before it began; they walked through the crowd and ordered him to stop. He took no notice. Two of them stepped on to the cart and, dragging him off, walked and ran him along the quay as far as the bridge. They let go of him and told him to get home. He tried to walk back. They seized him at once, kicking him and twisting his arms behind his back, and threw him forward on to the bridge.

Handel realized that he must give up. There were people standing about, watching, but there was no sympathy for him in any face.

He crossed the bridge, and walked slowly, followed along the dark narrow turbulent street by yelling children. A woman screeched at them and drove them off, and a man spoke to him in a rough anxious voice. Handel looked at him without answering. I still have friends, he said to himself.

Someone ran after him in the darkness. Mower. Handel did not stop and they walked for some minutes without exchanging a word.

Mower was breathing painfully. In a low voice, he said: "They've had orders to do it. And King in his editorial this morning approves of them in advance." He began to pour a torrent of abuse on the editor, seizing Handel's arm.

Handel freed himself. "No, no. Be quiet," he said sternly.

They were nearing the circle of light round a street lamp.
A young man sauntered out of a yard and stood under the lamp
watching them approach. He was a squat stunted youth and his
face had a bestial ugliness, flat-lipped, dull narrow eyes. As the
two men passed him he stretched his arm out and touched Handel
on the shoulder.

"They chivvied tha, did'a?" he said. "But we'll brekk
that —— Money's windows for 'n——"

Handel had halted and drawn back. He did not let the man
finish. Putting his hands behind his back he spoke to him with
an abrupt blazing fury, and walked on. Mower glanced over his
shoulder and saw that the youth had vanished. "That settled
him," he murmured.

Handel did not reply.

He and Mower climbed the Garth in silence. As soon as they
reached the house Mower was going to light the lamp. He was
fumbling in his pocket for matches when Handel spoke.

"Leave it alone."

"Don't you want a light?"

"Not yet."

They stood side by side in the darkness. The fire had gone
but the room was still warm. A chair creaked, startling Mower.
He thought of Vansittart.

"Am I right?" Handel said suddenly.

"You can't doubt it."

Handel made some sort of gesture which the other felt without
seeing. "But are men to be trusted?" he said in a barely audible
voice.

"I trust you completely," Mower said.

After a few minutes Handel sighed; he stood up and lit the
lamp. Looking at him anxiously Mower saw that he was frowning,
sunk in his thoughts. His mouth was thrust forward. His face
had a cold withdrawn air, and he seemed to have forgotten that
anyone was in the room with him. Mower turned away.

CHAPTER XXXVII

Tib awoke, as she did often, with the first light. The moments of silence when London is being re-created from the wastage of night are strangely poignant. It is not a natural miracle, like dawn in the country. Something monstrous is born afresh of the stirring of so many limbs and with the first thoughts of the sleepers. Tib had to struggle with this monster and to escape from it before she realized that she was lying quietly in bed looking at the roof of a house which rose into a sea of blue sky and hearing the shrill cries of birds. These cries formed a thin thread which stretched back, like the thread spun by a spider from leaf to branch, as far as her infancy. But it did not break off there; it passed from memory to memory until it joined the first and the last pinch of human dust blowing about the world. The fine-spun threads crossed the space between the young woman's body lying in the bed and the walls dividing her from the next house; they went up into that calm sky and down into the earth.

She was happy before she remembered that her happiness belonged to the child which had begun to live in her; then she murmured something to it and turned joyfully to fall asleep again. Children ought to sleep.

None the less she was awake again before six. She got up, dressed, and moved quietly about re-arranging the room, so that from being her bedroom it became the living-room with her few trifling possessions hidden, the floor swept, and the bed covered with a striped linen quilt so that it looked like a couch. As she worked she was thinking that before her child was born she must find a flat near Battersea Park, so that by getting up very early she could spend hours with him in the park. She felt so much energy in her body as though she would not be able to exhaust it if she walked with him the whole of the day.

At eight o'clock, when the coffee was almost ready, she went in to wake Andrew. He was lying on his side frowning, his hand clenched even in sleep, his reddish hair disordered and bristling; it was incredibly stiff and bright, and she wondered whether her son would have hair like it. She put her hand on his shoulder.

"Wake up, Andrew," she said gently.

He opened his eyes, saw her, and closed them again immediately. She did not go away until he sat up. If she left him he would sleep until it was time to go to the office at two o'clock and his morning had been wasted.

He came into breakfast yawning but wideawake. When she gave him his coffee and bowl of porridge she spoke to him about a new flat.

"You must find one," he said frowning. "We can afford to have more rooms. And you must have someone to help you with the work."

"No," Tib said lightly. "I don't want help. I'd rather do it myself. It's simpler, and it means that I work as hard as you— and that we're independent."

"But why should we be?"

"I like it," she said smiling.

She could not put into words her instinct—less formal than a belief—that a change had begun in the world which would undermine the sort of secure careful life her mother had lived and brought her up to live. In the future it was the people without possessions, without servants, living in a few rooms, able to be uprooted without difficulty, who could call themselves wise, careful, well-off.

"Very well, you must do as you please," Andrew said with a touch of impatience.

He turned over his letters. One was from his aunt and he put it aside unread: she wrote now every week complaining with extreme bitterness of his cruelty, raking over memories of the past when he had behaved badly, when he was a child, an infant, and in spite of his irritation these letters disturbed him. He carried them about unread for days. Looking at the envelope he said:

"Another letter from the old woman, curse her. I wish she would die. And yet I can't help being sorry for her."

His wife looked at him with her clear smile. "That's nonsense, darling, you needn't be at all sorry for that generation.

They were hard and possessive. They did exactly as they pleased. It's no use wishing they'll die, they're in us, not dying. Fortunately we have the future in us as well, so let's leave your detestable old aunt in the past, where she's quite at home and quite satisfied. She's not unhappy, but she thinks we ought to be."

The future? thought Andrew. Yes, I know; she is thinking of her child: in one natural sense the future is in her, but there is another in which it belongs only to me. A very strange but familiar sensation, the feeling of ice in his veins, seized him. His mind, teeming with images, teeming with a world, seemed closed. It was as though the future it carried about with it was, after all, his death. He turned impatiently back.

"All right, I'm not sorry for her."

"She wants you to be."

"I know, I know."

"This is 1908, darling—and you're writing a book. I'm going to clear the table and let you get on with it."

"Can't I finish my coffee?" Andrew asked. The mere thought of writing had made him want to talk. "We needn't envy the future; 1908 is precisely the year I would have chosen for us—I feel that this is an Elizabethan age of the mind. Instead of quays loaded with the newly-found Indies we have archipelagos of the mind; the world is dissolving into a flux, and any writer who wants to make something from it has to take his chance of finding the Spanish main . . . the *organization* of the bewildering rushing past of things seen with things felt. To see—when one looks at the ripples flowing downstream—to see them stiffen into the folds of a linen sheet and from that to discover what it must be like to wake up in a lodging-house in one of these streets, morning after morning, with the street entering your mind. An Elizabethan writer delighted in the world he saw, before he knew that he was different from the other objects in the world. The delight I feel is in joining one object to another before it disappears. But it has disappeared and what is left are the threads I spin towards it. When I was writing in here last night I heard a stair creak in the next house, and there was myself, a child eight or nine years old, lying in bed listening to steps outside my door, but at the same time, yes, the same instant, I was standing in the Queen's Hall hearing a thin note that belonged to another order of time altogether or to no time. How am I to find a way of writing in two worlds at once?"

Tib listened in her calm way. She was not certain that he was serious. He talked a great deal.

"But, my dear boy, no one will know what you are writing about. Neither of these worlds belong to anybody but you!"

"It doesn't matter."

"It does. If that clever young man who lives in the house opposite—I see him making his bed every morning before he goes out to work—can't understand you, you might as well not write."

Andrew put his arm round her, and allowed his hand to fall lightly on to her body, so little rounded that he would not have known that she was pregnant. The future, he thought again. He could only feel that it was alien; he had not with it even the partial sense of identity he felt with her. His hand passed gently up over her small breasts.

"Do you feel strong?"

"I am strong," said Tib quietly.

"You know I couldn't live with anyone else."

His wife's eyes sparkled with irony. "I don't want you to, my dear boy."

"If you left me I should have no one to talk to," he said, releasing her.

Tib moved away and began to clear the table, and he sat down to write. Lifting his eyes he saw the young man opposite opening his window before going out; his sullen face, the face of a boy perplexed by himself, roused in Andrew a strange and unexpected emotion—as though he could have loved the other man if he had known him. For a moment it was necessary that this young man should understand what he wrote. And—if Tib was right—he wouldn't. An Elizabethan writer could appeal still to an experience common to all men, but now an icy distance divided the journeyman setting off obediently to work at the same hour every morning from the masters of reality. And I, thought Andrew, am stifling in this icy cold, between two worlds. In the hour before daylight. The hour when the very old and the very young stumble aside. The hour of our deaths.

This slippery new reality is the Sphinx which is devouring us—but I shall find the answer, he thought; I shall find words as simple and decent as the look which brings me to the side of that young man. He will read my books.

As he began to write, crossing out a sentence he had written yesterday, the sensation of being shut in returned. Sense of isolation. He shook his head violently. "One needs practice in breathing a new air," he muttered.

Tib set down the bowl she had been washing in the scullery and pressed both hands on the little table. Her eyes were widely open. She might be listening to some sound. The first moment when a child moves in its mother's body has the quality of a sound more than of a movement. She felt an instant of weakness, as though her bones were being jerked apart. Then her life closed over her like a wave and she felt herself being drawn into depths where she was alone with her child. She was safe, but she could no longer see the sky. She was happy.

Now that I am twenty-three, she thought foolishly, there is no time to be lost. But what am I thinking? she cried instantly. There is a lifetime, there is all the time one could need. And if there is to be a new age my son is the one who will belong to it by right of birth; he will understand it: he will live in it. It will be his, not Andrew's. Not mine.

Andrew walked to the office after lunch for the sake of his health. He was proud of his country vigour and habits. In the streets, too, he was part of the life sweated out by the bricks; the smells; the greasy collar of a waiter; torn stockings; the little boy watering the corner wall of the dingy tenement house; geraniums in a window; the old woman shuffling along the gutter in her layers of soiled rags—she dropped her hat back and exposed a skull with a few hairs drawn across it; a Jew, young, pale, at work over furs in a cellar, his hands dirty yellow bones, sad starved cheeks; a woman yawning in a dressing-gown at the window of her room, last night's rouge smeared over her face; insolence and stupidity in a fur coat; stupidity and insolence in mercerized cotton.

All these fed the book he carried in him; half of it was already written: he had taught himself to use images which evoked the instability and inconceivable variety of this life—just as the thought of London itself was an image standing for modern life itself: *Per me si va nella città dolente.*

He stood still to watch a man slapping new play-bills over the old—the office of the grave-digger in *Hamlet*. And at the other side of the tumultuous street an old man turned the handle of a street-piano, playing *After the Ball is Over*.   The cheap cracked tune filled him with a longing all the more insistent because he could attach it to nothing.   It excited him by the promises it held out, as, when he could no longer hear it, he was excited by footsteps on the pavement beside him, by an autumn sharpness in the air from the river, by the delight of journeys not yet made.

CHAPTER XXXVIII

SITTING perched high up in the new dog-cart Ezekiel flew along the road into Wik. He was singing at the top of his strong voice, and out of tune, a song of which he remembered the entire air but only a few of the words: "Oh, you little darling! I love you, Oh, you little darling! are you true? . . ." His face was blazing with happiness. He flourished his whip and allowed the end of it to tickle the mare's flanks to encourage her; she was going so well that the dog-cart bounced on the sides of the ruts and flung him into the air, big and heavy as he was.

The air was as clear, mild, and sparkling as it can be on a September morning between sea and moor; on all the hills the trees were golden with tongues of flame, and the short grass at the edge of the road glittered with a fine grey mist of spiders' webs, woven thickly, one lying above the other.

In the town he drove straight to *The Swan*. While he stood in the yard watching the man rub the mare before turning her loose in the stable he caught a glimpse between out-buildings of the harbour. It was full tide and the water swayed and slipped, gleaming like the sides of a fish, and rubbing itself against the wooden piles. "Although I don't intend to wed," he roared, "to tut-to-tut in life. . . ."

He went into the bar parlour and ordered a brandy, then a second, carrying it over to the window so that he could stare down at the water lapping the walls of the room and across it to Under Wik. The sunlight transformed everything—water, the old houses, smoke from the chimneys—the brightness worked on them like an enchantment to make them seem far off and strange. There was a huge fire in the room. It was warm and quiet. Ezekiel sniffed the brandy before swallowing it: he was so filled with bliss that his body felt light as a feather, and the brandy made the back of his neck tingle.

He watched a sea-gull rising from the water, its long wet legs gleaming like flames, the sun dazzling on its wings. "By God! it's a beauty," he shouted at the landlord. "Just look at it!"

Without glancing round—he was moodily wiping over the glass of a picture of King Edward painted on satin—the other man answered:

"They're greedy birds. Sly—nasty—creatures."

Ezekiel felt vexed with him. He finished the brandy in silence, paid, and went out. On his way to the lawyer's office his annoyance vanished in the joy of thinking that at last Scoresby's Field had fallen into his hands. Ever since the letter the old man had written to him a fortnight since he had been living in a fever of happiness and expectation of this moment. I shan't pay him too much, he said to himself: if he's willing to sell—and since he offered—he must be in need of money. I shan't pay more than half. . . . All the time he knew that he would pay anything, any amount of money, rather than run the risk of losing it.

People were looking at him and smiling. What's the matter with me, he wondered, pushing his hat farther over his eyes. He did not know that he had begun to sing. . . . "If you only love me as you ought to do, Nothing in this world can cut our love in two. . . ."

He turned out of the dingy courtyard into the offices of Messrs. Semple and Hutton. The entrance room was low and very dark and smelled of dry rot. A clerk swung himself round on his high stool and came towards him.

"Good morning, Mr. Wikker," he said with immense solemnity. "Mr. Semple is expecting you."

"Oh! Good morning," shouted Ezekiel.

He followed the young clerk up the wooden stairs. They were so dark that he had to feel his way, and each stair was worn down in the centre to a depth of four or five inches. Cunning fellows, these lawyers, he thought: no show, no expenses—the place isn't even clean . . . the money pours in, and they hide it away so that no one can know how much they steal. The difficulty of walking on the stairs made him giddy, and to steady himself he fixed his eyes on the young man's thin legs. Not much grip in them, he thought; no good for a woman. He slapped himself gently on the thighs. That's better.

Mr. Semple stood up to shake hands with him. He was the senior partner, a man of sixty, red-faced, white-haired, with an expression of forced benevolence. "Sit down," he said in a weak grating voice. "Do sit down, my good sir."

Ezekiel sat down in a black leather armchair as decrepit as the staircase. Semple began to talk to him, and after he had listened for a few minutes and could make nothing of it he dismissed it as "lawyer's chatter." He stared about him at the deed boxes piled against one wall. Estate of W. S. Boulby, Deceased. With a shudder of cold he imagined a box—Estate of E. Wikker, Deceased. To avoid thinking of anything so hateful he began trying to attend to the solicitor's mumbling, unpleasant voice.

It seemed that Scoresby had not, as it had been arranged, brought his own solicitor with him. He had come alone. He was in the next room.

"What the devil does it matter?" Ezekiel said, staring. "Fetch him in."

"The fact is—it's not satisfactory," whispered Semple.

"My God, what next?" Ezekiel said, groaning. "Send for him. Can't you!"

The solicitor lifted his large white hands, like two dead fish hanging from his sleeves. But he rang the bell. The door opened and a clerk showed Scoresby in and half pushed, half supported him to a chair. He looked so shabby and seedy that Ezekiel felt a pang of triumphant pity. He imagined that the other man's heart must be bleeding for the loss of his field. Scoresby sighed, collapsed into the hard chair, and put his hand behind his sound ear, which was very flat and dirty, to listen better. After a string of inaudible remarks Mr. Semple came to the point.

". . . met here to discuss your offer to sell."

Scoresby lifted his head for the first time. "I never made no offer," he said distinctly.

Ezekiel jumped up. "What?"

Drawing one of the fish gently through the air in front of him, the solicitor went on unmoved. "My client, Mr. Wikker, has had a communication from you on the subject——"

"I never communicated," Scoresby muttered.

Dumbfounded, Ezekiel said, "You wrote me you'd changed your mind about th' field. Don't deny it." He felt as though he were going to be ill. The white lettering on the boxes advanced and receded . . . lbY DeceASEd.

"Allow me," Mr. Semple said in a surprisingly sharp voice. "Let us have everything clear. . . ."

Scoresby smiled slyly. "Y' don't come t' a lawyer's office t' have things made clear," he said with an impudence that infuriated

Ezekiel. "But all I want to know is what Mr. Wikker will pay m' for t' field."

Before his solicitor could stop him Ezekiel had answered: "Not a penny over five hundred pounds." He was beside himself with impatience. Cutting short the interminable and pompous chatter of the lawyer about procedure, he shouted into Scoresby's face: "You've had your offer, scoundrel."

Lifting his eyes, Scoresby gazed at him with a sly, pleased smile. "I hear you," he said softly. "I'm willing t' sell now, but I shan't give you possession before I'm deead."

Like a thunderclap it broke over Ezekiel's mind that the whole thing was a trick to annoy him. Bursting with rage he rushed towards Scoresby, but the seemingly weak old man had moved first, nimbly, behind the desk, and finding Mr. Semple in his way Ezekiel fell on him in impotent fury and shook him. Clerks came running in from the outer office and Ezekiel was pushed and pulled out of the room. His anguish was genuine. Just before they got him out of the room he fell silent. He had caught sight of Scoresby leaning against the window and rocking with senile laughter.

As soon as he was outside he rushed to *The Swan*, got out his horse and trap, and drove home. The wind had changed; it was coming off the sea, thin, cold.

He drove straight into the yard; leaving the dog-cart standing with the mare between the shafts he walked into the kitchen. His daughter was seated close to the fire, sewing. She was listless and pale and he gazed at her with a look of fury.

"Back. Back from the fire, girl. Back, back," he said, stamping.

Bessie stood up, holding her sewing in her skirt, and moved in silence to another chair. She did not trust herself to speak. His rages were so familiar to her that she had no need to look at him to know the expression of his face: without looking, she saw his old man's greedy lips, unsatisfied by all his self-indulgence, the powerful jaw, hooked fleshy nose, the cruel and yet humorous glint in his black eyes. She could forgive him everything but his humour.

Ezekiel felt that someone ought to suffer for what he had gone through. He began to turn over in his mind the most taunting remark he could make. At that moment his eye caught a glitter of gold in the armchair she had just left, a tiny pair of gold scissors; they had fallen into the space between the arm and the cushion. He sauntered over to the chair and slipped them deftly into his pocket.

In a minute or two Bessie began to look round for them, on her knee first and then on the floor. Glancing at him she saw the triumphant and delighted spite on his face and knew that he had them. She sank back in her chair, pressing her lips together.

"Ha' you lost something?" he asked.

"No, father."

He felt that he might burst with annoyance. His head swam. Turning to go, he shouted:

"If you ha'n't lost you won't find."

His exasperation drove him out of the house. He went into the yard, saw the dog-cart still standing there, and climbing in he set off without thinking, to his sister's house. The lane to Soureby Bog Hall was so wildly overgrown that he might have been driving through a wood; the branches of the hedge struck him over the head and shoulders and made the mare dance from side to side of the narrow road. The effort of avoiding them used up so much of his energy that he was almost calm when he reached the house. He knew that his sister would never pay a man to trim the hedges and he resolved to send one of his own men down before he came again. He was fond of Ann. She reminded him of his childhood.

She had seen him coming, and before he opened the side door she sent Lily flying out of the room with the tray of cups and the tea-pot. The minute he came in she cried joyfully:

"You're ovver late. We've had tea and I shan't send to make fresh for you."

Brushing this aside he sat down and began in a jeering voice:

"The world's going bad, I tell you. There's something wrong with it when an honest man can't manage his business in peace as he pleases. . . ."

Ann's pale eyes were sly and inattentive; she interrupted him. "Well, brother," she said eagerly, "I heard t' world crack th' other night. There was a crack—and then it leaped like a flea. And now t'pantry door doesn't shut properly, th' frame's sagged, and so I know it's true, t' world's shifted. I don't know what'll happen now."

"Will you stop talking, woman? You—you can't think of anyone but yourself, and here I am and you can see the state I'm in, I've been made a fool of, I've been tricked and forced to assault that wretched old fool Semple, because I'm an honest man and

can't control myself when I'm injured. Estate of Boulby, Deceased
. . . death staring him in the face while he sits telling his paltry
lies."

He went off into a fit of laughter at the memory of Semple's
face of helpless outrage. "His face . . . you should have seen
his face!"

"You'll have an apoplectic fit one of these days," said Ann
drily.

He wiped his eyes. "But you wouldn't let anything like that
happen to me, Ann, would you?" he said, pursing his lips, using
the words he used when they were children.

She softened a little. But, afraid that he might get something
out of her if she showed any weakness, she muttered:

"Don't say I didn't tell you." Then, guessing by his face
that he was going to talk to her about Bessie, she felt a generous
impulse—it would not cost her anything—to befriend her niece.
"I've been thinking o' your Bessie," she said mildly. "You
ought to let th' gel marry now she has t' chance. Heaven knows
marriage isn't much of a do, but it's better than nowt."

"What do you know about marriage?" exclaimed her brother.
"So far as Sweet William went, you can't ha' been certain you
were married!"

"I've Lily to show for it," Ann said coldly.

He was amazed, stupefied, that anyone could speak of Lily
as if she were a matter for satisfaction. He was going to speak,
but a glance at his sister's face with its expression of calm maternal
pride, pierced even his skin. He held his tongue.

CHAPTER XXXIX

STANDING as close to the window as it was possible to stand without breathing on the glass and so obscuring her sight, Bessie waited minute after minute. She tried to see her watch in the darkness but she could only see that the hands had moved; whether it was now midnight or earlier she could not guess. So far as feeling went she might have been standing there for hours.

She had been forced to shut the window. A terrific wind had sprung up in the evening. She had watched the trees being stripped as though hail were beating on them. During the day it had rained and the sky was heavy with clouds until the wind cleared it. Now—it could not be earlier than eleven o'clock—the moon shone with an extraordinary brightness. It was three days before the full, an October moon, hard, polished, pouring its icy light through the almost cloudless sky.

He isn't coming, she thought. Her mind refused to believe it.

Suddenly, she saw the figure of a man crossing the road near the house. He was wearing his overcoat. He had his head down against the wind. Although she expected him, her heart was beating violently. How is it I didn't see him when he passed the gap? Turning from the window she groped her way with desperate quickness across the room. She was afraid of making a noise.

She had left a candle on a chair by the door. Her fingers shook while she felt for it and lit it. On the landing she stopped to listen a minute outside her father's door. The yellow flame of the candle lit her throat, which was younger and smoother than her face, and painted a three-cornered shadow across her cheek. The puckered line below her chin was cruelly marked.

Satisfied, she straightened herself and began to walk downstairs, as noiselessly as her own shadow. In her haste she forgot to set the candle out of the way before she opened the door, and the wind blew it out the same instant. She scarcely noticed it. The ghostly light outside startled her; she saw Charles waiting

with his back to the wall of the house. He came in at once. She
shut the door and said in an eager whisper:

"I didn't keep you waiting?"

In the darkness of the hall she could see nothing of his face,
and she waited with a sharp anxiety for his anwer.

"Quite long enough in this wind. I could hardly get
along."

She did not relight the candle. When they were on the stairs
she turned her head to murmur: "The chest across the corner of
the landing—don't forget it."

She felt only anguish at the bad temper she detected in his
voice. In the silence of the night she heard his breathing and
his lightly-planted footsteps, and it was as though he trod on her
at each step. Opening the door of her room, she forced herself
to whisper, gaily, as if she were at ease:

"I couldn't light the lamp—I was watching for you from the
window."

She felt her way to the table and stooped carefully over the
lamp. When the yellow light sprang in it she did not turn
round. She waited a second, picturing to herself the first
glimpse of his face, with its look of sulky discontent. She
knew it so well—eyes smilingly ironical, inquisitive when they
were not strangely blank, his round chin and shapely petulant
mouth.

She turned, and without lifting her eyes murmured:

"Are you cold?"

"Freezing."

Actually the wind was not a cold one. But he could not help
wanting to punish her—he was in a ridiculous position—his friends
knew that she was in love with him, and they found it laughable
enough, and he could not turn the laughter by reminding them
that even if she was eight years older than he was, she had money.
Until the old man died he would not know certainly that she
had.

"Are you really?" she said timidly. Taking one of his hands
in hers she began to rub it. It was not cold at all. He drew it
back quickly. Bessie did not protest. She stood awkwardly,
silent, her arms hanging at her sides—as though she were trying
to repudiate their action.

Charles felt slightly ashamed of himself: with an attempt at
joviality he said: "Never mind—I'm here."

v

"Yes," murmured Bessie. She did not look up.

He drew her rather roughly into his arms; he kissed her and began to stroke her neck, running his fingers into her thick soft hair. The awkwardness she could not check made her stiffen. Slowly she yielded. She felt an extraordinary mingling of bitterness, joy, and humiliation. The violence of her passion for him could not silence her real shrewdness; even at this moment she knew that he did not love her; and some secret perversity of her nature turned the knowledge into another and sharper joy— much as a child who is ill-treated will find a happiness in thinking of the wrong that is being done to it. Her childhood seemed close at these moments: she wondered vaguely how it had come about that no man had ever looked at her or desired her when she was a girl. She knew she had been pretty.

Yielding suddenly to an impulse in which there was as much grief as love, she took his head between her hands and kissed it passionately. She drew back at once, certain that she was making herself ridiculous. He can't want it, she thought. She half closed her eyes, with a smile that pleaded with him to forgive her for being thirty-five and intolerably awkward.

"You knew I was expecting you to-night?" she asked.

"Yes, of course. That's why I came."

The pain of hearing him say this brought tears to her eyes. "Would you rather not have come?"

"Don't be silly," her lover said calmly, "if I didn't want to see you, do you suppose I should come out all this way, at night?"

She put her hand to her throat. Forcing herself to speak lightly, she said: "You're losing patience."

Charles shrugged his shoulders. He brought his face close to hers and said:

"Don't make a scene, my dear. I love you—if I didn't, should I be here?"

He was not deliberately cruel. If he had known what she was feeling he would justify himself by thinking of the happiness he must give her. What if she did suffer a little?—she could feel safe —he was not going to break with her.

His indolence, which he mistook for sensitiveness—he was sensitive about himself and about no one else—would keep him coming here, hoping that her father would die, waiting for him to die. And it was not cruelty, it was rather the special sort of boredom which lies in wait in small towns that made him take pleasure in tormenting her with the fear of losing him. It doesn't do, he would say fatuously, to allow women to feel certain; they take advantage of it, don't you know?

It was close on five when he left the house. The moon had set and the sky was thick with stars; they seemed nearer and more brilliant than usual. The wind was still high.

Bessie had opened her window cautiously. She strained her eyes to watch him out of sight, but the darkness was curiously disturbing, and the wind blew her loosened hair over her face. A sense of insecurity took hold of her. She could almost believe that the sea was going to rise above the cliffs three miles away and pour down on them. Anything could come of such a wind. The stars were inhuman.

She knelt down and rested her forehead on the glass. Gradually, the room, the garden, in which the trees were becoming spectral in the changing light, came back into focus. Her heart beat more slowly and quietly. She was beginning to feel soothed. To-day, she thought drowsily, to-day we make bread. The image of the warm kitchen stayed with her for a minute. In spite of poverty— and she was only poor because her father hated to give her money —and in spite of feeling herself less regarded than a labourer, she was proud of living in this house. The harvest was a satisfaction to her; she enjoyed bottling fruit, and the smell of new bread, made of their own flour. She was happy when, in February, she could take hot tea to the shepherd busy at night with his lambs. He was an old man, as old as her father, and the only one of his men who was allowed to be given anything from the house; any of the others would be sacked if he were seen speaking to Soal at the back door.

She knew something, a little, about looking after the land. She had even thought that, when her father died at last—he couldn't live for ever—she would be able to learn enough not to be at the mercy of a manager.

It was now—when she thought of these things—that she despised herself for clinging to Charles. She knew that she would never have the strength or the courage to send him off.

She was not unhappy.

CHAPTER XL

THE clearness of the air was startling; it might be the gale that had swept through it—or rain coming. Hills so distant that they were not visible from Wik more than once a year bounded across the near sky; there were no shadows, a fold in the moors was seen plainly for what it was, the broken lip of a quarry, a sunk road. In Wik, the dry October sunlight pointed each roof, stone, warped tree, with a sharp blade-edge of light. The windows of the grey ugly stone houses, pricked out in summer with the bathing-dresses of visitors hanging over the sills to dry, were shuttered to keep any arrow of light from piercing the dust-sheets; and with the weight of the empty house pressing on her, Mrs. Skinnerby shut herself in the basement living-room, and kept up a small fire, expecting winter and the rate-collector.

The houses of Under Wik tumbling into the harbour were as sharp as bones. Seen from a terrace of these shuttered houses, they quivered with life. The bright restless water in the harbour took it up and gave it back with the harsh screaming of gulls.

At the end of the terrace, one house had windows open, on the first floor. A curtain was blowing out. Someone, probably a girl, was playing the piano in the room, faltering, slurring the left hand, a restless scurrying sound, broken up like the water.

"Look at them curtains," said Semiramis. She jerked her finger in the stiff black kid glove. "They'll be raved to tatters, and serve her right for letting them fly out."

She stood close to Ann, sleeve touching jet-trimmed sleeve; they waited to cross the road until Lady Money's carriage reached them and went past. Sitting bolt upright on the dark-red cushions, she looked in front of her: her expression was bored and sulky; she was as pale as though she had been ill lately.

"How old is she?"

"She'll be ovver fifty," Semiramis said instantly. Sarah Money was only forty, but if Semiramis had known her age she would still have added ten years, obeying the instinct that told her there was nothing this woman dreaded so much as age; as the years which only increased her appalling boredom.

"She spends hours a day painting her face," said Ann. "And after she's coloured it red she puts white powder ovver it to look distinguished."

"Ay, and she drinks."

The carriage had gone past. They walked on. As they were approaching a house a woman reached it from the other side and hurried up the steps. She was so quick about it that neither of the old women saw her at all clearly, and they had to be content with a glimpse of her back before the door shut. There was something dashing as well as furtive about this back; a fur with six moth-eaten heads and little paws flew back from it, and her hat slipped sideways.

Pretending to have seen her face, Semiramis said: "She's wearing badly."

"She should never ha' taken on a house this size; the season's too short—if I was as poor as a rat I wouldn't take in visitors . . . always wanting something . . . and the trouble with servants—leaving you with a house full of visitors. I should hang m'self."

They stopped in front of the house and examined closely the blistered paint. The curtains in one unshuttered window had faded. "Blue's no good by t'sea. Th' salt takes the colour out. I could ha' told her." Their terrible eyes noted all the marks of decay and failure.

"She put two single beds in every room. They say there isn't a po in the house, she won't have them."

They went past. They turned a corner—the sea, grey-green, stood up between them and the sky. Neither of them looked at it.

"T'gale last night blashed the trees," Semiramis said.

Ann stood still—suddenly—her pale eyes, reflecting nothing at all, searched the distance.

"What's th' matter?"

She mumbled something. It was about spring, it was about a journey. "You'll go no more journeys," said Semiramis scornfully, "your next journey will be your long last."

"Th' Wikkers are long livers," Ann said, "I'm onny sixty-eight by your seventy—seventy-one, is it, or seventy-two?"

"We're both widows," Semiramis said meditatively.

"I daresay, but you've lost your Merry where I've got my gel still. My little Lily." A wavering smile crossed her face. "The main thing," she went on joyously, "is that we're both on us alive."

Semiramis laughed. It was a light, dry, creaking noise. "Can you remember us coming here one morning . . . we had yellow dresses and drawers, and there was a man sitting up on horseback, taking off his hat, bowing?" She saw the two children against her eyelids, but so faintly that she might have been looking at an old photograph: they slipped past in their yellow dresses, less visible than shadows—unseizable—gone, gone for ever. Opening her eyes, she saw the sea and the white-edged waves like knives.

"I remember something," Ann said after a moment.

They were standing still in the sunlight on the empty cliff. Their legs trembled a little; it was long since they had walked so far. Neither would say she was tired. They stood side by side, the sea stretching below their feet in tight buttoned boots; and first one and then the other turned her face to glance at the pale hoop of the sky. Some children ran past, shouting and screaming. I walked here with my mother, Semiramis was thinking. A strange and terrible excitement filled her. Something she had always wanted to know—she listened, her black eyes searching, staring—but what was it? It all vanished.

She looked sideways at her sister.

CHAPTER XLI

Ann Wellhem was lying in bed staring at the ceiling. Slowly and very cautiously she turned her head on the pillow to look at the clock standing with a wineglass and a cup of milk and other odds and ends on the night-table. Three o'clock—three o'clock on a November afternoon—in half an hour it would be dark.

She was vexed with the nurse for putting her wig into the drawer before the doctor came, so that for the first time he had seen her bald head.

"Well, old lady," he said, his eyes watching her, "they've skinned you."

She heard the nurse moving her chair in the next room; she had nothing to do but sit, and sit—and eat the meals brought to her by Horn. I'm dying, Ann thought. I got it out of him at last. He was speaking to her as they did, reeming off all his fond lies; and she said to him quietly:

"You drunken old fool, why don't you do the decent thing for once and tell me how much longer I've got; you won't regret it."

He stopped speaking then and looked at her. "Twenty-four hours," he said, rubbing his forehead; "you'll probably live about twenty-four hours. Another day."

That meant to-morrow afternoon. At three to-morrow she would be dead. With half-closed eyes she looked up again at the ceiling—it stretched away on all sides like a snow-field: the slats of the blind were open at the top of the window and a hard white light came in from the snow falling outside. At three o'clock, she thought. There was not a tremor in her body: even when he said it her heart felt nothing. It was—when? yesterday? —in the morning yesterday, she heard him tell the nurse in the other room, "The old lady's heart is giving out." As soon as he had said it the nurse rushed softly to close the door. He was speaking in a loud voice because he was deaf—perhaps he was drunk, even at that time of the day.

They say he never eats a meal now, she thought, he drinks whisky instead. She closed her eyes. She was proud of what was happening to her, it proved that she had always been remarkable, and not like other people. She had forgotten that everyone died.

She heard sounds in the other room. The nurse came silently into her room and stood by the bed. Although it disturbed her, Ann felt that she must lift her eyelids—to keep an eye on the woman.

"Mr. Sele has called," the woman said in the bright soothing voice used to a child; "would you like to see him?"

"I won't see him," Ann said into the pillow. "Set him off —and he's not to be given any tea. It's all he comes for." But before the nurse had reached the door she changed her mind and said: "Yes, I'll see him. Where is he?"

She watched him coming into the room, his shoulders drawn up; he was pinched with the cold. Thin and white-faced, he looked younger than he was, unfinished, harassed. It's them deacons, she thought.

"You should stand up to them," she said to him.

He looked at her, smiling and uncertain, rubbing his hands to warm them. "Who, Mrs. Wellhem?"

"Why, them deacons," she said impatiently. "They'll sup out of your hand if you make them, and if you don't they'll fairly harry you to your death." He listened with an embarrassed smile. He's a fool, she thought. "Do you know I'm dying?"

"Oh, I trust not," he murmured. He was looking nervously round for somewhere to sit. Near the bed, but not too near.

"Well, I am," she said abruptly. "And now I'll tell you what's to be done."

Her arm moved under the sheet; she actually brought it out, with a groan, and took hold of the young man's cold wrist, compelling him to stoop over her while she told him that she was being waited for in heaven; to be met at the river, to be honoured.

"Perhaps you would like me to pray," he said quietly.

"Pray? Pray now? No, certainly not." He'll be here until tea-time, she thought, vexed. "Whatever should you pray for?" Her exasperation with him, his mean cunning, offering to pray so that he could stay on and be given tea, buzzed in her head with the noise made by a bluebottle against a window; she could scarcely hear what he was saying. "Do you . . . you may wish, Mrs. Wellhem . . . repentance—and forgiveness——" A cold fury possessed her.

"I've done nothing that needs any forgiveness," she told him. Looking at his downcast face without moving her own, she thought, He's too young to know anything; my life has been far more honorifying—yes, honorifying, and splendid—than anything that is likely to happen to him. I ought to tell him about it, but if I once begin—and where can I begin? Her mind fled away like a startled animal, rushing through shadows, minutes, years. I can't, it's too much.

"Go away," she said spitefully, "go away and speak to the Almighty—isn't it what you do, what we pay you for? And tell Him I'm a'most there. To prepare for me. Go, go on—go away."

She shut her eyes until she heard him close the door on to the landing. The nurse came in.

"That young man is very far from the light," Ann said.

The door opened again. It was Lily. She crossed the room without looking at her mother, and stood silently in the window. It was almost dark; the snow was still falling thickly, from a sky as close as the chimneys. Ann remembered something—lost it; suddenly it came again into her mind and she saw Lily standing on the stairs, her hands folded, mouth open, singing *O Fair Dove, O Fond Dove*. Why? What possessed her? I know, she thought. She believed that she was laughing.

Lily came over to her when she saw her move. "What is it?"

"Your father——" Ann began. It had gone again. She waited.

Lily turned to speak to the nurse. "She's wandering, isn't she?" she said, pointing to her mother.

What next? Ann thought. She lay watching until Lily turned round. Mouthing silently, Send her away—meaning the nurse—she kept her eyes fixed on her daughter's face until suddenly Lily understood. She sent the nurse into the other room.

"Do you want something, mother?"

"Yes. Fetch my purse."

Lily brought it from the drawer where it lay hidden under piles of underclothes and stood with it in her hand.

"Have I a sixpence?"

She watched Lily feeling about in the soft worn purse. I've had it thirty years, she thought.

"Yes. You have."

"You're to put it, and a candle, in my coffin. Nothing else.

Sixpence and a candle . . . I want to see Semiramis. Send for her, I want her."

"It's dark," Lily said. She did not move, waiting: she knew by her mother's voice that she was falling asleep. In a few minutes she was asleep—it happened as suddenly as with a child. Her mouth opened and her head rolled over on one side. Lily looked at her with an inscrutable expression, stooping over the bed, and went away into the next room to look with displeasure at the nurse yawning in her chair.

Semiramis refused to believe that Ann was going to die. She came in the morning, when she got her niece's message and the news that the road was passable. Villages and houses farther inland were cut off, but Soureby Bog Hall was so near the sea that the snow did not lie until it had been falling a long time.

She got out of the carriage, and walked, dragging on Horn's arm, into the house, and marched upstairs. She saw that her sister was still alive and thought, Why should she die? *I'm* alive! When at three o'clock that afternoon there was no change in her, no sign of any change, she said drily:

"I told you so, H'Ann."

Ann was annoyed. "I'll go to-morrow," she muttered.

"Ha' you fixed t'time?" said Semiramis ironically.

"It'll be in t'morning," Ann said after a minute.

She did not, in the morning, feel herself any nearer death. With extreme anger, she put it off until three in the afternoon, and lay watching the clock. When three o'clock came and passed, she felt not simply angry but bitterly humiliated. It came to her that she had been overlooked, that Sele had made a fool of himself. As soon as I'm up, she thought, I'll leave and join t'Primitives; there's so few on 'em they'll be glad enough to have me.

Semiramis prepared to return to her house. She could not endure the discomfort of living in someone else's another night or day. If she had been alone—but Lily followed her about everywhere. Thinking her safely upstairs, Semiramis would go to the china cupboard and begin counting over the Rockingham tea-cups —and there Lily was, she had stolen into the room behind her and was watching, with her long face thrust forward, and her pale blue eyes brightened by curiosity and resentment, to see that her aunt put back into the cupboard everything she touched.

She fastened her sable fur round her neck. "Is t'carriage there?" she asked Lily.

Lily held the curtains apart. "Yes."

"I'll go up and speak to your mother before I go off."

The nurse, as usual, was sitting in the other room with the door open into Ann's bedroom. Semiramis walked past her without looking. Th' lazy beast, she thought; sitting and eating, eating and sitting.

As soon as she was in the room she noticed the difference in it —the silence. She stood leaning against the bed. She felt a furious annoyance, then nothing, blankness, a dull grief and pain. She bent over the pillow. "You shan't die, I say. *H'Ann.* H'ANN."

The nurse came running into the room.

Snow fell again during the night. Now it was lying even on the marsh. The tides crept towards it and fell back. On the moor the roads vanished and the hollows were filled with drifts in which a man could be drowned standing up. Ezekiel had had men at work clearing the road from his house, and towards noon Bessie was able to walk the five miles to Soureby Bog Hall between black glaring walls of snow until she came to the rough track circling the marsh itself. Nothing had been done here, but the snow was still only a thin covering, feathery, sliding off the branches of trees with every faint breath from the sea. Harsh reeds thrust through it on the marsh. Its flakes falling on the sea had flattened it into a grey sluggish plain, smooth, and narrowed by mists. On land wherever the snow could lie undisturbed, there was silence.

When Bessie had nearly reached the house she heard her name spoken in the silence. She turned her head and saw the Congregational minister hurrying to catch her up. Kicking the snow from her boots, she waited for him. He is like some lean eager bird, she thought; or like a hungry undergraduate—how can he have authority over other people or know more than others?

He was out of breath when he reached her. "We're both out, I think, on the same errand," he said anxiously.

"I don't know what your errand is," Bessie said.

His wrists were a bluish red between the ends of his woollen gloves and the sleeve of his overcoat; he must have had the coat a long time, perhaps when he was at the theological college; it was now much too small for him.

"I've been asked," he said; "I had a letter from your cousin, from Miss Wellhem—to come and pray over her mother. . . it's not quite usual, but if your cousin wishes it——" Her silence discouraged him. Trying to talk it down, he said: "It looks like more snow."

"Yes, it does," she answered, looking up at the sky; it was grey and distended, sagging heavily in the centre like an old quilt.

"If it snows again to-night the funeral won't be any too easy to-morrow. It's a long way from here to the cemetery at Upsal."

"Three miles by the church-road," said Bessie pleasantly. "Nearly eight if you're going the long way round. My aunt left directions for her funeral; she wanted to be taken by the church-road, which means carrying her for half a mile. I don't think anyone uses that road now. Although it's short, the last half-mile is so steep that carriages can't get up. You haven't had a funeral at Upsal, then?"

He was holding the gate open for her. They toiled, one behind the other, up the steep snow-covered path to the side door of the house. His harassed voice began again at her elbow.

"Miss Wellhem will be distressed by her mother's passing."

He's quite nervous, she thought. Why? All this is his business. "I don't think so," she said drily. "Not very much."

They went in. Horn—she had become very fat in the body and she was half blind—blundered along the narrow passage in front of them, her skirts brushing cobwebs from the panelled walls, and when they emerged into the front hall she pulled Mr. Sele's sleeve. "Will you come straight upstairs?" she said, speaking with the sullen authority of an old servant. Bessie watched him drawing his poor chapped face into firm lines. No, she thought; he's not a priest, he's too dry and young: he knows his doctrine, but—religion? Can you have a religion from which everything terrible and tender has been left out?

"Where is Miss Wellhem?" she asked Horn.

The woman pointed sideways. Bessie opened the door of the drawing-room. There, at the end of the long room, darkened by the lowered blinds, was her cousin. She was sitting perched up queerly on something; and the look she gave Bessie was very queer. In some curious way, she seemed to be not in her body at all. Her body was perched on some piece of furniture, toes pointed in like a bird, but her mind had hopped on to another perch somewhere else.

Bessie waited. "I came in," she said, "with your minister."

"Oh, yes," Lily said. "He ought to come and pray."

"Do you think it does any good, prayer?" Bessie asked.

Lily did not answer. She frowned as though she were seriously offended. Her eyes were red. After a silence she asked: "Well, aren't you going to help me down?" She was sitting, Bessie now saw, on the elaborate gilt and walnut commode which used to stand in Mrs. Wellhem's bedroom. But what is it doing here? she thought. A start of laughter went through her. Her lips twitched.

"Uncle Ezekiel, your father, came here last night," Lily said.

"Yes, but he was——" She had been going to say, He was angry because you wanted him to look at her. I wouldn't go, he said; I don't want to see poor Ann with her chaffs tied up.

Lily had begun opening drawers and cupboards; she took nothing out, but ran her hand over several things. Her lips moved, and her usually lustreless eyes were bright and alive. She is remembering that all these things are her own now, Bessie thought. She felt an uneasy disgust and sympathy. Abruptly Lily said that she wanted her cousin's advice about some clothes. They went upstairs to her bedroom. A pile of frightful dresses, so old that when she moved them they gave off an indescribable smell, was laid on the bed.

"But these aren't yours?" cried Bessie.

"No, they were mother's," her cousin said calmly.

"What do you——" Bessie said. The door of the room was wide open; she heard the door of her aunt's room at the other side of the landing open slowly, and Mr. Sele's soft, hesitating steps. He looked up and saw the two women staring at him. He stopped.

Lily beckoned the young man into her room. "Now you're here," she said in a flat voice, "you can tell me which of these dresses I ought to have dyed black. I'm not going to the trouble of buying any black, it's too old looking for me." She turned them over.

"Oh, burn the lot," exclaimed Mr. Sele, and fled downstairs. They heard a door shut noisily.

"I must go," Bessie murmured. She walked quickly across the landing. "Don't come." But Lily followed her down the stairs and stood in front of her in the hall, watching her fasten her coat, with an air of inquisitive friendliness, like a young child.   She even put her hand out and stroked the coat.   Bessie turned towards the side door.

"You can go out at the front," Lily said.

"I thought you kept that door bolted always."

"It has to be open for another four days.   Seven days since she died.   It's my house now—but I don't want her to feel shut out."

"Why for seven days?" Bessie asked.

"She'll never stay here longer than that," said Lily.   A sly, ironical smile passed across her face.   "She'll be off then—on one of her journeys."

CHAPTER XLII

WHEN they came in sight of the cross-roads the carriages stopped. The road to the right led after about half a mile to the narrow, steep church-road, steeper than a staircase and so narrow that the bearers of a coffin had to lean over it and duck their heads to avoid the hedges. This part of the road was half a mile long.

Ezekiel, who had been sitting in the first carriage behind the hearse, got out and spoke to the driver. Then he walked up to one of the eight men waiting behind the hearse—they were the undertaker and his men—and declared in a loud genial voice that he was not going to walk up the church-road, "not for God or man."

"Nor for woman, either," he added, remembering that the coffin halted on the snowy road held his sister.

Except his daughter he was the only mourner. The other carriages were all empty. They had been hired as the least number that could be sent to a decent funeral. The undertaker talked to him, expostulating, in a low voice, but he refused to listen.

"A dog couldn't get up the church-road in this weather. And as for carrying a coffin up it——"

His daughter, who had followed him out of the carriage when the argument had been going on for some minutes, now said timidly:

"She—Aunt Ann—wanted to go by the church-road. She left full instructions——"

"Hold your tongue," her father said. "She did it to be a nuisance." He took his hat off and glanced up at the sky; the cords of his neck swelled with the effort of bending his head backwards in his tight collar. "You can go that way if you like," he gasped, but "I'm going round—and I'll be there first."

He put his hat on and walked off to the left.

The undertaker hesitated. He looked at Bessie who was stepping back into the carriage with a jerky awkward haste to avoid having to speak to him, and at last shrugged his shoulders in their black morning-coat and told the driver of the hearse to turn to the right towards the church-road. The carriages followed at the slowest walking pace. A road had been cut in the snow for the funeral, but fresh snow had fallen during the night and the horses' feet slipped on it. As they trudged, the bearers kept up their spirits by talking in almost inaudible voices without moving their lips—it was good practice.

"If you ask me it's going to be no joke carrying the old lady up that hill. Why couldn't she go quietly?"

A smile as pale as the light ran from face to face. "Yes, she left a letter to say that she must be carried up the church-road, and if it wasn't done she would *come again.*"

"Did she say that?"

Ezekiel had marched off along the road to the left without looking back. He walked briskly, his head singing a little from annoyance and excitement. Actually he was pleased to be out of the stuffy carriage, where, in spite of the foot-warmer, he had been very cold. The raw air whipped his face. He grew warm, but when he removed his hat for a moment he put it on again hurriedly; the air was bitter. Before he left the house he had been drinking brandy and he was a little drunk.

It was not snowing, but the sky looked grey and heavy. Bluish white hills loomed through the mist, and wherever he looked he saw only white fields, and trees that the snow made spectral and surrounded with a grey mist like breath. It was as though the breath of the trees had frozen.

The road was almost clear, as far as a farm belonging to him. He turned in there, walking across snow stained yellow with dung and strewn with bits of straw, and went into the earth-closet. When he came out the wife of his tenant was standing in her back door; she offered him a glass of ginger wine; he took it and spat it out, it was too hot and tasteless.

Beyond the farm the road had not been cleared at all, but the snow was firm and not at all bad to walk on, and the road climbed gently. There was a hedge on either side. The hedges after a time came to an end, the fields gave way to moor, and the snow lay in an unbroken waste like a sea; its waves piled up over the furze bushes and it rose gently, with green and purple shadows, towards the distant line of the sky: dim forms of hills might have been clouds. A few stone posts, pierced for chains which no longer existed, marked the track at one side. The snow covered them more than half way. Sea-gulls walked about in the snow. They looked dirty and dejected, and he recalled with a sense of surprise their dazzling whiteness in the sunlight. He felt sorry for them, they showed up here so badly.

He was beginning to feel tired with the effort of walking in deep snow. He stood still, breathing painfully, and reflected. Had he not better turn back? He remembered boasting that he would be there first. He went on.

He did not want to think of Ann. Although he had refused to look at her in the coffin a vision of her lying in it kept coming into his head, a ridiculous painful vision. Her face wore the vague spiteful smile with which she used to listen to his stories, one pale-blue eye was open and the other closed. To get rid of this unpleasant notion he tried to recall what she looked like when they were both young. When they were very young—children—they were often together. She protected him from Semiramis, who wanted to force all three younger children to obey her and if she caught him would turn back his petticoats and slap him on his bare thighs. In summer he and Ann used to wake up very early; they could not lie in bed with the sun shining, and they got up and crept out of the house. There was one morning when they picked armfuls of yellow broom; very clearly he remembered the cool, bright air, the clear distance, and the smell of earth and broom.

With a start he found himself off the road, plunged up to his knees in the snow. He struggled back. There were no more stone posts, and he began to be uncertain of the road and to put his foot down cautiously, as though he could feel the road through the snow. He felt in his pocket for the flask he had filled with brandy before leaving the house, and remembered with a prick of rage that he had dropped it into a flap of the carriage. He toiled on. He felt worn out. He had been walking, struggling through the snow, for a long time, and surely by now he ought to be turning towards Upsal and in sight of the village or of the church. There was a huge mound to the left of him, one of those hills called hows— it must be Upsal How, he said to himself, but it ought to be farther off.

He went slowly forward. Suddenly he fell up to his neck in

snow, and realized that he had wandered off the road again. He
pulled himself out and, carefully groping his way, he came out on
to firm ground, where the snow was only up to his ankles. The
road, thank heaven!

He walked on slowly and with great difficulty. When, a minute
later, he fell into deep snow again he knew that he had not found
the road. A feeling of dismay seized him. He shook himself, and
exclaimed:

"I'm fat and very hot, but there's no sense in putting me on
ice in this weather."

He dragged himself out.

When he was once more on what might be the road or might
only be a barer and more level stretch of the moor he stood still to
look round. The sky seemed to him darker and nearer the ground.
He felt about under his coats for his watch and got it out at last.
When he saw that it was three o'clock he was shocked. He had
been walking since twelve. The funeral must be over. He threw
a long frowning glance over the miles and miles of snow. A horrible
sound, the sudden sharp screaming of gulls overhead, sent the blood
rushing to his head. He looked up, but could not see them. The
clouds are very low, he thought. They screamed again, a loud harsh
tearing noise that made every nerve start up in his body, and reminded him of Soal's fears when she heard the wild geese passing
over the house at night. When they screeched she said it was the
"gabble-ratchet"; it was supposed to be damned souls casting about
to take the soul of some man, woman, or child who was going to
die. He looked up again and grinned.

"If it's me you're looking for, our Annie——" he said in a
teasing voice.

If I keep to the left, he thought, I shall see Upsal. He walked
on, and in less than a minute he fell in head first. Panting as
he fought his way out he saw distinctly the old woman's greedy
malicious face.

"Go away," he shouted.

She moved away a short distance: he turned his back on her
and tried to walk quickly. He was now exhausted, and as he toiled
forward he thought, but I passed that hump in the snow before.
Turning about to look for his foot-steps he saw Ann. "You're
leading me a pretty do-dance," he muttered. He went on, slowly.
It was certainly darker. Ann hobbled just in front of him; he
shouted to her to go away, then to stop.

"Wait, wait for me."

She took no notice of his shouts. Losing his temper he threatened to give her a good beating.

He stood still. The snow and the silence were everywhere. Trembling with exhaustion, he sat down. He got up again at once, struggled forward a short distance and sank down with his back against a hard ridge—it was probably a limestone rock under the snow.

There was no sign of Ann now, when he would have been quite glad to see her. He closed his eyes. After a minute he opened them again, and thought he saw her standing a short distance from him.

"Is that you, Annie?" he said.

He stood up, but his legs doubled under him and he sat down again in the snow. Now we shan't be long, he said to himself. He felt very drowsy. A few flakes of snow were falling and one landed on his nose. Brushing it off he saw a bush blazing with yellow broom just in front of his face. All was still and clear. How it smells, he thought. He felt deliciously warm.

Bessie spent the night at the farm on the Upsal road. With the undertaker and two of the bearers she had driven here after the funeral. They waited an hour for Ezekiel to turn up, and when he did not and it seemed that he was lost, one man suggested that he might be at this farm, the only one on the road. It was dark when they reached it. After searching with lanterns for a time they gave it up.

They found him in the morning. Actually he had not walked far. He was alive. They poured brandy into him and took him back to the farm where they rubbed him with brandy until the doctor came. He lay in bed for a week, then one morning, when he was alone in the room, he had a seizure and fell out of bed on to the floor.

In three days he had almost recovered. His left arm was still paralysed and he was weak. The doctor told Bessie to keep him quiet and unexcited and take care not to annoy him—another stroke might kill him.

Soal came to the farm to help her to nurse him. He was a cruelly exacting invalid. His mind was confused and sometimes childish, but she thought that part of the childishness was assumed;

it afforded so many ways of plaguing her and Soal. One afternoon when he had been asleep he insisted that it was breakfast-time; he demanded ham and eggs and as soon as he had eaten them he began to ask what she was giving him for dinner.

"You had your dinner before you went to sleep," Bessie said. "You have just had tea."

"No, that was breakfast," he said. "Then comes dinner. What's for dinner?"

She explained to him patiently, several times; he scowled and she said gently: "You know I wouldn't try to mislead you, father."

"I shouldn't allow you to mislead me," he said, coldly and drily. When she tried to distract him by talking of other things he silenced her. "I don't want to hear anything from you except what is for dinner."

Fortunately he fell asleep. He awoke in an almost dark room, with the yellow sickle of the new moon hanging outside the window, as thin as the blade of a knife. It is unlucky to see the new moon through glass. Bessie was in the room and he wanted her to draw the curtains at once; the trouble he had in speaking was worse after he had slept, and he could not make her understand. In his excitement he tried to lift himself in the bed.

"Glass . . ." he said, "fool . . . glass, glass."

She looked round in despair. There was an old glass on the dressing-table; she went over to it and touched it, looking at him. "Fool," he stammered, "fool."

She blushed crimson, and twisted her hands with worry and helplessness. Suddenly her father closed his eyes, and said calmly:

"The window—cover the window."

She hurried to draw the curtain. Then she felt cold—there was a small grate in the bedroom and it was difficult to keep a good fire in it. She sat down as close to it as possible. At once her father said:

"Back, back, girl."

"It's cold, father."

"Nonsense."

She moved back. There was silence. She placed her chair against the wall, as far away from the bed as she could get in the small room, and began to think of Charles. She imagined him coming into the room—not this room, another, a large, airy well-warmed room. Her body felt languid, as though she were experiencing the weakness of love and with such pleasure as she never felt when she was with him. Take me, love me, she said. A shudder passed through her. Opening her eyes, she tried to edge her chair nearer to the fire, but her father was watching and at the first movement she made, he repeated: "Back, back," in such a voice that she dared not disobey.

She sat shivering, horribly ashamed. Here I am, a woman of thirty-five, she thought; and my father speaks to me as if I were a fool or a child. She tried, by reminding herself that she had a lover, to revive a little self-respect and happiness, but she felt too much resentment, as well as being too cold.

"I want," her father said in a thick, slow voice, "to speak . . . I want to speak to you——"

She stood up. "What is it?"

"I want you to go for Semple," he stammered. "Go—or send for him."

"Why do you want him?"

A malicious look crossed his face. "I'm going to—to——" he strove for words—"I'm going to cut—cut you out of th' will."

She went out of the room without a word. He lay chuckling and dozing for an hour. She came back then, made up the fire, and seated herself near it. He noticed it but said nothing. After a time he said:

"Here."

Bessie looked round. "What do you want?"

"Semple," he articulated, "where is Semple?"

She did not answer. Resting her head on her hand she moved her fingers to shield her face from the fire. Ezekiel became agitated. She could hear him groaning and panting as he struggled to sit up. Yes, yes, kill yourself, she thought. A terrible excitement filled her.

He began to talk with senseless haste, a flood of incoherent words. "Get—get—mother. . . ."

Bessie got up and came to the side of the bed, and looked at him, at his crimson, perspiring face, webbed with black veins, the grey hair matted on his forehead, his thick neck, his eyes, rolling and vacant. He had given up trying to speak. She bent over him and said distinctly:

"I haven't sent for him, and I'm not going to send. I don't think you'll live much longer. And when you go I shall take all your money and marry Charles."

While she was speaking an extraordinary expression came over his face—a look of anger followed by a childlike grief and hurt. He began fighting for breath. Alarmed by his struggles, she broke down and wanted to help him. She called. She heard Soal and the other woman coming up the stairs, and she leaned against the wall, unable to turn her eyes from the bed. Her father, who had not had the strength to move himself, was twisting in it and arching his body like a trout leaping out of the water; a frightful noise came from his throat. As the two women entered the room he collapsed.

So I've done it, I have killed him, she thought.

Soal turned her out of the room and told her to go to the kitchen. She was shaking with terror. "Warm yourself," the other woman said.

In the kitchen she sank into a chair near the fire. "No, I won't think of it," she muttered. Her body arched itself in the chair, then she sat upright, and forced herself to stop trembling. "I'll never think of it again."

She stood up and walked up and down the kitchen, then—since there was nowhere else to lie down—she stretched herself on the hearthrug and almost succeeded in falling asleep. Soal came downstairs for water. Without disturbing Bessie she emptied the water from the kettle into a basin and refilled the kettle, leaving it at the side of the stove. After a long time Bessie heard the two women coming downstairs together. She stood up. Soal was excited; her wrinkled face was wet with tears or sweat, and she sighed heavily and noisily. "Go up and look at him," she said to Bessie, "he looks a fine figure of a man now, exactly as he looked when he——" She broke off, confused, her voice dying away under Bessie's stern and sardonic gaze.

"That will do, Soal," she said drily. "You'd better lie down and get some sleep." She apologized to the other woman for the trouble they were causing in the house, and asked her whether she would feel repaid by a return of the year's rent.

Cutting short the woman's thanks, she went quickly and with a firm step to look at him.

The very next day he was nailed into his coffin and taken back to Upgang House. It was a heavy coffin and to avoid carrying him upstairs she had it placed in the drawing-room. It stood in front of one of the tarnished gilt mirrors with its elaborate scrolls, leaves, and eagles, and to make room for it the men moved aside a couch of which the tapestry was worn through to the wool in several places.

To look at this couch, and to remember that she had lain on it with Charles, gave her an exquisite sense of power, and yet the coffin standing in its place embarrassed her. She thought that she would not feel safe—though why safe?—until it was out of the house, and then she would begin the renovation of the whole house, together with this room. But I should like to keep the couch as it is, she thought; then blushed with shame for having had so stupid an idea. I might be an unpleasant schoolgirl, she thought sternly: she imagined Charles's mocking and inquisitive stare if she suggested it.

Since she could not begin at once to refurnish the house, she tried to think of something she could do to impress on everyone that a new life had begun for her, that she was no longer the last person to be regarded. She decided to make the funeral an occasion. She had no need to consult anyone—Handel Wikker had been ill for some time, too ill to leave his house—she could do as she liked without asking the opinion of any member of the family.

It was still usual in the country behind Wik to bid guests to a funeral. She sent the regular bidder—he was also the Upsal sexton and the pig killer for the district—to every tenant, even the cottagers, as well as to her father's friends and some of her own. Altogether, with the wives and children of the tenants, she expected to have to provide food for three hundred people. As part of her new life she engaged three young servants, and with Soal they began to prepare cold joints, pies, jellies. Four hundred-weights of beef and cold bacon were dressed and put on the tables, with fifty raised pies, a hundred dishes of jellied creams, and as much ale and wine as all this would need. The guests were fed in batches in the dining-room. Those who had eaten went into the other rooms to wait and talk. Only Semiramis Jordan never moved from the seat she had taken at the head of the table, where she could see everything and cram food into her mouth with fingers as nimble as they were predatory and dirty.

All this serving and talking took longer than they expected. The undertaker came several times to whisper in Bessie's ear that the time was getting short; they must start soon. She listened to him, smoothing with her fingers the front of her new, elegant dress, nodded, smiled slightly, and left him in order to speak warmly to some young farmer's wife or merrily to a child whose red cheeks she could not help touching and stroking. So at last he took it into his own hands, and told her that they were going to lift the body.

This was the moment for two of the farmers' wives, acting as servers, to go round with glasses of wine and the spiced averill-bread.

They set out an hour late, crowding into the eighteen carriages; when these were full the others started out on foot. Bessie saw old Scoresby rush for the last carriage and in his tipsy haste fall sprawling over the step. He had to be hoisted in to avoid a scandal.

Semiramis was not coming. She preferred to stay behind and go through the house from top to bottom—a delight which would never come her way again. The mere thought of it intoxicated her; she trembled with pleasure: her black eyes glittered as though they had been enamelled, and she kept taking the cotton-wool out of her ears to hear better, and lifting one old dirty silk petticoat after another to get at the pocket where she kept the aniseed balls she ate to keep off infection in company.

The carriages started at last. It was a mild day—promise of a green Christmas. There had been heavy rains during the week, followed by days of gentle south-west wind; the last frill of snow had melted from the hills: almost a spring day, except that there was no liveliness in the air—it was a false spring, sapless and barren.

But the sun shone, although low in the sky as it was it had little warmth to give here, and the earth smelled fresh. Everybody felt cheerful. At the cross-roads they stopped to discuss the road, and it was decided, without asking Bessie, that so heavy a coffin could not be carried uphill, and they took the longer road. The sun set as they were passing the farm, and when they reached the cemetery it was dusk, and the Vicar of Upsal, who had been waiting for two hours, looked with bored displeasure at the people jumping out of the carriages and stretching arms and legs after the long drive. They were more like revellers than mourners. They crowded into the chapel after the coffin; there was another delay while candles were fetched from the vicarage, and subdued talk, even laughter, hummed through the chapel.

The vicar hurried his reading of the service. When it came to the hymn it was too dark in the body of the chapel for anyone to see the books, and the old clerk gave out two lines at a time in a quavering voice. "Lay the precious body In the quiet grave," he droned. The congregation hesitated at first, then took it up and sang lustily. The strong untrained voices flew up.

Bessie did not sing, but she listened with an extraordinary feeling of excitement and happiness. The singers rollicked through the verses, with energy and joy. "Here the casket lieth, Waiting for repair. . . ."

As she walked out of the chapel behind the coffin she felt dazed. She caught sight of old Scoresby looking up at the roof with a blissful, ironical smile on his wrinkled face.

Outside, the dusk seemed light after the darkness of the un- lighted church. The air was cool, transparent, tender. A thin yellow flame, shaped like a river between mountains, burned softly in the sky. A feeling of unreality possessed her senses. She imagined that she could hear his voice saying, "Back, back." Her body stiffened itself, and she gripped her hands in their new gloves. None of that, she thought fiercely.

The sexton had zealously taken two candles from the chapel, and he held them so that the light fell on his own face with its wet pursed mouth, on the vicar's hands, and on a wall of clay thrown up from the grave. None of the light fell into the grave, and the coffin disappeared into blackness.

Beyond this feeble glow the dusk was clear and watery; a few trees glistened with moisture; the distant fields were hidden by darkness. Bessie tried to listen, but she was shaking with fatigue and excitement and did not realize that the service had ended until she felt the sexton nudge her. The other people were walking away and she followed, stumbling. The undertaker came to her help; taking her by the arm he led her towards the carriage. She saw the circle of light cast by a lamp on the wall, and a man rubbing one of the horses with a cloth.

As soon as the carriage started she let down the windows. The cold air pouring in soothed her. She leaned back, still trembling, and tried to think only of Charles. Fear, instantly suppressed, seized her with the thought that this carriage, in which if she chose she could drive into Wik and perhaps contrive to meet him somewhere, was bringing her from her father's graveside and that she had killed him. She sat upright. Closing the window against the influence of the night she began to think calmly and sternly of the changes she would make in the house.

CHAPTER XLIII

HANDEL had had a sudden attack of pain over his heart when he was getting ready to go to Ann's funeral. It was so severe that it stopped his breathing for a minute and afterwards he breathed only with difficulty. A woman had come up to clean the house when he went out, and he sent her for Nock.

Surprisingly sober, the doctor examined Handel again and told him that nothing would do him any good but a long rest—and afterwards he must live a quiet life. "Serve you right," he said, chuckling.

Handel lay in bed for three weeks. Then one afternoon—it was the day after his brother's funeral, which he had not attended and had already forgotten—he went downstairs and began to work again on his history of common law.

He became aware of the sound of footsteps in the other room; someone crossed the room quickly, hesitated, then knocked sharply on the door of his workroom.

"Come in," he said. "Who is it? Come in."

The door opened quickly. Lady Money stood, smiling a little, while she explained that she had knocked at the outer door until she found it open, and—"It is a long way up here. I wanted to see you if it's possible," she said softly.

Handel frowned in surprise and some embarrassment. "You see how possible it is," he said. "Please come in."

"If you'd rather not see me I can go away." As she spoke she was settling herself in the chair he drew out for her; she took off her hat and gave her head a shake so that the curls that had been pressed down flew out on either side of her narrow face.

She had become haggard without ceasing to be attractive; her wide mouth and the extraordinary brilliance of her eyes would attract men to her when she was an old woman, as readily as the speeches which sprang from that mouth frightened them. She drew a deliberate happiness from the contemplation of her body, which was still childishly slender. When she undressed at night she would pass her hands over it in much the way that a surgeon might look at and handle a sharp instrument hè had never used.

She allowed her fur coat to slip off her shoulders, and lit a cigarette. "I don't want to be a nuisance to you," she said. Her smile would have been lascivious if it had not been almost mechanical.

"If I can be of any use——"

"I heard yesterday—have you been ill?" She saw that he had become extremely thin: his white hair, brushed from his high forehead, stood on end; his eyes, deeply sunken and burning with a cold light, had concentrated in themselves all the passion and energy of his body. He must have been older than I knew, she thought. He is an old man. She had, in fact, adjusted her mind to this knowledge as she came in, but she could not at once give up hoping to attract him. It was intolerable to her that he did not admire her in the least—as she put it to herself, he did not respect her. Since the ineradicable purpose of her nature was to please, it forced her to try to impress even this man.

"Yes, but I have recovered."

"You don't look strong," Sarah murmured.

"I assure you that I'm strong enough to do anything I want to do," said Handel drily.

"Does that include pulling down railings?" Sarah asked recklessly. She knocked the ash off her cigarette on to the floor.

Handel gave her a cold glance. "Have you been sent to make inquiries?"

Sarah looked down gravely. "Surely you don't think——" she said.

"It is really difficult," Handel said, "to guess what could have moved you to pay me a visit, in winter, to this house."

"So you rule out any idea that I might be moved by friendship?"

"I don't rule out anything," Handel said in the same tone.

Sarah lifted her eyes suddenly and looked him full in the face. "Why don't you respect me?" she said quietly.

Handel laughed shortly. "I have always been certain that you were a clever woman," he said, with an effort at courtesy.

"But you don't trust me?" she said smiling.

He made a gesture of impatience. "What possible occasion could there be for me to trust or distrust you?"

There was a silence, during which Handel's glance moved to his papers, and he sighed heavily.

"I must tell you the truth," Sarah murmured. "I came for a definite purpose, but it doesn't involve asking you about your— your intentions. That was something I ought not to have said. Will you overlook it and listen to me without prejudice?"

"You know I'm prejudiced," Handel answered ironically. "If you want to tell me something, please do. I'm ready to listen."

Sarah blushed with shame and a curious excitement. If she could, she would have punished him for making her feel small, and in the same moment she felt an impulse to ask him to forgive her. Why did I come here? she thought. She might have answered, Because I was bored, and inquisitive. But that would have left out the other more powerful reason—she wanted to impress her husband; she winced when she recalled the indifference with which he had given her permission to come here and "go through her tricks."

To calm her nerves she lit another cigarette, crushing out the first on the edge of the bare wooden table.

"The scheme to turn the Piece into Spa Gardens has gone too far to be given up," she said slowly. "The plans have been passed and some money has been spent. Your—your campaign has embarrassed us, you're well known outside Wik. And—you see how frank I am—we should like to placate you." Noticing instantly his involuntary contempt, she went on hurriedly: "You object to the word *placate*."

"No; not at all. To your idea that it is necessary."

Sarah narrowed her eyes. "Do you know what?" she said, lightly and almost merrily, "it's vanity—it's your quite extraordinary vanity which feels insulted at the thought of people wanting to placate you."

"I don't think I'm vain," said Handel simply. He stretched himself, yawning. He is like a peasant, thought Sarah; she felt repelled by him.

"Let me finish," she said drily. "My husband——"

Handel lifted his eyebrows. "Your husband sent you?"

A smile of peculiar slyness and impudence altered her face. "No, I asked to be allowed to come," she exclaimed. His glance embarrassed her; she faltered, and said quickly: "My husband and the other persons involved know that it would be tactless to ask you simply to withdraw. . . . Please let me go on," she said, looking at him. "We have a suggestion to make. One of the yards in Under Wik—it's called Ash Yard——"

"A filthy and revolting place," Handel said abruptly. It was dark and narrow, and the stench both inside and outside the houses was indescribable and human. The inner rooms had no window and the others were not made to open; to balance matters, the doors did not shut.

"Yes, I know," Sarah said. She pulled a face. "Very well, the suggestion is," she said easily, "that you should give up your opposition to the scheme . . . and, in return, my husband—or I can do it if you prefer it that way, but it would be his money—will put down five thousand pounds to rebuild Ash Yard. It can be renamed Handel's Yard," she said lightly, "if you like." She stopped and added, with the simplicity she could use when she wished: "I've kept nothing back. You have only to decide." In a lower voice she went on: "A moment ago you asked me if I had been sent. I wasn't. I came. But don't forget that I shall be forced to go back . . . and justify myself."

Handel looked at her. "You are exceedingly kind," he said quietly.

She was confused and began to shake.

Leaning back in his chair, Handel gave himself up to his thoughts, as oblivious of her as if she were not in the room. The patience of his face gave it a look of simplicity and commonness like that of a private soldier.

He was thinking, not without excitement. To cleanse Ash Yard was not nothing. He saw that it tempted him. What must I pay for it? he thought. I must only retract all I have been teaching about justice. Ought I then to renounce it if by doing so I can give a score of families decent room? He was tortured by indecision. It was an almost bodily anguish. Suddenly he was calm. If these poor men and women see me selling justice for the good of a few of them what will they think? They will think that justice is something you talk about, but only that you may be bought off. Then he thought of a child he had seen playing in Ash Yard with a handful of dirt he had made into the rough shape of a doll and was pressing to his lips. Am I to leave him there?

A movement she made reminded him of the woman sitting in his room. She had drawn her fur coat over her shoulders. She finds the room cold, he thought impatiently. He himself was sweating.

That child in Ash Yard is not the only one, he thought with pain. There are God knows how many thousands, who by poverty are starved even in the womb; their enemy is not Ash Yard; their enemy is injustice, the lust of power, the pride, the hardness of heart, the insolence of office, the cruelty, the greed by which England is fouled with Ash Yards, more than can be thought of.

"No, it's no use," he said quietly. "I'm sorry, I can't do it."

So I've failed, Sarah thought. She was seized with a feeling of dismay and discouragement. She tried not to show it.

"Can you explain?" she said in a low voice.

"No; it would take too long," Handel said after a moment.

"Do you think you have the right to refuse to rebuild Ash Yard?"

"It's not my refusal," he said ironically. "If you and your husband can afford to rebuild it, why don't you? Why make it depend on my doing something?"

She turned crimson, and said: "Don't you think . . . five thousand pounds is a great deal of money, Mr. Wikker!"

A look of profound sadness came over his face. "You feel that you ought to get more for it than the mere happiness of changing a vile place into a decent one?" he said wearily.

Sarah stood up. "You're intolerable," she said. "Are you quite sure it's not your vanity? You're afraid to climb down?"

Handel smiled slightly, looking at her with mild friendliness. "To tell you the truth, I'm afraid of not climbing down far enough, or of forgetting that I don't need the good opinion of respectable people—nor security."

He started to walk across the room to help her with her coat, but she had it on before he reached her, and was walking swiftly to the door. She gave him a jaunty smile. She was mortified by her failure. A feeling of profound dissatisfaction had seized her. It seemed to her that her life was unbearably dull and empty, like the life of a prisoner. I must go away, she thought; but where? How?

When Handel spoke to her she could not answer him. She trembled with hatred of him. The disorder in his room now seemed to her mean and vile. He has become a peasant, she thought again, trying to feel contempt. What she really felt was shame and dislike—and frightful, bitter dissatisfaction.

As soon as she had gone Handel went back to his work. He soon gave it up, and sat with his head in his hands, thinking. I sank so low once, he thought, as to ask myself whether I shouldn't have done better to marry a woman—not this woman—but one less simple-minded and ignorant than Kezia. He began thinking about Kezia. He thought of her with self-reproach, as though he had injured her, and then with a strange eagerness. He remembered that she was so simple she liked this poor house. She was humble, and lived in it without wanting anything for herself. And how kind she was, he thought. How brave! She would have come with me even if she had known that it meant she would die in less than a year.

He stood up and began to walk about the room, but stopped in a minute and put his fingers over his eyes, as though what he wanted to see could be seen more clearly without light. "It was when you left me that I began to lose my way," he murmured.

Sinking his head on his chest, he stumbled towards the window. The light was going. He brushed the books off a chair and sat down, as though he were no longer sure of himself. An hour passed. He sat looking in front of him with the laborious immobility of age, in which remembering and suffering takes the place of thought.

He was roused by hearing Mower's voice in the other room. In the instant of standing up, to go to him, he thought, How fortunate I am in having a friend. Mower's unshakable loyalty and affection were the unfailing sources of happiness in his life. It is a part of my life on which I can really congratulate myself, although I have done nothing to deserve it, he thought with an ironical smile.

"You're up, then?" exclaimed Mower.

"Yes, I couldn't lie there any longer. Besides, I'm better. . . . Have you come to supper?"

"I've brought my own," Mower answered. He was carrying a package under his arm; unwrapping it, he brought out a potato turnover and put it on the table.

"That's enough for two meals," said Handel.

"My wife made it for you."

"Very kind of her," Handel said absently.

He took a few hesitating steps towards the cupboard that occupied one corner of the room, stopped, and at last turned round and said with an air of confusion:

"I have nothing for you to drink."

"But I don't want anything," said Mower. He was surprised. It was a long time since Handel had been able to buy wine, and he had never spoken of it until now.

During the meal Mower in a nervous jocular voice asked Handel whether he knew that the railings had been put up round the Piece.

Handel made a vague gesture. "I'm almost well again," he said in a meditative voice.

There was a silence during which Mower got up and walked agitatedly up and down the room.

"I hadn't wanted to say all this now," he said abruptly, "but if I must I must, and you, Handel, must listen to me. You're barely recovered, and already you're thinking of continuing your mad efforts. Yes, mad—let me finish—I can't hold my tongue any longer, or pretend not to be anxious and unhappy when I see you losing your health, your time, strength, reputation, in a useless effort. The Piece is lost; it's finished as common land. It is inevitably going to be enclosed and built on—and a number of people are pleased. I've said what I think. Why should you, you, Handel, try to force unwilling people to accept your ideas of justice——"

"My ideas?" Handel said mildly.

"Oh, they are mine, too. I agree whole-heartedly with you, the whole thing is shameful. But it's finished, settled—there's nothing to be done about it! Why not accept it? All this—persecution is useless."

"We've had all this before."

"I know," Mower cried, his voice suddenly trembling with emotion, "and I can't sit still and watch you doing yourself this harm. I—forgive me for saying it—I care too much for you. You don't consider what it's like for me . . . for all your friends."

"Have I any others?" Handel said softly.

Mower did not answer.

Handel looked at him with love and a relentless pity. "I'll tell you what I was thinking when you came in," he said gently. "My whole life—when I was in the church—and afterwards— even to now—has been made up of actions done to my own credit. As a priest I enjoyed having authority. More than I wanted to help people I wanted them to obey me. When I left the church I became proud of what I called my liberalism; I wanted to help people by improving them. If I could have changed them by force, against their will, I would have done it. But I did not feel love towards any of them." He stopped. The look of sadness

x

came into his face again, but as it were at an infinite distance. "It seems to me now that I have never cared enough for anybody. Not even Kezia. Nor you. Not Vansittart."

"You did everything for Vansittart," interrupted Mower eagerly. "Without you he would have remained in that place."

"Let me tell you——" Handel began.

Mower made a quick gesture. "My dear Handel, you saved Vansittart's life."

"Perhaps on the contrary I killed him," said Handel quietly.

"What do you mean?"

"He killed himself," Handel said in the same restrained voice. "It wasn't—as we all assumed it was—an accident. I know it, but it's only just lately I've known it."

Mower was so astonished that he jumped up, knocking over his chair. A glance at Handel's face calmed him; he stooped for the chair and said immediately:

"You're talking nonsense." He paused. "Even if he did kill himself," he said in a low voice, "how are you to blame?"

Handel looked at him with a distorted smile. "I let him guess that he was in the way here," he said. "I had no time to give to him. He knew it, he knew I was bored. One day——" he still smiled—"he tried to kill me."

"Vansittart?" exclaimed Mower.

"It was entirely my fault," said Handel. "You see, I had destroyed his confidence in himself."

"But why do you say that he—that suicide——"

"He must have been afraid that he would attack me again, and perhaps next time. . . . You see," he went on, "how good he was. What he did at the end shows the genuine goodness of his nature, and—the poorness and arrogance of mine."

Mower dropped into a chair, and took his head between his hands. "Oh, nonsense," he muttered, "you were not——"

"Not arrogant?" interrupted Handel smiling.

"If you are arrogant you have the right to be," Mower said roughly.

There was a long silence. Handel had lit the lamp, and when he turned it up the room seemed to become smaller, drawn together under the pale double circle of light on the ceiling. Suddenly the sofa creaked. Mower looked at it with a startled expression. He opened his mouth, but said nothing.

Handel lifted his head.

"Let me tell you something," he said. "All my life I have lived for myself. When I have helped a man or a woman I did it despising them for their weakness. It is only during the last weeks that I have discovered—myself. I'm too old for the discovery to matter to anyone. But to you, you, my dear John, I'll tell you that all these years when I've seemed to condemn the rich and powerful, to loathe humbug, I never separated myself from the people I hated. In my own mind I still remained one of them." He stretched his hand out over a book on his table and quoted: "I became to myself a barren land."

"I don't understand you," Mower said.

Handel shrugged his shoulders. "It's unimportant. I don't care whether you do or not. I understand—at last—that the only way to be of use to the people is to become vile, viler than they are—poorer than they are. To have no shame. You must own nothing——" he glanced at his books and instruments— "nothing that you are afraid to lose. To be indifferent—oh, not to death, that's actually nothing—to failure." He added slowly, searching for his words: "Christ believed he had failed." A sardonic, sly smile crossed his face. "The only useful thing I've ever done is to pull down those railings. It's the only time in my life I wasn't a coward. You say they don't matter very much, they're nothing, the surrender of a piece of common land is nothing—some people are actually pleased. But those are the people I want to scare. I deny them—that is, I deny them in myself. I separate myself from them, I become vile, a felon, a man who wants to pull society down. What you say is true: the railings will go up again—but something will have been gained. Some one person will have learned the truth——"

Mower moved his hands. "The truth?" he murmured. "Did you say the truth? Do you know the truth?"

"I know a truth," Handel said calmly. "I know that a society which turns the Piece into a pleasure ground for the well-to-do is rotten. I shall protest against it until my tongue dries up in my head."

He stopped and coughed.

"I don't agree with you," said Mower at last. He hesitated, and went on: "But if you're determined to get into trouble I'll come with you. You can count on me."

"I expect to," Handel said simply.

He began to hunt through the papers on his table and on the

floor. In the end he found the letter he wanted in his pocket with a dozen others.

"We're not the only ones. One of the men I wrote to in London, a politician, is coming down to speak about it on Sunday night."

He gave Mower the letter. Mower looked at the writer's name, and asked in a surprised voice:

"But do you . . . is this man really coming?"

Handel laughed slyly. "Certainly. Read it."

Mower left shortly after this. Handel walked with him as far as the bridge to Over Wik. When he was walking back alone through the street by the harbour he looked into the uncurtained window of a room in which a boy was reading and frowning over his book; he held his hand to the lamp to warm it: there was no fire in the grate. Handel walked slowly past. In spite of the late hour and the cold, children were playing in the light round the lamp-posts: one of them looked at Handel with a merry chapped face, his nose blue and running down over his chin. A woman with a shawl over her head ran past him carrying something in a bundle. Between the lamp-posts the street was pitch-black, and the houses hanging from the cliff were flocculent with shadows.

To walk on a winter's night through Under Wik was to think that in some rooms children huddled together for warmth: in this house a pregnant woman moved, preceded by her shadow in a room overcrowded already without this new scarcely living creature; in that, a man and a woman gave life to another soul so that it might play in the slippery narrow street for a few years before they and everyone else declined responsibility for it.

Handel found that he was tired and walked slowly. Towards the top of the Garth a lane went off to the left, passing behind the uppermost and craziest gap-toothed row of houses. This same lane could be reached from the street by the harbour, by ten flights of steps that served each a row of houses. Handel walked along it as far as the gate leading into the small graveyard, no longer used, on the very lip of the cliff pouting over the sea. He went in. The stones leaned at crazy angles or fell flat in the long grass.

When he stood there he thought he could hear voices, of the dead, and of the living, the same voices, speaking about hunger, cold, happiness, childbirth, lust, need, poverty, as though the cliff were alive with men, women, and children, like worms, "with all the fury of a spiritual existence."

Should I, he thought, give thanksgiving for creation? Should I offer myself for these? Should I pray for the righteous, for sinners, the sick, poor, imprisoned? Should I desire and earnestly long for the love of the Creator of these?

He took hold of one of the stones, more nearly upright than its fellows. If I am to be born again, he thought, let me be born below this stone, this grass, this heavy earth, let me be born in and of Under Wik, let me marry Kezia and have children, let me be the poorest, the most debased, and the least patient; let me be a laughing sword.

He thought that he understood in another sense the promise, "in *returning* and rest shall ye be saved." Let me, he thought, return to the angry and rebellious womb.

The cold entered his fingers and passed through his arm to his heart. It burned him. He felt it in all his veins. "Let someone hear me," he said aloud.

He turned away, and walked along the lane to the Garth and so home. It was late and dark. He lit his lamp and sat down to prepare his address for the next night.

CHAPTER XLIV

AFTER this address—call it an address if you like, but it was more of a sermon than many he preached in the old days—Handel was regarded as disreputable, silly, indecent, by most even of those who had supported him. He announced the text, "thou hast taken usury and increase, and thou hast greedily gained of thy neighbours by extortion," and beginning at once, "What is usury?" "Who are our neighbours?" he so scalded with words the skins of his listeners that only the poorest and most disappointed felt safe from him. Even of these some were shocked.

When the time came for the collection, Lamb, who was one of the men used to take it up, walked out of the hall.

The trade union secretary did not go alone. When he turned round for an instant he saw that he was being followed by a number of people. None of them were friends of his.

On the Saturday an editorial in the *Wik Times* pointed out with gross dignity that agitators who incited ignorant persons to violence could hardly complain if it were turned against them.

"While we should deplore any untoward acts committed as a natural consequence of the indignation and resentment roused in the minds of patriotic citizens of Wik, they could hardly surprise us. Undoubtedly the moral responsibility for them would lie at the door of any person whose intemperate speeches and deeds outrage . . . undermine . . . society which tolerates him. . . ." King was earning his reward.

In the afternoon Handel walked to the Piece, spoke for only a minute, then made his assault on the railings. With two of the young fishermen from Under Wik he threw down a few feet of iron railing. A band of young men, who had been waiting in the nearest house, rushed out, and while eight or nine of them dealt with his helpers the others seized Handel, beat him about the body, and began to drag his clothes off.

One of them could not help laughing. "With no Sarah Money!" he stuttered.

Handel struggled with them to prevent himself being stripped.

At the same instant he saw Mower run forward with his arms out. His mouth was wide open and he was stammering: "For God's sake someone stop this." A big youth turned round and struck him on the side of the head. He stumbled, and fell heavily.

The police had been looking on. They came forward and with energy and good humour rescued Handel before he was worse than very sore and bruised.

"Now, now, gentlemen, this won't do—you'd better go home."

By this time two policemen had picked Handel up, wrapped his coat round him, and shoved him into the road. "Take yourself off, now," one of them said to him.

Mower was pulling himself up slowly and with an obvious effort, and Handel turned to go to him.

"Do you want to be told twice?" the man said. "Go on. Be off."

It struck Handel that his help was more likely to injure Mower than do him good. He stumbled away, walking laboriously and with pain: he was exhausted now. Looking back over his shoulder, he saw Mower being helped into a house by two men.

Somebody in the town—who?—sent an account of the affair to one of the London newspapers. It appeared on the middle page under a sensational headline. Next day Handel had a letter from his friend, the well-known politician, explaining why he could not fulfil his promise to come to Wik and address a meeting about the enclosure. He had had a tooth out. Handel read his letter with an exultant satisfaction and pride. One feels more confidence in disgrace than in triumph; and it is easier to exult in it.

CHAPTER XLV

HE was astonished to see Vawn. The vicar had left his carriage at the bottom of the Garth and toiled up on foot. It was hardly friendship that had brought him. Looking round Handel's room, he allowed his expression to speak for him. An undusted table, the floor covered with papers and books, the half cheese left on a chair with one boot and a handleless cup, disgusted him. The jacket Handel was wearing had a large stain of ink across the front. His hands were still earthy from digging in the garden. His hair was on end, his linen dirty.

Vawn had come because of his sense of duty, and because the man had once been his friend. He would not allow distaste to turn him aside.

"You can't expect sympathy," he said at once, "for your way of life."

"But do you imagine I do?" Handel asked.

"Nor personal respect," said Vawn drily. "An educated man toadying to the rabble to satisfy his vanity. . . ." Blotches of colour came into his thin, rather sickly, face. "I have shrunk from saying these words, but I feel compelled for the sake of sincerity and truth to say them."

Handel did not seem angry. "No one," he said quietly, "will question your sincerity. The actual question is whether you can be said to be honest? Mightn't I retort that you toady to the Thomas Moneys of your parish?"

"It wouldn't be true."

"Yet you're not ignorant that human beings living in places like Ash Yard pay him rent for those unspeakable walls."

"What has that got to do with your conduct?" Vawn asked coldly. "We all—I—profoundly deplore Ash Yard——"

"You don't rebuke the man who draws a profit from it."

"I beg your pardon, it doesn't lie in my province. Thomas Money attends church regularly—I have no reason to suppose that he is a hypocrite. If he were, it wouldn't alter a single one of the facts——"

"What facts?" murmured Handel.

Quietly and civilly Vawn said: "You want to overturn society itself in the hope of remedying certain things——"

"Things which you deplore."

"Which I deplore," Vawn said, bending his head stiffly. "My opinion of you is that you are a criminal," he went on calmly. "If you could succeed it would be at the cost of crushing out every decency, every advance, tradition, kindness. You would let loose ignorance and violence—civil war. Frankly, I would rather see you locked up. You're not dangerous, but you might be."

Handel looked at him with an expression of irony. "So you want to keep things as they are—even if it means keeping Ash Yard?"

"Not at all," Vawn said in the same colourless voice. He rested his hands on the table, the long fingers intertwined. "Ash Yard will disappear in due time. . . . As a Christian, and as an educated man, I prefer not to destroy society in the silly hope that Ash Yard can be altered overnight."

"Why *as a Christian?*" Handel smiled.

For the first time Vawn seemed likely to lose his temper. "You're perverse."

"Oh, no," Handel said. He continued with an unbearable calmness: "If you have the honesty to tell me that you support Thomas Money because society supports both him and you . . . and you don't care to upset an arrangement so convenient and comforting to people like yourself . . . I shall at least understand you. But you ask me to believe that the Founder of your Church —the Man who hated usurers, and enjoined poverty—would preach a mild piety and meet Thomas Money at dinner afterwards. I have no more respect for you than for any other self-deceiver —myself, for instance."

Vawn had turned extremely pale.

"I——" he said, "I have no patience with the—the cant of people who pretend to know how Christ would behave if He were alive now." He raised his voice. "I don't believe He would try to overthrow society——"

"And if He did——?"

"My mind rejects such a thought."

"If He did you would reject Him," said Handel softly.

Vawn leaned forward. "Do you think you are above society?" he asked violently.

Handel crossed one leg over the other so that his ankle rested on his knee, and Vawn saw that the sole of his shoe was worn through. For some reason the sight offended him.

"Do you think that we are living in a Christian society?"

"We are living in a society which has accepted Christianity," Vawn said, trembling with irritation. "As Christians we are called on to do our duty in it—and our duty does not consist in over-turning it. As you would if you could."

"It seems we have different views not only of Christianity but of our duty," Handel said, smiling.

"Can you point out one word of Christ's in support of your —your wretched ideas?"

Handel rocked himself to and fro, nursing his foot.

"Oh, well, there's the Sermon on the Mount," he said.

"It's not a code of conduct!"

"You mean," Handel said in the same bland, biting tones, "that it is not a code which can be practised in society—in the society you find so much more than tolerable that you can endure Ash Yard—for other people."

Vawn stood up. "I ask you again," he said, looking at Handel with a sharp distaste and contempt, "do you consider yourself above the laws of society?"

Handel lowered his head and the other man could not see his face at all clearly. After a long silence he said in a low voice:

"I consider that Christ would not spare Thomas Money."

Vawn interrupted him. For the moment he was beside himself with anger.

"Are you comparing yourself with Christ?"

Handel gave him a long, quiet, penetrating look; at last he smiled curiously.

"There is only one way of believing in Christ. That is, to be like Him. But all those things—giving your cloak to the man sueing you for your coat, giving to anyone who asks, loving your enemies, refusing to lay up treasure on earth—are folly—worse than folly—according to society. And those who follow Him must inevitably be opposed to society——"

"Nonsense," Vawn said.

Handel did not answer. He sat still, nursing his foot in its dirty broken shoe. Silence fell between them, broken by Vawn's hand striking the table as he turned to go out.

"I came to make a last appeal to your reason," he said drily.

"Very good of you."

"I wasted my time."

"I'm afraid you did," Handel said, with his almost inaudible laugh. "You'll have the satisfaction of knowing that you did it."

"Don't see me out," Vawn said. He walked rapidly to the door and without stopping as he reached it said: "If we happen to meet at any time I should be glad if you would recall that I don't know you."

Even if he had had time to speak Handel had nothing to say to this. He stood for some minutes, when he was alone, with an expression of perplexity on his face. He was surprised to find that he was angry. Then the anger left him without any impulse of his will. It was as though a cool breath blew through him, sucking out every emotion.

He sat down and began to write.

The next day he had to appear in court. After the affair on Saturday he had been served with a summons. He was charged only with pulling down the railings, and fined ten pounds, and the magistrate added sternly that no blame could be too severe for the conduct of an educated man whose actions caused damage to property.

Handel answered civilly that he had no intention to pay the fine; he was then arrested. While he was still waiting in a corridor of the jail a clerk came with the message that the fine had been paid for him. He was set free. A few children and idle youths followed him through the streets. He met Lamb, and his former sidesman hurried down a side street to avoid him.

Mower had not been in court. He was still laid up at home with a broken rib, and when Handel called at the house, Mrs. Mower, very red in the face, declined shrewishly and rudely to let him in.

On his way home he spoke to three or four people, and received no acknowledgement at all or one meant to discourage him.

Before his address on Sunday evening he felt ill. He had a pain, and the effort of walking to the Temperance Hall made him breathless. Not more than thirty people had come to hear him, and they, he noticed, were what Vawn would call rabble. Very well, he thought, I accept them, I accept the rabble.

After the meeting he went into the room behind the hall to get his overcoat. As he reached for it he was seized by a sharp pain, followed by another and another. It was so severe that he fell on to his knees and crawled up the stairs to the entrance. Sweat was running into his eyes. More pain. He lay down and closed his eyes.

He was still lying there unconscious when Nock came, and had him carried to the cottage hospital.

CHAPTER XLVI

HE was ill for four months. When he got up, after a month spent in bed in his own house, he was so thin that he could hardly hold himself upright. His skin had the glazed pallor of extreme weakness: the bony ridge round his eye-sockets showed through it, and his eyes conveyed a strange impression of light, a cold light.

He was growing stronger daily. A week before Easter he decided that he was strong enough to give an address on the Sunday evening. He went down on Tuesday to make arrangements, and the next day he had a letter from Semple informing him that he would not be allowed to speak there again. He learned that the hall belonged to a private company, of which Sir Thomas Money was chairman.

He had handbills printed calling a meeting for Saturday evening, at the Dock End. Easter Saturday.

During his long illness Mower had visited him in the hospital and at home. Nothing was ever said between them about the occasion when Handel was turned off the doorstep by Mower's wife, and Handel had had no chance to tell her he was sorry to be an offence. Soon he forgot all about her.

On Good Friday evening Mower came up to see him. Coming into the room he put his hand into the pocket of his coat and brought out one of the bills about the meeting. He laid it on the table without a word. Still holding it, he let himself drop into a chair; the arm stretched over the table shook steadily, although he made efforts to control it by clenching his hand.

Handel watched him.

"What do you intend to say at this meeting?" he managed to ask, after a minute.

"I'm going to give the address I should have given on Sunday," Handel said serenely. "I may—mark you, I may—preach on the verse, *And all that believed were together, and had all things common.* Why do you ask?"

Mower leaned forward. "Do you mean to do anything else?"

"What are you thinking about, John?" Handel asked easily.

"You know."

Handel did not answer at once. He sat looking down, as if reluctant to look at his friend.

"Yes, I mean, if I can get there, to pull down some of the railings," he said in a low confident voice. "Why?"

"Because I promised to go with you," Mower said. "I told you to count on me."

"Yes?"

Mower had become very pale and his arm still trembled continuously: he seemed to notice it for the first time; he slowly drew it back and let it fall at his side. He sat upright.

"I can't have anything more to do with it," he said, with an anguished smile. "I've been ordered—told . . . you know I have another two years to work before I retire on a pension. If I were dismissed before then I should lose it. In fact——" He faltered, and went on in a louder voice: "Handel, I beg you to give it up."

Handel hesitated for such a short time that it was barely perceptible. He leaned back in his chair, one hand resting on the seat beside him, the other playing with a button of his coat. It was already loose and he twisted it so that it seemed likely to come off altogether.

"You've saved me an awkward moment, my dear fellow . . . I was about to ask you if you would mind staying away to-morrow. In fact, in future. It embarrasses me to see you there. I find myself saying less or more than I mean simply because I'm conscious the whole time of your awkward position. You'll really be doing me a favour."

Mower was standing up.

"I don't believe you," he whispered.

"You can," Handel said simply. "I have never lied to you."

"You are now."

"Come, you must believe me," Handel said, smiling persuasively. "I can't have misunderstandings between us." He hesitated. Standing up, he said smoothly and deliberately: "Have I ever misled you?"

"No," answered Mower. He turned his head restlessly. "No, no. I believe you." He gripped his hands together. For the first time he looked like a very old man. "Give the meeting up," he muttered. "It's no use—no use at all."

"Yes, I think you're right," Handel said.   He was still smiling.
"I think it's no use."

"I'm glad——" Mower said.   He broke off and began moving
towards the door.   "Forgive me, but I must go, my wife will be
waiting for me at supper . . . I've upset your work.   I should
never have come."

"You're always welcome."

Walking to the door with him, Handel said in an amused voice:
"You'll hardly believe me, but I have some parsley growing.   I'll
give it to you.   Your wife will appreciate it."

Mower could see nothing in the darkness, but he put his hands
out and closed them over the firm rough sprigs his friend laid
there.   What have I done? he thought.   Crushing the parsley
in his fingers he walked off, and soon dropped it in the street.
The smell of it remained on his hands and he remembered when
he got home that it had been given to him.   He was in despair
because he had dropped it.

When his friend had gone Handel could not stay in the house.
He went out and walked without knowing where he went, until
he found himself close to Upsal Wood.   He had been walking
for three or four hours.   The small, cold Good Friday moon had
risen, so that he knew it must be nearly midnight.

He stumbled among the trees to the Stone.   Kneeling down
he pressed his head and arms against it.   The scent of young
leaves came to him, and when he looked up he saw through them
the intense blue of the sky, in which the moon burned like a large
star and gave only a slightly keener light.   The cold penetrated
to his skull.   He felt it behind his eyes and at the roots of his tongue
and in his cheekbones.

He had never felt so alone.   An agony of doubt possessed him.

If in all Wik he were the only man to whom it seemed worth while
to struggle against injustice, could he be in his right mind?   Or
was he mad?   In his agony he could not be sure that he was not
mad.

His teeth chattered with cold, but he had the impression that
he was feverishly warm, and his body felt weak.   His bones
seemed to be dissolving.

"Help me," he said.   He answered himself at once.   "I am what
I am, and what I shall be; I am not alone, after all."

He lost the feeling of the stone against which he was kneeling,
and seemed to be stretched on the earth, which moved and breathed

under him. Its breathing mingled with his. Its limbs parted
to receive his, its veins opened into his, too; he felt the seed stirring
in it as though each seed were a man. My children, my brothers,
the numbers of my friends, he thought.

He got up to go home. He was less tired, and his despair and
doubt had given way to a new joy.

*He saw a man coming slowly across the earth to him, walking
through it as it might be a street. The man was laughing and shaking
the dirt from his clothes, which looked as though he had been buried;
perhaps by a fall of earth. He strode past Handel, towards Wik,
and that was the last Handel saw of him.*

CHAPTER XLVII

In the afternoon a man climbed the Garth from the street by the harbour to speak to him. He was a man named Redman, by trade a plasterer. Although a good workman he was not—because he held opinions he was eager to talk about—often in work. His wife helped him by going out to work, charring. He had two sons and three daughters and they were never without enough. They had their bad times—but they made out.

Redman was independent by nature. He read in the evenings, and when his children were not playing he made them read. He had a laugh, as his wife said, like a fair day. Pig-headed, he believed firmly that if not his sons, then his sons' sons would help to govern England for their kind—but he did not believe that it would fall like a ripe apple into their hands. You can see the kind of man he was—shrewd, obstinate, cautious, painstaking, kind, not easy to trick or frighten.

When he came into Handel's room he sat down, setting his hands on his knees, and said carefully:

"Now, Mr. Wikker, I don't want you to take offence at any-thing I say——"

"Why should I?" Handel said, looking at him.

"Some would," Redman said easily. "The fact is, I've had a few words about you with some friends o' mine, and I've talked it over with the wife, and we've decided someone ought to call on you in a friendly way, as you might say, and ask you not to go on about th' Piece. It's a fair waste o' time—you'll mebbe get hurt, seeing th' police are sick o' the trouble you give 'em—and no one a penny the better for it. Us chaps would gladly have helped you, but we can't waste time and run ourselves into a muck of trouble for what, practically speaking, is nowt." His blue eyes, small, twinkling, guarded, searched Handel as shrewdly as an east wind, but with more kindness. "There's ways and ways o' doing things. Knocking ovver railings isn't one o' them. It swatters away energy for nowt, sitha!"

Handel looked through him.

"I daresay you're right," he said shortly.

"You'd better hang with us," Redman said, laughing. "If there's to be Dock End meetings some on us ha' plenty to say. I could talk m' tail off about Under Wik. But it's bound to be facts, Mr. Wikker. What's the use in fligging off into t' clouds wi' men as have problems and troubles enough under their own seats? Tell 'em *why* th' bairns are half starved, drive it intil them with nails—that's the right road, not running your crown into t' railings."

Handel laughed. He shook his head slowly, his eyes empty, waiting.

"I'm too old to learn a new trick, Redman. I shan't try to learn what you know without learning. You know how to live in the skin of a poor man, a man born to do what and go where he's told. You've had the consolation of killing that in yourself. I had another enemy—spy, Judas, call it what you like—to reject and kill. The effort has fetched me up where I am now. It's the last thing I shall have time to finish." He hesitated. "I shan't try again to remove the railings. Other men get into trouble —I can't pull them down alone."

"Most o' t' lads went up there for a lark," Redman said, grinning.

A look of anger crossed Handel's face; it was followed at once by grief, then sly mirth. He laughed to himself at some thought.

"I remember a man coming here about six years ago," he said, "to try to make a speech at the Dock End. He ended up in the harbour. I haven't come to that yet!"

"You'd best not. Not in April," Redman said. He stood up. "If you change your mind about joining us, you know where you can find me."

Redman went home. Over tea, when he was telling his wife about his visit, his youngest girl of thirteen burst out laughing.

"Now what's t'matter?" he asked, smiling. "What's up with Cath?" She was his favoured child, because she was clever and very eager.

"Eh, our dad, I was laughing at Handel Wikker. He's balmy, isn't he?" she said.

Her father's face became hard and cold, like a stone. Leaning across the table, he slapped her deliberately across the face, a slap meant to hurt.

"That's to make you remember Handel Wikker as long as you live," he said sternly.

She was too astonished and mortified to cry. She rushed out of the house and ran along the street as far as the bridge, without hat or coat. Her anger was already softening to grief, and to avert the tears that would disgrace her she leaned against the railing of the bridge and stared fixedly at the water. The light shook across it, mimicking the vanished sunlight. A familiar and unmanageable happiness seized her, and in order to endure it she pressed her thin body against the rail. Other people were idling on the bridge in this lucid hour between dusk and light. As light-footed and dusty as in summer, children were coming back with handfuls of the primroses they gathered first on Easter Saturday. Forgetting her unhappiness Cath ran across the bridge and along the quay.

At the Dock End a large crowd was waiting to hear Handel. The child worked her way through it. Her quick eyes noticed that among the fishermen and the rough mischievous lads from Under Wik were a goodish few others, gentlemen and ladies from Over Wik, keeping to the back of the crowd. They think good of themselves, she thought, with her father's rough cynicism.

It was a warm evening, a little airless, one of those spring evenings when the blood seems to lapse slowly through the veins. There was a smell of dust and new rope, and the peculiar salty smell of the mud in the harbour at low tide.

She saw Handel walking slowly along the quay. He went round to the back of the crowd, and there must have been something placed for him to stand on for he appeared well above the people's heads. Cath Redman examined him carefully, seeking in him the reason for the slap she had received. He is old, thin, he is like a dry tree—*Lo, on the inglorious tree*—she was recalling the hymn sung yesterday at the Good Friday service.

He was not wearing an overcoat. She could not help seeing how stained and shabby all his clothes were. He was bareheaded.

She squeezed her way as far as a low wall. Iron railings rose from the top of the wall; she pulled herself up and stood, holding on to the railings, so that she felt safe and could look down on the crowd. Eight or nine rough idle youths, from one of the "bad" yards near the harbour, were shoving and knocking up against the people near them. Plainly they were out for mischief. On the edge of the crowd there were policemen, nine, eleven, fourteen. Every bobby in Wik must be here, the child thought. She felt a spasm of fear and sick excitement. Perched up on the wall, with people squeezed against her legs, she could not run away easily if there were a row. She gripped the railings in her long-fingered not clean hands, listening to Handel when he began to speak.

Her attention could not remain fixed on him but kept wandering off into the crowd. A hunger in her mind wanted to seize the least fragment of the evening and hoard them, the light sliding from the roofs, molten corner of a window, the quay-side crane, squat smoky ship lying against a wharf, voices, the confused torn-off voices from the crowd.

Handel stood with his hands clasped behind his back; he was repeating verses the child knew already.

"Go to now, ye rich men, weep and howl for your miseries that shall come upon you. Your riches are corrupted, and your garments are moth-eaten. Your gold and your silver are rusted; and their rust shall be for a witness against you, and shall eat your flesh as fire. Ye had heaped treasure together for the last days. Behold, the hire of the labourers which have reaped down your fields, which is of you kept back by fraud, crieth; and the cries of them that reaped are entered into the ears of the Lord. Ye have lived delicately on the earth, and taken your pleasure; ye have nourished your hearts in a day of slaughter."

A woman with a shawl round her shoulders stood immediately below Cath Redman. The shawl was of black wool, the strands knotted together like a net. She was a poor, thin, ungainly creature. The listless child she was carrying dragged at her.

". . . every year we speak in our churches of the birth of Christ. She brought forth her first-born son, and wrapped him in swaddling clothes, we know, because women do the same now. And laid him, we hear next, in a manger. The mother of Christ was a poor woman and thought nothing of lying down in a stable to be delivered. But what do we think of this birth? That it was hard? poor? bitter? Do we think that, if we had been as fortunate in time as to be there, we should have brought comfortable things, luxuries, suitable to a childbed? Well, there will be a woman in Under Wik bring forth a child this evening in a room meaner than a stable, cold, with one lamp for two rooms, for two rooms one window, a handful of fire in the grate; she will be forced to ask her neighbour to lend her even clean rags. What should we think? One thing does not change. The son of man is neglected by us whenever he is born—unless he is born in a family which can spend money for his birth. Yet the womb is not kinder to the poor, nor cruelty excusable because it has happened an infinite number of times since the Birth we talk about once a year, and ignore. . . ."

Looking at the woman below her, Cath saw her lips moving as she listened. There was some shouting and quarrelling in the middle of the crowd.

". . . in that day you will be told: We were hungry because they took away our tools and our goods, we shivered with cold because these made us so poor we could not buy, we were maimed by our labours, we were homeless because evicted; their feasting was our famine, their joy our bitter scorn, their plenty our want, idleness, and squalid deaths. . . ."

There was a movement, people trying to step aside, as a woman standing a short distance from the wall pushed her way to it. She joined the other shawled woman, who gave up listening for a minute to gossip with her. The second woman was pregnant; she was young and thin, so that her swollen body seemed hideously too heavy for her.

". . . complaints of the moth in her furs. Then she says: I must have a new coat, new soft furs. . . ."

One woman was saying with a familiar smile to the other: "I've a shawl you can tek for t'time. . . ." Turning their faces again to listen, they were remarkably like each other. It is the eyes, thought the child; the same look in both of them: they see the same room, the walls, the sink, the chipped basin under the tap, the bed crowding the chairs, the curtained window. I see it, but I see other things, the fuschia plant, the gull hovering. I shall go away. I shall live and shall not die.

". . . as Christ hired himself that we might live, so these labouring men and poor women are born to be hired, or not hired. If they refuse their labour, if the wombs we expect to breed for us still more factory hands, more servants, more conscripts, dry up and are seen to be barren. . . ."

A lady who was standing near Cath Redman turned to her husband, and said in biting tones: "This really is disgusting. We must go." The child missed what Handel said next because she was watching the lady and her husband edge their way between people as gingerly and politely as they could. When she listened again he was saying the strangest thing.

". . . to be like Christ is not enough. The scorn, the anger, the logic of Christ is in me. His pity might be. Learn to seek Christ in the men and women you. . ."

She heard a harsh scandalized voice. "He compared himself to Christ. How abominable!"

". . . . it is in vain that men ask God to save them while they engage in crucifixions at a profit. God cannot save the world until he is worshipped in man. I say we must worship man himself. I say that every man is Christ and every woman the mother of Christ. The son of man. . . ."

The voices distracted her again.

—how shocking. . .

—he would actually have preached it on Easter Sunday if he had been allowed. . . .

—he rubbed my hands. . .

The spasmodic disturbances in the crowd were centred round the youths from the "bad" yard. One of them would push a quietly listening man or woman with his elbow, then turn round and pretend to shout angrily: "Here, who'r'y'shoving?" Suddenly one of these yelled:

"Aren't y' going to pull t'railings down?"

"Awa, let's get at t'railings."

There was a rush of people to get away. A stone flew over their heads and cracked against the wall behind Handel. Cath heard the older woman say fearfully: "You shouldn't ha' come, Lil." A shower of stones and pieces of wood came from the middle of the crowd. Pressing herself to the wall Cath saw her father, who must just have come, seize on one of the trouble-makers and clout him over the head. To make *him* remember Handel Wikker, she thought joyously. The police were pushing their way in among the crowd, their arms threshing right and left. Shivering with excitement, the child looked at Handel at the moment when two men were pulling him down. The rest of the police were driving the crowd away from the Dock End, and people were running along the quay. She lost sight of Handel; then, just as she was wondering whether to cling to the railings or try to run away, he was dragged past her. She saw that his jacket had been torn off him, and he was bleeding from a cut on the head. A man driving an empty dust cart had stopped to look. The police half lifted and half threw Handel into the cart; four of them got in with him and told the man to drive to the police station.

During these few moments Cath Redman's bones seemed to be turning to water; she slipped from the wall, her heart throbbing at the base of her throat; her body was almost paralysed. For a moment she was scarcely able to breathe. Then suddenly she sprang forward and began to run after the cart. She saw one of the men lift his foot and kick Handel, another struck him on the face. She stood still. The tears ran down her cheeks; she felt such despair and rage that she thought she was going mad.

The cart had to move slowly in the road from the Dock End because it was filled with people walking and running to get away from possible trouble. Looking up for a moment Handel saw a single person walking in the opposite direction, towards the cart.

His sister, Semiramis Jordan.

She walked, her head poked forward, with stiff, short steps, and when she had almost reached the cart she halted and stood in the middle of the road, so that the driver was forced to pull up. Ignoring him, she came forward until she could strike the front of the cart with her fist.

"I see I've come too late for t'meeting," she said to Handel. Her face twitched slightly. "What ha' you done to him?" she exclaimed, taking hold of the rim of the cart with both hands, as though she wanted to overturn it. The police sergeant leaned forward and told her to stand out of the road.

"Hold your tongue!" she answered. Snatching at the driver's arm, she said sharply: "You. Help me into t'cart."

He glanced helplessly at the policemen and seeing that they were silent, he got down and pushed the old woman into the cart, as decorously as possible. She sat down on the floor of the cart beside her brother. Her face had assumed a vindictive expression. Biting her lips, she stared round her with bright, viperish eyes at the people hurrying past the cart. She saw a woman she knew, and shouted spitefully:

"Good evening to you, Mrs. Lasselles. Ay, you may well look t'other road. Standing gaping like a ninny while people make beasts of themselves. You'll come to——"

She was jerked so suddenly by the cart moving that her last

word was cut in half by a scream. Recovering herself, she muttered: "Great mucky maunsells. All of them."

She took no further notice of Handel. He exasperated her by his folly; it was an instinct of family loyalty that had brought her to his side, and it was that, with her jealous contempt for everyone she had ever known, which kept her seated stiffly upright on the dirty floor of the cart, sending venomous glances over the edge. She was indifferent to the police, whom she thought of as her servants.

As the cart reached the end of the dock road a man with a barrow set it down and began slowly taking off his jacket. He walked with it to the cart and offered it, with a smile that showed decayed stumps of teeth, to Semiramis. Wagging his head he said something in a hoarse voice.

Semiramis snatched the jacket and drew it over Handel's torn blood- and dirt-stained shirt.

"It will be spoiled," Handel said, looking at the man.

"Ay, let it," the fellow said slowly. "Luckily, it's t'warmest I have."

At the police station Semiramis found herself being respectfully and ruthlessly pushed into the street. There was nothing for it but for her to give way and return home. She spat into her handkerchief, to express the contempt she felt for the law as symbolized by the inspector, and went away without speaking to her brother.

Handel was stripped roughly and searched. In the pockets of the jacket he was wearing were a clay pipe, a piece of twine and a rag. They were given back to him with his clothes and he was shut up for the night in a cell.

He lay down as soon as he was alone. The cell was damply cold, and he had not been given a blanket. After a few minutes he felt that he had been lying for hours, days, in the same attitude, but he could not move. He seemed to have no strength, not even the strength to raise his hand to his face, on which the blood had dried into a false scar. His body shivered with cold, but he was unconscious of it.

He could not sleep. When he closed his eyes his mind seemed only to become more awake. He tried to think, to decide what he must do—but his thoughts slipped away from him with the movement of light among leaves.

A sense of intolerable humiliation weighed on him. Everything he had done, that had brought him to this moment in time, seemed to him ridiculous, unnecessary, useless.

He was pursued through all his distracted efforts at thinking by the figure of the man with the barrow, and the gesture with which he took his coat off and held it up. Here, he felt, was something important, and it stubbornly eluded him. He groaned.

The pain of which he had been half aware during an hour became insistent. It was as though a hand were drawn across the stretched nerves of his chest and arms. In his half delirium he imagined that he was being plunged into icy water; he saw the face of the young Jew he rescued, and called out to him: "Help me, I have failed."

When the man brought him his food in the morning he asked if he could have a doctor.

"It's Easter Sunday," the man said civilly, as if that were the answer to the request.

Handel might have persisted, but the pain had suddenly withdrawn. It left him infinitely tired and he lay still. His fingers strayed towards the pocket of his coat; he remembered that there was nothing in it but the other man's few poor possessions.

By no authority could I have obtained this coat, he thought. The words echoed in his mind as though they were something he had forgotten, yet they were what he had not, not ever, known. And the past he had not lived became confused with his actual past, and with this moment in a cold ill-smelling room. Sunlight glittered among the leaves and, whitened with the morning, the grass supported long shadows. He saw himself cross it. The walls of the cell drew close, hiding him. He lay still and the stillness became actual; he was aware of his body as a swimmer is aware, joyously, of the water lapping and sustaining him. His body was still and yet it moved, released and held.

It came to him that everything that was of value in his life was one and the same thing: that was the narrow energy of his love. It was the stone in the middle of Upsal Wood, the stream turned by the moon to silver in the dark flesh of the moor, the talks with his friends, the meal prepared for Mower. It was Kezia. . . .

The cell was neither light nor dark, and he had lost the sense of time passing. When he heard distant singing he remembered that the Congregational chapel was at the back of the police station, behind a yard bordered in spring with flowering currant. It was the morning service, therefore after ten. Listening, he could distinguish nothing but the repeated and triumphant "Alleluias."

Ha-a-a-a-al-e-e-lu-u-jah.

He seemed to descend below the voices into a deeper stillness. Here was only light, yet not light, but light answering darkness as the silence became a word; words; the calling and twittering in the shadow; the gull's wing—*and of all changeful things, the changeless springs abide with Thee.* The words slipped through the silence, and the silence flowed unfractured round them, above them, below. He walked through the fire under the tree, feeling its cool fingers cleansing him. There was now only darkness and the ascending shaft of light.

The man opening the cell door took a step or two forward and stopped.

"Hi! run and fetch sergeant," he called back.

"Why, what's up?"

"He's hopped it; he's dead."

The other man stood uneasily in the passage. He avoided looking into the cell because he was not certain that he wanted to see anything.

"Well, he'll give no more trouble," he said slowly.

"Don't you be too sure."

CHAPTER XLVIII

LEFT alone in the garden, after Skelton had brought her in turn chair, sealskin cape, shawl, and finally a hassock and a large drawing-room clock, Semiramis stared about her. She shivered a little. Her eyes, unused to so much naked sunlight, blinked, and she sneezed, and spat over the side of the chair. Fixing her gaze at that turn in the road round which Andrew must come from the station, she waited.

There was a light fragrance of lilacs from the half-open buds hidden in the dark leaves. The wind slanted across the hedge. The garden was full of birds, scolding, chattering, strutting along the paths, listening for worms with body tilted from an impudent tail.

The old woman's eyelids scarcely moved. She looked as one looks into the past when the past is a world. Here I am, the eldest, she thought; they've all gone, and I'm only left. Triumph sharpened in her like an appetite: her eyes darted their glances from side to side with the greedy motion of the thrush she was watching. Trying to think of Handel lying upstairs in the house behind her, she could only see a child waving a bare plump arm.

In front of her a bush of laurel was shaken by birds scuffling behind the leaves; the leaves glittered, and the bird noises jetted among them like a child laughing excitedly—yes, like Merry.

She was distracted from these vague images, shadows of the shadow in her deceitful mind, by a twinge of hunger. With increasing anxiety she thought about her supper. Looking at the clock standing beside her on the grass she saw that she had more than an hour to wait yet. She wondered whether Skelton had remembered to order fresh white bread. She imagined the savour of new bread on her tongue with voluptuous sharpness—it was infinitely closer and more friendly to her than thoughts of Handel or Merry.

A cloud passed, throwing a shadow over the garden. She

felt that fingers were exploring her scalp among the few hairs at the back of her neck. A shudder of cold crept over her, and for the space of a second she had the impression that she was held down, unable to move, on the turning earth; she felt giddy and stared defiantly and spitefully in front of her.

Then the clock began ticking loudly and hurriedly again. The air round her and above her became sunlight, falling on her dry twitching cheek and hand; she noticed the smell of lilacs, of fresh young grass, and earth.

A rough, jeering voice said: "Leuk at owd maunsell sitting there! Wheer's Handel Wikker now, missus?"

She looked up sharply to see the upper halves of three lads outside the railings. They had pulled themselves above the wall, and were hanging to the railings like monkeys. Seeing her look up one put his tongue out, and another, twisting his arm round the rail, made a hideous noise with the fingers of the other hand in his mouth.

She did not say anything, but fixed them with her black eyes in a malevolent staring face. One lad threw his arms up and dropped to the ground out of sight, and the other two followed him at once. She could hear them running off.

This incident would not have sent her indoors, but she was cold, in spite of the April sun. She pulled herself up and walked slowly towards the house. Stopping suddenly, she sent a vacant look over the garden.

"H'Ann," she said, meditatively, with inquiry, with resignation, with finality.

Andrew Wikker was suffering a transient sense of defeat and anger. When the old die it is as though we had abandoned them, not they us. Living our own lives, we have let them go unattended into the darkness. It is a desertion, an unkindness.

"You can't forgive my father, can you?" he said with a sharp smile. "Why? What's the matter?"

Semiramis struck her hand on her knee: she held her hand flat and struck sideways, a curious and rather murderous gesture.

"Your father was ovver proud," she said stubbornly. "Everything he did—from leaving t'sea, and marrying your mother, and now this moil he's getten in—was pride, self-seeking, wilfulness, pride. He tramped an ill road. He could ha' given up any time and taken th' offer they made him. But he had to have his way. He had to be jailed like a common thief. He let them insult him and put upon him. Time and again I told him of it—but he was unsayable."

"It scarcely seems pride," Andrew said wearily.

"The way ordinary people live wasn't good enough for him. He must throw himself away for nothing. For a set o' drunken trash. Fine thanks he got for it—it wasn't onny t'police hit him—others cobbled him as well." She added sarcastically: "Perhaps you know why he shouldn't have agreed to Thomas Money's offer!"

"He was striving for perfection," Andrew said in a low voice. Whether she thought him an imbecile or not had ceased to matter.

"He had only to hold his tongue—and think of himself. Like any decent sensible man. However long I live I shan't forget t'figure he made in t'cart. We'll be t'laughing stock of th' town for years to come."

"I'm only sorry I wasn't there," Andrew said.

"I daresay you'll find some way of making a fool of yourself," the old woman said drily.

"Oh, undoubtedly," Andrew said, grinning.

Semiramis gave him a look full of contempt and a sort of malicious joy.

"Yes, you'll come to it," she said spitefully.

"So will the rest of the world!"

Semiramis shook her head vigorously.

"Oh, no," she said in a loud voice, quivering with harsh scorn. "Oh, no! Wik won't ever come to it. London and t'rest may. But not Wik."

She was sitting a little huddled in her chair, as Andrew had seen her so many times and would see her whenever he remembered her. He looked at her, with a compulsive need to remember. Malicious as she was, lying and wicked as she was, indomitable and without pity, not asking to be pitied, she was his childhood, time past and time eternally present, in his bones, in his senses, in his mind. He could never get rid of her, and he was not certain that he wanted to. An obscure fear, joining him to her by a nerve which he had not been able to find and sever, now touched him lightly. In order to forget it at once he thought of Tib—who lives, he thought, as though her life were a stage through which she is always passing.

From her his mind leapt aside to think again about Handel. What do I believe? What is left that is more than a reproach? He made his protest against the usury he hated; it was ill-advised; it was useless: when he died everything remained exactly as it was before. Was it for nothing?

An obstinate, invincible joy answered him.

No man when he dies knows whether he has lived at all. If anyone says of a man, "He will give no more trouble," the answer now, here, now, always, is: "Don't you be too sure." As they say in Wik, "Ovver sure comes to it afore night."